DARK 丨DE
OF THE
RIVER

DARK SIDE
OF THE
RIVER

BRIAN FORMBY

Matador
9 Priory Business Park
Kibworth Beauchamp
Leicestershire LE8 0RX, UK
Tel: (+44) 116 279 2299
Fax: (+44) 116 279 2277
Email: books@troubador.co.uk
Web: www.troubador.co.uk/matador

ISBN 978 1783061 303

British Library Cataloguing in Publication Data.
A catalogue record for this book is available from the British Library.

Typeset in Minion Pro by Troubador Publishing Ltd
Printed and bound in the UK by TJ International, Padstow, Cornwall

Matador is an imprint of Troubador Publishing Ltd

For Viv and Sarah

PROLOGUE

Unemployment Protest – Liverpool 1922

The crowd of protesters had gathered at Everton Brow. Jack Finney checked the time on his pocket watch, it was almost midnight. The men were milling about uneasily and Finney could sense their tension and uncertainty. It was so different from the series of meetings running up to the protest. The atmosphere then had been determined, militant and resolved. Amber sparks blew upward from a bonfire of old wooden fruit boxes and the men jostled to get their share of the warmth. Finney looked around the crowd and could see many faces like his own, tired, pitted and old before their time. The bulk of the protesters were skilled men and unskilled labourers who had reached the end of the line and were desperate for work.

The men looked nervously at Finney, most of them just wanted to get it done quickly but others relished the opportunity to fight back. Finney took a deep breath and nodded toward a small group of men who immediately broke way and headed toward the city. He checked his watch again and prayed that his group leaders could keep the rest of the men calm for fifteen minutes until they were due to leave for their destination. Their plan was to gain entry to the town hall and occupy it for as long as possible as a protest against growing unemployment.

Constable John Bridle stood firmly in the front rank of the biggest men he had ever seen in police uniform. He was a raw recruit and had only taken the oath three days before, but all available men had been drafted in to deal with the protest. Bridle was in the first of three ranks of hand-picked men who were selected for their size and strength or in his case for his reputation as an amateur boxer. He felt intimidated due to his lack of experience but he was determined not to show it in the presence of the formidable Sergeant Mcleish.

Mcleish was a powerful, square shouldered scot in his early thirties. His chiselled face told the story of his early army experience. He was battle hardened by the time he was twenty and his subsequent decade on the force had given him a legendary reputation. Mcleish turned his head sharply toward the door then slowly drew a riot baton from his belt and held it up. The men followed his lead and Bridle felt so awkward he almost dropped his baton. Mcleish threw him a look that Bridle thought could root a cobra to the spot. They had been ordered to maintain silence as they waited in a large room on the upper floor of the town hall. Bridle cursed himself then froze as he heard a crack from the ground floor. He realised Mcleish must have heard something before anyone else and wondered at the man's instincts. Bridle gripped the handle of the baton firmly and kept his eye fixed on Mcleish.

The window frame at the basement level had cracked open easily under the force of the crow bars wielded by Finney's men. Finney whistled through his teeth and a Foundryman they called Mickey the whippet for his speed and agility leapt forward and was through the jagged window frame in seconds. Moments later they heard the heavy draw bolts being pulled back on the rear door and Mickey appeared with a toothless grin. Finney grinned back and slapped his shoulder then led the small group through the door.

'Good work Mick, secure the door and try to block up that window, we'll get upstairs and sort the watchman out.'

Finney led the group up a dark set of winding steps and nervous tension was so high they all felt their hearts drumming against their chests. As Mickey slipped the top bolt into place a shadow fell across the door. He turned around but was stunned to find his way blocked by two huge policemen. He stalled for a moment but quickly pulled himself together and drew a breath to shout a warning. A baton was driven straight into his solar plexus and Mickey fell gasping to the floor in agony.

Finney and his men reached the main entrance hall at the foot of a long central staircase and found a crusty old nightwatchman staring blankly at them. Two men went forward and opened the main doors and the rest of the protesters spilled through shouting and cheering at their success. The hall was soon full of men celebrating but Finney stood halfway up the impressive central stairway and looked around cautiously. His instincts felt something was wrong. Finney scanned the room carefully and saw the watchman slipping through the raucous crowd toward the main door and his heart sank when he realised the man wasn't trying to escape. The watchman rammed the doorbolts into place then turned around and glanced at Finney with a thin, nervous smile.

'Get them doors open' Finney screamed but his voice was drowned out by the crowd. He tried desperately to silence the men but then he heard it, the shrill whistle blowing in short bursts and the sound paralysed him. Doors on the ground floor burst open and a blue wall of screaming policemen surged out.

There was no way for the men to escape and Finney watched with cold fascination as the line of blue uniforms clashed with the startled rabble of men. As rage and panic exploded all around him Finney stood and watched all of his hopes for a peaceful protest fall apart in one crazed and riotous moment. Then he saw Sergeant Mcleish striding triumphantly down the stairs with more officers behind him and the anger surged through Finney so powerfully that he felt his head would burst. Finney lurched forward and grabbed the lapels of Mcleish's great-coat but Mcleish just stared back at him with dead eyes.

'It had to be you Mcleish' Finney seethed 'what are you doing man?'

'I'm doing my duty what else do you expect?'

Finney slowly released his grip on Mcleish's great-coat. What did he expect? The feeling of total failure hit him in the pit of his stomach. Finney's arrogant belief in his cause and his leadership was like a lump in his throat choking him.

'These men are desperate' Finney said shaking his head.

'These men are criminals Jack and so are you' Mcleish half-whispered.

'I trained you Mcleish… I… ' Finney's voice broke with emotion… 'who informed on us?' Finney spat the question out 'just give me a name.'

Mcleish straightened his great-coat and and gave a hint of a smile on his granite features.

'I won't nick you Jack for old time's sake – I'll leave that feather for someone else's cap.'

Mcleish turned away and quickly merged with the battling crowd. Finney tried to pull his racing thoughts together. The protest was lost and all they could hope to do was fight their way out and escape a prison sentence. He had warned them from the beginning of the dangers and the consequences but the risk they took was a measure of their desperation. Finney had driven them to stand up and be counted, to rise up and show strength but in the chaos of the moment all of that naive rhetoric dissolved in his guilt and his fury.

Finney broke through the line of fighting men and sprinted up the long staircase pushing at uniforms left and right. A baton came down toward his head and he deflected it with his forearm. There was a loud crack and a burning pain shot through his elbow joint. Blindly rushing on he crashed through a side door and into a long, dim corridor with a window at the far end. His injured arm was limp at his side and he had blood in his eyes from a head wound as he scrambled down the corridor toward the window. The shouts and screams from the men downstairs cut through him as he launched himself at the window frame which looked barely wide enough to squeeze through. Bracing his limp arm with his good hand he kicked at the frame again and again with his hob-nail boot until it cracked apart. He thrust his head out but couldn't see the ground, only blackness. Finney kicked his legs over the sill and eased himself into a sitting position. If it was suicide he didn't care. He leaned forward and began to slip into the open blackness but two powerful hands caught his shoulders from behind and held him like a child.

Constable John Bridle pulled Finney back from the darkness and into the corridor where he fell limply to the floor. Finney crawled across the floor and propped himself against the wall. His face was streaked with blood and his arm was at an unnatural angle. He looked up and studied the young constable's pugilistic face.

'I could murder a smoke' Finney gasped but could see the dark look in Bridle's eyes. 'What are you doing up here constable?' 'Shouldn't you be downstairs cracking heads and sticking chains on good men?' Finney wheezed and he struggled to breathe but he was determined to stand up to his young captor.

'Are you Sergeant Finney?' Bridle asked.

'I was once… I resigned on principle… but no doubt you've heard another story.'

'I've heard you're a communist' Bridle said and leaned back against the wall. Finney stared hard at this young man who seemed so detached from the situation going on around them and he battled to hold off the faintness that was drifting over him.

'Communist, agitator, radical, take your pick lad, but I was a good copper, once.'

'What was the point of this Mr.Finney?' Bridle was incredulous and Finney almost felt sorry for him.

'Radical action generates change' Finney said and closed his eyes for a moment.

'So you had to break the law?'

'Sometimes there's no other way lad.' The pain burned through Finney's arm and he had no energy left to argue. The two men just looked at each other in silence then Bridle eased the chinstrap of his helmet.

'I've been up here taking stock of myself' Bridle said thoughtfully, 'I've only been in the force for two weeks but I didn't join up for this madness. I didn't realise it would get out of control.'

Finney couldn't help admiring the naive young constable but his cynical mind wondered how long it would be before the lad turned into another Mcleish. Finney propped himself up to reply to Bridle but he suddenly lost consciousness and slipped back against the wall.

Bridle walked over and squatted beside him. Gripping his armpits he pulled Finney up the wall to his feet, then bending his knees he easily threw him over his shoulder. As Bridle carried him along the corridor Finney opened his eyes. All he could see was the floor looming up at him like a dark grave. He was in intense pain but he managed a smile at the thought of this new recruit getting a flying start to his career by catching the ring leader.

The rush of cold air struck Finney like a bucket of ice water. They were outside the building. Bridle carefully slipped Finney from his shoulder and propped him against the wall. Revived by the cold air Finney got his bearings, they were on Exchange Flags and there was a bitter wind howling around the courtyard. Finney stared into Bridle's stern, enigmatic face and wondered what made him tick. There was something about Bridle he could not pin down.

'If you can run Mr. Finney, run now and don't stop.'

Bridle turned to walk away and Finney grabbed his arm. He wanted to say something to Bridle but he didn't know what. He had never felt so helplessly grateful to anyone before and it made him feel weak.

'Stay with it lad, be better than them.'

Bridle walked into the building without saying a word or looking back. Finney watched him until he disappeared into the shadow of the doorway, then he turned slowly and limped away like a wounded animal. High up at the broken window Sergeant Mcleish stood in the shadows and watched Finney slip into the darkness of the city.

CHAPTER ONE

Liverpool Docklands 1936

Detective Sergeant John Bridle stood away from the crowd as the bareknuckle bout drew its first blood. A howl of satisfaction erupted from the clamouring pack of roughnecks and dock workers surrounding the fighters. It was a balmy night and the atmosphere in the dock warehouse was heavy with acrid dust. Bridle loosened his tie and scanned the crowd of twisted and screaming faces. They stank of sweat, beer and tobacco and Bridle wondered if the stink would suffocate the boxers before the end of the first round.

The fighters kept their distance and held their guards high. The crowd sensed they were taking a rest and gave out a volley of abuse so the boxers circled and jabbed but the crowd were not convinced. A powerful man with a thick neck leapt forward shouting for more action but the referee caught him on the jaw with a sharp elbow strike and he groaned as he was catupulted backwards into the howling spectators.

Bridle moved around the perimeter switching his gaze from the fight to the assortment of local villains controlling the proceedings. The small access gate was covered by two of the hardest men on the dock and both well known to Bridle. The main entrance was at the opposite end of the warehouse so Bridle knew someone wanted to slip in discreetly. As he moved through the crowd they watched him with a mixture of suspicion and grudging respect. To them Bridle was just another scuffer in plain clothes, a city 'Jack' who wasn't to be trusted.

An old, rum soaked deck-hand with white hair shuffled over to Bridle and stood at his side with a grin that exposed stained and rotten stumps of teeth.

'Your man's doin' well Mr. Bridle what do yer feed him on?'

'Red meat and Irish stout' Bridle replied as he turned and looked at the cracked face grinning at him.

'Arthur your mouth looks like Anfield cemetery on a wet night.'

The old man let out a wheezy laugh that reeked of cheap rum and tobacco. Bridle slapped him on the shoulder and kept moving steadily toward the access gate. He knew something was happening and he wanted a closer look. A shout went up from the crowd as one of the fighters was knocked to the floor but he leapt to his feet again just as the referee called an end to the round. Bridle turned his full attention to the activity at the gate.

Three people stepped through the gate. Bridle recognised Billy Doyle one the most powerful of the dockside foremen who had that section of the docks under his control. A man had to know Billy Doyle if he wanted work on the dock but there was something reptilian about him that made Bridle's skin crawl. Doyle was followed by a young man and woman of class and both dressed for a party. Doyle was fawning over them and it made Bridle squirm to see him working so hard for the biscuit they would eventually throw him. As they approached the ring Bridle recognised the young man as David Grant son of Sir Edward Grant a local shipping magnate. The Grant-Hollister shipping line was well known in the city and had been established for over a hundred years. Like many of the local shipping merchants the line had begun with dubious trading links with West Africa. Bridle knew the family were influential and very wealthy and he felt uneasy that Doyle was so familiar with the son and heir.

Bridle took in the detail of the girl. She was smaller than Grant and slightly older, late twenties he judged and very slim with dark bobbed hair. Her lipstick was deep red and Bridle's attention was drawn to her mouth. Her lips were full, and her teeth were white and even. She laughed at something Grant said and Bridle suddenly felt that warm excitement that only a really beautiful woman can stir in a man she has never met. Bridle looked back at the ring as the fight went into the second round. He quietly cursed himself as he was sure the girl had caught his stare.

One of the roughnecks opened the gate and another bright young couple wandered in and looked at the chaos as if they had stepped over the threshold to another world. Bridle didn't recognise the man but he could see a monogram on the silk handkerchief he was using to wipe something unsavoury from the lapel of his well-cut suit. Bridle guessed from his demeanour that he struggled to hold down his drink. He wore a homburg tilted at a rakish angle which Bridle guessed was supposed to make him look artistic. His partner was loud and had a grating squeal that substituted for a giggle. She was thinner and taller than her partner and her manner was nervous and jittery. They joined their friends with lots of noisy banter which Bridle found irritating.

They quickly entered into the spirit and roared with the crowd at the best punches. The jittery girl held a handkerchief over her mouth to filter the smell but lifted it regularly to shout at the fighters. Bridle watched the group with fascination. His attention was constantly drawn to the girl with Grant. She didn't seem to fit in. She paid lip service to the fight and spent her time looking around and taking in the whole experience. She had a cruel look about her. Each time Grant demanded her attention she was vivacious and adoring but then she would turn away and her face would change to a cold mask.

'Can't keep me eyes off that one either Mr. Bridle.'

Billy Doyle was at his right shoulder and Bridle couldn't believe he'd been caught off-guard.

'Which one would that be Billy?' Bridle asked and Doyle sniggered. Bridle subdued the urge to punch his smug face.

'She's a cool one Mr. Bridle with perfume to make yer head spin, and those dark eyes.'

Bridle had to pull himself together as Doyle was almost reading his thoughts and he wasn't comfortable with it. Bridle faked a laugh.

'Never heard you wax lyrical before Billy.' Doyle chuckled at Bridle's response.

'I'm only a man Mr. Bridle… only human… just like you.'

Doyle sniggered again and Bridle took a deep breath. He had to get control of the conversation. It was the first time Bridle had felt any threat from Doyle and he had to remind himself of his own rules, never drop your guard and never show any weakness. He felt in danger of doing both and with a lizard like Billy Doyle.

'Mixing with the elite eh Billy, what's going on?'

'These rich kids get bored easy, they need a bit of entertainment' Doyle shrugged.

'So they come to Uncle Billy?' Bridle said flatly 'you'll be doing the puppet show on New Brighton pier next.' Doyle gave out a deep laugh and shook his head.

'That dry humour of yours Mr. Bridle I bet you're a great man to drink with.'

Bridle ignored Doyle's professional crawling. Bridle was uneasy with these well dressed and nicely scented people at the ringside. It had an air of nobles watching gladiators in the arena. It was an uncomfortable feeling for Bridle.

'How much is he paying you Billy?'

Doyle dropped his chin and exaggerated a shrug of his shoulders.

'More than you earn in a month I'd guess Mr. Bridle.' Doyle nodded, turned slowly and ambled his way back to his guests. Bridle was glad to be rid of him. He always felt a little unclean in the presence of Billy Doyle so he turned his attention back to the fight.

Grant's party hissed and booed as if they were at a pantomime and Bridle wondered if they had any idea how much danger was around them. But he knew it didn't matter because Grant was paying for protection and Bridle guessed that the danger was part of the thrill for them. The boxers clashed then held on to each other for a brief rest. The younger boxer looked up furtively and held Bridle's stare. Bridle gave a short nod and the boxer grinned. He pushed himself away from his opponent and stood back with his guard loose and low. He suddenly had an air of confidence and the crowd could sense that something was coming. The older fighter wiped the sweat from his shaven head then he took the bait and launched himself forward. His tall opponent timed his next move perfectly. He stepped lightly forward and to the side, at the same time he fired three very fast snapping punches, two to the head and one to the floating ribs. The cry of pain silenced the crowd as the older man went down clutching his side. Blood poured from a cut above his eye as he lay hunched on the ground. The referee hesitated and looked nervously in Doyle's direction but the crowd began to scream for the count to start.

'Stay down' Bridle whispered to himself 'stay down.'

The count started slowly as the cut and bloodied fighter raised himself from the ground and stood with his guard up. The crowd knew it was over but they wanted to see the kill.

Grant's party were shouting for blood and Grant held out his fist with his thumb pointing down to the rabid amusement of his friends, except the dark-eyed girl. She was staring at this broken fighter with detached interest and Bridle wondered what was going through her head. There was no expression on her face. Everyone stood in silence as the fighter rocked on his heels squirming to see through swollen eyes. Suddenly his knees began to buckle. Bridle had great respect for this veteran prize-fighter and he wasn't proud to be part of his downfall.

The shouts got louder and Grant's party were amused to the point of hysteria and joined in the calls to finish him. Bridle started forward through the crowd. He couldn't let it go on. As he was about to step into the ring the fighter's legs began to shake violently. The baying crowd fell silent again. Bridle watched as the old boxer fell to his knees then crumbled to the floor as the crowd roared their approval. Bridle rushed forward and turned the fighter over onto his back. He was still breathing. He let out a long groan and Bridle tapped his face until he opened his eyes.

A commotion broke out in the crowd and Bridle looked up to see Billy Doyle ushering his party through the gate. The dark-eyed girl stopped at the gate and looked back. She scanned the room slowly absorbing the wild atmosphere. There was a hint of decadence about this girl that unsettled Bridle. As she turned to leave she caught his stare and held it. Then she turned away without any reaction and slipped through the gate.

Unlicensed bareknuckle fights were illegal in the city and as a serving police officer Bridle had to be careful and discreet. It was recognised in police circles that organised bouts eased tensions among the unemployed and petty criminals in the community. Street fights either organised or spontaneous were endemic and Bridle took advantage of them to train his boxers. Bridle's man strolled over with an arrogant grin on his face. Bridle looked up and nodded.

'Well boxed Malone.'

'How is he?' Malone responded.

Malone was one of the best fighters in the police boxing club and Bridle knew that his killer instinct wasn't just kept for the ring. He was a tough and ambitious officer and his show of concern didn't really convince Bridle. The broken prize-fighter was well known in the city. His reputation gave him a degree of hero worship in his community especially among the tough, teenage bucks. But his time had past.

'He wasn't much trouble' Malone said.

Bridle stepped back as two men propped the crumpled fighter between them and shuffled him away.

'No he wasn't much trouble' Bridle muttered. He looked at Malone and wondered if anyone would weep for him when his time came. Bridle flicked out his pocket watch and checked the time. His wife Stella would be fast asleep and they had hardly seen each other over the past week. He sighed heavily as he slipped the watch back into his pocket and made his way to the gate.

A drunken stoker lurched across the dock searching for his ship through the numb haze of rum and whiskey. He staggered against a pile of cotton bales then fell through a gap in the stack and collapsed onto the damp and stinking dockside. It felt strangely comfortable on his back on the hard ground and he fell unconscious within seconds. It was dawn when he came to his senses but he had no idea of the time as he hauled himself up into a sitting position and tried to focus his eyes. He felt a desperate need for a cigarette and tapped his pockets in a vain search for a pack or a stub. The stoker cursed his luck then felt around the ground in case they had fallen out. He cursed again when he put his hand in something wet and pulled it away quickly. He baulked at the sight of thick blood all over his hand and searched himself frantically for a wound. Slowly he looked up.

The body was hanging from a winch pulley with the rope pulled tight around it's neck. The stoker was riveted on the face. The eyes and tongue were protruding in a grotesque death-mask and the head was covered in coagulated blood. The stoker lifted himself from the floor and tried to shout but couldn't make any noise. He pushed his way out from between the bales and desperately looked around for help. Dock men were gathering to start their day's work and the stoker began to wave, shout and jump up and down. As the dock men noticed him he had a sudden thought and dashed back between the bales to his grisly discovery. He frantically searched the pockets of the corpse. Loose change clanged across the dockside but he managed to grab two cigars from the breast pocket before panic made him back away. He wiped the blood from the cigars and rammed them into his pocket before the first men got to him.

'In there lads – dead as a fuckin' doornail – right mess – get the dock Sergeant – would yer have a bottle on yer lads just for me nerves?'

Bridle sat in the tram staring blankly at the newspaper and cursed the events that followed the unlicensed fight. The newspaper report quickly turned from the gruesome killing of David Grant to hinting at scandalous rumours of his private life. The fact that he was the son of a respected businessman and philanthropist gave the story more potential for scandal. Bridle looked around the tram. It had already caught the public imagination. The tram was full of people talking about Grant's lifestyle. Working men sneered at the artless son but spoke highly of his father. Two middle-aged ladies shook their heads in disgrace but lapped up every paragraph in the newspaper. Detective Sergeant Bridle was beginning to wish that he wasn't one of the last people to see David Grant alive as he jumped off the tram at Castle Street.

Bridle took a slow walk to Dale Street. He had to report to senior officers at eleven o'clock and he had an hour to kill and a load of excuses to explore. Detective Constable Tommy Lodge was smoking a cigarette as he leaned against a police box with his nose in a newspaper. He looked up as Bridle approached and offered him his cigarette. 'Might be a good time to try one boss' Lodge said but Bridle ignored him so he mumbled 'you must be the only Jack on the force who doesn't smoke.' Bridle stared at the headline of Lodge's newspaper then he read it out loud.

'Heir to city shipping line found murdered' Bridle shook his head 'why Tommy?'

Lodge was a little amused to be asked for an opinion. He flicked the stub of his Woodbine away and folded his newspaper.

'Who cares?' Lodge shrugged 'just means more donkey-work for the likes of us.'

Bridle looked at Lodge. He saw a tall, heavy boned man, baggy eyed with a pallid complexion and stained teeth. All ambition had been drained from him by years of dull routine and regular rejection for promotion. Sarcasm and resentment seeped through all aspects of his work. Most of the Jacks in the division found him to be too cynical even for their cynical world but Bridle had learned by experience that Lodge was a solid copper, not very sharp but dogged. Bridle preferred that to having to watch his back with a young ambitious partner.

'What time are you on the carpet boss?' Lodge asked with a smirk.

'Eleven o'clock in Crowley's office' Bridle replied then braced himself for Lodge's response.

'Crowley?' Lodge stopped and stared at Bridle. Lodge's opinion of Chief Superintendent Crowley had been formed many years before and Bridle knew that Lodge was about to launch one of his tirades of abuse and sarcasm.

'What the hell is goin' on?' Lodge spluttered 'How many people did that bastard walk over to get where he is?'

Bridle sneaked a look at his pocket watch then slipped it back into his waistcoat.

'He knows people Tommy' Bridle said with a wink and Lodge sneered and spat a lump of phlegm into the gutter.

'Yeah the funny handshake brigade – shower of bastards' Lodge snarled. Bridle grinned at Lodge's favourite description of any group that annoyed him. Uniformed officers, politicians, Liverpool football supporters and many others would receive Lodge's colourful dismissal.

'Will some tea and toast brighten that sour gob of yours Tommy?' Bridle knew Lodge would be easier to handle after a mug of tea and a rant about Everton's place in the league. He also needed some time to prepare his mind for the imminent interrogation by his superiors.

Sir Edward Grant sat at the oak desk in his study. The French windows directly in front of his desk gave him a clear view across the Dee estuary to the Clwyd hills. Further to the right he could faintly see the pinnacles of Snowdonia stabbing their way into view. The constant stream of family, friends and general sympathisers had left him drained. The vicar was in the drawing room having tea with his daughter Amelia but he couldn't face joining them. Grant walked over to an ornate cabinet and opened the exquisitely lacquered doors to reveal a number of crystal decanters and glasses. He drew two tumblers from the cabinet then poured malt whiskey from a decanter very slowly as he was aware that his hand was trembling slightly.

Simon Greenstein swept into the room unannounced and threw his heavy document bag on the leather chair under the window. His eyes widened when he saw the whiskey

'Ah thank you Edward.' He picked up the glass and sipped the whiskey as if to approve the quality then downed it in one.

'Good morning by the way... may I?' Greenstein gestured toward the decanter. Grant nodded impatiently and strode back to his chair and set his glass down carefully. Greenstein filled his glass and sat down opposite Grant puffing heavily. His rotund head was bathed in sweat and his round-framed spectacles were too small for his bloated face.

'Still moving at full throttle Simon?' Grant scowled and Greenstein looked sheepish for a moment.

'First of all Edward may I give you my condolences. It's a terrible business. How is Margaret?'

'Exhausted' Grant replied wearily.

'Yes I'm sure, David was her favourite' Greenstein said and winced slightly.

'Is the malt not to your taste Simon? You have a sour look.'

Grant was aware of Greenstein's opinion of his son but he felt he should make an effort under the circumstances.

'The stories in the papers wouldn't help Margaret's condition at all' Greenstein mumbled, side-stepping Grant's question.

'That's the reason I contacted you Simon' Grant said firmly 'can I do anything about the press?' 'I've had enough of the gossip and innuendo.'

Greenstein shifted in his chair, took a deep breath and looked Grant squarely in the eye.

'Edward I have been your legal advisor for many years' Greenstein hesitated and Grant snorted.

'Spit it out Simon.'

'Very well I shall be frank. You suspected David's private life was outrageous so you had me engage an enquiry agent last year to keep an eye on his activities' Greenstein nodded toward the document bag on the chair. 'The file is in that bag and makes alarming reading. If you decide to sue the press they will dig up some of his, dare I say, more colourful escapades which began at Oxford and have continued since.'

Grant leaned forward and placed his hands firmly on the desk as if the solidity gave him some security.

'Read the file yourself Edward' Greenstein continued 'that girl Miranda Shaw, she's like something from DH Lawrence. No propriety, total disregard for convention. She mixes with scruffy bohemians who no doubt call themselves artists and poets.'

Grant looked at Greenstein with distaste.

'What would you call them Simon?

'Idle and incapable' Greenstein responded drily.

'Are you telling me Simon, that my family has to endure this nightmare and I can do nothing about it?' Greenstein pondered

Grant's question but his legal mind could only see the logical route.

'If your family were exposed to the details in that file Edward I can assure you it would devastate them. My advice is let it lie.'

Grant looked incredulously at Greenstein.

'You have no choice Edward. David led a colourful life. He was often drunk in public. He made dubious business deals. He had no scruples. He was a cad with women, especially married women, shall I go on?'

Grant stood up sharply thrusting his chair backwards and strode over to the window. Greenstein recoiled as he knew Grant's temper was explosive. Grant could see a small fishing boat making slow progress along the River Dee taking advantage of the fine weather. He watched it for a quiet moment then exploded.

'What the hell was David doing at the docks?'

Greenstein stared at the carpet for a moment then looked up slowly.

'Read the file Edward.'

Bridle stood in the corridor outside Chief Superintendent Crowley's office and considered his situation. He was aware that many officers fell by the wayside due to circumstances. He had spent most of his working life listening to burned-out police officers cursing their fate due to mysterious circumstances and he vowed he would never fall into that deluded trap. But as he stood in the corridor that stank of pipe tobacco and disinfectant he suddenly understood what they meant and felt his own circumstances were staring him in the face.

Officers of varied rank wandered up and down the corridor. They cast him a sideways glance and some that he knew even risked a furtive nod. Everyone knew why he was there. He drew a deep breath and let it out slowly remembering how proud Stella had been when he was promoted to Detective Sergeant five years before. He was confident he could make Detective Inspector or even higher but the thought of going back into uniform was coursing through his head like a slow poison.

'Detective Sergeant Bridle.'

Bridle looked up sharply and almost stood to attention. He knew the voice immediately as Superintendent Mcleish's bark was unmistakeable. Mcleish stood at the open doorway. His brooding face glared in Bridle's direction but he had an unnerving ability to look straight through a man. Bridle was a hardened police officer but Mcleish's presence always reduced him.

His Superintendent's uniform was impeccable. The buttons gleamed and the creases in his trousers were ramrod straight. His boots were polished to such a high finish that the toe-caps looked like black mirrors. His face still had a chiselled firmness but his eyes had dark rings and his cropped hair was white against his skull.

'Sir' Bridle responded sharply.

Mcleish paused and tilted his head back to focus his stare.

'When you enter the room you will stand directly behind the chair in the centre of the floor. You will not sit down until directed to do so by the senior officer present. Is that clear Sergeant?'

'Sir'

Bridle knew it was suicidal to display any informality to an officer like Mcleish although inside he felt like a recruit on a parade ground.

'You will follow me into the room after a count of thirty seconds, understood Sergeant?'

Bridle snapped his response and Mcleish gave him a suspicious stare, then he turned swiftly and stepped back into the room. Bridle counted slowly in his head and it reminded him of playing games as a child. He felt he was still playing games as he stepped forward and rapped his knuckles firmly against the door panel. Mcleish's voice barked from inside.

'Enter.'

Bridle entered and moved quickly to the chair and stood behind it with his hands behind his back and feet apart. Seated at a long table were four senior officers, two in uniform and two detectives in suits. The room was hazy with pipe-smoke and cigarettes. Bridle watched the blue haze drifting out through an open window and wished he could go with it.

'Sit down Sergeant Bridle' Chief Superintendent Crowley's tone was flat and Bridle prepared himself for the onslaught. Crowley's pinched and officious face studied him as he sat down. His thin military moustache was perched on his lip like a smudge and it seemed to dance around his mouth as he spoke. Crowley paused for effect then leaned forward in what he considered to be a menacing way.

'Sergeant Bridle we feel under the circumstances you should come here today and answer some very serious questions.'

Crowley's use of the word 'circumstances' was ironic and almost made Bridle smirk but he knew better and looked as serious as he could and responded confidently.

'Now do you understand the gravity of the situation Sergeant Bridle?'

Crowley's condescending attitude irritated Bridle and there was something about the man that seemed to demand insubordination.

'Gravity Sir?'

Bridle responded with a poker face. Crowley shifted in his chair and cleared his throat.

'Do you understand what I mean by gravity Sergeant?'

Bridle looked directly at Crowley and said firmly,

'I understand it to mean very serious and nothing at all to do with Sir Isaac Newton Sir.' Crowley stared back at him and wondered if he was being insubordinate or if he was really that stupid. Superintendent Mcleish stifled a chuckle and Detective Inspector Radford seethed quietly. Crowley's clipped moustache danced nervously around his reddening face.

'Perhaps you have a misplaced sense of humour Sergeant.'

Bridle tried to look contrite but Mcleish stepped in.

'You are in a serious position Sergeant Bridle and you will treat all questions with due respect.'

Detective Superintendent Webster took a briar pipe from his mouth and pointed it at Bridle. He nodded his head slowly as he spoke.

'The head of the body had been battered with a spiked weapon, the face and neck torn diagonally, quite frenzied'

Webster drew the pipe across his face sharply to illustrate the angle of the injuries.

'My guess would be a bale hook'

Webster thrust the pipe back into his mouth with a look of triumph. Bridle tried not to look bemused. Webster was known for his crusty and eccentric manner which irritated his peers. He had the dusty appearance of an ageing professor but everyone knew he had the most incisive mind in the department. Inspector Radford cast Webster an impatient glance then turned his narrow eyes to Bridle.

'What were you doing in the warehouse Sergeant?' Bridle stared hard into Radford's face which seemed to disappear in layers of fat. He had lost count of the times he had carried Radford through a case and saved his professional skin. Bridle knew Radford was fully informed of the events in the warehouse but he also knew Radford wanted to make him walk over hot coals. He knew he had to play the game.

'I was involved in a bare knuckle contest Sir. One of my best boxers from the division team was fighting.'

'But the fight was unlicensed Sergeant' Radford said and cast a look at his colleagues. Bridle could feel the heat and tension rising in his chest. Crowley shook his head and pulled a quizzical face as he spoke.

'Are the amateur contests not good enough for your boxers Sergeant Bridle?'

A cold determination came over Bridle as he looked along the line of inquisitors and held the stare of each man for a moment.

'My superiors in division are aware I use the fight game in this town to keep my ear to the ground. It's a practical way to contact and recruit informants. My own ability in the sport and my reputation as a trainer has helped me to be accepted.'

'You are a city Jack and they'll never accept you' Radford sneered 'what success have you had with your ear to the ground?'

Bridle subdued the impulse to rise to Radford's sarcasm and promised himself that if he survived this he would give Radford enough rope to hang himself at some point in the future.

'The record shows intelligence from my informants closed a number of cases successfully over the last few years. They contributed to my promotion and possibly one or two others.'

Bridle stared hard at Radford. Crowley cleared his throat nervously and thrust his finger at Bridle.

'You were still involved in an illegal gathering where gambling was taking place Sergeant.' Bridle nodded slowly.

'Yes Sir that's true, but every officer in this room knows it's impossible to make any progress in criminal detection in this city without fraternising and without loosely interpreting the law on occasions.' Radford crushed his cigarette into the ash tray exposing dark nicotine stains on his fingers.

'Loosely interpreting the law?' Radford repeated, 'what exactly does that mean Sergeant?' 'Does it mean you can make things up as you go along?' 'How does it make us look when the son of Sir Edward Grant is murdered under the nose of a serving police officer and he knows nothing about it?' Radford finished his rant with his face deep red from the neck up.

Detective Superintendent Webster lowered his already extinguished pipe and screwed up his face as if deep in thought then said.

'To be fair we don't know the exact time Grant was murdered, pathology has been vague in this case.' Webster spoke slowly and calmly as if he was deliberating out loud. 'Sergeant Bridle can't be expected to carry responsibility for that. In fact Sergeant Bridle's presence in the warehouse is a bonus. Have you written a report Sergeant?' Bridle sensed that Webster was throwing him a lifeline.

'Yes Sir I submitted it to Chief Superintendent Crowley's office yesterday afternoon.'

'Yesterday' Webster looked over to Crowley 'we should have had a copy prior to this meeting.' Webster chuckled and shook his head as he knocked the black tobacco from his pipe into the ashtray. Crowley's cheeks flushed and he cleared his throat awkwardly.

'Sergeant Bridle did you see any threats to David Grant or his party?' Webster asked as he fiddled idly with a pipe cleaner. Webster had a way of appearing lethargic and disinterested but Bridle knew that this was all technique. Webster's method appeared casual but he could take a man apart faster than any investigating officer on the force.

'No Sir, no direct threats. He was under the protection of Billy Doyle and his cronies as far as I could see.'

'And he left the warehouse with Doyle?' Webster tapped the bowl of the pipe against the ashtray to irritate his colleagues.

'Yes Sir, all of Grant's party left with Doyle.'

'Just Doyle' Webster said indifferently.

'No Sir, two of Doyle's roughnecks went with them.'

Webster dropped the pipe into the ashtray and linked his hands across his chest.

'I am assuming all of these details are in your report Sergeant?'

'Yes Sir, together with the names of Grant's party and as many of the dock men that I could positively identify.'

Bridle knew Webster was using his report to score points against Crowley. Superintendent Mcleish broke his silence and fixed his stare directly at Bridle.

'Doyle is a yard-dog. I've known his family for years and they're all yard-dogs but they haven't got the balls to kill anyone. It takes a lot to kill another man at close quarters. Doyle isn't capable. He's just a bully boy.'

Everyone in the room looked at Mcleish. He unnerved people but they respected his opinions and no one doubted his ability to recognise the killer instinct in a man

'I feel Sergeant Bridle should be officially reprimanded for his actions' Radford said and looked around for support.

'I disagree' said Webster 'Sergeant Bridle has a good record and he's a competent officer.'

Bridle kept his face blank but clenched his fists against his thighs. Mcleish noticed the whitening of his knuckles but was impressed at no other outward sign of his anger. Anger and the desperate need to keep calm pulled Bridle apart but he knew any sign of cracking in this situation would finish his career.

'Who have you assigned to lead the murder investigation Chief Superintendent?' Mcleish knew the answer but he wanted Crowley to acknowledge it.

'I have assigned Detective Inspector Radford' Crowley muttered.

'In that case I suggest you have Sergeant Bridle seconded as an investigating officer on the team. As Detective Superintendent Webster pointed out he was at the scene and he's a methodical detective with a sound record.'

'I agree' said Webster.

Radford's face darkened.

'I'm not sure that's a very good idea' Radford said looking at Crowley for support. 'My investigation is already underway. My men have all been assigned their areas of enquiry' Radford's face grew a deeper shade of red as he spoke.

'Perhaps he should be on your team' Crowley said avoiding eye contact with Radford 'being at the scene makes him an asset to the investigation.'

Mcleish smiled at Crowley's submission and Bridle wondered what was going on.

'That's settled then' Webster said with a wry smile at Radford and Crowley. 'Oh yes, Inspector Radford I suggest you get your men to read Sergeant Bridle's report before they begin their areas of enquiry.'

Bridle knew he was being used politically but at that moment he didn't care. He needed to get away from the room and get some air. It wasn't the outcome he had expected and he knew that Radford felt the same way.

CHAPTER TWO

Stella Bridle put the final stitches in the dress she was altering and smoothed the fabric against the hips of the mannequin. It was a superb evening gown. Stella had gained a reputation for quality work in altering gowns and dresses and the city department stores offered her regular business. Stella knew that most of the initial interest was due to her father's contacts but the quality of her work had assured her reputation and modest success.

The concentration required for her craft helped to pass lonely hours as the wife of a serving police officer. The long shifts and debilitating night duty often made their lives confused and disjointed. When Bridle was on night duty she would work on an alteration all night just to keep on the same time pattern as him. She also worked hard because if she wasn't occupied she was prone to dark moods when she would dwell on their lack of success in starting a family. Their semi-detached villa on Wallasey promenade was high up on the rock overlooking the River Mersey with a good view of the waterfront buildings of Liverpool except when they were covered by the dense smog of industry. She used the front bedroom as her work-room and was fascinated by the river traffic that came in from all over the world.

The gown on the mannequin belonged to her sister and she was to wear it for an annual ball held in the Cheshire countryside. This was the summer ball where the gentry would display their offspring for partners of the right class and breeding. Stella felt that it was no different to the way they managed their live-stock but her views were scorned by her affluent family and friends. They teased her by calling her the little socialist. It was a priveleged world she had rejected for her marriage and she had no real regrets. It was only when she looked at a ball gown that she did miss the glamour and all the giddy excitement of those occasions.

The sound of a familiar car engine drawing up outside brought a smile to her face and she jumped up to look out of the window. Her father had parked his maroon, two-seater Alvis directly outside her front gate. He was looking at himself in the rear-view mirror and obviously admired what he saw. Stella was always amused by her father's vanity and took every opportunity to tease him about it. He climbed out of the car and closed the door then caressed the edge of the body work with his fingertips as he walked around the vehicle. Stella giggled as she knew he was stalling just so the neighbours or passers-by could admire the car.

Stella glanced at the clock. Bridle was due home at anytime and the sight of the Alvis parked outside the house would irritate him for certain. He might even visit the pub at the top of the promenade until the car had gone. Stella was desperate to avoid that situation. She made her way down stairs and opened the door just as her father was reaching out to knock. He smiled broadly when he saw his youngest daughter and kissed her lovingly on the cheek.

'Hello darling how are you?' He said as he eased himself into the hallway.

'Hello, Daddy I'm very well thank you' Stella was always

genuinely happy to see her father but knew that he only visited when he had something to say.

'Is mummy alright? She isn't sick or anything?'

'Your mother is fine' he sighed 'can't I pay my daughter a call without any strings attached?'

Stella grinned at the rakish good looks of her father which were always enhanced when he smiled. His debonair charm was legendary on the social circuit of Cheshire and even in his late fifties he still had a glint in his eye. She stole a quick glance up and down the promenade then closed the door.

Sir Nigel Carver K.C. had distinguished himself in the criminal courts of Liverpool and Manchester and was renowned for his incisive intelligence and cruel wit. As he wandered around the tiny parlour removing his driving gloves the look of disdain on his face was obvious to Stella.

'And how is life in court daddy? Are you still cutting a dash in your wig and gown?'

Carver looked at his daughter's mischievous grin and laughed.

'Estella you have my sense of humour I do miss you.'

He looked around and shook his head. Stella took a deep breath. She knew he was trying to goad her but she was on to his tricks. The fact that he used her full name of Estella was designed to needle her. Bridle had called her Stella from the day they were married and she had grown used to it.

'I take it from your furtive glance up and down the promenade that the Detective Sergeant isn't home, but you are expecting him anytime now?' He looked in the mirror and straightened his tie as he spoke.

'You never miss a trick do you daddy? Is it any wonder you're the scourge of the criminal classes?' She folded her arms and looked him squarely in the eye.

'I have always loved your spirit Estella. Even as a child you would question me and argue with me' he sighed heavily 'I had such high hopes for you.'

'By that you mean a good marriage to a doctor or God forbid, a dusty barrister' she put on a bored expression.

'Don't pull that silly face darling' he chuckled 'I find it very endearing.'

'You are impossible daddy' she punched him playfully on the shoulder.

'So doctors and lawyers are boring. What about that concert pianist chappie? He was very taken with you as I recall.' He looked at her and grinned as she shook her head slowly.

'Daddy you know he had no interest in girls whatsoever. He was more interested in my dress designs than he was with me.'

Bridle, standing outside the front door could hear them laughing together. He looked back at the Alvis. It was a beautiful car and it seemed to symbolise the life that he could never give Stella. He heard the laughter again. He turned on his heel and walked down the steps but stopped at the car. It was highly polished and the chrome-work gleamed in the sunlight. A young couple strolled past arm in arm. The young man looked at the car with a wide grin on his face and gave out a long whistle of appreciation. The girl looked from the car to Bridle and gave him a waspish smile. Bridle grinned at the irony of the situation. He decided he couldn't face his father in law. He'd spent the day fencing with people and he wasn't in the mood to carry it on in his own house. Sir Nigel was a sharp opponent and always got the better of him. In fact Bridle felt so intimidated in his presence that he could never relax.

Just as he made the decision to run and hide in the bar of the Queens Hotel the door flew open and Stella ran down the steps with a dazzling smile on her face. She ran straight up to him and kissed him on the cheek. She held both his hands and just looked at him as she smiled that glorious smile. She didn't have to say anything, she knew him inside out. Stella tugged his hands gently and nodded toward the house. He hesitated and she could see that uncertainty in him like a little boy out of his depth. She linked his arm and started to lead him up the steps.

'Is this the masterful brute I married?'

She looked up at him and grinned again. He didn't know what to say. He felt a little ashamed of his own cowardice but all he could think about was to take Stella up to their bed and make love to her there and then. He stopped on the top step and pulled her to him. He kissed her long and hard on the mouth and he felt her body go limp in warm submission. She pushed him away with a gasp. Her cheeks were flushed and her eyes were languid. Bridle cursed the presence of his in-law.

'Now there is the brute I married' she giggled.

'Please let me know if I'm interrupting anything you know how much I hate to intrude.' Carver was in the doorway leaning casually against the frame. Bridle took in the vision of suave sophistication before him.

'Hello... Sir Nigel... father... dad'.

Stella crumbled with a snorting laugh and Bridle crumbled with her.

'Please show a little restraint. You are far too happy for a married couple' Carver murmured as he brushed an imaginary speck from the shoulder of his sports jacket. He turned back into the house and they followed him sheepishly into the parlour where he stood by the window. He cleared his throat then glanced out of the window as if he was scared to lose sight of his beloved car.

'As you are aware Estella the Whitley Ball is coming up and your mother has asked me, or perhaps, directed me to talk you into accepting your usual invitation.'

Carver was aware of Bridle's frown but chose to ignore it.

'It has been some years since you attended and it would give you the opportunity catch up with your old friends not to mention your sisters.'

'Elizabeth and Caroline could catch up with me anytime Daddy. Do I have to attend a country knees-up just to make contact with them?'

Bridle grinned at Stella's response.

'A country knees-up?' Carver almost choked. 'This is the most prestigious ball on the Cheshire circuit, as you well know my girl. There will be people there who could be of great help to your ambitions. I mean, do you want to scrape work from department stores forever? If you want to achieve your potential you need contacts. To be honest it wouldn't do your career any harm either.' He said looking sideways at Bridle. 'There will be some very influential people attending.'

'I'm not a great believer in using people Sir Nigel' Bridle said.

'Oh yes of course I forgot that Catholic, working-class ethic of yours. Tell me, how are things in purgatory?' Carver smirked and raised an eyebrow.

'Daddy' Stella placed her hands on her hips and stared him down.

'Well really Estella this man of yours can be such a bore.'

Bridle seethed quietly as Stella stormed around in front of her father and crossed her arms in defiance.

'Look daddy...

Bridle placed his hand on his wife's shoulder and gently moved her to one side. The two men stood toe to toe. Carver prepared himself to relish a verbal spar with an unworthy opponent. Bridle's hard, punished face stared back at him.

'It must be painful to lose your daughter to such a working class bore. It must really hurt that she would rather be with me than one of your well-bred polo club boys.'

'To be fair old boy, that one hurts her mother more than I.'

Carver thrust in his response and checked Bridle's face for a reaction. Bridle could hear Stella sobbing lightly behind him. He held Carver's stare for a moment then broke into a smile.

'I think Stella could do with a good night out, we would love to come to the ball.'

Stella hated to see her two favourite men fighting each other as they always did. Carver smiled but he felt Bridle was trying to disarm him and he wasn't going to fall for it. Carver decided to call his bluff.

'Excellent that's settled then' Carver said then turned and strolled into the hall.

'Your mother will be so delighted darling, oh by the way' Carver turned back as he opened the front door, 'Guy Charlton has just come back from Europe, made an absolute fortune I believe, he was asking about you. You can catch up at the ball.'

He gave a mischievous grin as he made his way down the steps to the car. Stella pursed her lips and closed her eyes tightly. Bridle stepped up behind her and whispered.

'And who is Guy Charlton?'

The Police car sped along the dockside and slammed to a halt outside the foreman's shed. Detective Inspector Radford stepped out and adjusted his hat against the wind. A uniformed Sergeant climbed out of the driver's seat and followed Radford in a slow walk to the shed door. Sergeant Bentley went forward and tried to open the door but it jammed against the frame. Without any hesitation he put his shoulder to it and the door crashed open. Billy Doyle was sitting behind a battered desk and he looked up with alarm as the Sergeant stepped into the room and towered over him.

'It's got a handle yer know' Doyle snapped.

Sergeant Bentley lunged forward and slapped Doyle with a backhand across his jaw. Doyle was knocked sideways and crashed to the floor with a grunt.

'Don't talk to me like that' Bentley snarled.

The Sergeant gripped Doyle's leather jerkin and hauled him up then tossed him into his chair. Doyle stroked his jaw then shook his head as if it made any difference to the pain. Radford lit a cigarette and looked out of the window across the river indifferently while Sergeant Bentley jammed the broken door back into the frame.

'Don't think I deserved that one Mr. Radford' Doyle mumbled 'I've done you some favours in the past.'

Radford flicked his cigarette through the window into the river and watched it float for a moment then he sat on a crate and looked at Doyle with contempt.

'Billy I hate your guts and you hate mine.'

Doyle's thin face darkened at Radford's response.

'You don't do favours Billy you just look after yourself like a gutter rat.'

'You have a short memory Mr. Radford.'

'When did you get brave Billy boy? Don't answer me back lad or I'll let Sergeant Bentley teach you the rules' Radford's face burned.

Doyle squirmed slightly and his nose began to bleed. He wiped the blood away with his shirt sleeve.

'If you don't want a favour what do yer want?' Doyle sneered.

'I need to know what happened on the night of Grant's murder.'

'I've been over it a hundred times I've already given a statement' Doyle snapped.

Radford hesitated then continued.

'I want to know everything Sergeant Bridle did at the fight and who he spoke to.'

'Bridle' Doyle was puzzled. 'What's he got to do with it?'

Radford looked at Sergeant Bentley and nodded. Bentley darted forward and Doyle threw both hands up in surrender.

'Alright, alright, I don't give a toss about Bridle just lay off.'

Doyle looked at Bentley. At least six feet four in his boots Bentley had the reputation of being Radford's mad dog. Doyle realised something was going on but he was wise enough to think of his own skin first. Doyle turned to Radford.

'Bridle puts some of his fighters in bare knuckle meetings. They go to most of the bouts around town. It gives them an edge I suppose' Doyle shrugged.

'What about prize money?' Radford asked.

'Never takes any.'

Doyle knew that this was the wrong answer but he perversely relished the thought of firing Radford's temper.

'You mean you haven't seen him take any. Maybe he takes it from one of your gang of dog shit. Maybe you can find someone who pays Bridle off. What do yer' say Billy boy?' Radford didn't try to hide his contempt.

'Don't get me wrong Mr. Radford I know what yer' sayin' but… '

Radford stood up sharply then moved forward slowly. Doyle instinctively leaned back.

'It's like this Mr. Radford … Bridle has got some… respect from the men… it'll be tough to find one who would set him up.'

Radford glared at him and Doyle was beginning to enjoy it.

'Maybe you gave Bridle a backhander yourself Billy? Maybe I can find evidence in this stinking shanty of yours' Radford looked around.

'Why bother Mr. Radford? You know I'll do what you want in the end.'

Doyle sighed, he knew how the game was played and he knew his position on the pitch. Radford grinned at Sergeant Bentley then turned to Doyle.

'Course you will Billy.'

The police boxing club was in a dim basement on Victoria Street. The steps down to the basement were damp and reeked of stale urine but that gave way to the pungent smell of sweat and liniment as the gym door was opened. The room was dominated in the centre by a regulation size boxing ring. To the right was a large training area with leather and canvas punch-bags hanging from steel hooks. To the left was a small area with various pieces of weight-training equipment, dumb-bells and bar-bells, all looking the worse for wear in the damp atmosphere. On the far wall was a rack holding a full set of Indian Clubs. Detective Constable Lodge was cleaning a pair of clubs with an uncharacteristically delicate touch.

A number of men were hitting bags or skipping furiously. Two young featherweights were sparring in the ring. They were both very skilled but too young to be policemen Lodge thought as he wandered over to Bridle who was watching them intently.

'Got some new recruits?' Lodge asked as the fleet-footed boxers skipped around the ring and clashed with impressive ferocity. Bridle ignored Lodge for a moment as he concentrated on the ring.

'These are the best lads from the Boys Club' Bridle said without looking away from the ring.

'Oh yeah, I forgot about your charity work' Lodge said with a smirk.

Lodge often sneered at Bridle's involvement in the club for street boys in the south-end of Liverpool. He saw it as a weakness in Bridle and took every opportunity to try and put him off it.

'How does it feel to be on Radford's murder squad?' Lodge tried not to sound too bitter but he didn't make a good job of it. Bridle sighed quietly.

'I heard the big boys asked for you personally. You must have impressed them when you solved that shopping bag snatch from that old lady in town last week.'

A mocking grin spread across Lodge's face but Bridle responded with a chuckle.

'What's so funny?' Lodge snarled.

The question made Bridle break into a laugh as Lodge grew more exasperated until he exploded.

'Look boss, I've been in the job a long time, I didn't go to grammar school like you but I'm a good copper. I never get a chance.'

He slammed his huge fist on the canvas and the two boxers stopped and glared at Lodge for breaking their concentration. Lodge looked at them sheepishly and they resumed their sparring.

'Grammar school' Bridle laughed again 'that's a new one Tommy anything else on your mind?'

Lodge thought for a moment.

'There might be but don't let me kick off.'

'Grammar school didn't impress Stella's family' Bridle said thoughtfully.

'Oh yeah I forgot about them' Lodge sneered 'Sir Nigel put in a good word with the brotherhood did he?' 'Shower of bastards.'

Bridle knew it was never wise to interrupt Tommy Lodge in mid-rant.

'Sir Nigel wouldn't put in a good word for me unless it was in a divorce court Tommy.'

Lodge grunted in frustration. Bridle understood his anger. Lodge had spent many years watching younger men go above him. It happened to everyone but it had happened to Lodge too many times. He seemed to deflate as he always did when his anger subsided.

'So when do you go boss?' Lodge sighed.

'Go?'

'To HQ to join the team' Lodge snapped.

Bridle took a long look at his partner.

'We report on Monday morning.'

Lodge nodded vacantly for a moment and then a light seemed to switch on his eyes. It was as if a lifetime of mistrust and bitterness had been interrupted by a glimmer of redemption.

'Don't let me down you miserable old duffer.'

Bridle murmured then jumped into the ring to speak to the fighters. Lodge knew that Bridle must have taken a big risk to get him a transfer. He looked at Bridle and wondered what made him tick. He was the kind of man who was either liked or hated and Lodge knew Bridle had made enemies in the service. His habit of blunt speaking hadn't done him any favours and Lodge felt a twinge of guilt for the times he had back-stabbed Bridle himself. But Lodge reasoned that he had betrayed just about everyone in the department at some point so Bridle shouldn't take it too personally.

'I must be a good copper' Lodge muttered to himself' 'I'm still suspicious even when someone does me a favour.'

Bridle made his way along the promenade in the late evening and could see the light still burning in Stella's work-room. It always made him smile but it filled him with guilt to think of her stitching away in the evening to finish a job to a deadline. Stella had turned her back on a comfortable middle-class lifestyle to be with him and had alienated her family. He was haunted by a dark feeling that one day she might realise that he wasn't worth it.

Bridle looked back as the setting sun appeared to extinguish the city he policed across the river. He was trying to remember what was for supper when he heard the clatter of boots running up behind him. He turned quickly and saw the ragged figure of Joey Vance run up to him breathless and gasping.

'What's wrong Joey?' Bridle was stunned for a moment 'breathe deep Joey and calm down'.

Joey was nineteen but he was considered to be slow witted. He was well known around the south end of the city and had a habit of turning up unexpectedly and in the strangest places but Bridle had never seen him on this side of the river before.

'Where are you going Joey?' Bridle held his arm.

'To me see me aunty.'

'Where does your aunty live?' Bridle knew he was lying.

'Up der… somewhere' he pointed vaguely up the promenade.

'Does she live in New Brighton?'

34

Joey shrugged his shoulders. Bridle knew that the more nervous Joey got the less coherent he became.

'Look Joey I live up the prom, you can walk with me, we can have a chat.'

Joey instinctively pulled away and tried to look over his shoulder but Bridle held firm. He had never seen Joey in this state before and he wanted to get to the bottom of it.

'What's scaring you? Have you been caught nicking stuff Joey?'

'No… not been near any shops… been on the boat.'

'Did you bunk over on the ferry? Did the gateman chase you up the landing?'

Joey had to think about it for a moment. As if he thought Bridle might turn him in for the boat fare.

'Didn't get caught… he didn't see me… I was quick Mr. Bridle.'

Joey relaxed for a moment and Bridle eased his grip.

'Come on we'll have a walk up the prom.'

Bridle grinned and started to walk casually away and Joey stood motionless for a moment and then ran to catch up with him. Bridle slipped his hand in his pocket and pulled out a lumpy paper bag and started to open it slowly. He threw a glacier mint into his mouth and offered the bag to Joey. Joey slowly reached out and took a mint from the bag and held it under his nose to smell it then stuffed it quickly into his mouth.

'My dad used to buy these – kept him going on long shifts.'

Bridle said walking slowly and glancing at Joey to judge his state.

'Was your dad a Jack like you Mr. Bridle?'

Bridle chuckled 'No he worked on the railways.'

'Was he a train driver?'

Joey stopped and looked at Bridle with wide eyes and gaping mouth. Bridle looked at Joey's face and didn't have the heart to tell him his dad was a labourer more likely to clean a train than drive one.

'My dad was the best train driver that ever left Lime Street Station.'

Joey became more animated.

'Did he take you up in the front where the driver sits?'

'Loads of times' Bridle lied.

'Did yer blow the big steam whistle?'

'Yeah my job was to blow the big whistle for me dad' Bridle grinned.

'Wow.'

Joey sucked on his mint as he walked along pondering the idea of blowing the big whistle on a steam train.

'So which way are you going from here Joey?'

'Not sure.'

Bridle stopped outside his house. The light in Stella's workroom was still on and he wasn't sure what to do with Joey.

'You haven't got an aunty over here have you Joey?'

Joey pulled a face and slipped his hands in his pockets.

'No'

'And you haven't just bunked over on the ferry have you?'

Bridle had noticed dry sand on his trousers and boots.

'Been to the seaside'

'You said you'd been on the ferry.'

'I was lyin' Mr. Bridle.'

'Why?'

Joey gave Bridle a puzzled look.

'Cos you're a Jack, everyone tells lies to Jacks.'

Bridle stifled a laugh. It was endemic not to trust a copper least of all a Jack. A car came in to view along the promenade and Joey instinctively tried to run but Bridle caught him within a couple of fast strides. Joey was strong but Bridle held on fast as he tried to hide his face from the car as it idled past.

'Are you in trouble Joey?'

Bridle looked Joey straight in the eye which unsettled him.

'Is someone after you?'

'Can't say Mr. Bridle'

'Is that because I'm a Jack?'

Bridle knew it was a stupid question to ask. Bridle pulled him toward the front door of his house but Joey pulled back.

'Are yer gonna lock me up Mr. Bridle?'

'Does it look like a bridewell Joey? This is my house and I'm going to give you a hot cup of char and something to eat.'

Bridle knocked on the door with one hand and held on firmly to Joey with the other. Stella answered the door and was a little startled to see the scuffle on her doorstep.

'Is everything alright?'

Stella looked at the state of Joey in his ragged clothes and boots as Bridle pulled him over the doorstep and into the parlour.

'This is Joey Vance an old friend of mine from the south-end. He's been sleeping rough and could do with a hot drink and a something to eat.'

Bridle grinned and motioned with his eyes to Stella who realised she had to treat the situation as normally as possible.

'Hello Joey, my name is Stella it's very nice to meet you.'

Stella held out her hand and smiled at Joey. Bridle could see that Joey was smitten as most men were with Stella. Joey wiped his grubby hand on his trousers and Stella looked at Bridle who was grinning. Joey shook her hand timidly and stared at her face.

'You look like a film star.'

Bridle was shaking with silent laughter behind Joey and Stella fought to keep her face straight.

'Why that's the most charming thing any man has said to me in a long time.'

'You even talk like a film star.'

Bridle stepped in and took Stella's arm.

'I think I'll have to keep my eye on you Joey I didn't know you were such a charmer.'

One of Stella's sketch pads was lying open on the parlour table and it caught Joey's eye.

'Can I draw Mr. Bridle?'

He sat down quickly at the table and picked up the pencil.

'Of course you can' said Stella. 'Can you draw me something nice while I put the kettle on?'

Joey blushed slightly and started to scribble away at the pad with his nose almost touching the paper.

The tiny kitchen was just off the parlour and Bridle spoke quietly as Stella put the kettle on the gas ring and deftly lit it with a match.

'I found him on the prom, something's wrong. He's been sleeping rough and I don't think he's eaten anything for a while.'

'He hasn't had a wash either' Stella wrinkled her nose and looked over at him scribbling on the pad 'where does he live?'

'He lives in a slum tenement with his Mother. She's a part-time whore and a full time alcoholic. All their money goes on booze. Joey hangs around street gangs, runs for them, anything to stay out of the house. He wants to tell me something. He wouldn't just turn up here out of the blue.'

Stella put two buttered scones on a plate and Bridle had a horrible feeling that they were part of his supper.

'Were they for my… '

'Supper' Stella smiled 'yes they were.'

Stella marched through to the parlour and set the plate down next to Joey.

'There you are Joey enjoy those while I make the tea.'

Joey looked up from his drawing and saw the cherry scones on the plate. His eyes widened, and he hesitated for a moment then he took a scone and bit it in half. He swallowed it quickly and treated the other half just as harshly. Bridle knew that Stella hated housework and he winced as he saw the remnants of the scones hitting the parlour floor.

'You were right he hasn't eaten anything for some time.' Stella said with genuine concern.

They both watched as he scraped every crumb from the plate and then from the table. When he leaned back and eyed the crumbs on the floor Stella turned her attention back to the tea-pot very quickly. Bridle wandered back into the parlour and idly looked over Joey's shoulder to see his drawings which appeared to be match-stick men. Joey covered the pictures with his arm.

'Just looking Joey'

'You'll laugh.'

'No he won't' Stella said brightly as she carried the tea things on a tray and placed it on the table. Joey was puzzled by the array of dishes, cups and saucers, spoons and pots.

'Which one's got tea in it?'

Bridle grinned as it took him some time to get used to Stella's posh teas.

'Here let me pour' Stella said.

Joey watched with nervous anticipation as she placed a small china cup on a saucer in front of him. It had an ornate, floral pattern on it but to Joey it looked about the size of thimble. Stella poured tea from a patterned china tea pot.

'Milk'

Stella held up a small jug with a pattern that matched the tea pot and looked at Joey. He nodded.

'Help yourself to sugar.'

Joey picked up the sugar bowl and dropped three lumps of sugar into his cup then, after pondering for a moment he dropped in another one. Then he set about stirring it so hard that it splashed over the rim of his cup. He picked up the cup and saucer and considered what to do with the spillage. Bridle knew what was coming next but Stella could only watch open-mouthed as Joey put the saucer to his lips and drank the spillage with a heavy slurping sound. He grinned sheepishly at Stella then wiped his mouth and nose on his filthy sleeve.

'Are you going to tell us why you're here Joey?'

Bridle spoke calmly as he sat down at the table as casually as he could. Joey looked suspicious but felt more relaxed with Stella in the room.

'Are you gonna put me in a cell?'

'Why would I do that Joey?'

'Dunno.'

'Have you done something wrong?'

Joey grew more agitated.

'No, not me Mr. Bridle'

'Who then, why are you so worried?'

'I didn't do anything I just saw the man.'

Bridle looked at Stella. He could see she was genuinely concerned for the boy.

'Want more tea Joey?' Bridle knew he had to take it slowly.

'Got any more of them cakes?'

Stella turned and made her back to the kitchen and Joey looked at her with the kind of smitten face Bridle had seen so many times on so many men.

'What man did you see Joey?' Was he doing something wrong?'

Joey looked at the floor and mumbled.

'I saw the feller in the paper… talkin' to another feller on the dock… I was hidin' after the fight… they both saw me and the little bloke chased me but I lost him easy.'

Bridle didn't understand what he was talking about at first but then it struck him and he couldn't believe his luck. Bridle took a deep breath.

'Which feller was this Joey?'

'The one that got topped on the dock, I saw him talkin' to this little feller after the fight, you was there Mr. Bridle' Joey sighed in exasperation.

Bridle paused for a moment but had to ask the question.

'Did you see the murder Joey?'

Joey was getting impatient and ignored the question.

'The little feller chased me. He was fast. Not fast enough though' Joey said with pride and a side glance at Stella.

Bridle grinned and nodded but his mind was racing.

'You've always been fast down the wing Joey.'

'Only when they let me play Mr. Bridle, they don't always let me play.'

'You're too fast for them' Stella said and Joey blushed.

'So why were you hiding after the fight?' Bridle asked carefully.

Joey looked at the floor. Bridle didn't want to get heavy-handed but he was getting a little frustrated now.

'I nicked some of the stake money Mr.Bridle, only ten bob, but they all started fightin' so I legged it.'

Bridle recalled the commotion that had broken out after the fight and how Doyle and his heavies had ushered David Grant's party out of the Judas gate in a hurry.

'So you think he chased you for the ten bob?'

'Dunno… they were shoutin' at each other… the little feller was pokin' the posh feller in the chest with something… think it was a blade.'

Joey looked toward the kitchen for his scones. Bridle couldn't help feeling that this was too good to be true.

'Joey I know you don't like talking to a Jack'…

'They'll call me a snout Mr. Bridle.'

'No Joey if you give me as much detail as you can I might be able to find this killer without calling you to trial or ever naming you, do you understand?'

Stella stepped back into the room with the tea-tray and set it down on the table firmly then threw a hard glance at her husband. Bridle caught the look but ignored it. Stella was seeing her husband's professional face for the first time and she wasn't comfortable with it. Even she knew that the chances of keeping Joey's involvement quiet were nil and she felt her husband was manipulating this slow-witted boy. She glared at Bridle but he refused to meet her stare.

'You said the man was small, can you remember what he looked like?' 'Was he stocky or thin, dark haired or fair?' Bridle knew he was rushing Joey but felt he had to.

'Can I have a cake Mrs?'

Joey's brow was furrowed and it seemed to Stella that he was looking to be rescued.

'Of course you can Joey but only if you help me with the dishes.'

Bridle threw a sharp look in her direction then he shoved the plate of scones under Joey's nose.

'Joey I need to know what this man looked like' Bridle was aware that Stella had folded her arms which meant her temper was on the rise.

'He was only small.'

'You already said that... have you seen him before?' 'Do you know him?'

Stella turned on her heel and went into the kitchen.

'Do you know him Joey?'

'No never seen him before Mr. Bridle.'

'You know everyone in the city Joey so this feller must be from out of town.'

Joey's face brightened as he slowly understood.

'Yeah... I think he was foreign anyway.'

Bridle took a deep breath and rubbed his forehead in frustration.

'Foreign?'

Bridle had to think about his questions. Liverpool was a major port and crews from all over the world were a common sight in the town. Joey was used to seeing lots of faces of varied race but many of them were born and bred in Liverpool.

'What makes you say he was foreign Joey?'

'The way he talked.'

'The way he talked to David Grant?'

'Yeah, and the posh bloke spoke the same back to him.'

Bridle paused for a moment. This was hard work and his patience was wearing thin. Stella had slammed every dish and pot into the cupboards with as much noise as possible which added to his frustration.

'Joey, are you saying that David Grant spoke to this stranger in his own language?'

Joey nodded his head and made a grab for a scone which he pushed into his mouth as though Bridle might take the plate away at any second.

'Do you know what language it was?'

Joey's mouth was full of scone and the butter dripped out over his lips and down his chin. He shrugged his shoulders and spoke through the debris.

'Dunno.'

'What do you think it sounded like?'

Joey shrugged his shoulders again and Bridle let the frustration show on his face. This made Joey withdraw into himself and he folded his arms and pouted.

'Are you pleased with yourself now?' Stella said.

She was at the kitchen door with her hands on her hips. Bridle stood up and strode over to her and ushered her back into the kitchen.

'Look Stella, you don't know how important this is. This is a murder investigation.'

'All I can see is a man I thought I knew bullying a simple-minded boy.'

'I am going easy on him. If some of the bastards in the station got hold of him God only knows where he'd end up. He's come here to talk to me but he's scared. Wake up Stella.'

'Perhaps I have just woken up, perhaps I'm seeing the real you.'

'Look I've got a job to do and I have to get results.'

'By being a bully' Stella's eyes flashed.

He knew it was pointless arguing with Stella when she was in this mood. He glanced into the parlour and let out a loud curse. Joey had gone. Bridle dashed through the parlour and out of the front door. He almost fell headlong down the steps to the promenade and glanced quickly left and right. There was no sign of him and it was too dark to see far. Stella strode up behind him and punched him on the shoulder.

'This is your own fault – you bullied him.'

Bridle had let a golden opportunity get away from him and he was furious about it.

'Stella I was trying to get his trust and you got in the way. You know nothing about my work you know nothing about the world I move in. Joey was an important witness.'

'He was a frightened boy' Stella snapped back.

'Yes I know and I had to use that.'

'Oh I see! It's alright to use people when you see fit. What was it you said to my father about not using people?'

Bridle had no answer to that.

'Stella I was trying to help the lad. I got frustrated because he was scared and he was slow. You shouldn't have interfered.'

Stella opened her mouth to respond but thought better of it. She let out a squeal of frustration and stormed back up the steps. Bridle noticed the curtains next door twitching frantically. He cursed under his breath and walked over to the promenade rail and looked down into the black river. He knew Joey was like an alley cat and could look after himself. He also knew Radford's methods and had no intention of throwing Joey to him.

Bridle turned around and looked at the house. The front door was wide open and the hall light burned across the prom. The light in Stella's workroom came on and he could see her shadow storming across the room aimlessly. He suddenly became aware of his stomach rumbling as he made his way back up the steps to the door. By the time he reached the parlour he had resolved to tell Radford nothing. His priority was to find

Joey and make the most of the opportunity. He could hear Stella crashing around her work-room and for a moment he thought about making up to her but his stomach led him directly to the kitchen instead.

CHAPTER THREE

Councillor Jack Finney sipped his pint of mild in the corner of the saloon bar of the Lighthouse pub on Lime Street. The pub was one of many along the street packed full of sailors, dock workers, whores and other revellers in varied stages of drunkenness. He sat in his favourite bench-seat under the main window which was long enough to accommodate other members of his group of socialists with himself as the centre of attention. Outside the window a Salvation Army band was playing abide with me, very slowly and a middle-aged lady in full uniform was rattling a collection box and singing off-key but with great enthusiasm. The cheap scent used by the whores was pungent enough to disguise their body odour and they squealed as loud as possible at the raucous jokes of potential customers.

The animated group around Finney smoked and talked casually about local and world news. Finney was something of a legend among the young guard of the party. His leadership and drive to improve the conditions of the working class in the city had won him many loyal friends and a dangerous number of enemies. Finney enjoyed the adulation and never tired of recalling his early involvement as a serious political activist. Left-wing intellectuals courted his company as if proximity would give them credibility. The local newspapers hung on to his every word because he was always good for a controversial quote.

Finney's old instincts had never left him. Even in deep conversation he would have one eye on the door or on the stranger in the next seat. He could never drop his guard. The door of the saloon was opened so cautiously it immediately caught Finney's attention but he relaxed when he saw the face of Harry Croft peer through the smoky gloom. Croft nodded when he saw Finney then turned back to the door and ushered two companions to follow him. Finney stood up as Croft approached with an outstretched hand and Finney shook it enthusiastically and those of his two Spanish companions. He shouted above the noise to make their way upstairs to the meeting room.

Harry Croft was a short but powerfully built man in his early forties. What was left of his hair was cropped and steel-grey. His face was tanned and lean and he moved with the physical assurance of a trained man. Croft had distinguished himself as a young professional soldier in the latter stages of the Great War. He was a natural leader and had become one of Finney's most popular leaders and hard line activists.

Finney led the group up two flights of stairs and into a spacious but dimly-lit room. At the front was a long, shabby wooden table with four chairs behind it. Rows of rickety wooden chairs were ranked tightly across the room and as Finney, Croft and his Spanish friends took their seats at the table the rest of the group sat around in small pockets excited at the prospect of the talk. The room began to fill with people from all backgrounds. A few were academics and Finney nodded graciously as they entered. Some were trade unionists and others were young political students. The number had grown to over forty when Finney decided to stand up and start the meeting. He thrashed the gavel until the chatter around the room died down.

'It is my great pleasure to welcome you here tonight. I am proud to introduce Mr. Harry Croft and his Spanish patriots. As you all know Harry has been in Spain fighting as a volunteer with the International Brigade. He has come here tonight to inform and motivate us as only he can. I give you Harry Croft ladies and gentlemen.'

As the wild applause faded Croft moved around the table and stood confidently in front of his audience. He stared hard at their faces for a moment as if to paralyse them with his piercing blue eyes then he began.

Finney watched with admiration as the charismatic Harry Croft held the audience with his graphic account of the Spanish Civil War. Croft's natural leadership shone through as he shocked and inspired his audience. His appeal to raise funds to arm the Spanish people was received with emotional applause.

'I beg you to give these noble people the means to defend themselves against ruthless oppressors, thank you ladies and gentlemen.'

Croft returned to his seat as the audience stood up and applauded furiously.

'Harry is usually a man of few words' Finney said above the applause.

'Not like you Jack!' A voice chipped in to the amusement of the audience.

'Thanks for that contribution brother' Finney grinned 'I was about to say Harry is a man of action not words. He won't tell you this but he has been recognised for his conspicuous bravery in many campaigns and he has now distinguished himself for the cause in Spain. Harry is touring the north of England for the next seven days talking about the civil war and recruiting interest in our forthcoming rally and protest march against unemployment.

He's not going back to Barcelona he's staying here to help lead our fight.' Finney raised his fist and the crowd cheered. 'The bar's still open if you want a glass and Harry will be here to answer any questions, thank you ladies and gentlemen.'

Another round of applause cracked through the air and Finney turned proudly to Croft and shook his hand.

'Spot on Harry nicely spoken.'

'Thanks Jack. I hope I get the same response in all our meetings this week.'

Finney and Croft left the stage and mingled with the chattering audience. The Spaniards had been cornered by some academics eager to hear a first-hand account of the uprising. A tray holding four pints of stout was placed on a table next to Finney by a dark haired man who turned to Finney with a quick smile. Croft stepped forward.

'Jack I want you to meet a friend of mine. We fought together until he joined the American contingent. Meet Callum Riley. He's reckless, dangerous and full of Irish charm.'

'All that and handsome too' Riley said with a grin.

They both laughed as Croft slapped his friend on the back.

'Callum is a veteran of the Irish war of independence as he likes to call it.'

Finney shook his hand and took in the detail of the man. He was about six feet tall and in his late thirties. His hair was jet black and his eyes were dark brown but his face was dominated by a broad smile that exposed large and perfectly straight white teeth. He looked like a charmer not a fighter but Finney knew better than to underestimate anyone. He trusted Croft's judgement but remained cautious.

'A man of your size is an easy target on a battlefield Mr. Riley' Finney said.

'I learned to keep me head down on the streets of Derry' Riley grinned.

'Why did you join the American militia?'

Riley broadened his dazzling grin and looked Finney squarely in the eye.

'Do I really have to answer that one Mr. Finney?' Riley's grin disappeared as he raised his glass to his lips.

'Irish Republican' Finney said quietly.

'Till the day I die.'

'Which won't be too long eh Callum' Croft laughed.

'Harry thinks I take too many risks but what the hell' Riley said with a wink then moved off to mingle with the crowd. Finney turned to Croft and spoke quietly.

'Harry we are raising money for a legitimate political cause do you think it's wise to have a rebel with us?'

'He's not active anymore Jack I can vouch for him.' Croft's face turned a little dark and Finney tensed 'don't you approve of my friends Jack?'

'You know what I am trying to say Harry. The last thing we need is any undue attention.'

'Never change do you Jack? You see bogey-men everywhere.'

'It's not like a battlefield out here Harry. No one wears a uniform. The enemy dress the same as you and they eat at your table.'

Croft laughed and took a swig of his beer then pointed at Riley who was entertaining a group with stories of his adventures in Spain.

'Look at him Jack. He's a great fighter but he's also a drunk and a womaniser. One of those three will kill him eventually and I wouldn't bet good money on which one.'

Croft laughed and shook his head as he made his way over to join his Irish friend who was relishing all the attention.

Finney trusted his instincts but decided to reserve judgement on Riley. He took his pint and wandered around the edge of the room absorbing the excitement. It was Finney's habit to look out of the window at regular intervals to appease his deeply rooted paranoia. He drew the curtain back and peered at the street through the dirty window panes. He had a good view across Lime Street to the soot blackened monolith of St. Georges Hall. Hard memories came back to him as he gazed blankly across the street. His reverie was broken as a figure below caught his eye. Two police officers were wandering slowly along the opposite side of the street and one of them held Finney's attention. He knew that slow, deliberate gait and the way he carried his swagger stick. There was no mistaking the man. Finney stared hard at Mcleish and sneered at the badge of rank on his epaulettes.

'Superintendent Mcleish' Finney whispered through gritted teeth. His mind swiftly fell into a dark place and not even the party atmosphere could lift him out of it.

Bridle and Lodge hesitated outside the office of Radford's murder squad and glanced at each other then Bridle opened the door forcefully and stepped through. The office was large and cluttered with typewriters, filing cabinets, open box files and telephones. There were a number of small rooms off the main area including Radford's office which was at the far-end and had his name emblazoned on the glass panel of the door. As they entered there was a classic moment of silence as all heads turned to look at them. Then the ice was broken by a heavy accented drawl from the back of the room.

'Tea boys have arrived lads.'

The room erupted with laughter and Bridle and Lodge knew that such initiations were an evil that had to be endured with detached humour.

'It's big, bad Tommy Lodge' another voice chipped in 'bloody hell Tommy what are you doing here?''Are yer knocking off Radford's wife or something?'

The laughter went round the room again but Lodge was determined to match their banter.

'Nah I wouldn't shag Radford's wife again, I spent too much time in the queue.'

The office burst into laughter then dipped sharply into silence and Lodge knew immediately that Radford had entered the room. In the short space of time before Radford stepped into his view Lodge reflected on the good and bad luck in his life. He rated this very highly on the bad side.

Radford stepped slowly around Bridle and Lodge and looked them up and down as if they had just crawled out of a sewer. Radford was of medium height but over-weight and beer-bloated. The hair on his balding head was swept back at the sides and had the slick look that could only be achieved by an excessive use of hair-cream.

'Look what they're sending us now lads, the dregs of CID' Radford sneered.

Bridle gritted his teeth. He had endured Radford for many years in the department and he knew the only way to handle his sneering and sniping was to ignore it until he got bored with it. But Bridle never found it any easier.

'Try and find something to do but don't get in my way' Radford said looking at Bridle.

Radford strode across the room and nodded at two

Detective Sergeants who followed him into his office. Lodge turned to Bridle.

'That's me finished.'

Bridle nodded in agreement.

'Good start Tommy.'

Bridle looked around for anyone he knew. They were all familiar but he didn't really know any of them and then he saw a grinning row of crooked teeth in the far corner and he let out sigh of relief.

'George Sullivan, that's a bit of good luck' Bridle said in a low voice.

Lodge was genuinely pleased to see the chubby face grinning at them from behind a heap of files. Sullivan stood up as they approached and he shook their hands with enthusiasm.

'How did you two manage to get stuck with Radford again?' Sullivan chuckled at them and he had the kind of jolly face that forced them to smile back.

'Long story' Bridle said 'good to see you George I thought they might have pensioned you off after that accident?'

'No such bloody luck, it's another three years to my retirement' Sullivan lifted his leg to show his ankle strapped in a thick bandage.

'I'm on light duties so I do all the filing and most of the typing for this lot.'

'Radford's cronies' Lodge muttered.

'You said it' Sullivan chuckled again then his big round face suddenly turned serious 'they don't want you around so watch yourselves.'

'Shower of bastards' Lodge sneered.

Bridle smirked at Lodge then took in the atmosphere of the room. They were getting furtive glances and the occasional snigger. Bridle took a deep breath and vowed to himself that he would make a success of this even if he had to do it alone. Bridle turned to Lodge.

'Look Tommy I got you into this. I didn't know it would be so hostile. If you want to go back to Division I won't blame you.'

'I'm tempted' Lodge grinned 'but you'll get more knives in your back than Julius Caesar so I'll stay for the assassination.'

Lodge's big shoulders bounced up and down as he laughed but Bridle appreciated his backhanded show of loyalty.

'That's your desk over there by the toilet door and believe me if they could have put you in the toilet they would have done' Sullivan said.

'What have they got George?' Bridle stood casually and tried not to draw any more attention.

'If you want the truth they've got sod all. A lot of statements no real suspects and a load of pressure from the big-wigs.'

'What big-wigs?' Bridle knew how sensitive the case had become and Sullivan kept his voice down as he replied.

'The Grant family are really influential. The pressure is on Radford from all sides and he's feeling it. If he doesn't get a quick result that bastard will fix somebody up for it.'

Lodge gave out low whistle through his teeth.

'It's complicated because you were at that fight' Sullivan said looking at Bridle 'Radford's mixing a toxic bottle for you and if he can wreck your career he will do.' Sullivan's cheerful face darkened slightly but then he changed his mood quickly and spoke loudly.

'Anyway I've put loads of reports on your desk so you can catch up – don't worry lads it'll only take forever.'

Sullivan's comment sent a snigger around the room. Bridle

glanced at the stack of files on the desk then grinned at the look of horror on Lodge's face.

'Look George you've read everything so where the hell do I start?'

Bridle knew he was taking a risk by trusting Sullivan so completely but he had no choice.

'Start by not getting too cocky' Sullivan hardened his look and Bridle sensed he was being tested.

'I can't afford to show any weakness in this snake pit' Bridle snapped.

'That's for sure' Sullivan nodded his head slowly.

'Are you thinkin' of going it alone on this boss?' Lodge asked.

'What's the alternative Tommy? Just settle for the donkey work?'

'Radford will crucify you' Lodge responded.

'Radford won't take any notice' Sullivan said 'as long as you keep out of his way and file a few reports now and again.'

Bridle knew Sullivan was right and he was prepared to take the risk.

'Read the files before you do any leg work – that's basic' Sullivan said 'then I'd start with Miranda Shaw. Her statement is just too sketchy for my liking.'

Sullivan was an old warhorse with good instincts and Bridle trusted his advice.

'Thanks George' Bridle said 'I'll make a start on these files.'

Bridle let out a heavy sigh threw his coat over the chair and sat down. Lodge squirmed and fiddled with the other chair.

'Two sugars in mine Tommy' Bridle said without looking up from the desk.

'Three in mine Tom' Sullivan grinned at the relief on Lodge's face.

Lodge made a quick exit for the tea room which was on the floor below and Bridle knew that by the time he'd had a smoke and a chat to whoever was passing it would be at least an hour before he saw him again.

Sir Nigel Carver sat quietly in Sir Edward Grant's garden and sipped a cup of strong Indian tea. It was late afternoon and the sun was now partially shaded by the tall oak at the bottom corner of Sir Edward's substantial lawn. Carver genuinely loved this garden. The lawn was manicured but the rest of it was designed to look as natural as a walk in the country. The garden ultimately ran down to the shore of the Dee estuary where Grant had a fishing boat moored up at his small private jetty.

Carver's wife Lady Marion was sitting some distance away in a shady wicker arbour with Grant's wife Lady Margaret and her daughter Amelia. Amelia was an accomplished musician and though not an outstanding beauty she was tall and slender and her almost spiritual innocence appealed to Carver's predatory nature. Though he was over twice her age it never occurred to him that she would not find him attractive and though she was grieving for her murdered brother it never occurred to him to change his attitude toward her. It was a curse to him that as he got older sexual interest in women of his own age had waned. To his personal shame he had to rely on vague fantasies about younger women that he knew would never be realised. Ageing was a cruel process for the ardent philanderer.

Carver reached into the breast pocket of his jacket and took out a silver cigarette case which was engraved with his initials in copperplate. The silver glistened in the sunlight and holding the smooth elegant case was as much of a sensual delight to him as the smoke itself. He opened the case and selected a cigarette then placed it between his lips. The immediate smell and then taste of the tobacco made him feel mellow even before lighting it. He savoured it for a few moments and then took a match from an ornate box on the table and lit it. He leaned back as he drew the smoke deep into his lungs and saw a kestrel cut a fast, straight line across the clear blue sky. He felt a great contentment at that moment in the warm sunlight of the afternoon.

Then he remembered the file. He had spent almost an hour reading it with a mixture of admiration, amazement and envy. The file on David Grant compiled by a private enquiry agency had made salacious reading which had ignited his lust for the fragrant young Amelia. He looked across at the young girl chatting with the older women and suddenly felt consumed with self-loathing. He was distracted by the sight of Sir Edward Grant striding across the lawn toward him.

Grant looked distinguished in white flannels a sharp navy-blue blazer and cravat. Carver thought Grant's style a little too staid, though acceptable for a man of little imagination and military bearing. Grant nodded and smiled at the ladies as he passed then Carver noticed the dour change in his demeanour as he turned back toward him.

'I hope the tea is to your taste' Grant said as he pulled out a chair and sat down.

'Excellent Edward and such a beautiful afternoon what more can a man ask for?'

Carver could see the tension in Grant's face and took a long draw on his cigarette.

'Margaret didn't see the file?' Grant snapped.

'Please have a little faith in my discretion Edward.'

'I'm sorry but these are trying times.'

'Yes for everyone involved' Carver said and gestured toward the ladies.

'I don't know how Margaret and Amelia have come through this' Grant sighed 'I owe Marion a great debt for her support.'

Carver nodded with a consoling smile and looked at his wife as she entertained and diverted the Grants with her wit and knowledge of all things horticultural. She was still a beautiful woman and their daughters had inherited her tactile charm. Often when he looked at his wife Carver would question his many infidelities but his conceit didn't allow him to dwell on the question for very long.

'Edward you do realise that you will have to hand this file over to the police?'

'I thought you would say that Nigel' Grant replied 'but the content.'

'Quite scandalous' Carver chuckled and took another long draw on his cigarette.

'That's the reason I can't give it to the police. My family would be devastated. I can't have that Nigel.'

Carver realised he had to be a little more sensitive to the situation and sat up in his chair to give Grant more of his attention, then he stubbed out the remainder of his cigarette in the ash-tray. He was distracted for a moment by an infectious laugh from Amelia then fixed a hard stare at Grant.

'The file is very detailed. David had an adventurous sex life. I am absolutely staggered at one or two of the names on the list – Lady Georgina… '

'Spare me your misplaced admiration Nigel.'

Carver sighed and sat back in his chair.

'Edward you do understand that any one of these women have a potential motive for murder. Two of these girls are no more than gutter prostitutes. They could have procurers who wouldn't think twice about murder or extortion.'

Grant's face turned grey and Carver had seen that look many times before. He reached into his jacket for his cigarette case. He deftly flicked open the case and offered it to Grant. Grant shook his head and took a leather cigar pouch from his jacket and drew a long cigar from it.Carver struck a match and lit his cigarette then sat patiently as Grant went through the ritual of lighting his cigar. Grant frowned at the look on Carver's face. It had changed from suave flippancy to the stern countenance of the courtroom.

'Edward how long has the blackmail been going on?'

CHAPTER FOUR

Bridle caught a tram for the south-end of the city. He had to clear his head. He'd spent most of the day reading through the case files and going over details with Sullivan. The tram was only half-full as it passed through the shadow of the Anglican Cathedral on St James Hill and made its way along Park Road toward the Dingle. Unemployed and war-injured men stood outside the many public houses along the road smoking stubs and making a pint of beer last as long as possible. It was common to see amputees on crutches and Bridle, like everyone else, had become accustomed to the sight of war veterans made prematurely old by injury and ill health.

Bridle watched as two beat officers approached an unlicensed street trader. His young runner gathered up his stock and sped like lightening down an alleyway. Bridle chuckled at the gormless look on the faces of the policemen. Further on a number of black-clad women carried washing wrapped in sheets to the bagwash on Peel Street. Their small, rotund frames distorted by regular and unplanned childbirth seemed to waddle in unison as they held their laundry bundles against their chests.

He jumped off the tram at High Park Street and strolled down toward Princes Road. The street was littered with ragged children playing games. This was an area where black and white children played together happily and where their parents fought each other regularly. As Bridle made his way down the street unemployed men were sitting on doorsteps in small groups sharing a newspaper and taking in the sun. They eyed him suspiciously as he was well known in the area but some gave him a furtive nod. He expected nothing more as he was a Jack and considered to be the enemy by most of the community.

As he passed Nelly Foster's sweet shop a group of very young girls were pretending to pick their favourite sweets from the jars in the window. Their clothes were dirty and ragged and some were shoeless but they laughed and giggled as they made their pretend purchases. Bridle had toughened himself to these scenes over many years on the beat in the area. He crossed the road to a tenement and made his way down the steps to the basement. As he descended the stench became so overpowering he gagged but composed himself as he banged on the door.

'If yer lookin' for the rent you can fuck off' a croaky female voice came from the other side of the door.

'Mrs. Vance I'm Detective Sergeant Bridle I need to talk to you about Joey.'

Bridle heard the door-bolt slam back and a number of curses as the door swung open. Mrs Vance flinched at the daylight and narrowed her eyes. She was in a cotton dressing gown which Bridle guessed might have been purple once but was difficult to tell with the amount of staining on it. Her greasy hair was bottle blonde and her make-up from the night before was caked on her face like a grotesque mask.

'What's the little bastard done now?'

She looked up the steps to see some street urchins leaning over the railings. An angelic-faced little girl looked at Bridle and shook her head.

'Watch it mister she's got the pox.'

Bridle stifled a laugh as Mrs Vance leapt out of the doorway 'fuck off yer little bitch' she shook her fist and they all squealed and ran off.

'Come inside quick I don't want no Jack seen on my doorstep' she turned and walked into the dark hall.

Bridle closed the door behind him and turned toward the damp and filthy parlour. He felt as if he was descending into some kind of hell as he slowly made his way forward in the dim light. The coal fire was burning hot which gave the room an oppressive atmosphere. Bridle's shoes were sticking to the rancid carpet as he made his way into the parlour. He looked around the room and saw a cluttered mess with filthy mugs, plates and dishes strewn across the table. There was an eye-watering stench of liniment which was made worse by the excessive heat and Bridle knew he wouldn't be able to stay in the room for long. In the centre of the room close to the fire was a tin bath and sitting in it was very big West Indian sailor.

'Take no notice of this bastard' she said pointing with her thumb 'he's from Jamaica, that's why it's so fuckin' hot in here. He can't understand a word we say so what d'yer want scuffer?'

Bridle and the Jamaican looked at each other passively as if it was a normal situation. The Jamaican was so big he was jammed into the bath with his knees bent up to his chest. The dirty water barely covered his waistline. Bridle was grateful that it did.

'I'm looking for Joey – where is he?'

'How the hell should I know?'

'Because you're his mother and he lives here.'

'Only when he feels like – sit down scuffer.'

Bridle looked at the greasy wooden chairs around the table and the tattered armchair near the fire.

'No thanks I'm not staying long.'

'Suit yer self' she sat down at the table and started rummaging through a full ashtray selecting and rejecting stubs until she found one that pleased her.

'When did you last see him?' Bridle's eyes were beginning to sting with the smell of the liniment.

'Weeks ago and I've had no upkeep money off the little sod either'. She turned the stub over in her fingers.

'Has he left for good?'

'He comes and goes, how should I know?'

'He's your son I thought you might have some idea.'

'The little bastard is nearly twenty it's not my fault if he's got the brains of a ten year old.'

'Do you know where he goes?' Bridle sighed as he knew it was a stupid question.

'Why would I tell a Jack even if I knew?'

She put the stub between her lips as though trying it for size and then started rummaging for a match.

'I saw him recently Mrs. Vance and I was a bit concerned for his welfare.'

'What about my welfare? No one gives a rats arse about me do they?' She croaked.

The Jamaican reached down for a small saucepan at the side of the bath then dipped it in the water and began to baste himself. Bridle stared at him until he put the pan down and resumed his blank look. Bridle loosened his tie a little as Mrs. Vance gave a piercing squeal. She had found a match. Bridle knew he was wasting his time as she was so hung-over on cheap gin it didn't seem possible to unscramble her brains.

'Who's this?' Bridle nodded toward the Jamaican 'one of Joey's uncles?'

'Well he can't be his fuckin' dad can he?' She squealed at her own joke and Bridle smirked and turned to walk out.

'Why is everyone looking for my Joey all of a sudden?' She struck the match and lit the stub with loving care. Bridle turned back quickly.

'What do you mean by everyone?'

'An Irish bloke came lookin' for him yesterday. Good lookin' bastard. I'd have shagged him for small change' she chuckled to herself and Bridle moved a little closer.

'What did he say?'

'He said I had beautiful blue eyes' her wistful smile revealed stained and rotting teeth 'only the Irish can fake that kind of genuine charm' she coughed loud and hard then took another drag on the stub. Bridle winced.

'Mrs Vance when I saw Joey he seemed scared of something or someone. Any information you can give me might be of help to him.'

'I don't talk to stinkin' Jacks' she snapped.

'Maybe I can change your mind down at the station' Bridle was losing patience.

'Oh sweet Virgin Mary, St Joseph and all the Archangels doesn't anybody care about me?' She slammed the stub into the ash-tray. 'Yer not takin' me down to the Bridewell, I've done nothin' wrong' she waved her fists in the air then knelt at her statue of St. Francis and joined her hands in prayer.

'How about soliciting for acts of prostitution?' Bridle said coldly.

'Can yer' hear this Jack callin' me a harlot up there in heaven St Francis?' She started howling as loud as possible 'I'm beggin' yer' St. Francis to get this Jack off me back. I'm just a poor mother abandoned by a wastrel of a husband. I try my best as

God is my witness. I love my son I love the bones of the useless little bastard.'

'Then where is he?' Bridle wasn't impressed by her performance.

'How the fuck should I know?' Her tears turned into a sneer.

'Get your coat Mrs. Vance I'm taking you in.'

'Yer can't collar me, I've done nothin' she squawked in desperation.

'I'll think of something by the time we get there' Bridle sighed.

'All you Jacks are evil bastards' she squealed and then began to sob.

'So you keep saying, now get your coat or go as you are' Bridle turned toward the door.

'Alright alright if I give you some information will yer leave us alone?'

She continued sobbing. Bridle turned back slowly and looked at Mrs Vance's emotional act. The tears had cut a channel through the make-up under her eyes and her mouth sagged at the sides. He tried not to laugh.

'What information Mrs. Vance?' He gave her a hard look and it occurred to him that they were both play-acting in their own way.

'Just give me a minute yer stinkin' Jack'

She staggered up from her knees and kissed the statue of St. Francis then started going through a pile of papers on the mantelpiece. Bridle looked at the Jamaican. His head was back and he was studying the ceiling so intently that Bridle looked up. A black stain covered a large portion of the ceiling and it looked to Bridle as if it was sagging slightly.

'Here it is' she squawked triumphantly and held a small piece of paper out toward Bridle with a huge grin on her face and no sign of any tears. Bridle took the paper and looked at it. There was no name just an address.

'Is that it?' Bridle wasn't impressed.

'The handsome Irish bastard said it was a nice hotel.'

'It's a doss-house off the Dock Road – what else did he say?'

'I'll get a bad name talkin' to scuffers like this.'

She pulled the sad face again and Bridle slipped the piece of paper into his pocket.

'Mrs. Vance this is your last chance' Bridle snarled.

'He said to tell Joey, Friday at two o'clock' she pulled a face as if the effort to remember was painful.

'When did he give you this message?'

'Er, what day is it today?' She looked puzzled and Bridle's patience was spent.

'Was it two in the morning or afternoon?' Bridle snapped.

'Joey is an alley cat, he only goes out at night' she spluttered.

The heat in the room was too oppressive for Bridle and he'd had enough of the atmosphere and the woman, he scowled and turned to leave. He was feeling nauseous.

'Call on me anytime Sergeant. I knock a few bob off for Jacks.'

Bridle looked back from the parlour door to see Mrs. Vance leaning forward provocatively with her gown open, partially revealing her huge breasts. He turned away and walked along the hall with a sick feeling in the pit of his stomach. As Bridle opened the front door he was confronted by a tall, square-shouldered man in his early forties.

'Who are you?' He asked glaring at Bridle.

'A police officer on my way out' Bridle noticed he reeked of ale and cigarettes. Bridle pushed past him and made his way up the steps to the street desperate to get some air. He stood at the top of the steps for a moment then looked back to see Mrs. Vance holding onto the stranger at the front door.

'He's a scuffer I swear on me fuckin' mother's life Charlie and the Jamaican only came round for a wash because his bath sprung a leak, honest to God. Would I cheat on you Charlie?'

Bridle turned and made his way along the street as some of the locals gathered to watch the commotion. Charlie broke free from Mrs. Vance and ran up the steps screaming at Bridle.

'Come back you, I'll tear yer apart.'

Bridle turned to see Charlie bearing down on him at a lumbering pace. Then he glanced right and left to see most of the street staring his way and waiting for a show.

'Don't be stupid I'm a police officer' Bridle shouted but knew it was already too late.

'You've been with my woman' Charlie screamed.

As he closed in on Bridle his fists were driving like pistons but Bridle ducked away easily then stepped to one side causing Charlie to stumble forward. The crowd roared with laughter. Bridle held both hands up in a gesture of parley but Charlie was now humiliated as well as angry. He ran at Bridle and threw out both arms in an effort to catch him in a bear-hug. Bridle ducked under his grip and deflected him sideways allowing his weight and momentum to carry him down the street and into the gutter. The crowd cheered and Bridle wondered how he was going to end it as there was no sign of a beat officer anywhere. Charlie pulled himself off the floor and looked around at the jeering crowd. Their goading was driving him mad. The ragged girls who had been playing at the sweetshop were watching intently and one of them shouted at Bridle.

'We'll get the scuffers for yer mister.'

The girls ran up the street at a good pace and Bridle felt an urge to smile until he saw Charlie holding an empty bottle of pale ale.

Charlie knocked the bottom of the bottle against a wall leaving a jagged edge of broken glass. He pointed it at Bridle like a knife. The crowd were completely silent now as the two men circled each other. Charlie lunged forward stabbing and swinging the bottle wildly as the screech of police whistles began breaking up the crowd. But it had come too late. Bridle stood his ground until the last moment then he caught the wrist of Charlie's bottle hand firmly. Charlie looked him in the eye and tried to pull his hand away but Bridle's grip was too strong. As Charlie drew back his free arm to throw a punch Bridle drove a powerful uppercut under Charlie's jaw. Bridle released his grip and stepped back. Charlie stood wobbling for a few moments as the crowd looked on in silence then his eyes rolled upward and he collapsed face-down on the street. The crowd cheered as two policemen pushed through and dispersed them. The younger policeman bent over Charlie and checked to see if he was still breathing then he grinned at Bridle.

'Looks like a broken jaw.'

'You took your time' Bridle said to the older policeman.

'Had to deal with unlicensed traders up the road Sarge' he said uneasily.

'I saw that from the tram' Bridle said with a smirk.

'It was those girls who alerted us Sarge a good bunch of kids they are' he said trying to change the subject.

'My rank is Detective Sergeant, not sarge' Bridle said flatly.

'Sorry Sergeant Bridle what do you want us to with him?' The officer asked contritely.

'Do what you want with him I'm not interested' Bridle said

and walked away. The policeman turned to his young colleague and spoke in a low voice.

'That's Detective Sergeant Bridle, runs the service boxing club, big-headed bastard.'

Nelly Foster's tobacconist and sweet shop hadn't changed much since Bridle's time as a beat copper. It still had ranks of sweet jars standing on dark varnished shelves. There was a strong smell of tobacco as he entered the shop because Nelly would sell it by the ounce for pipe or roll-ups. It looked a little shabbier than he remembered it and looking at Nelly's grinning face behind the counter he could see that she wasn't in the best of health. A tall woman in her late fifties she was a widow and lived alone having lost her only son in the war. Bridle could see that she was stooped and had a regular cough but she smiled just the same.

'It's about time someone sorted out that big bully.'

'Hello Nelly how are you keeping?' Bridle smiled.

'I'm fine Mr. Bridle I haven't seen you in a long time. Is it still Glacier Mints?'

Bridle laughed and nodded as Nelly set about weighing a quarter pound of his favourite sweets then she poured the mints from the scales into a paper bag and twisted it closed.

'I've been trying to find Joey Vance I don't suppose you've seen him around lately?'

'He came in yesterday afternoon and bought two sticks of liquorice and an ounce of baccy.'

'Did he now?' Bridle said quietly.

'I suppose she said she hadn't seen him?' Nelly sniffed.

'Yeah she did' Bridle nodded.

'She's an evil bitch. Joe only came home to give her some money.'

'Did Joey tell you that?' Bridle slipped the bag of mints into his pocket and she nodded.

'He used to tell me everything when he was growing up. Joe would spend hours in here just to keep out of the house while she entertained her customers.'

'So he had money on him?'

'He had ten shillings but I didn't ask where he got it. I've heard he's mixed up with Paddy Finch's gang but I don't ask questions it doesn't pay to ask questions.'

'Thanks for that Nelly you've been a big help.'

Bridle took some coins out of his pocket and noticed Nelly was smiling over his shoulder. He turned to see the band of ragged little girls had resumed their game of pretend sweet-picking on the other side of the window. Bridle put the coins for his mints on the counter and threw down an extra few pence then walked over to the door.

'Give those girls a mixed bag of sweets when I'm down the road. Thanks again Nelly' Bridle opened the door to step out and Nelly shouted.

'You're a good man Mr. Bridle.'

Bridle closed the door and made his way down the street. He pondered the story from Joey's mother. He assumed she was making it up to get rid of him but he knew he would check it anyway.

The tea room on Church Street was busy with afternoon shoppers and theatre goers having a cup of tea before the matinee at the Playhouse. Stella loved to come to town just to see the energetic hustle and bustle of the city. Her own lifestyle had become so grey and predictable she was beginning to doubt her ability to endure it. Meeting her sisters Elizabeth and

Caroline in town was always a giddy experience but not one that occurred very often. It had been almost a year since they had met socially and that was mainly due to embarrassment on their part. Stella's marriage to Bridle had been viewed by the family as a misjudgement due to her rebellious nature. It was generally considered that it would never last and Stella would go back to her own home and class and become Estella again.

As she sat alone at the table sipping her tea and waiting for her sisters she noticed disapproving stares from matronly ladies who no doubt thought it unseemly for a young lady to sit in a tea room alone. At another table three young men in their late teens were staring at her with stupid grins on their faces. The spottiest one seemed to be the most confident and he threw her an awkward wink which made his two friends fall apart with laughter. She almost blushed but decided to give them the obligatory look of contempt while stifling a giggle.

Elizabeth and Caroline burst into the tea room like a cyclone squealing and waving at Stella as best they could with hands full of shopping bags from the department stores. They shuffled quickly over to Stella's table and hugged her and kissed her on both cheeks with genuine affection. Elizabeth was the oldest but by far the most immature whereas Caroline who was two years younger than her sister was the sensible one. Elizabeth and Caroline had quickly conformed to the family expectation of a good marriage and Stella was determined to keep them off the subject of their husbands. She loved her sisters but found their husbands to be arrogant bores who could only talk about their own careers in law and banking to anyone unfortunate enough to be cornered by them.

'I know you enjoy playing the girl of the people Estella'

Caroline said looking around the room 'but really we could have met somewhere… '

'More appropriate' Stella said and Caroline pursed her lips.

'Don't look now' Elizabeth whispered 'but three very spotty youths are giving us the glad-eye from across the room.'

'Ignore them Elizabeth' Caroline snapped 'they are so uncouth they wouldn't even see the rings on our fingers.'

Elizabeth and Stella burst into laughter at the dour look on Caroline's face.

'Oh you two are impossible' Caroline sniffed.

Stella signalled a waitress and ordered tea and scones as her sisters brought her up to date on all of the news and gossip. Stella knew they were keeping the news of Guy Charlton's return till last and that they were desperate for her to ask about him first. But Stella also knew that Elizabeth wouldn't be able to hold it back for long. Elizabeth gave Caroline a playful glance and Stella guessed it was coming next.

'Estella we've got some very interesting news about the Whitely Ball.'

'Really Elizabeth and what could that be?' Stella asked.

'Someone is back from the dark and mysterious continent' Elizabeth said wide-eyed.

'I would hardly call southern Europe a dark and mysterious continent' Caroline said exasperated by her sister's sense of fun.

'Oh Caroline you are such a bore you've given it away' Elizabeth pouted.

'To be honest Daddy has already told me' Stella interjected.

'Guy Charlton in all his gorgeousness' Elizabeth couldn't contain her excitement.

'Elizabeth, do remember you are a married woman' Caroline said but studied Stella's face to discern any reaction. Stella sipped her tea and was so desperate to change the subject that she asked about their husbands.

Stella kept a straight face as they extolled the success of Malcolm and Gerald but she knew she was wasting her time trying to side-step the issue of Guy Charlton. She also didn't want to spoil their fun as anyone who had to go home to Malcolm and Gerald needed as much entertainment as they could get. Elizabeth shoe-horned Guy Charlton into the conversation again and Stella sighed.

'Alright, alright so Guy has come home and everyone thinks I am supposed to go all glassy-eyed. I've moved on. I'm happily married now.'

'Estella, Guy broke your heart when he left for Europe. You married the policeman on the rebound.' Caroline spoke bluntly and Elizabeth stared at her as if she couldn't believe what her sister had said.

'Really Caroline is that what you think? His name is John by the way' Stella folded her arms and looked her sister in the eye.

'That's what everyone thinks Estella' Elizabeth spluttered with excitement.

'I married John because I fell in love with him and I still love him' Stella kept her arms folded and her face stern.

'Of course you do dear' Caroline gave her a sympathetic smile and a condescending pat on her hand. Stella felt furious and was about to explode when Elizabeth let out a squeal.

'Oh I think John is so handsome and much more rugged than Guy. Don't you think so Caroline?' Elizabeth was desperate to lighten the conversation.

'He is hardly in the same class as Guy' Caroline sniffed.

Caroline was determined to make Stella crack as she did when they were children. Their spats were legendary in the family. Elizabeth was petrified that an eruption was about to occur in the middle of a tea room and amongst so many common people. Stella suddenly felt the emotion build up inside her and her eyes filled with tears but she was determined not to let them fall. Caroline saw the tears immediately then leaned forward and took her sister's hand.

'Oh I'm so sorry darling I didn't realise it was so bad for you.'

Stella hadn't realised it either until now.

'It's not that it's bad it's just not what I hoped it would be.' Stella couldn't believe she'd said it out loud and neither could her sisters. She took a sip of hot tea and looked at their concerned faces. She knew that they wanted her to leave Bridle and go back to the fold but she was equally determined not to.

'You can talk to us Estella' Caroline said with such an earnest look on her face that Stella almost laughed.

Stella pulled herself together and immediately regretted her moment of weakness. Sometimes it felt as though she spent her whole life in her work-room with no one to talk to. She found her husband's world to be rough and alien. Her loneliness had turned to confusion and she knew that she had to talk to him and clear the air. The return of Guy Charlton had also added to her confusion and her head was beginning to ache because she knew her sisters were not finished with her yet. Stella kept quiet as Caroline fired broadsides at Bridle and their relationship. Her headache grew worse and she stopped listening to the tirade until she heard Caroline's final suggestion.

'Why don't you move back in with mummy and daddy until you sort yourself out? They would love to have you home.' Caroline was serious and Stella was horrified that her expression of doubt had escalated into a separation in Caroline's mind.

'You don't know him Caroline. John is uncomfortable outside his own world.'

'His world Estella are the back-streets of a stinking city. Brawling with drunks in alleyways, scrambling for a promotion, that's his future, what's your's?' Caroline held Stella's gaze for a moment then Elizabeth sat up and brushed her blonde curls away from her face.

'So are you going to see Guy?' Elizabeth had to ask.

'It's been almost eight years Elizabeth. People change. I'm sure he must have a wife and family' Stella didn't want to be interested but couldn't help herself.

'Apparently not' said Caroline.

'Too busy making pots of money' said Elizabeth gleefully.

'I'm sure we can all catch up at the ball' Caroline glanced at Stella and sipped her tea.

CHAPTER FIVE

Miranda Shaw yawned as she stood motionless under the skylight in the studio of Hugh Tobias on Rodney Street. Tobias and a number of students were seated at easels around the room. A classic plinth stood in the centre of the stage with an arrangement of flowers on top. Miranda Shaw posed at the side of the plinth with her arm outstretched over the flowers looking vaguely heavenward toward the glowing sun pouring through the skylight. A tiara of flowers circled her auburn wig of ringlets which ran down her back to her waist. She was barefoot with one foot flat on the ground and the other raised on the ball as she reached up toward heaven. Her gown was white and diaphanous which gave her naked body an angelic glow. A heavy knock on the door broke the intense atmosphere of concentration.

'Door' Tobias bellowed.

The door opened before anyone could respond and Bridle stepped into the room followed by a bemused Lodge. Lodge had no time for academics and even less for artistic academics and his opinion was reinforced by the the sight of the bohemian students around the room. Then he looked up at the stage and his jaw dropped at the sight of Miranda Shaw bathed in sunlight and virtually naked. Lodge couldn't believe his eyes and even Bridle found himself staring.

'This is not an end of pier peep-show identify yourself or get out of my studio.'

Tobias hardly looked away from his canvas as he spoke. Miranda Shaw took a long look at Bridle. She had seen him before. Bridle tried not to stare back and was about to introduce himself.

'Never mind' Tobias boomed 'it's obvious from your vacuous attire that you are policemen in what your fevered imagination calls plain clothes. Please state your business.'

'I'm sorry to disturb your class Sir, I am Detective Sergeant Bridle and this is Detective Constable Lodge' Bridle and Lodge exchanged uncomfortable looks. Lodge had begun to sweat and was trying to look anywhere but at the stage. A bespectacled female student giggled at Lodge which made his discomfort even worse.

'Gentlemen have you never seen a naked Roman Goddess before?'

'Not in Liverpool I haven't' Lodge spluttered and the class laughed out loud.

'Darling put on your gown before these panting heterosexuals have heart failure.'

Lodge leaned toward Bridle's ear and whispered.

'What did he just call us boss?'

Bridle ignored him. He held Miranda Shaw's gaze as she made slow work of slipping on her silk gown.

'Mr. Tobias we're here to interview Miss Shaw.'

'What if I said it was just too inconvenient Sergeant' Tobias huffed.

'In that case Sir I would have to ask Miss Shaw to accompany us to the station.'

Tobias threw his hands in the air and shook his head.

'Who am I to obstruct the course of justice? You must conduct your civic duty Sergeant albeit at my expense' Tobias bowed his head as if he had just delivered a speech in a melodrama and the class laughed again. Lodge felt out of his depth.

'Take no notice of him' Miranda Shaw said as she stepped off the stage tying her gown. Lodge noticed how the silk gown hugged the curves of her body and he thought she was stunning naked but the gown just made it worse for him. She slipped the wig from her head revealing her dark bobbed hair. She tossed her her head from side to side to shake out her hair but her dark eyes never left Bridle.

'I am Miranda Shaw and I'm convinced I know your face Sergeant.'

'Is there anywhere we can talk privately Miss Shaw?' Bridle asked.

'I've already been interviewed by the police' she said firmly.

'We just need to clarify a few points if you don't mind Miss' Lodge responded.

She gave them a charming smile then looked at Tobias who rolled his eyes.

'Use my study darling but keep your eye on the big one, he looks hot under the collar.'

Lodge squirmed as the students laughed again. He was glad to leave the studio and go into a small study across the landing with a large window that overlooked Rodney Street. Miranda Shaw slid onto a leather chair under the window and curled up like a kitten. Lodge sat on the edge of a cluttered desk and Bridle sat opposite Miranda Shaw. Lodge took out his notebook and pencil and settled himself.

'Where would you boys be without your little notebooks?'

'We'd be lost Miss' Lodge said and she looked away coldly.

'Miss Shaw I was at the fight on the night of David Grant's murder and I saw you there.'

'I knew I'd seen you before, yes I noticed you. You stood out in a brooding sort of way.'

Lodge coughed and raised his eyebrows but Bridle ignored her comment.

'How long had you known David Grant?'

'It must have been three years.'

'Where did you meet?'

'We met in Oxford. He was pretending to study history and I was studying sex most of the time.'

Lodge nearly broke his pencil but Bridle made no reaction as he stared him down.

'You are from an Oxford family.'

'Yes I have been through this with the other officers' she leaned forward slightly and fixed Bridle with her dark eyes 'but I'll tell you something I didn't tell them – I hated David Grant.'

She sat back in the chair and giggled which Lodge found irritating.

'That's an interesting admission under the circumstances' Bridle said.

'Does that make me a suspect? How delicious' she giggled again.

'You were one of the last people to see David Grant before the murder.'

'That's true Sergeant but do I look like a killer?' She gave him a coy smile 'you both look like street brawlers, hardly the kind of police officers I'm used to in Oxford.'

'No Miss' Lodge said without looking up from his notebook 'up here we have to deal with hardened criminals not angry yokels or tipsy parsons.'

'Why that was quite droll and I was just thinking how boring you are' her eyes narrowed but Lodge didn't flinch as he replied.

'I suggest you answer the questions clearly and precisely Miss Shaw otherwise we might have to take you down to the station for questioning.'

'Is that a threat? I do like strong men but not quite so prehistoric.'

Lodge smirked and turned his attention back to his notebook.

'What happened after the fight?' Bridle asked ignoring their spat 'where did you go?'

'We were ushered into a filthy taxi by that rancid little man.'

'That would be Billy Doyle' Bridle said.

'I've no idea.'

'Where did the cab take you?'

'To the Adelphi Hotel we had rooms there' she looked at Bridle seductively and Lodge was beginning to tire of her femme fatale act.

'Grant must have left the hotel at some point' Bridle said.

'No he didn't Sergeant' she smiled in the hope it might annoy him.

'But he was murdered on the dock.'

'Yes but he didn't leave the hotel room because he didn't come with us' she giggled.

Bridle was confused and increasingly irritated.

'Are you wasting our time Miss Shaw? You didn't say that in your original statement, neither did Miss Porter or Mr. Swain.'

'Oh dear I seem to have let the cat out of the bag.'

'If that's true you will have to revise your statement Miss Shaw' Bridle was losing patience.

'What about spineless Swain and prissy Porter?' She asked with a smirk.

'Why did you all lie in your statements?' Bridle snapped.

She threw her hands up in the air in exasperation then shook her fists with a grunt. Bridle looked at Lodge for support but he returned a look that said you're the boss and you can deal with her. Bridle knew she wasn't stupid and it was obvious she wasn't scared. It was rare to find a woman who didn't show some fear or nervous tension when being interviewed by the police. It was something they relied on.

'Why did we lie in our statements? Fear Sergeant and I don't intend to say another word about my statement without legal representation' she sat back and folded her arms. Bridle sighed then took a deep breath.

'Why did you hate David Grant Miss Shaw?'

'Let me see what day of the week is it?' She looked Bridle playfully and Lodge rolled his eyes.

'Miss Shaw I don't think...'

'You see Sergeant I hated him for a different reason each day of the week, so on Monday I might hate him for being a drunk on Tuesday for being rich and spoiled on Weds...'

'I think we get the picture Miss Shaw. Did you hate him enough to kill him?' Bridle fixed his stare on her dark eyes. They widened as he asked the question and she uncurled herself from the chair.

'I considered killing him on a number of occasions Sergeant as did most of his inner circle.'

'And who exactly are his inner circle Miss Shaw?'

'That would give you too many suspects and I was so enjoying being suspect number one' she giggled and coiled herself back into the chair. Bridle knew he was getting nowhere and he found her difficult to read.

'Did you ever hear David Grant speak another language fluently?'

'I like you Sergeant' she said ignoring his question 'I don't really know why' she tipped her head to one side and looked at him quizzically.

'Miss Shaw, do you know who Grant spoke to on the dock that night?'

'Now let me see... '

She put her finger to her lip and Lodge let out a long impatient sigh. Bridle knew Lodge was telling him to get on with it or get out as she was making fools of both of them.

'Are you married Sergeant?'

'I don't answer personal questions.'

'Only you don't have a ring on your finger.'

Bridle glanced at his hand. She was right. The loss disturbed his thoughts for a moment as he was sure he had put it on that morning.

'Perhaps you left it off when you knew you were coming to see me' she giggled.

Lodge coughed loudly then snapped his notebook shut. Bridle got the message immediately.

'That will be all Miss Shaw for the moment.'

Bridle stood up sharply as Lodge thrust his notebook into his jacket pocket. If Lodge had his way he would have given this girl a hard time. He couldn't understand Bridle's reticence. Miranda Shaw folded her arms and gave them a cold look.

'If you do remember anything Miss Shaw...

'Thank you Sergeant but I believe an Inspector Radford is in charge of the investigation is he not?'

'Yes Miss he is.'

'If you'll excuse me I must get back to work.'

She slipped gracefully out of the leather chair and swept between the two men and through the open door. They followed her out and watched her as she strolled back into the sunlit studio. Lodge was transfixed as she let the gown slip from her shoulders then took her time replacing the wig. The sunlight exposed her long naked body through the white shift and Lodge gasped quietly. Bridle turned quickly and made his way down the stairs to the street followed by his angry and over-heated partner. Lodge was glad to feel the cool air on his face.

'She was taking the piss out of us boss' Lodge said stretching his collar 'you should have leaned on the teasing little bitch.'

'She might have complained and I can't afford Radford on my back.'

'Why would she complain?'

'Because of your lecherous leering for a start' Bridle retorted.

'There's something going on with her boss. I don't trust her. She's playin' games.'

'I didn't like her comment about Radford' Bridle mused.

'That was a veiled threat' Lodge said flicking open a packet of players.

'She really lit your furnace Tommy has the fire gone out with you and Betty?' Bridle grinned and walked away.

'Betty can't even find the matches anymore' Lodge said wistfully then followed his partner along Rodney Street.

Chief Superintendent Crowley sat at his desk bolt upright with his hands clasped. He had considered this pose in the mirror for some time before trying it on the assembled officers before him. He felt it gave him an air of confidence and informed authority especially if he nodded his head in a light but positive way as someone spoke. For Superintendent Mcleish it just confirmed Crowley's crass and affected manner which irritated him to the point of impatience.

The meeting was to assess the progress of the Grant murder case and Mcleish could see the pressure building in Inspector Radford's face like a balloon about to burst. Radford had brought two Detective Sergeants from his squad and for the last hour he had systematically sacrificed them on the altar of incompetent scapegoats. Mcleish knew that their only function was to take the blame for Radford and he quietly despaired at the calibre of men the force was producing. The whole investigation was no closer to a positive solution than it had been at the beginning.

'We have no hard evidence to arrest our main suspect we are snookered at the moment.'

Mcleish felt that Radford had made no solid case against Billy Doyle the man he suspected of the murder. It seemed the only reason he was a suspect was because of his past record, the fact that he had organised the trip to the fight for the dead man and the fact that he was there on the night.

'You haven't given any clear-cut explanation as to why you suspect Doyle' Mcleish growled.

'I have information from my sources that Billy Doyle had a substantial amount of money only days after the murder' Radford responded.

'Are your informants reliable Inspector?' Crowley held his chin high as he spoke which he felt increased his air of authority in the room.

'My informants are one hundred percent reliable Sir' Radford stabbed his finger in the air.

'Inspector Radford we know that Grant's wallet was still in his breast pocket with cash in it. Fifteen pounds as I recall. If the motive was theft would the killer leave fifteen pounds?' Mcleish sneered 'I know I wouldn't and I'm amazed the stoker who found the body didn't nick it.'

'We know that Grant had a solid-silver pocket watch and that was found in Doyle's lock-up' Radford said 'he claims Grant gave it to him as a gift and he has witnesses of course.'

'Billy Doyle could have lifted that off Grant anytime during the fight he's a light-fingered little bastard' Mcleish said wearily 'well known for it. It doesn't make him a murderer. I still say he hasn't got the guts to kill anyone.' Mcleish looked at Radford for a response.

'If I could bring him in I know I could crack him. I'd get a confession in no time' Radford pulled a tough and determined face and Mcleish sighed heavily and looked Radford squarely in the eye.

'Why should an innocent man confess to murder Inspector Radford?'

'I know its Doyle Sir. Everything points to him.' Radford was becoming exasperated.

'Then come up with some evidence Inspector because all you've done for the past hour is lay the blame on these two officers. You are responsible for this investigation and it's time you delivered some results' Mcleish barked at Radford.

'Sir I accept your criticisms with reservations' Radford spoke quietly and Mcleish drew a breath to relaunch his attack when Crowley decided to assert himself.

'What concerns me gentlemen is the public and press interest in this case.' Crowley's moustache started to twitch nervously 'the press is following the case too closely for my liking. We need some results and we need them soon'.

Crowley's attempt at aggressive determination drew Mcleish's contempt but he knew Crowley was right. The editorial comments in the press were starting to cause embarrassment and affect morale among the investigating officers. Detective

Superintendent Webster stirred in his chair as though waking from a deep sleep. He cleared his throat with a heavy cough and spat into his large white handkerchief which made Crowley wince with disgust.

'Excuse me gentlemen, thank goodness my wife puts out a clean hankie everyday.'

He chuckled to himself then fixed Radford with a stare that made him and his Sergeants feel uneasy.

'What do you know about corruption Inspector Radford?' Webster wiped his nose with his handkerchief as he spoke and Radford looked outraged by the question. He exchanged glances with his Sergeants which made them all look a little conspiratorial.

'It's not a difficult question is it Inspector?'

Webster's relaxed attitude had the immediate effect of putting the fear of God into Radford and his officers. Mcleish sat up in his chair with amused interest. Webster was something of an enigma in the service with his photographic memory and his apparent ability to manipulate and penetrate the psyche of his subject. Mcleish accepted that Webster was unique. Not the kind of man Mcleish would ever socialise with but he had great respect for him as a detective.

'Corruption Sir?' Radford asked with a quizzical look on his face desperately buying time in order to decide how to answer the question. Webster grinned and nodded and Radford felt immediate hatred for the man.

'I'm not quite sure why you asking me the question Sir. Is it relevant to this investigation?'

'I hoped you could tell me Inspector' Webster said.

'I'm not quite sure what you are getting at Sir?' Radford's mind ticked over fast.

'This case has all the hallmarks of corruption within the squad Inspector wouldn't you say so?'

'No Sir I can't agree with that statement' Radford shifted in his chair.

Crowley cleared his throat and looked up and down at the men before him.

'Superintendent Webster this isn't on the agenda' Crowley sniffed.

'No Chief Superintendent Crowley it isn't' Webster said scratching his ear casually.

'Can you explain yourself Superintendent?' Crowley wanted control and Mcleish scowled.

'In my experience any investigation that makes such little progress is often the result of corrupt rather than inept officers.' Webster said and waved his hand in a matter of fact way as the two Sergeants looked at each other and shifted uneasily in their chairs. Radford and Crowley exchanged glances and Webster sat back in his chair like a contented dog falling onto its blanket.

'I can vouch for every copper in my squad' Radford said haughtily

'Is that so' said Webster 'very loyal however it is not very astute for a senior officer.'

'I have no reason to question any of my officers Detective Superintendent Webster' Radford said through gritted teeth.

'I can't really see how corruption would come into this case' Mcleish said enjoying Radford's discomfort but not quite sure where Webster was coming from. Webster scratched his head and pulled a slightly puzzled face.

'I was speaking generally but in my experience corrupt officers tend to be lazy and unproductive. I am merely suggesting that Inspector Radford should take a hard look at his squad.'

'Yes Sir' Said Radford seething 'thank you for that advice but I can assure you that we will have a result on this murder enquiry within a month or I will resign.'

Mcleish smirked as he knew Radford was now up against a wall.

'Very well' said Crowley officiously 'that will be all Inspector.'

'Thank you Sir'

Radford nodded to his Sergeants and they stood up together and left the room. Mcleish shook his head slowly and Webster smirked as he lay back in his chair. Crowley cleared his throat nervously and looked at his two colleagues. Mcleish made Crowley nervous with his blunt military approach but it was Webster who worried Crowley most of all.

'Within a month' said Mcleish 'or he will resign.'

Mcleish looked at Crowley for a response but Crowley kept his gaze on the pencil he was nervously tapping against his thumb.

'I'm sure Radford is doing his best' said Crowley with more than a little hesitation in his voice.

CHAPTER SIX

Lodge drove the police car along the country lanes of the Wirral like an excited schoolboy on a day trip. He had driven through the Mersey tunnel with a sense of expectation and Bridle had to hold tight as Lodge took the winding curves of the tunnel like a racing driver. Bridle could see he was excited by the strange grin on his face which had replaced the usual glower he wore in town. Bridle had tried to read through the initial questioning of Sir Edward Grant as best he could while bracing himself against the dashboard to prevent being thrown out of the vehicle. Bridle looked sideways at Lodge who broke into a laugh.

'I know boss I can't help it. I always get excited over this side of the river. My grandad used to bring me over to Moreton shore to dig for cockles on the beach when I was a lad.' Bridle abandoned trying to read the report and threw it onto the back seat as Lodge continued.

'I loved cocklin' on hot summer days away from the stinking city. I'd take my lad now but he's not interested.'

Bridle noticed that Lodge had taken the scenic route from the tunnel and was running down the Dee coast through Hoylake and West Kirby. It was a stunning stretch of coastline and one that Bridle knew well because his in-law's house was just a short run along the coast from Sir Edward Grant's. He remembered the long walks along the cliff tops with Stella during their short courtship. Bridle made sure they were long walks because he detested spending time in the big house with her family who treated him as an outsider. He felt a slight twinge in his stomach as they turned off the main coast road and down into Gayton village which held so many uncomfortable memories for him.

'Don't your in-laws live round here somewhere boss?' Lodge knew he was being mischievous.

'Just past it' Bridle sighed knowing Lodge was going to make the most of it.

'What?' Lodge took an exaggerated look over his shoulder and Bridle knew he was about to launch into his repartee.

'You don't mean that stunning detached Victorian mansion looking over the Dee to the Welsh coast by any chance Sarge?'

'Sergeant' Bridle said idly because Lodge was aware of Bridle's distaste for the shortened slang for his rank.

'Is it the one with the long gravel drive lined by pine trees with the classical Roman fountain at the top with water pouring out of a jug held by a semi-naked nymph Sarge?'

'Sergeant' Bridle sighed.

'I've always wanted a house with a semi-naked nymph holdin' her jugs' Lodge grinned.

'You need to turn in here you tosser' Bridle flicked his thumb to the right. Lodge reacted fast and swung the car through a wide gateway with black iron gates secured in the open position. The gateway and drive had been designed for horse and carriage initially and though the drive wasn't very long it was enhanced by stunning gardens to the left and right.

'I always thought heaven would look something like this' Lodge said and whistled through his teeth. Bridle had seen it all before and wasn't impressed although Lodge's reaction made him smirk.

'The Dee smells fresher than the Mersey' Bridle mused as he climbed out of the car.

'A corpse smells fresher than the Mersey' Lodge said as he pulled his bulk from the driver's seat and slammed the door shut. Their shoes crunched on the gravel as they made their way across the drive to the steps leading up to the classical porch. The double doors were solid and imposing and Bridle pulled on the metal rod that rang the doorbell.

The door was opened by a Butler who Bridle estimated to be in his mid-forties around six feet tall with thinning grey hair. His clothes were immaculate and his bearing was so superior that Bridle and Lodge immediately felt a little uneasy.

'I am Detective Sergeant Bridle and this is Detective Constable Lodge we have arranged to see Sir Edward Grant.' The Butler looked Bridle up and down and his mouth twitched slightly and then he held Bridle's gaze a little too long.

'You are expected gentlemen please come this way.'

The Butler kept his eyes on Bridle as they stepped through the door into an opulent hall dominated by a curving staircase. The walls of the stairwell were covered with portraits and classical busts stood on plinths around the walls.

'If you would like to step into the study I will inform Sir Edward of your arrival.'

He opened the door of the study and stepped back to allow Lodge to walk in but as Bridle stepped through he deliberately leaned forward slightly to allow Bridle's shoulder to brush lightly against his chest. Bridle was about to apologise but thought better of it. The Butler bowed his head slightly as he withdrew and closed the door and Lodge chuckled as he looked around the room. Bridle gave him a puzzled look.

'Bent as a nine bob note boss and I think he's got his eye on you.'

Bridle frowned and ignored his comment as he wandered around the room full of dark oak shelves ranked with leather bound books. A number of framed prints hung on the panels around the room and Lodge went from one to another looking in disbelief.

'Have you seen these dirty pictures boss?' Lodge was dumbfounded as Bridle looked over his shoulder.

'Victorian erotica' Bridle said casually 'it's fairly common in big houses especially in studies and smoking-rooms were the men take their brandy after dinner.'

'I guess you should know havin' married into all this middle class decadence.' Lodge leaned as close as he could to one of the pictures when the door suddenly opened and Sir Edward Grant walked in. Lodge pulled back so quickly he cricked his neck and let out a grunt. Bridle stifled a laugh as he turned to introduce himself.

'Good afternoon Sir Edward I am Detective Sergeant Bridle and this is Detective Constable Lodge.'

Grant stared at Bridle for a moment and then cast a dismissive glance at Lodge.

'Bridle you say, are you the rake who stole young Estella from her tyrannical father?'

Bridle wasn't sure what to say when Grant's stern face cracked into a smile.

'Don't worry Sergeant Sir Nigel Carver is an old friend of mine. Estella was always a free spirit. Please take a seat.' He sat behind his desk and motioned them to sit down. Lodge took out his notebook and pencil and Bridle cleared his throat.

'I realise that this is a difficult time for you Sir Edward but our investigation has become a little stagnant and we feel that a few more questions may help with our enquiries' Bridle spoke as gravely as he could.

'Yes of course Sergeant. It has been difficult especially for my wife and daughter. What can I do for you?'

'I'm interested in your son's state of mind on the evening of the murder. Did he show any sign of agitation or concern Sir?' Bridle looked Grant directly in the eye as he spoke.

'David hardly had any contact with me Sergeant on the night of the murder or any other night for that matter.'

'So you didn't see him on the evening of the murder. When did you last see David Sir?'

'The last time I saw my son alive was the morning of the day before.' Grant leaned forward and took a cigar from a silver box then struck a match and lit it. Lodge savoured the aroma as Grant blew the smoke out into the room.

'How did he seem to you then Sir?'

'He had a hang-over as I recall' Grant's eyes dropped as he spoke.

'So you had no conversation with him?'

'No he was hardly coherent.'

'Did he ever confide in you Sir? Ask your advice? Relate any problems?'

'No I'm sorry Sergeant we never had that kind of intimacy I'm afraid.'

Grant's face was as blank as a poker player and Bridle was beginning to understand why the initial report was so sparse.

'What can you tell me about your son's companions on the night of the murder?'

'His companions' Grant looked slightly puzzled and Bridle nodded to Lodge who flicked through his note-book.

'That would be a Miss Miranda Shaw a Miss Jane Porter and a Mr. Peter Swain' Lodge said casually and flicked his note-book to its original page.

'Oh yes them. As far as I know Peter Swain is the dullard son of Dr. Mathew Swain quite a renowned surgeon. Jane Porter is a feckless socialite desperate to find a husband of the right class in order to please her mother and the other one?' Grant shook his head slightly.

'Miranda Shaw Sir' Bridle said.

'Yes quite a character I believe' Grant blew out the cigar smoke slowly.

'A character Sir' Bridle repeated.

'I believe she is rather Bohemian, artistic, loose morals.'

'And who told you that Sir?' Bridle held his gaze.

'I'm not sure Sergeant. It was just gossip I suppose.' Grant shifted in his seat.

'Did it concern you that your son had a relationship with Miss Shaw Sir?' Bridle noted his discomfort.

'Why should it concern me?' Grant looked firmly at Bridle.

'You described her as Bohemian and of loose morals Sir.'

'Sowing wild oats is not a crime Sergeant.'

'You don't feel it was a serious relationship Sir Edward?'

'Serious' Grant almost choked on his cigar 'I'd have… ' Grant thought twice about his response and sat back in his chair slowly.

'You'd have… what Sir? Bridle asked and Grant smiled slightly as he glanced at Lodge taking notes.

'I'd have disinherited him Sergeant.'

'Have you ever met any of his three companions personally Sir?' Bridle asked tentatively.

'Porter and Swain I may have met socially but I cannot honestly remember when.' Grant was beginning to tire of Bridle's questions.

'And Miss Shaw Sir' Bridle watched every detail of expression on Grant's face.

'No Sergeant I have never met Miss Shaw and I never want to' Grant was becoming irritated.

'Did you know your son was going out that evening Sir Edward?'

'No I didn't.'

'What about your wife Sir? Did she have any idea where your son was going?'

'I very much doubt it Sergeant but perhaps you should ask her yourself?'

'Is Lady Grant up to it Sir?' Bridle asked sympathetically.

'Do you people actually care Sergeant? I'm not sure if she will ever fully recover.'

'I understand Sir but it would be helpful if we could speak to her today.'

Bridle knew Grant was agitated but he had no intention of missing an opportunity. Lodge winced slightly as he thought Grant might explode at any moment. Grant drew long on his cigar then stubbed it out in the ash tray as he blew the smoke out of his lungs like a train letting off steam.

'I suppose it would be best to get this over with. Give me a moment Sergeant.'

'Thank you Sir Edward.'

Grant got up from his chair and straightened his jacket then left the room with a forceful slam of the door.

'What do you make of him Tommy?' Bridle asked with a sigh of relief.

'Thoroughbred bastard' Lodge replied without looking up from his notes.

'Yeah and I think he's lying' Bridle said as he scanned the literature on the desk for anything of interest.

'You lit his fuse and it's burning fast' Lodge said closing his notebook with a slap 'what makes you think he's lying?'

'Just something about his reaction when I mentioned Porter and Swain, as if he knew nothing about them' Bridle tapped his fingers on the desk as he considered the situation.

'I'd tread careful if I was you boss' Lodge took out a penknife and started to sharpen his pencil.

'He's a businessman used to asking questions not answering them' Bridle pondered 'men like him have to be in control but he has no control over us, he's not comfortable.'

'Very analytical boss but maybe he just feels guilty cos he fiddles his taxes or something.' Lodge leaned over the desk and opened the cigar box and sniffed the strong aromatic tobacco.

'I wish I could afford one of these beauties' Lodge frowned and closed the box carefully.

'Have a look on the gravel when we leave Tommy you might find yourself a stub' Bridle said dryly and Lodge's face brightened.

'Good idea boss.'

The door opened slowly and they sat back quickly like guilty schoolboys. The Butler stood at the open door and Lodge gave Bridle a furtive nudge with his elbow and a sly wink which Bridle ignored.

'If you would follow me gentlemen I am instructed to direct you to the conservatory.'

He motioned toward the open door and Bridle and Lodge got up and sauntered through into the hall. He carefully closed the door and with a slight twitch of his nostril he led them across the hall, through a drawing room and into a large conservatory which was noticeably warmer than the rest of the house. Many varieties of plants stood in large pots around the edge of the room and there was a mixed aroma of flowers, vegetation and fresh coffee. The conservatory was metal framed and the rows of arched windows reached to the ceiling. The view across the beautiful garden made both men stop and gaze for a moment.

Grant and his wife and daughter were seated at a large table in high-backed wicker chairs. They turned and looked at the policemen with mixed expressions. Sir Edward looked taciturn, his wife Margaret looked pale and tired and their daughter Amelia was grinning from ear to ear. Grant stood up as they approached and motioned to the Butler to start pouring coffee.

'My wife Margaret and my daughter Amelia, this is Detective Sergeant Bridle and Constable?'

Grant waved his hand impatiently.

'Lodge Sir, Detective Constable' Lodge said with a frown.

'Yes, yes of course. Amelia I think you should go to your room. Please sit down gentlemen.'

The two men sat down and the Butler hovered with the coffee pot as Amelia stamped her foot in frustration.

'Oh father please can't I stay? Aren't you married to Estella?' She said grinning at Bridle who was a little surprised at the question and looked it.

'Do forgive my daughter Sergeant' Lady Grant said graciously 'she does get very excited in company.'

'I wasn't aware you knew my wife Miss Grant' Bridle said.

'Oh yes I love Estella, she is so up to date with fashions and designs and things and gosh you are just as handsome and rugged as all the girls said you were.'

She broke off into a giggle and the Butler raised an eyebrow. Lodge cleared his throat noisily and took out his notebook. Bridle felt his face redden. He dreaded to think how much fun Lodge would get out of this back at the station.

'That's quite enough Amelia' Grant said.

'Yes darling would you mind leaving us for a little while?' Lady Grant smiled gently.

'Yes mother.'

Amelia was petulant and Bridle felt she was far too childish for a girl of her age but put it down to pampering. She left the table as noisily as possible and Bridle and Lodge glanced at each other then at the floor.

'I'm sorry gentlemen' Lady Grant said with a smile 'but she is an excitable child, would you like some coffee?'

'Thank you m'am' Bridle nodded and the Butler leaned forward and poured the thick black coffee into his cup. He leaned so close that Bridle could feel his warm breath on his ear and he shifted slightly to avoid it. Lodge slowly flicked through the pages of his notebook as the Butler poured his coffee and they eyed each other suspiciously.

'Really Margaret you shouldn't call her a child even though she acts like one at times' Grant was impatient as if he had said it a hundred times before. 'She is nineteen years of age.'

'I know Edward but it's merely a term of endearment I'm sure the officers understand that.'

Grant made a grunting noise as his wife picked up the silver jug of fresh cream.

'Cream gentlemen?'

Bridle declined but Lodge held out his cup with a broad grin on his face.

'Yes please m'am' Lodge said enthusiastically as Lady Grant poured the cream into his cup.

'Sugar'

She held up the bowl of sugar cubes with a charming smile as Lodge leaned over and took four cubes and dropped them into his cup with a splash then stirred it up noisily. Grant looked at him with total distaste but his wife was mildly amused

'I hope you don't mind answering a few questions Lady Grant, I know it's a difficult time'

'Not at all Sergeant' she smiled graciously and Bridle wondered for a moment how she ever got herself involved with a man like Grant.

'When was the last time you spoke to your son m'am?' Bridle asked but was aware of Sir Edward's intense stare.

'I spoke to David on the afternoon of the day he died' her speech wavered slightly.

'How did he seem to you? Did he seem upset in any way or was he unusually tense?'

'I think he was little unwell' she said with half a smile.

'Hung over again' Grant muttered and his wife glowered at him.

'David was a young man and he liked his fun Sergeant' she said painfully.

'Did he say anything that would make you suspect he was worried in any way?' Bridle asked.

'No Sergeant just the opposite he was quite elated.'

'Do you know why m'am?' She was about to answer when Grant butted in.

'God only knows' Grant sipped his coffee and Bridle and Lodge exchanged glances.

'Sir with all due respect I am trying to interview your wife' Bridle spoke forcefully and Grant's eyes burned through him. Lodge made no reaction but noticed the Butler twitch his mouth and shift slightly. Lady Grant just stared at the table.

'Do you know why he was so elated m'am?' Bridle continued.

'He mentioned a business proposition with an old friend and

he was excited about it. I was so pleased that he had found some direction at last' she was animated for a moment then the cloud crossed her face again.

'Business proposition' Grant sneered and Bridle threw him a hard glance. Grant raised his hand in mock contrition.

'I hate it when you sneer Edward. David just needed an opportunity' Lady Margaret said defensively but Bridle felt that she was trying to convince herself.

'Do you have any idea what the nature of the business was?' Bridle asked.

'No I don't Sergeant but I do know a number of partners were involved.'

'Can you give me any names?'

'I only know one name Sergeant.'

She looked tentatively at her husband but he looked blankly ahead as he sipped his coffee.

'And who would that be Lady Grant?' Bridle asked flatly.

'A man called Guy Charlton' she said with a wistful smile and Bridle was stunned for a moment to hear that name again.

'Guy is a very dashing character Sergeant. He has been away for some years making his fortune abroad' Lady Grant was cut short by her husband's grunt of disapproval.

'Do you know Mr. Charlton Sir?' Bridle said looking at Grant.

'Guy Charlton is another one with big schemes but no backbone for hard work' Grant said slamming his cup onto the table.

'Guy's family are in farming and livestock and his father breeds racehorses' Lady Grant said quickly 'I am on very good terms with his Mother.'

'Do you know where I can find Mr. Charlton?' Bridle was intrigued.

'I'm not sure where he is. The family estate is near Chester but Guy is a bit of a gadabout I'm afraid.' She cast a sideways glance at her husband as she finished her sentence.

'Thank you Lady Grant you've been very helpful' Bridle smiled at her and she looked sheepishly at him.

'Will that be all?' Grant asked curtly.

'Yes, thank you Sir.'

'In that case Barton will show you out.'

Grant nodded to the Butler who bowed slightly and walked to the door. Bridle and Lodge stood up together and made their way toward the door.

'Thank you for your time Lady Grant' Bridle said turning back 'and thank you Sir Edward.'

Grant took a sip of his coffee and stared vacantly out of the window.

'Oh there is just one other question if you don't mind' Bridle said almost casually and Grant rolled his eyes impatiently.

'Was your son fluent in any foreign language?'

The Grants cast a puzzled glance at each other.

'No Sergeant' Grant said bluntly 'he had no acumen for education.'

'Thank you Sir' Bridle said and nodded to Lodge.

They turned and followed the Butler in a silent procession through the house to the front door. The Butler opened the door and Bridle felt slightly uncomfortable and he left quickly. Lodge followed behind and winked at the butler only to be met with a blank stare. They made their way quickly down the steps and across the gravel drive toward the car.

'Grant is a thoroughbred bastard just like I said' Lodge looked pleased with himself as he cast his eye over the gravel in the hope of seeing a discarded cigar stub.

'Guy Charlton' Bridle mused.

'Sounds like another posh bastard to me' Lodge said sliding his foot over the gravel.

'Come on Tommy I'll stand you a pint in one of these quaint country pubs around here. It might straighten your face.'

Bridle grinned at Lodge but he was thinking about Guy Charlton and Stella.

CHAPTER SEVEN

Councillor Jack Finney's house in Wavertree was a comfortable two up and two down that was kept in immaculate condition by his softly spoken wife Bernadette. Her hair was white and she was much smaller than her husband but her face was round and jolly and quick to smile which made her approachable and a popular figure in the community. She pushed at the parlour door with her back as she was carrying a large wooden tray loaded with three enamel mugs of tea and a plate of thick-cut sandwiches. She swung around into the parlour to see her husband, Harry Croft and Callum Riley hunched together at her best dinner table. She frowned when she saw that no one had bothered to put a cloth down to protect the surface of the table.

They stopped talking as she entered the room and Riley's face lit up when he saw the tray. He leapt to his feet and whistled through his dazzling white teeth.

'Mrs Finney only a Killarney girl could stack a plate like that. I'll be runnin' off with yer meself so I will.' Riley took the tray from her so forcefully she was swept forward and she gasped as she recovered her balance. 'My God woman how many glasses have yer had and it's only two in the afternoon?' Riley winked and she blushed as the men laughed at her embarassment.

'You are a cheeky one Mr. Riley' Bernadette said casting a glance at her husband.

'Mrs Finney you have a lilt to your voice that reminds me of my one and only sweetheart back in Donegal' Riley said with a frown.

'I thought you were from Kerry' Croft said and winked at Finney.

'English fool' Riley said 'never tell a handsome woman were yer from just in case the husband comes after yer.'

'Be off with yer now I'm old enough to be your mother' she said slapping his shoulder.

'What?' Riley was in full flow 'are yer tellin' me there's no hope for us?'

'You'll be turning me head Mr. Riley and with me own husband sitting there' she giggled like a teenager and Finney laughed and shook his head.

'You always were a soft touch Bernadette' Finney said reaching out for his mug of tea 'now be a good woman and leave us men to our work.'

Riley threw her a furtive wink which made her chuckle and leave the room without any argument.

The three men sat quietly for a moment as they enjoyed their hot tea and sandwiches then Croft took out a packet of Woodbines and handed them around to his companions. The room was soon full of blue smoke and Croft took a long look at Finney. He could see an ageing man who had battled for the working class for most of his life but the strain had begun to show. He was once tall and physically powerful but now in his mid-sixties he was slightly bent by arthritis.

'Will you be up to this Jack?' Croft said.

'I'm fine Harry' Finney snapped.

'I had to ask' Croft said holding his hands up.

'I was an activist when you were still at yer mother's teat Harry.'

'The man's a legend' Riley said dismissively.

'Look Harry, this is the biggest rally for unemployment this country has seen' Finney said earnestly 'keeping control is the main issue for us and that's why I need you and Callum' Finney glanced from Riley to Croft. 'I need tough, experienced men like you to control the subversive elements. I won't have it wrecked by violence. I've seen it happen too many times.'

'You can rely on us Jack' Croft said and looked at Riley who winked and smiled confidently. Finney stood up and turned to the two men with a stern look on his face.

'I don't want anybody hurt. The protesters are all working men trying to survive an economic depression. They are marching for the right to work and feed their families. I don't want any of them hurt in any way' Finney went pale and slumped on to his chair.

'Not like back in 1922 eh Jack?' Croft said stubbing his cigarette into a glass ash tray. 'Most of those protesters ended up in hospital or prison or both. It was a fiasco if you want me to be brutally honest' Croft could see the pain on Finney's face but he had no intention of holding back.

'We were betrayed from the inside' Finney said quietly.

'So the legend goes but you never found the traitor did you?'

'No we didn't Harry' Finney sighed.

'I'm not trying to needle you Jack I'm just pointing out that things can go wrong, but God forbid they go as wrong as that.'

Finney's temper exploded and he leapt to his feet with Croft just a second behind him. Riley was instantly between them.

'Come on me boys let's calm it down. We've got to get something straight here. This isn't just another rabble rousing protest were a bunch of flat-foots storm in and crack heads open. Jack has worked hard to give it credibility, to keep it peaceful.

The coppers are workin' with us right Jack?' Finney nodded slowly and Riley's stern face suddenly cracked into a dazzling smile.

'Now I've got a thirst that tea can't quench me lovely boys so let's get our arses down to that saloon on the main road and I'll stand us all a pint and a chaser.'

Finney and Croft softened to Riley's infectious enthusiasm then they gripped hands and shook hard without saying a word.

'That's more like it boys' Riley said as he made his way over to the window and drew the net curtain back slightly.

'You won't find any bogey men on this street Riley' Finney said.

'Yer wouldn't want a man to drop his guard now would yer?' Riley responded.

'Callum's instincts saved our lives more than once in Spain' Croft said.

'Now what have we go here boys?' Riley said softly.

Finney and Croft stepped over to the window and looked across the street at the man Riley indicated. He was standing opposite the house and he wore a long, grey overcoat and a dark bowler hat. Riley estimated him to be in his early forties. The man had a brown leather satchel and he was studying what looked like a standard rent book.

'Well done Riley you've spotted the rent man' Finney said bluntly.

'He's just walked up the street and stopped across the way there' Riley said thoughtfully.

'Mind you, I can't say I've seen him before' Finney said tentatively.

'You don't sound sure Jack' Croft said.

'When the usual rent man is sick they send someone else, it's not that unsusal.'

'But you've never seen him before?' Riley emphasised.

'No, but he could be a new man at the rent office' Finney said with a shrug.

'We seem to have a problem here boys' Riley said seriously 'now this lovely fella here is a tall, strong lookin' man wouldn't yer say? He's carryin' a heavy satchel of coins which would normally pull the shoulder down with the weight. But yer man is standing up tall and stiff like it's no effort. I've just watched him walk up the street and he moved like a cat. I'd say there is no weight in that satchel.'

'Maybe he's just started' Finney said.

'At this time of day' Croft said.

'He could be doing recalls' Finney reasoned 'most people round here are on the bones of their arses, they hide from the rent man.'

'I think we'll be havin' a little look round the back anyway' Riley said glancing at Croft.

'You'd best have a look from the back bedroom' Finney said. 'There's a yard out the back with a high wall and a gate.'

Riley nodded and the three men made their way quickly up the stairs and into the tiny back bedroom cluttered with junk and piles of socialist and communist literature dating back almost thirty years. Riley carefully looked around the edge of the open curtain to see a long alley between drab, grey houses lined with cobblestones and litter.

'Seems clear' Riley said unconvinced.

'Who would be following you anyway?' Finney asked suspiciously.

Riley and Croft looked at each other then Riley turned back toward the window.

'You've been out of the country for a year' Finney said

turning the situation over in his mind 'and the police don't dress up as rent collectors so who the hell is after you?'

'Now look what we've got here boys' Riley said ignoring Finney's question. Croft moved forward carefully and looked over Riley's shoulder. A tramp was looking through the bins and pieces of litter in the alley-way. He was quite tall and was bent over an overflowing bin and they could see his filthy hat bobbing up and down as he fumbled through the rubbish.

'Have many tramps round here Jack?' Riley asked with a smile.

'No' Finney said sternly 'they usually get arrested for vagrancy.'

'I'm not taking any chances' Riley said as he darted from the room and raced down the stairs with Croft and Finney following behind him. Riley strode up and down the parlour looking more worried than Finney had ever seen him.

'What the hell is going on?' Finney snapped.

'Maybe nothing' Croft said calmly but Finney could see the tension in him.

'So why are you both so coiled up? What's going on Harry?' Finney was determined to get an answer but neither man said a word. Riley dipped his hand inside his reefer jacket and drew out a Webley .38 service revolver. He inspected the chamber to make sure it was fully loaded.

'What the hell are you doing?' Finney suddenly felt sick.

'I'm not doing anything Jack' Riley said quietly as he slipped the revolver back inside his jacket which he left open and slightly pulled back. 'We are just going to leave quietly like there's no problem at all' Riley grinned but this time Finney saw menace in his smile.

'We leave together Harry' Riley said firmly 'you go left down the street and I'll turn right. If all goes well I'll meet you at the

Golden Lion. We can't go back to the digs till after dark. They might be watching the place' Croft nodded.

'Who are they? I'm not having Bernadette involved in this. You should never have come here' Finney could see the situation getting worse by the minute.

'Don't worry Jack these boys aren't here for our kick at the system' Riley grinned 'they just want me.'

'Who are they Riley?' Finney could see the perverse excitement on Riley's face and it worried him.

'You've been on their files for years Jack. If they wanted you they'd have lifted you long ago' Croft said with a hard edge to his voice. Finney let out a sigh as he realised who they were dealing with.

'Intelligence service' Finney said quietly 'I don't want to go through all that again' Finney knew he was getting too old to take the strain.

'They must be keeping an eye on you Jack, that's how they've found me.' Riley was enjoying the experience.

'You cocky bastard' Finney said trying to subdue his anger.

'To be sure I am Jack' Riley laughed 'I've had fisticuffs with those public schoolboys since Derry but I don't think they'll arrest me this time.'

'What does that mean?' Finney snapped.

'Expediency' Croft murmured.

'You mean murder' Finney said grimly.

They quickly moved to the front door. Riley placed one hand on the door handle and shuffled the pistol into a smoother drawing position with his other hand then covered it with his coat. Riley and Croft held each other's stare for a moment

'If they want you Riley why don't they just walk in and take you?' Finney asked.

'They want to know what I'm up to' Riley said quietly but his mind was already engaged on his next move.

Finney paced up and down the hall and pondered what to do. If Riley started anything in the street all of their plans for the protest march would be wiped out. Finney wasn't afraid of radical action but gunplay was out of the question. He had to get Bernadette away from it. He would send her over to Ireland for a long stay with her sister for her safety and his own peace of mind. Finney had always admired Harry Croft but he cursed him now for bringing the mad Irishman into their circle.

'We'll have to cancel the protest march. We've been compromised. It's too dangerous' Finney said as he paced up and down the hall.

'Running scared already Jack?' Harry Croft said through clenched teeth and Finney stiffened with anger.

'Don't you ever talk to me like that Harry I'm not too old to meet you on the street anytime you say.' Finney clenched his fists and his eyes turned dark with rage as Croft broke into a slow steely grin.

'You disappeared from the scene pretty quick back in nineteen twenty two when most of the marchers got collared and thrown in the Bridewell' Croft said glowering at Finney.

'It was bloody chaos' Finney said trembling with anger.

'You never told anyone how you got out of the town hall did you Jack?' Croft sneered.

'What are you getting at?' Finney snarled 'I had a broken arm and a cracked skull.'

Finney moved before Croft could speak and gripped his throat with both hands. Both men crashed forward toward the scullery. Bernadette screamed as Riley spurted forward and pulled Finney away. Riley expected Croft to lose control and take

Finney apart but Croft burst out laughing as he picked himself off the floor.

'That's the spirit Jack. I thought you'd lost your nerve. That anger in you inspired me as a kid and inspired dozens of men to follow you. We can't give up now. We can fight back and you can still lead us' Croft threw his head back and laughed.

Finney leaned against the wall and took a deep breath. He glanced into the scullery and could see Bernadette sitting on her wooden stool with a handkerchief to her mouth as she always did when she was worried.

'I don't know where I am with you two mad bastards' Finney said gasping for breath.

'Cheer up Jack and stop worrying' Riley smiled 'it might just be the rent man and a tramp after all.'

Riley winked then swiftly pulled the door open and walked out followed by Croft who went in the opposite direction. Finney rushed forward and slammed the door then thrust the bolt across quickly. He leaned back against the door and held his breath. He listened for any sign of a scuffle or even worse a gunshot. It seemed a long time to Finney but he heard nothing so he went into the parlour and had a look up and down the street. There was no sign of anyone so Finney slumped down into his armchair and let out a sigh of relief.

He knew that Riley was a liability and he had seen a different side to Harry Croft but they were too far down the line to call off the protest march. Finney had reached a stage where he was prepared to take greater risks for his political vision and if it took men like Riley and Croft to achieve his aim then he had to use them. There was no going back.

George Sullivan sat at his desk and pondered the nature of the pain he still felt in his injured leg. Sometimes it was a light throbbing sensation and other times it was dull-ache. He hated the dull-ache more than anything else and today was a dull-ache day. The office had been deserted for most of the shift as Radford had been on the rampage about lack of progress and most of the officers had taken themselves off to look for straws to clutch. It was days like this that made him look forward to his retirement. The sudden ring of the telephone made him jump in his seat and he snatched the receiver from its cradle as the ringing in an empty office seemed so much louder than normal. He paused for a moment as he heard the coins drop in the public telephone box. The line just crackled in his ear.

'Hello?'

'I'd like to speak to Detective Sergeant Bridle please' the female voice was young and raspy.

'I'm afraid Sergeant Bridle is out at the moment can I take a message?'

'I don't really want to speak to anyone else except Sergeant Bridle' she giggled quietly and Sullivan began to think he was being taken for a ride.

'Can I take your name and phone number Miss and I will ask Sergeant Bridle to contact you.'

'That won't be necessary I will contact him.'

'Can I ask the nature of your enquiry Miss?'

'I don't have an enquiry I have some information.'

'Can I ask what the information is related to?'

'It's confidential' she giggled again which began to annoy Sullivan.

'In that case Miss I suggest you call back later today' Sullivan was about to replace the receiver heavily when she cut in abruptly.

'Tell Sergeant Bridle that people are telling lies about David Grant' her voice became steadier and less childish.

'And who would that be Miss?' Sullivan was suspicious because 'crank' phone calls regarding investigations had increased dramatically. The oddness of character had never ceased to amaze Sullivan in his long career.

'I can tell by your voice that you don't believe me' she sounded petulant and it occurred to Sullivan that she might be a little drunk.

'Have you been drinking Miss?' There was a clunk as she put another coin in the slot.

'Drinking?' She giggled louder this time and Sullivan felt sure she was drunk.

'Alright Miss, I'll tell Sergeant Bridle to expect your call' Sullivan felt she was wasting his time.

'Everyone is saying he was a bad person but he wasn't a bad person I should know' her voice was a little weepy now.

'How do you know Miss? Was he a good friend of yours?' Sullivan asked sympathetically in the hope that she might drop her guard.

'He was more than a friend we were lovers.'

Sullivan's reaction was to roll his eyes and think not another one but he stayed with the sympathetic approach.

'I see Miss it must be very difficult for you at the moment.'

'It is' she began to weep quietly and Sullivan felt a little guilty but he knew she would be easier to crack if she was upset.

'Are you alright Miss?'

'Yes thank you but it has been a struggle with the baby and everything.'

Sullivan's mind was racing now as he ran through names

from the files on the Grant murder and tried to place this girl in the picture.

'I understand it must be difficult to talk about it Miss, is there's anything I can do?'

The line went quiet for a moment then the annoying giggle started again and Sullivan wasn't quite sure what was going on.

'I lied about the baby.'

'Miss I hope you know it's an offence to waste police time.'

'I can't help it I'm a compulsive liar apparently.'

If it hadn't been such a quiet afternoon Sullivan would have hung-up the phone but he felt he was getting an education in the quirks of the human mind. He heard another coin drop into the slot.

'Is there anything else Miss? If not I'll tell Sergeant Bridle to look forward to your call' Sullivan didn't hide his sarcasm and was about to hang up.

'Tell Sergeant Bridle that Joey Vance is in danger' her voice was firmer but Sullivan was becoming angry now.

'Look Miss, I suggest you get off the line and go and sober–up because I've had enough of this rubbish.'

'I swear this is true. I know Sergeant Bridle is looking for Joey Vance but he could be dead by now. Tell Sergeant Bridle I will be in touch.'

The line clicked as she hung-up the telephone and Sullivan was relieved to get rid of her. He sat staring at the telephone for a few moments wondering just how mad people can be. Then he considered her information about Joey Vance. Sullivan had no idea if Bridle was looking for Joey Vance or not. If he was then how would she know it without being involved somewhere along the line?

Sullivan was more than intrigued he was rattled by it. He got up from his desk and wandered out along the corridor and lit the cigarette he was saving. The smoke trailed him as he made his way down the stairs being careful not to put too much weight on his healing leg. Police officers were milling about on the ground floor but most of them were on their way to the mess-room in the basement. Sullivan followed his nose down the basement steps as the aroma of cabbage and potatoes wafted up the corridor.

The canteen was full of animated blue uniforms and occasional plain-clothes all talking and eating at the same time. He made his way over to the tea urn and helped himself as blue uniformed shoulders jostled him left and right in a scramble for sausage, mash and gravy. The thronging room was a mass of noise but one voice still boomed out above the rest. Tommy Lodge was arguing the toss about a disputed goal at the last Derby game inbetween mouthfuls of mash and gravy.

'It never crossed the line – I was right behind the goal – I saw the whole thing.'

Lodge went on mashing his dinner and was desperate not to let anyone else into the argument. As he ranted on the gravy was running down his chin. He saw Sullivan approaching.

'How are yer doin' George?' Lodge boomed then immediately skewered a pork sausage with his fork and bit it in half.

'I'm looking for Bridle' Sullivan had to shout over the din.

'Eh?' Lodge feigned deafness to amuse the rest of the table and Sullivan knew it.

'Bridle' Sullivan leaned forward to make himself heard but got a closer look at Lodge shoving the remainder of the sausage into a mouth that was already dripping gravy. Sullivan took it in his stride.

'I think he's gone to interview that chinless git' Lodge spluttered gravy out as he spoke.

'Peter Swain?' Sullivan asked.

'Yeah' Lodge let out an enormous belch as he answered and the table erupted in laughter.

'I thought you were goin' over to Chester today' Sullivan said

'Give us a chance George just havin' some dinner first' Lodge shovelled in more mash.

'Do you know if he's looking for Joey Vance?' Sullivan wasn't hopeful that Lodge would know too much.

'Joey Vance? Oh yeah he is, don't know why though.'

Sullivan took a deep breath. Bridle was looking for Vance and the girl knew it. That changed things in Sullivan's mind as it gave her more credibility.

'What's goin' on George? You look like you've just bagged a blonde and found out it's a bloke.' Lodge laughed at his own joke and looked around the table for a response but he had lost the momentum of his repartee.

'Just a message for Bridle it can wait.'

Bridle drove south of the city through the slums of the Dingle into the suburban area of Aigburth. The main road was a wide and pleasant avenue lined with trees which ran parallel to the river, with many substantial detached and semi-detached houses along the route. He passed Liverpool Cricket Club then turned right into Cressington Park, an area of Victorian property which ran down to the banks of the Mersey. It had its own private promenade with views across the river and was originally occupied by the wealthy shipping merchants of the city. Now it was home to the city's professional elite.

Bridle followed the lane down to the promenade and parked the car within splashing distance of the river. He took in a deep breath of fresh air as he always did when he was out of the smog laden town. Swain's sandstone mansion house was surrounded by an orchard of apple and pear trees. It was a short walk along the gravel drive to the door and as he rang the bell he wondered if he was to be confronted by yet another stiff-necked butler. The door was opened by a maid. She was small and pretty and Bridle guessed her age to be around eighteen or nineteen. The girl had a smile that lit up her face and demanded a smile in return. Bridle grinned as he announced himself and the maid blushed and showed him into the library.

'If you would wait one moment Sir I'll tell the family you've arrived.' Her voice was local but not common and Bridle wondered if the family insisted on her improving her elocution.

'Thank you' Bridle smiled again and she blushed as she flitted out of the room. Bridle looked around and reflected on his first impression of Peter Swain when he entered the warehouse on the night of the fight. Bridle recalled Swain wiping vomit from his suit as he walked through the door and the hat he wore made him look foolish. He appeared to be a wet and over-indulged socialite but Bridle ws prepared to reserve judgement.

The library was stocked mainly with books relating to the medical profession as Bridle expected. He took a volume from the shelf and flicked through the detailed sketches of the human skeleton. There were diagrams of muscle composition and blood vessels all of which he found fascinating and he marvelled at the intelligence required to become a doctor. Further along he noticed a number of books on Christian theology and leather-bound volumes of Charles Dickens. He pulled a copy of Bleak House from the shelf and noticed that it was a first edition. Being curious to see if the others were also first editions he took down the copy of David Copperfield just as he heard the door creak open behind him.

'I had no idea police officers had the inclination to read Dickens.'

The female voice was commanding and Bridle turned to see a woman he judged to be in her late forties. She was tall and slim and her hair was pinned back which gave her face a taut and severe attitude. She had high cheek bones and almond shaped eyes which gave her face an attractive feline quality.

'In fact I had no idea police officers read books at all.' Her face showed no emotion or reaction as she gave out her insult and Bridle decided that she might actually believe it to be true.

'I'm sorry I didn't mean to be forward m'am.'

Bridle closed the book quickly and awkwardly placed it back on the shelf. It didn't help that the maid was behind her mistress stifling a giggle at Bridle's discomfort. She turned and gave her maid a stern look and the girl blushed and stood still.

'I am Detective Sergeant Bridle of the city constabulary' Bridle said shakily.

'I hardly thought you were from Scotland Yard' her delivery was so unemotional that Bridle wasn't sure if he had been insulted or not.

'It seems Sergeant that you are the kind of man who makes young girls blush very easily' she turned to the maid with an impatient manner 'you may go and bring Master Peter to the library immediately.'

The maid's eyes widened at the order which Bridle felt made her look even prettier.

'Yes m'am' she turned and fled from the room accidentally slamming the door behind her. Her mistress turned impatiently back to Bridle and shook her head as she strode over to him and held his gaze firmly.

'I am Beatrice Swain and I will be here throughout your

questioning of my son. Do you have any objections Sergeant?' Bridle recognised the kind of steel in her eyes that he had only seen in hardened criminals.

'I have no objection at all Mrs. Swain. I know your son has already been questioned so I am only here to clarify a number of points I shan't keep you long.'

'Good then we understand each other Sergeant please take a seat' she motioned to a small suite of brown leather armchairs in the window bay. Bridle followed her and waited until Mrs. Swain was seated then sat in the chair opposite. She sat on the edge of the seat with her back bolt upright and placed her hands on her lap linked at the fingers. Bridle had noticed her bearing and grace of movement and now with her obvious posture it occurred to him that she may have had some degree of training, possibly ballet.

The area was well lit from the bay window which had stained-glass upper panels and a central window depicting an Arthurian tableau of a knight holding the Holy Grail.

'Do you read Dickens Sergeant or were you being an inquisitive policeman?' She fixed her gaze on him.

'I enjoy his works m'am. My father in-law is an expert on Dickens and holds readings for his club. He named his daughter – my wife that is' Bridle stumbled slightly.

'Obviously' she said tersely.

'He named her Estella after the character in Great Expectations' Bridle knew he was punching fresh air trying to make polite conversation with this woman but he knew he had no option.

'A strange choice I would have thought Sergeant. Estella is such a cold reflection of Miss Havisham.'

'But she does redeem herself m'am' Bridle responded.

'Where would we all be without redemption Sergeant?' She sighed heavily.

Bridle was saved from trying to answer the question as the door opened slowly but noisily and Peter Swain appeared like a phantom looking pale and tired. Bridle was struck by the redness of his hair which was hidden under a hat when Bridle first saw him in the dock warehouse. He was wearing an expensive silk dressing gown which made him look effete. As he sauntered over to join them his face was squirming like a petulant schoolboy who had just been told it was bath time. He dropped himself into the chair with a heavy grunt and the look on his face made Bridle wish he could adjust it with a swift right hook.

'Really Mama have I to go through all of this again?'

He draped himself across the arms of his chair and his head lolled to one side. Mrs. Swain kept her composure and her face remained stone-like.

'Detective Sergeant Bridle is here to clarify some points concerning your statement is that correct Sergeant?' Bridle nodded.

'Oh thank God I couldn't cope with another interrogation. I had such a head-ache last time and those policemen were so rough. I'm sure they didn't like me.'

He remained slumped in the chair as Bridle took his notebook from his jacket. Bridle flicked through the pages slowly in order to give himself time to think. He was beginning to tire of the arrogance of the so-called elite he was investigating in this case. The idea of going back to normal duties on the street was starting to appeal to him.

'How long had you known David Grant Mr. Swain?'

'Oh really Sergeant' Mrs Swain said indignantly 'I'm sure you will find that Peter has answered that question. Please refer to your records.'

Bridle hesitated and pretended to read his note book for a moment.

'Did you like David Grant Mr.Swain?'

'Like him?' Swain looked puzzled.

'Yes sir would you say you were good friends?'

'Good friends?' Swain began to laugh 'don't be absurd Sergeant.'

'But you socialised with him.'

'Socialised' Swain sniggered behind his hand.

'Come along Peter don't be silly' Mrs Swain said.

'What would you call your relationship with David Grant Sir?' Bridle said slowly.

'I would call it necessary Sergeant' Swain sniggered again and Bridle tensed.

'I would like to remind you Mr. Swain that I am investigating a murder and you were one of the last people to see the victim alive. You are a very important witness and if you don't wish to co-operate in your own home then I will be forced to ask you to accompany me to the station.' Bridle barely disguised his anger and Swain immediately sat up straight with look of terror on his face.

'That won't be necessary Sergeant' Mrs Swain said dismissively.

'I'll decide that Mrs. Swain and I would ask you not to interrupt while I question your son otherwise I will have to ask you to leave the room.'

Mrs Swain's jaw dropped open and wavered as if she was about to be very outraged but the firmness of Bridle's voice and attitude seemed to quell her. Bridle wondered if she had ever been challenged in her life and was prepared for a tirade of righteous indignation. But none came and Peter Swain looked pitifully to his mother for support. She stared vaguely out of the window.

'Now Mr. Swain can you tell me what you were doing at the dock warehouse on the night of the 14th August?'

'I was invited to attend'… he looked at his mother with a hint of desperation in his eyes.

'Go on Mr. Swain.'

'I was invited to attend after we had been to a musical show and dinner.'

'Who invited you Sir?'

Swain cast another look at his mother who answered it by looking at the floor.

'David Grant.'

'But you didn't like David Grant.'

'No Sergeant but I was in company, we were a party.'

'That would be Jane Porter and Miranda Shaw?'

'Yes I thought you knew all of this' Swain screwed his face up as if he was in pain.

'So you were attracted to the idea of watching a bare-knuckle fight?'

'Not in the least.'

'Then why did you go Sir?' Bridle looked at him blankly.

'It was the girls they were giddy at the idea of a prize fight, especially Miranda. She can be very persuasive.'

'Persuasive'

'Yes Sergeant persuasive, dominating and slightly intoxicating if you get my drift.'

Swain looked at his mother who kept her eyes downcast but was now pursing her lips very tightly.

'Did David Grant tell you about the fight initially or did he bring it up later?'

'Tell us about it? Of course not Sergeant he would never admit he had planned it. He liked to play the big man. I'm sure you know how it goes. David knew a man who knew another man with underworld contacts. It impressed the girls anyway, need I go on?'

'Were you jealous of David Grant Mr. Swain?'

'Jealous of course I was jealous. He had Miranda and I was stuck with Jane the husband hunter.'

'Did Miss Shaw ever reject you Sir?' Swain broke into his sniggering laugh again but broke it off when he saw the look on Bridle's face.

'Miranda never had to reject me. I just let myself get swept along in her whirlwind Sergeant. She is a free spirit and she likes bad men. Not men like me.'

'Was David Grant a bad man Sir?'

'Bad enough.'

'Were you upset by his death Mr. Swain?'

'Of course I was he owed me money' Swain sniggered again.

'Mr. Swain I have reason to believe that Miss Shaw, Miss Porter and yourself lied on your original statements. Initially you stated that the whole party boarded a taxi and returned to the hotel. I now understand that David Grant never left the dock that night.'

Swain's head started to shake and he stammered a few inaudible words. Then he cleared his throat and sat upright with his hands clasped tightly on his lap.

'He did get in the taxi but he got out again – further along the dock.'

He looked at his mother for guidance but she turned her head and gazed out of the window.

'Why did you lie in your statement Mr. Swain?' Bridle could see he was a nervous wreck and a little more pressure would crack him open.

'He told us… he warned us to keep quiet. He said he had business with some ruffians on the dock and we all had to keep our mouths shut… ' Swain hesitated.

'Go on.' Bridle's stare unnerved Swain as he stumbled on.

'I told you he was always trying to play the big man. I thought he was just showing off. He knew Miranda was impressed by that kind of thing.'

'Was she impressed Mr. Swain?'

'Yes indeed her excitement was palpable' he glanced at his mother who continued to stare vacantly out of the window.

'What exactly did Grant say to you that made you lie in your statements?'

'Just a melodramatic warning, it amused us at first but the outcome was frightening.'

'What did he say to you Mr. Swain?' Bridle said firmly and Swain frowned.

'He said he had arranged to meet some people for a very lucrative deal. He said they were ruthless, violent capable of murder.'

'Did you believe him?'

'Not then, I thought it was his usual flannel. He got in the taxi because he was told that police were often at bare-knuckle fights and he wanted to be seen leaving. David loved all the cloak and dagger stuff.' Swain took a spotless handkerchief from the pocket of his gown and mopped the line of sweat that had formed on his brow.

'Go on Mr. Swain.'

'Look Sergeant, will I go to prison for lying in my statement? I really couldn't cope I think I would die. I really do.'

Bridle felt no pity for the man. The fact that he was privileged and spoiled was obvious enough but it was his self-serving vanity, his bitter jealousy and his venal personality that turned Bridle's stomach.

'The important thing Mr. Swain is to tell the truth now. If you had lied in a court of law then I'm afraid no one could help you.'

The relief seemed to take all of the energy out of Swain and he slumped down in the chair like a crumpled rag. Bridle looked at Mrs. Swain and wondered how she really felt about her son. The strain seemed to tighten her features and he could see that she was outwardly composed but her breathing had deepened as she maintained her calm.

'Can you remember where he got out of the cab?'

'We seemed to drive for a long time I didn't know the docks were so big. I was feeling a little queasy with all the twists and turns.'

'How long were you driving before he got out? Just a guess will do Mr. Swain.'

'I really couldn't say Sergeant.'

'So Grant told you he was dealing with dangerous men what else did he say?'

'He really laid it on thick, he said if anything happened to him then we had to deny all knowledge of his rendezvous or we might also be in danger. I just rolled my eyes and lit another cigarette but the girls lapped it up. They were all over him.'

'You didn't believe he might be in danger?'

'Not for a moment it was like one of those cheap crime novels you can buy at Lime Street Station.'

'Did you see anyone else with Grant when the cab pulled away?'

'Only that horrid little man who organised the shindig'

'Billy Doyle?'

'Don't know his name, thin with greasy hair and narrow

eyes. He was fawning all over us during the fight, quite a disgusting person really.' Swain closed his eyes and put his handkerchief to his mouth as if the strain was too much for him.

'You left the warehouse with Doyle as I recall.'

'Did we? I can't remember Sergeant we were surrounded by ruffians. I tried not to look at them I just had to get out of the noise and the smell. The smell was atrocious then we had to wait for the damn cab.'

'How long did you wait for it?'

'I've no idea but I had time to smoke a cigarette. If it wasn't for Miranda keeping us entertained I'd have gone mad.'

'How long does it take you to smoke a cigarette Mr. Swain?'

'It depends on my mood. If I feel irritated I smoke faster than normal.'

'And were you irritated Sir?'

'Very.'

Swain was beginning to feel the contempt coming from Bridle and he drew his knees up onto the chair and hugged them like a child.

'Would you say ten minutes? Fifteen minutes? It's important Mr. Swain.'

Swain continued to hug his knees as he rolled his eyes in thought. Then he blew out a petulant sigh and sat up straight in the chair.

'It was probably less than ten minutes but seemed longer. Do you know what I mean Sergeant?' Bridle ignored his question and flicked over another page of his note book as he thought about the taxi. He knew the driver had to be one of Doyle's cronies and it was going to be difficult to trace him.

'I know you said you couldn't describe the driver in your statement but can you recall anything about him or the cab?'

'I only saw the back of his head, he never spoke a word'.

'Did you notice the taxi plate number on the meter?' Bridle knew he was wasting his time.

'I didn't even notice the meter Sergeant.'

Bridle sighed as he closed his note book and slipped it inside his jacket.

'Oh thank God that's over' Swain put his hand to his forehead and closed his eyes.

'One last question Mr. Swain have you heard of a man called Guy Charlton?'

'What's Guy got to do this?' Swain looked startled.

'I can't discuss that Sir but you obviously know him.'

'Of course I know him but he's been away for some time.'

'Have you ever seen him with David Grant?'

'I haven't seen him at all since he came back – what's this about Sergeant?'

Bridle stood up briskly and managed a slight smile as he turned toward the door.

'Thank you both for your time you've been very helpful' Bridle lied. Mrs Swain stood up and followed him silently.

'I won't be seeing you again will I Sergeant?' Swain asked nervously. Bridle turned and saw that the haughty confidence had returned to his face.

'No Sir, only if I need to arrest you. Goodbye Mr. Swain.'

Bridle didn't wait to see the look of horror return to Swain's face as he made his way to the front door with Mrs. Swain walking gracefully behind him. Bridle opened the door sharply but Mrs. Swain caught his arm. He turned around and expected the overdue tirade of indignation but was confronted by a face that was softer than before.

'I'm sorry Sergeant I wish I could have been more help.'

In the sunlight Bridle could see she had been a very beautiful woman in her prime and he could see in her pale blue eyes that she had warmed towards him. But he could also see loneliness and a longing that made him feel very sorry for her. He held her gaze for a moment then with a slight nod and an awkward smile he turned and made his way down the gravel path to the lane. He didn't look back but he knew she had watched him all the way before she closed the door.

CHAPTER EIGHT

Tommy Lodge sat opposite Jane Porter in the drawing room of her father's Georgian town house near the Roman wall in Chester. The idea of Roman soldiers walking along the wall directly outside the window excited Lodge like a schoolboy. He tried to imagine the Roman sentries in their armour and red cloaks armed to the teeth and battle hardened. He admired elite armies and in his mind they didn't come more elite than the disciplined Romans.

Jane Porter finished reading the copy of her statement and placed it on the small oak table at her side. Lodge could see the nervous tension in her face but he was accustomed to people being nervous and intimidated during police interviews

'Thank you for reading that again Miss Porter. Are you satisfied with your statement?'

Lodge tried to speak as nicely as he could as he felt that his physical presence was making her uneasy.

'Why wouldn't I be satisfied with my statement?'

Lodge noticed the pitch of her voice rise as she spoke. 'It's just in case you remembered something else Miss and the fact that Miss Shaw has stated that you all falsified your statements.'

Her face turned into a pallid mask and Lodge thought for a moment she would faint.

'This is just a review Miss there's nothing to worry about. We understand why you did it and it's important that you amend it in due course.'

'I'm just sick of the whole affair. I wish I'd never set eyes on David Grant or Peter Swain or that bitch Miranda.'

The strain contorted her face and she looked as if she was about to cry but somehow held it back. Lodge put on the most sympathetic face he could manage and leaned slightly forward as he lowered his voice.

'It's a very nasty business Miss I'm surprised a nice girl like you got mixed up in it.'

'Mother pushes me to mix with certain people. She just sees their status she has no idea what they are really like.'

'You mean David Grant?' Lodge asked tentatively.

'And Peter Swain' she grimaced 'mother says he's artistic but I think there's another word for men like him.' Lodge cleared his throat and shuffled in his seat.

'Is your mother trying to match you?'

'I think she would sell me to the highest bidder of the right class of course.'

Lodge smiled in what he hoped was an understanding way but he wasn't good at faking sensitivity.

'Why did you go out with them if you felt that way?'

'Reputation you see. They are the people to be seen with, they go to the places to be seen at. I want a social life. The alternative is total boredom.'

She folded her arms and began to look less nervous and more impatient. Lodge didn't take an obvious look around the well furnished and ornate room but he wondered just how bored rich people could get. He felt she was holding something back but he was unwilling to push her too far due to her highly strung nature.

'So you are not a good friend of Miranda Shaw Miss?' Lodge could see the explosion about to occur so he braced himself.

'Why would I be a good friend of that slut?' She squealed 'she has a dangerous reputation and I don't mind associating with dangerous people. I don't want to be seen as boring. To be considered a bore is just social suicide.'

Lodge nodded and smiled but wondered how he ever got the idea that this was a nice girl. He was already looking forward to a stroll along the Roman wall and down to the nearest pub when he remembered that Bridle had asked him to check a name with her. He flicked through his note book and looked up at the impatient face sitting opposite him and smiled.

'I'm sorry to keep you Miss' he found the page and pressed it down with his hand 'do you know a Mr... Guy Charlton?' Lodge was amazed to see a bright smile appear on her face.

'Of course I know Guy' her smile suddenly vanished 'he's not involved in this is he?'

'Not directly Miss we are just checking all of Mr. Grant's known contacts.'

'Yes I've known Guy since childhood really. Guy was mother's first choice in her breeding plans for me.' Lodge wasn't sure if he should laugh because he wasn't sure if she was joking so he just nodded and listened.

'Guy is the kind of man every woman wants and every man hates because of that' she couldn't help smiling as she thought of him.

'Does he have a profession or a career of any kind Miss?'

'Not Guy he's far too dashing for a stuffy career. He went abroad to make his fortune and I believe he has.' She cocked her head slightly to one side as if she was proud of him and Lodge was beginning to hate the man himself.

'I see Miss.' Lodge had heard enough and a pint pot of Irish stout was clogging his thoughts.

'Of course we all thought he would marry Estella and settle down as the country gentleman but I'm not sure what went wrong. She actually married a policeman, no one could believe it. Mother always said Estella was too independent and she would end up a spinster or take a husband in desperation. She was obviously desperate, no offence of course.'

'None taken Miss' Lodge was intrigued 'would this be Estella Carver by any chance?'

'Why yes, do you know her husband?'

'Vaguely Miss' he lied confidently.

'Her father is a famous Barrister, very suave and sophisticated. I think mother had a crush on him, perhaps you knew him officer?'

'Our paths did cross in court a number of times Miss' Lodge murmured.

'Was he very dashing?'

'Dashing is not a word I would use Miss.' Bastard was the word Lodge was thinking of.

'Estella was devastated when Guy left, inconsolable. The policeman got her on the rebound and I've heard he's a Liverpool roughneck.' She squealed with amusement.

'Yes Miss an unsavoury character I believe' Lodge stifled a smirk 'but malicious gossip can be a dangerous thing Miss.'

'It's not malicious gossip, just juicy gossip' she said almost playfully but Lodge registered no interest in his face at all. 'The latest word on the circuit is that Estella is so disenchanted with married life that she might just go running back to Guy.'

'But she's a married woman Miss' Lodge said.

'Yes but they have no children. Apparently he can't produce in that department if you know what I mean.' She squealed again and Lodge winced.

'Is this Guy Charlton the kind of man who would break up a home Miss?'

'You can hardly call it a home officer. They have no family and are totally opposite in social class Estella's family can't abide him.'

'Would you happen to know where I can find Mr. Charlton Miss Porter?'

'I don't know where he is staying but I do know he was here in Chester this week. He'll be at the Whitley Ball next weekend, absolutely everyone will be there. Gosh you won't repeat what I've told you officer?'

'No Miss my job is to deal in facts not gossip. If you do remember anything else about the evening in question you can contact me on this telephone number.' He handed her a slip of paper and she glanced at it then discarded it. Lodge picked up his hat, notebook and paperwork and made his way to the door. She made no attempt to move.

'Thank you Miss I'll find my own way out' he tried not to sound sarcastic. Lodge made his way out quickly and was happy to find himself on the stone steps to the Roman wall. It was a fine afternoon and the thought of a dark pint almost put a skip in his step.

Stella Bridle strolled across Foregate Street in the centre of Chester and walked up the hill toward the town cross. She was wearing a thin summer dress belted at the waist and the flowing skirt billowed in the warm breeze causing male heads to turn from all directions. A grocer's delivery boy nearly fell off his bike as the wind caught her dress and revealed more above the knee than he could deal with. She was oblivious to the attention as her mind was absorbed in the dress she was completing for the

Whitley ball. She had just purchased some material for the final touches and she wanted to look special for her husband. She knew he would be uncomfortable and she also knew that her family would try their best to make him uncomfortable. He would be dour and moody but that image suited his looks and Stella wanted them both to stand out like Laurence Olivier and Vivienne Leigh. She giggled at the thought.

Stella had worked hard to lift herself out of the feeling of stagnation that had engulfed her in recent months. The idea of attending the ball had lifted her spirits immensely. Stella was aware that the pressures from her family had affected their marriage but she was determined to make it work. She hardly noticed the jaguar sports car keeping pace with her until the beep of the horn made her jump.

'I hope you realise what a danger you are to traffic Estella. You've almost caused two accidents already. How are you?'

Stella recognised the voice immediately and as she turned she saw the familiar smile on Guy Charlton's face. She was stunned for a moment as she took in the detail of the man she hadn't seen for so many years. He seemed broader than before and his blonde hair was a little darker than she remembered but his face still lit up as he smiled. He was very tall and she thought he looked funny with his knees bent up so much to fit in the sports car. But he hadn't aged at all and though she knew this moment would occur sooner or later she failed to keep the promise to herself that she would feel nothing.

'Hello Guy, are you keeping well?' She tried to appear friendly but not too warm.

'Very well thank you. I have to say you look stunning, married life agrees with you.'

'Yes it does' she said a little too quickly.

'Can I give you a lift somewhere? I think we need to talk.'

'Do we?' Stella knew how persuasive Guy could be and though she was trembling slightly she had no intention of falling to pieces.

'I think I need to apologise, about the past, the way I left.' He tried to look humble but couldn't quite manage it.

'There's really no need to apologise Guy, I'd completely forgotten about it.'

Charlton's conceited nature didn't allow him to believe that for a second and he smiled at her condescendingly.

'We can't talk here Estella' he said as he took his sports jacket from the passenger seat and threw it in the back of the car.

'Jump in and we'll nip round to the Grosvenor for a light lunch.'

'I don't think so Guy.'

'It would give us the chance to catch up. We don't want to bore everyone at the ball on Saturday by talking about the past. Let me buy you lunch please Estella.'

Charlton looked sincere and Stella bit her lip. He was right about the ball as there were things she wanted to say to him privately. She looked left and right as though she was searching for an escape route then she opened the passenger door and climbed in. She slammed it shut. Charlton knew better than to say anything at all as he slipped the car into gear and pulled away with unnecessary speed.

On the Roman Wall overlooking the street Lodge finished his cigarette as he watched the Jaguar pull away. He didn't know Stella Bridle very well but she was the kind of woman a man didn't forget in a hurry. Lodge tossed the stub of his cigarette over the wall and turned away. He decided not to bother with a pint after all.

Bridle stepped into the smoky lounge bar of the Cross Keys pub and scanned the room. It was busy with merchants and legal types discussing their business of the day and the air had a sweeter aroma of pipe and cigar smoke than most local bars. He had arranged to meet Lodge and Sullivan at five o'clock but he was already late. He saw them burrowed into a corner seat and Lodge indicated that a drink was ready on the table for him. As Bridle sat down he cast a doleful eye at the pint of stout then at Lodge's cigarette.

'It's about time you gave them up' Bridle said as he lifted his glass 'think of your training.'

'Been tryin' boss but I can still hit a bag as hard as any of them' Lodge said testily and Sullivan shook his head.

'How did you get on in Chester?' Bridle asked getting down to business.

'Thanks for that job boss. All she did was squeal and get touchy, it was a nightmare.'

'Get anything?' Bridle asked casually.

Lodge paused as he considered the gossip Jane Porter had squealed at him and the sight of Stella getting into a sports car with another man. Lodge shook his head as he blew out a blue plume of smoke.

'Nah it was a waste of time.' Lodge felt uncomfortable but he was too experienced to be convinced by gossip or a coincidental meeting between two people. Bridle had not shown any outward signs of strain in his marriage and Lodge was prepared to accept that someone like Jane Porter and her circle would be happy to dote on gossip and trivia. Lodge swallowed the beer that was left in the glass and placed it on the table carefully and deliberately. Bridle and Sullivan glanced at each other.

'I had a funny phone call about this case' Sullivan said ignoring Lodge's signal for another round.

'I could do with laugh' Bridle said as he squeezed himself into the seat.

'Not that kind of funny' Sullivan replied.

'It's always the same with a murder cases, brings out every crank in town' Lodge dismissed it as he reached for his cigarettes.

'What did he say George?' Bridle asked.

'It was a woman or a girl and she sounded a bit dizzy. She was definitely under the influence.'

'Cranks are always pissed' Lodge said and lit his cigarette.

'Yeah I thought so until she said something interesting' Sullivan paused as if to add some drama.

'Don't milk it George' Bridle said grinning.

'I couldn't get much out of her as she wanted to talk to you, but she said that David Grant wasn't a bad person. She said people were telling lies about him.'

'That is interesting' Bridle murmured.

'She was an odd one, said she had a baby then said she didn't have a baby. Then she says she's a compulsive liar.'

'That's it then you can stick her in the bin' Lodge said looking at his empty glass.

'I thought so too, but then she said Joey Vance was in danger.'

'Joey Vance' Bridle repeated.

'Yeah I was suspicious but I thought if you were looking for Joey that put her in a new light. She must know something about the investigation somewhere down the line.'

'Did she give a name or a phone number?' Bridle asked but Sullivan shook his head.

'It'll be that Miranda no-knickers from the artist's studio I'd put ten bob on it' Lodge said 'she's a queer one.'

'Did you tell Radford?' Bridle asked tentatively.

'It wasn't relevant to his investigation' Sullivan said with wink.

'Thanks for that George' Bridle said 'has he been looking for us?'

'Nah he's still ranting after that bollicking he got from upstairs' Sullivan replied 'he's gone into a sulk now.'

'That's not unusual' Bridle said. He looked at Lodge 'how was Chester today Tommy?'

'Why?' Lodge asked sharply.

'Stella was there shopping for the ball on Saturday' Bridle noticed Lodge's discomfort.

'I didn't see her' Lodge said flatly.

'What ball is this then?' Sullivan was intrigued.

'The Whitley Ball, a shindig I avoid every year' Bridle replied.

'Upper class shag night' Lodge sneered.

'I'm concerned about this phone call' Bridle said ignoring Lodge 'I know Joey was seen recently. Tommy I need you out with me in the early hours on Friday.' Lodge knew from Bridle's tone of voice that it wasn't worth an argument.

'George I need any background information on Guy Charlton you can find' Sullivan nodded 'I could also do with some detailed background on the Swain's, the Porters, Miranda Shaw's family and also the Grant family.'

Lodge took a long drag on his cigarette and scowled. He hated it when Bridle was enthusiastic as it usually meant more work.

'Very decisive today boss' Lodge said and crushed his cigarette into the ash tray. Bridle picked up Lodge's irritation but ignored it as he always did.

'I need to know how connected these families are' Bridle mused 'something isn't right.'

Tommy Lodge glanced at Bridle and thought about Stella and the man in the sports car.

Superintendent Mcleish sat in the front passenger seat of the Black Maria and took a quick glance over his shoulder at the officers swaying around in the back. He smirked at the glum and serious faces of the men but knew they were more than ready to take on the drunks and the brawlers that littered the street after closing time. Mcleish enjoyed his late night excursions into the city although his rank was above the task. This was an aspect of police work that he felt was essential for all ranks to experience and maintain because it was so fundamental and generally entertaining.

As the van made its way along the street the numerous pubs were letting out and the sight of the Black Maria caused many to scurry along faster or duck into alleyways. This made Mcleish laugh as he was aware that the public had various nicknames for his particular group of officers. Mcleish's favourite was The Bastard Brigade.

The people were disappointingly well ordered and Mcleish signalled to Sergeant Hurst to turn around and do another sweep along the opposite side of the street. Men cast worried looks over their shoulders as the van caught them in the headlights. They were waiting for that dreaded moment when the engine stopped and the blue uniforms spilled out of the back. They knew that to be pulled into the Black Maria meant an overnight stay in the stinking drunk tank at the bridewell and then a visit to the magistrates court the following morning.

'Is that fat Freddy pissin' by the wall over there?' Sergeant

Hurst said with a smirk on his face and Mcleish chuckled as he heard the groans coming from the rear of the vehicle.

'Please Sarge don't pull that fat bastard tonight, not again' the pleading voice spoke for the whole group.

'We have to uphold the law constable' Mcleish said firmly but grinned at Sergeant Hurst.

'But Sir the man stinks. He can't stop farting, his pants are covered in stale piss and his armpits make yer eyes water.'

'Is that right constable? Are we supposed to stand by while he pulls his dick out in full view of all and sundry to have a piss? Isn't that an offence in your book constable?' Mcleish kept his face straight and his voice stern.

'Yes Sir' the voice said submissively like a balloon deflating slowly.

'Fat Freddy it is then boys' Sergeant Hurst said as he swung the van around to catch Freddy in the headlights.

'What a sight' Mcleish said stifling a laugh as Freddy turned into the glare of the headlights still holding his manhood in both hands.

'Come on yer big bastids I'll take on the lot of yer' Freddy pointed his manhood at the van like a loaded gun and every officer in the vehicle burst into laughter. Sergeant Hurst slammed the van to a halt then looked back at the squirming faces in the van.

'He's all yours lads' Sergeant Hurst said laughing.

The rear doors were opened slowly and the less than enthusiastic officers climbed out and lined up reluctantly in a standard ready formation. Freddy was trying to stand without swaying and still had his trousers defiantly open in contempt for his opponents. He held his fists up and threw random punches to the left and right.

'Come on scuffers what are yer waitin' for?'

Freddy's open trousers slipped off his waist and down to his knees and as he tried to move forward he lost balance and fell flat on his face. Mcleish and Sergeant Hurst broke into uncontrolled laughter but the officers just looked at each other because they had caught a whiff of him as he fell. Freddy cursed and rolled over onto his back. He was so heavy all he could do was roll from side to side and his trousers had fallen to his ankles which made it impossible for him to stand. He punched his fists aimlessly into the air.

'I'm not finished yet yer bastids.'

As the reluctant officers moved forward to subdue Freddy a sudden crash of glass came from the pub followed by the unmistakeable sound of a bar-room brawl. Mcleish nodded to Sergeant Hurst.

'Leave him and get in the pub on the double' Sergeant Hurst growled.

The jubilant policemen leapt over Freddy's helpless body and into the pub with renewed energy followed by Mcleish and Hurst.

'Where the fuck are yer goin?' Freddy rolled over to one side to see the officers storming the bar then fell onto his back like a helpless tortoise on its shell.

Mcleish stepped through the door and was met by a stevedore on his way out. The stevedore drove both hands into Mcleish's chest to push him back but was halted by a truncheon slammed into his groin from Mcleish's right hip. There was a look of shock and agony on the man's face as he dropped to his knees and passed out. Mcleish calmly stepped over him and surveyed the mayhem in the bar. The room was full of shouting men and women who had turned their attention away from the brawl to shout abuse at the police. A screaming woman with red hair leapt onto a policeman's back in a wild effort to free the man he had in an arm-lock. As Mcleish walked forward he casually cracked her on the elbow with his truncheon and she fell howling to the floor.

The sight of Mcleish strolling through the broken glass and upturned furniture was enough to make the majority of revellers dive for the exits. The few brawlers left had been subdued and Mcleish made his way over to the bar.

'What happened here landlord?' Mcleish fixed the landlord with a glare.

'It was an argument Mr. Mcleish' the landlord's bald head gleamed with nervous sweat and he wiped his hands on a towel just so Mcleish wouldn't see them trembling.

'An argument was it? I would never have guessed' Mcleish sneered.

'Over politics Mr. Mcleish'

'This scum would find any excuse' Mcleish said looking sideways at an old woman in the corner who gave him the two finger sign.

'Had some of Jack Finney's lads here talkin' about an unemployment march, they left these leaflets. A couple of them stayed back for a drink and next thing I know this mad bastard is head-buttin' one of my regulars.'

Mcleish picked up one of the leaflets and held it at arm's length in an effort to see it without his glasses.

'Which one started it?' Mcleish asked nodding toward the apprehended men.

'He's gone, he just kicked it off then got out fast' the landlord spluttered.

'Was he one of the organisers?' Mcleish strained his eyes to read the flyer in the dim light.

'Not sure Mr. Mcleish, he was a gobby bastard, he stirred everyone up. Finney's lads usually drink well and don't cause trouble.'

'A rally and a march to St. Georges Plateau – A demonstration against unemployment – Saturday 21st June – We urge all working class men employed and unemployed to march for the sake of their brothers.' Mcleish sneered as he finished reading the flyer then folded it and slipped it into the breast pocket of his tunic.

'Sheep and cattle' Mcleish mumbled.

'It's organised by Councillor Finney so it must be above board' the landlord said enthusiastically and Mcleish just stared at him.

'Was the Councillor here tonight?' Mcleish asked quietly.

'Yeah but he left early. I know Jack Finney he's a good man' the landlord dropped his guard for moment and Mcleish stared him down.

'Is that so landlord?' Mcleish peered out from under the sharp peak of his cap and the landlord shrank back and sidled away cursing Mcleish under his breath.

Mcleish looked around at the mess and at the small number of men that had been arrested. The woman that Mcleish had cracked with his truncheon was lying on the floor holding her elbow and moaning in agony. Mcleish looked at her with disgust then stepped over her as he moved toward the door. He kicked a broken chair sideways across the room then turned to Sergeant Hurst.

'Get this shite in the van and get them down to the bridewell.'

'What about her Sir?' Sergeant Hurst said nodding toward the injured woman.

'The bitch is parish fed so the parish can look after her'
Mcleish strode out through the open door without looking back.
Sergeant Hurst glared at the men.

'You heard Superintendent Mcleish get moving.'

CHAPTER NINE

'But you know we are at the ball on Saturday.'

'I have to go Stella, it's a tip-off to do with young Joey' Bridle said quietly but firmly.

'How long will you be out?' She stopped cutting her fish altogether and placed her cutlery on the plate which Bridle knew was a very bad sign. He could see from the tightness of her lips and the narrowing of her lovely hazel eyes that she was ready for a battle.

'I don't know. The tip-off is for the early hours. We'll have to watch the place, maybe follow someone. We could be wasting our time I just don't know at the moment Stella.' Bridle cut a large portion of fish and put the fork in his mouth quickly. He made an ecstatic face as if it was the best food he had ever tasted in his life. His idea was to make her laugh but his tactic fell flat.

'You know how much I've been looking forward to the ball' Stella said firmly and Bridle almost choked on his fish. 'And you always put too much on your fork. You can be such a lout at times.'

Bridle chewed and swallowed his fish slowly. When Stella was angry with him she would often resort to criticising his lack of manners in some department.

'I'll try not to embarrass you at the ball Stella' Bridle said patiently in an effort to defuse the imminent explosion that he could see building up.

'What kind of state will you be in? Up all night chasing God knows who through the back-streets.'

'That's my job Stella' Bridle said quietly.

'Is it?' Stella picked up her cutlery again and resumed cutting her fish in silence and Bridle held his breath.

'Did you get the material you wanted in Chester?' He asked as cheerily as he could.

'Yes thank you' she placed a sliver of fish into her mouth and chewed it almost imperceptibly as if to emphasise Bridle's uncouth approach to eating his dinner.

'Have you finished your gown for the ball?' Bridle smiled but immediately regretted asking the question.

'What did I tell you this morning at breakfast?'

Bridle sat open-mouthed desperately trying to remember any conversation over breakfast.

'You mentioned Chester' he spluttered.

'And... ' she folded her arms'

'You mentioned material for the gown' he grinned as charmingly as he could but it was obvious from her expression that he was wasting his time.

'You don't listen to me any more.'

'Stella that's not true.'

'We hardly see each other. You are obsessed with work and you spend your spare time at the boxing club.Where is our marriage going to?'

'We are going to the ball on Saturday and you are going to knock them all dead in your new gown. I'll be the proudest man there.'

Bridle smiled and reached over for her hand but she pulled away and stood up then turned and ran out of the room. Bridle sat and listened to her footfall on the stairs and suddenly felt sick in his stomach. He stood up and slowly made his way upstairs to her work-room where she was sitting at her sewing table with her head in her hands. The room was full of the clutter of Stella's craft and it occurred to Bridle as he looked around that he didn't really appreciate how hard she worked. He sat on the floor beside her chair and knew it had gone beyond any clowning around to recover her mood. They sat in silence for a few moments then she looked at him sitting beside her on the floor with his legs crossed like a school boy and she couldn't help giggling despite her gloom.

As she giggled Bridle broke into a grin then a smile and before long they were both laughing but neither were sure why.

'Stella I can't do without you' Bridle looked up at her wet face and the sick feeling in his stomach increased.

'I know' she whispered.

She smiled as he stood up and pulled her to him. He kissed her hard and she responded warmly. He wiped the tears from under her eyes with his thumb and kissed her again.

'Things will get better for us Stella.'

He smiled as he looked into her glistening hazel eyes but he could sense that something had changed and it worried him.

'I would love to see you in that velvet dress' he glanced at the dress standing sleek and tight on the mannequin.

'That is a very expensive dress for a very good client' she said wiping her eyes.

'There can't be two women with a figure like yours Stella.'

'I think you are a bit of a wolf Mr. Bridle' she tilted her head back as she spoke.

'It would look perfect on you' he kissed her firmly on the lips.

'Keep dreaming' her eyes widened as he kissed her neck.

'I will' he whispered hoarsely' he kissed her again then lifted her off the floor and easily carried her across the landing to their bedroom.

Tommy Lodge sat in the saloon bar on City Road with a slow burning Woodbine on the edge of an ash-tray, a pint of mild at his right hand and the Liverpool echo on the table in front of him. It was a quiet night in the bar and he was disappointed that he had no audience to enthral with his knowledge of football and politics. Lodge had left his wife Betty asleep in an armchair and slipped out just after their fish and chip supper. He knew she would be asleep until ten o'clock sharp when she would normally wake up with a start and call out the name of her cat that had died years before. Then she would get up and put the kettle on for a cup of tea before bed. The routine never failed to depress Lodge but he had grown perversely accustomed to it. He was engrossed in his paper but was fully aware that a figure was approaching him from behind so he planted both feet firmly on the ground and braced himself ready to move.

He turned and looked over his shoulder. Billy Doyle was standing behind him with two pints of beer. He looked like he hadn't shaved for days and Lodge judged his body odour to be about the same vintage.

'Have you been sleepin' rough Billy?' Lodge asked pointing to the empty seat at his table. He was not the kind of man to refuse a pint from anyone.

'Thanks Mr. Lodge.'

Doyle sat in the chair and placed both glasses on the table. He took out some cigarette papers and tobacco and started to roll a cigarette with a speed and dexterity that fascinated Lodge.

149

'Want a roly?' Doyle asked holding up a completed cigarette.

'I'll stick with the Woodies thanks' Lodge stubbed out the remains of his Woodbine then immediately took another from the packet on the table. He struck a Swan Vesta and lit Doyle's cigarette then lit his own and threw the dead match into the ash tray.

'Cheers Billy' Lodge held up his fresh pint and took a gulp.

'It always tastes better when someone else buys it' Doyle said and Lodge wondered what the pint was going to cost him. Doyle's face was bruised and he had cuts above his eye and one on his lip that had just begun to heal.

'Looks like you upset the wrong people' Lodge said flatly.

Doyle took a long drag on his cigarette and caught a glimpse of himself in the wall mirror.

'Radford' Doyle said with disgust.

'Why?' Lodge responded.

'Does he need a reason?' Doyle shrugged.

'Inspector Radford isn't stupid Billy, he wouldn't risk doin' that without a reason' Lodge said looking at his paper.

'No wonder you're still a constable' Doyle sneered.

'Detective Constable' Lodge snapped and Doyle stifled a laugh although it obviously hurt his ribs to do so.

'You Jacks stick together even when you hate each other's guts' Doyle said shaking his head then said suddenly 'Radford wants me to take the drop for the Grant murder.'

Lodge could see that one of Doyle's front teeth had been knocked out and he felt uneasy about his condition.

'Radford needs someone to swing for it soon' Lodge replied.

'He's got no evidence so he tried to persuade me to confess' Doyle said and took a drag on his cigarette 'so I had to disappear like a fairy in a fuckin' panto.'

'I guess you want something from me' Lodge looked at his paper and waited for a reply.

'I need to talk to Bridle' Doyle said quietly.

'So why come to me?' Lodge felt a little irritated 'how do yer know I won't go to Radford?'

Doyle started to laugh then almost choked on a hacking cough.

'You and Bridle are shit on Radford's shoes' Doyle rasped 'everyone knows it.'

'What kind of shit?' Lodge didn't look up from his paper. 'Dog shit' Doyle responded confidently and Lodge looked up slowly.

'Are you a brave man Billy?'

'Not really' Doyle nodded toward the bar then toward each exit. Lodge looked around to see Doyle's cronies covering each area. All of them sipping pints and staring at Lodge intensely.

'Looks like a funeral wake to me' Lodge said calmly.

'It'll be yours if you go to Radford' Doyle whispered then he pulled his chair closer to the table and leaned forward toward Lodge's face.

'Don't get high-handed with me Lodge. Paddy Finch has been toppin' up your wallet for years, everyone knows it. You Jacks are all bent bastards except for Bridle and he's a fuckin' boy scout. That's why I need him.'

'I joined the boy scouts recently Billy. I get my first badge next week, the one for disposing of a dead body in open country' Lodge showed no expression or emotion and Doyle slowly broke into a rasping laugh.

'Let's be men about this, we don't need to fall out. Just arrange for me to see Bridle that's all I ask' Doyle winked at Lodge and stood up from the table.

As Doyle moved away with his loping strides Lodge cursed him under his breath and then cursed his own life. A dark feeling crept over Lodge as Doyle slipped through the door. It was a feeling of no going back. He had put himself in a position were scum like Doyle could call the tune and it sickened him. He threw the remainder of the pint down his throat and slammed the glass down onto the table. The rain was hammering down outside and Lodge could hear the water spilling over a blocked gutter. He remembered he had a half-bottle of whiskey stashed away in the house and he was in a mood to walk home very slowly and get very wet.

Jack Finney stood on the stage of the community hall on Park Lane flanked by Harry Croft and Stan Myers of the docker's union all taking the good wishes and handshakes from the departing crowd. Myers had organised the meeting to generate interest and gain some commitment for the forthcoming rally for the unemployed. He was a stout man in his late fifties with a large pot-belly and ruddy cheeks. The meeting had gone well and the audience had been slow to leave as everyone wanted to shake the hand of Harry Croft and ask him about the civil war in Spain. As the last of the audience slipped away the three men sat back in their chairs. Exhausted with the effort of the last couple of hours they failed to notice the figure standing at the back of the hall until he started to walk slowly down the central aisle. The slow thump of his boots on the wooden floor made them look up but Finney already had his eyes fixed on the cold face of Superintendent Mcleish.

'It's the boys in blue' Croft said smiling until he saw the looks passing between Finney and Mcleish. Croft recognised the look. He had seen it many times in his life. The tension between the two men was palpable.

'What exactly is the Ted Dunn Militia?' Mcleish asked as he strolled down the aisle to the stage with his hands clasped behind his back. Croft hesitated for a moment before answering.

'It's a division of the International Brigade... '

'Fighting fascism in Spain' Mcleish butted in 'why would they name a militia after a union trouble maker like Ted Dunn?' Mcleish sneered.

'Ted Dunn is a legend around here Mr. Mcleish' Stan Myers said firmly.

'A hero of yours Mr. Myers' Mcleish said with a smirk.

'I am proud to say yes to that' Myers sat upright in his chair as he answered and folded his arms. Mcleish ignored Myers and stared at Finney as he came to a stop at the edge of the stage.

'Jack it's been a long time' Mcleish's granite face cracked into a grin.

'Not long enough' Finney said flatly and Mcleish laughed at his response. Croft looked to the back of the hall and could see the silhouetted figures of uniformed policemen ranked along the back wall and it made him uneasy.

'The unemployed riot of nineteen twenty... two wasn't it?' Mcleish said coldly.

'I don't remember' Finney lied.

'There you were fighting the good fight in the town hall of all places. A peaceful demonstration that turned into a riot, a total disaster, I thought we apprehended everyone that night so tell us how you got away Jack' Mcleish looked at each man and grinned.

'What do you want Mr. Mcleish?' Stan Myers asked.

'What do I want Mr. Myers? I want law and order.'

The three men looked at each other and then back to Mcleish.

'Are we breaking the law officer?' Harry Croft asked smugly.

Mcleish placed both of his gloved hands on the stage and leaned forward slightly as if he was about to push it away. He studied Croft in detail for a moment to test if it unnerved him. It didn't.

'You must be the famous Harry Croft, man of the people, legend of the spanish civil war and general all round communist flag waver.'

Harry Croft felt such a powerful surge of anger that he braced himself to leap at Mcleish but Finney caught his arm and held him firm.

'Ah well done Jack, always the sensible one. I can't arrest a legend like Harry Croft it might spark a riot, son of the late Alan Croft another socialist hero.'

'And proud of it' Croft snarled and Finney whispered 'don't let him get to you Harry.'

Mcleish put his hands behind his back and began to stroll up and down the front of the stage as if deep in thought.

'Alan Croft was a hard drinking man as I recall' Mcleish said quizzicaly 'cost me a few quid every time I saw him but it was worth it, he was one of the best snouts I ever had.'

Harry Croft leapt up and dragged Finney with him. Myers caught Croft's other arm and both men held him back as he cursed Mcleish

'You lying poisonous bastard' Croft snarled and the rank at the back of the hall took an instinctive step forward.

'Did he drink himself to death?' Mcleish asked casually 'wouldn't surprise me, I guess his conscience made him drink so much, the way he betrayed all his mates eh Jack.'

'Liar' Croft screamed.

154

'Threw all his money away on the drink and the nags' Mcleish shook his head slowly 'no wonder he was a snout.'

'Liar' Croft screamed louder.

Mcleish stopped walking up and down then turned swiftly and slammed his fist down on the stage.

'Your dad was a worthless inebriate and a police informer.'

Mcleish's words numbed Finney but drove Croft into a wild rage. Finney knew Mcleish was making mischief and didn't want to believe it, but as he held Croft back his mind was racing with doubt.

'Jack knows I'm telling the truth don't you Jack?' Mcleish said with a mocking tone.

'He's trying to split us Harry' Finney said struggling to hold Croft 'he wants to stop the rally before it starts, he's an evil bastard but he's a clever one.'

'It's easy to smear a dead man copper, step outside with me and we'll sort this out like men'

Croft's rage caused the vein in his temple to pulse with blood.

'You know I'm right Jack. You know you were betrayed that night because I was waiting for you. It was your partner in socialism and my snout Alan Croft.'

'Go to hell Mcleish' Finney didn't want to listen.

'You know we had a man on the inside Jack, you said it yourself, our inside man was Alan Croft.'

'No' Croft struggled to pull free.

'Oh yes Harry, hero of the oppressed, your dad was a traitor to the cause but don't worry' Mcleish looked left and right conspiratorially then whispered 'I won't tell anyone.'

Mcleish broke into a loud laugh as he turned on his heel and walked up the central aisle of the hall. He walked through the main doors and the shadowy figures of the rank fell into step behind him and they melted into the dim light of the doorway.

'I'm going to kill that bastard one day' Croft said coldly and Finney knew by the look on his face that he meant it.

Sir Nigel Carver strolled along the narrow path of his garden and contemplated trimming the borders but gave up the idea to savour a rather sweet cigar from a batch he had recently collected from Turmeau's. He thought he had fooled his wife by dutifully changing into his gardening clothes and making a lot of noise about pruning and tidying but she could smell the aroma of the cigar from the house and sighed yet another sigh of resignation. Carver settled himself in a wicker chair in their large greenhouse and pondered the Grant case.

The file that Sir Edward Grant had passed into his keeping had been troubling him for some time. He didn't know what to do with it. He was aware that the information in the file could be of great assistance to the murder case but there was nothing conclusive in it. He was professional enough to know that an investigation could be swung in the right direction by even the slightest piece of information and he was holding on to a lot more than that.

On the other hand he knew that the Grant family were being dragged through the mud thanks to David's antics and he considered whether it was necessary to continue their pain. He asked himself two basic questions. Did he care that David Grant was dead? The answer was no. Did he care that David Grant was murdered? The answer was yes he did care. He'd had a lifetime dedicated to the rule of law and a murder was to him a heinous crime. The victim was irrelevant.

His main quandary was deciding on the best pair of hands to drop the file into. He knew many senior police officers through his social circle and he wasn't keen to enhance any of their careers. He considered most of them to be uncultured dullards that had to be tolerated due to their standing in the community. Having crossed most of their paths in the courtroom over the years he had beaten them at every turn and he found it a little distasteful when they openly fawned to him during Lodge meetings.

Another alternative occurred to him earlier that day when he lunched with his daughters Elizabeth and Caroline. He doted on the company of his girls and relished the diversity of their personalities which always entertained him. He listened straight-faced to embellished stories of their husband's talents and successful careers which amused Carver because he knew Malcolm and Gerald were full of the deluded self-belief that their social standing gave them. Carver didn't care that their husbands were mediocrities. Estella was a different case entirely.

Carver savoured the taste and aroma of his cigar for a moment then the image of John Bridle loomed up in his mind. He knew from his contacts that Bridle was a talented police officer. But he also knew that his personality, sometimes aggressive, other times amusing, very often sarcastic, but more often taciturn, hadn't endeared him to his superiors. Carver had a grudging respect for Bridle but he would never be good enough for Estella. He was fixed on that.

Elizabeth and Caroline had informed him of their conversation with Estella in the tea room and it pleased him that cracks had begun to appear in Estella's marriage because he always knew it would happen. He rolled the cigar between his lips and drew the smoke into his mouth then put his head back and blew a long blue plume of smoke up the roof of the greenhouse. Carver smiled as he realised the perfect use for the file.

CHAPTER TEN

Rain speckled the windscreen of the car and Lodge turned the handle of the manual wiper at regular intervals which eased the monotony of staring out into the darkness of the street. Bridle himself was in a morose sort of mood and had hardly spoken since they had parked the car just off the Dock road near Park Lane. Lodge had amused himself by reading and re-reading the sign for a ship's chandler but that had become tedious. All attempts at conversation with Bridle had resulted in a grunt or a snapped reply so Lodge had backed off in a huff. Lodge began to turn the wiper to the rhythm of a ticking clock and even started making a ticking noise under his breath until he caught the look on Bridle's face.

They had arrived just after one in the morning and had parked the car with a clear view of the doss house across the road. In the past hour Lodge had counted seven prostitutes going in and out of the place which was no more than a whore's den for sailors. Lodge didn't ask Bridle why he was so miserable. Having seen Bridle's wife climb into the sports car in Chester he assumed there were domestic strains that couldn't be discussed. Lodge hadn't told Bridle about seeing Stella with another man and he had no intention of doing so. As far as he was concerned it was none of his business.

'How many whores have you counted so far?' Bridle broke the silence.

'Seven' Lodge said flatly.

'Eight' Bridle said.

'Eight?' Lodge responded.

'There's one down the alley banging sailors in a doorway' Bridle murmured.

'I thought they were just goin' for a piss, not takin' long are they?' Lodge said with a smirk.

'I think it's Daisy' Bridle said.

'Daft Daisy' Lodge sniggered 'That explains it.'

Bridle resumed his silence and continued his concentration on the doss house. It seemed to Lodge that the man had an on and off switch.

'I had a visit from Billy Doyle in the pub' Lodge said idly 'he bought me a pint' Lodge glanced at Bridle.

'He'll be a mate of yours for life then eh?' Bridle said and Lodge smirked.

'Says Radford kicked the shit out of him'

'How did he look?' Bridle asked.

'Kicked shitless' Lodge said sniffing.

They both began to chuckle but Bridle stopped abruptly and continued his hard stare through the windscreen. The off switch again Lodge thought.

'He thinks Radford's tryin' to mark his card for the Grant murder' Lodge struggled to spark Bridle's interest.

'Something else is going on' Bridle said quietly 'Joey Vance knows something.'

'Oh so that's why we're sat here in the pissin' rain at two o'clock in the mornin' Lodge scowled.

'That's about it Tommy' Bridle sighed.

'Doyle wants to talk to you' Lodge said after a long pause.

'Why?' Bridle replied.

'He says you're a boy scout and he doesn't trust anyone else' Lodge looked for a reaction but Bridle didn't flinch. Lodge squirmed in his seat then shook his head.

'Sorry boss I need a serious piss.'

'Keep it quiet when you get out and don't close the door' Bridle snapped impatiently.

Lodge knew better than to reply when Bridle was touchy so he carefully opened the door and slid out as gingerly as his bulk would allow. He scurried to the rear of the vehicle and fought with the buttons of his fly then let loose a jet of steaming urine into the gutter.

As Lodge stood immobile in the rain Joey Vance appeared from the shadows, his head darting left and right as he moved toward the doss house. Lodge thought about knocking on the window to alert Bridle but as he raised his hand Bridle was already slipping silently out of the car. Lodge watched helplessly as Bridle moved through the rain toward the doss house as another figure appeared from the alleyway to the left. Lodge could see this figure was a tall and well built man and Joey approached him confidently as though he was expected. Lodge finished his task too hastily and sprayed urine down his trouser leg and over his shoes. He frantically buttoned his flies as he tried to keep low and out of sight.

Lodge slipped around the side of the car and looked up carefully over the bonnet. He couldn't see Bridle but knew he was somewhere in the darkness and moving toward Joey and the other man. The only light was from a gas lamp above the door of the doss house and the pelting rain limited its range. Lodge squinted through the rain. He didn't want to move in case he alerted the men and he had no idea what Bridle was up to. The rain fell heavier drumming the car roof and obscuring any of the conversation. Joey and the man moved closer to the wall to shelter from the rain and Lodge could see the taller man was becoming agitated and getting into a temper. Lodge assumed that Bridle had moved close enough to overhear the conversation and was waiting for the right moment to move.

As Lodge watched the argument develop he thought he could hear a motor above the drumming of the rain getting louder from behind him. He turned to look just as an unlit saloon car sped past him at high speed. Without headlamps on it was virtually invisible until the last moment and it almost gave Lodge a heart attack. He swung around to see it speeding toward the doss house. The driver slammed on the brakes and lit the headlamps at the same time which caught Joey and his companion in a blinding rain-speckled light. Like two actors on a stage Lodge thought in the heat of the moment.

Joey Vance froze to the spot squinting into the headlamps but the tall man reacted instantly and threw himself sideways just as the first gunshot exploded from the car. Lodge jumped up with shock and saw the impact of the bullet hit the wall behind Joey who remained rigid and stunned.

'Fuck this' Lodge said in a panic then stood helpless guessing the next shot would probably drop Joey.

Bridle screamed at Joey to get down as he broke cover and raced directly toward him. Lodge looked on in disbelief as Bridle sprinted through the rain and caught Joey with a low rugby tackle just as a second shot smashed through a window above their falling heads. Screams of panic came out of the doss house when another gun was discharged from the alley to the left. Lodge saw the flash of the barrel and the bullet shattered the side window of the police car then passed close enough to his ear for him to hear it whistle as it passed. Lodge dropped down low and his stomach churned.

'Shit.' Lodge felt helpless as he crouched behind the car knowing Bridle and Joey were lying in the rain in the direct line of fire.

'Call yourself a man Tommy Lodge, get yer arse up.' He pushed himself up as more shots were exchanged but all he could see was Bridle lying motionless on top of Joey close to the wall of the doss house.

Lodge looked around frantically and saw some loose building bricks that had fallen from a crumbling wall. He picked one up and launched himself forward toward the rear of the gunman's car with the brick raised above his head and howling wildly. The car immediately reversed straight at him as he rammed the brick through the rear-window causing the driver to slam the brakes on. Lodge threw himself sideways into the rain filled gutter and shut his eyes tightly as he braced himself for the car to reverse over him. Lodge opened his eyes slowly then sharply as he stared in disbelief. He saw Bridle hurling himself at full speed into the glare of the headlamps screaming like a man possessed. The car slammed into forward gear and the tyres screeched as it sped forward straight at Bridle. Lodge watched as Bridle sprinted forward on a collision course in a duel that he couldn't possibly win.

The car had little time to accelerate and at the point of impact Bridle leapt up onto the bonnet. The forward motion of the car projected him up and over the roof. His natural reaction was to drop his head into a forward roll across the roof and into a ragged fall over the boot onto his back in the gutter next to Lodge. He grunted as he hit the rain soaked ground and lay motionless. The car sped off into the darkness as the panicking residents of the doss house spilled onto the street. The whores were screaming and crying and the men were making quick exits into the darkness. Lodge could hear the police whistles responding to the gunshots and it all seemed unreal to him because it had happened so fast. Bridle stirred with a low moan then sat up quickly.

'Careful boss you've just had one hell of a fall' Lodge spluttered through the rain.

Bridle and Lodge looked at each other for moment sitting in a gutter in the pouring rain and they both started to laugh at the absurdity of it. Bridle could feel pain in his back and shoulder but suddenly remembered Joey Vance and jumped up to look around. There was no sign of him. Bridle cursed under his breath as Lodge pulled himself up and brushed the debris of the gutter from his coat.

'You should go to the hospital for a check over boss' Lodge tried to hold Bridle back.

'I've got to find Joey Vance.' Bridle moved off toward the alley and felt another sharp pain coming from his forearm.

'There's another gunman out there boss are yer forgettin' that?' Lodge shouted as Bridle broke into a jog and soon merged into the darkness of the alley.

Bridle ran through the rain into the next street lined by huge cotton warehouses on both sides. He could cope with the pain in his forearm but his shoulder ached badly. The next street was exactly the same as the last one and as he made his way through the darkness and rain he knew it was hopeless His shoulder was irritating and he prayed nothing was broken. He stopped and listened. All he could hear was the commotion around the doss house in the next street and the piercing shrill of police whistles. He called Joey's name and it echoed around the alley. The rain was still pounding down and he slowly realised that he was soaked to the skin and was beginning to feel very cold. He reluctantly turned into the alley to make his way back to the doss house but came to a sudden halt as a pistol barrel was pressed into his neck from behind and his injured shoulder was gripped by powerful fingers.

'If you move or shout I'll blow your brains out Englishman' the Irish accent was softly but menacingly spoken and Bridle froze to the spot.

'I've had enough excitement for one night' Bridle said quietly and slowly turned his head.

'Don't move your head, if you see my face you are a dead man, now who the hell are yer?'

'I'm a police officer, a Detective Sergeant' Bridle's stomach churned as he answered.

'What do yer 'want with the boy?'

'I just want to talk to him Joey knows me.'

'How did yer know we'd be here?'

'I was just looking for Joey no one else' Bridle lied.

'Who tipped you off copper? Someone told you we'd be here.'

'Where's Joey?' Bridle snapped 'If you fire that thing you'll bring a dozen officers from around the corner.'

'With all these warehouses around the gunshot would echo all over the place. By the time they work out which direction it's come from I'd be tucked up in bed.'

'You've done this before' Bridle knew he was in dangerous hands.

'I shot my first Black and Tan when I was fifteen.'

'For sport' Bridle regretted the remark immediately.

'No yer English bastard for shooting dead my Da' and my brother. So believe me I would kill you then piss all over yer, do I make myself clear?'

'Crystal clear' Bridle could hear his heart pounding above the noise of the rain

The sound of police boots and Lodge's curses grew closer from the other side of the alleyway and Bridle's heart rate increased even further. He knew the Irishman would have to make a decision very quickly.

'Must be your lucky day Sergeant. I'm gonna back away slowly. I've got a 9mm pointin' straight at yer back, if you make any sound before yer mates get here I'll blow yer heart out through yer fuckin' chest. If yer try to find me Sergeant I will finish the job.'

Bridle stood motionless in the rain as Lodge and four constables gradually appeared with torch lamps making flashing images dance around the walls of the alley.

'You look like you've seen a ghost boss' Lodge quipped.

'A ghost' Bridle shivered 'I think I've just met the devil himself.'

Stella Bridle pretended to be asleep when her husband tried to slip unnoticed into bed at six o'clock in the morning. Bridle knew she was awake because her breathing was silent and her body was rigid but he hoped she would keep up the pretence because he was desperately tired and couldn't face an argument. He had boiled a kettle of water and had a wash in the scullery in the hope that he wouldn't disturb her. Bruises had started to come through on his shoulder, hip and knee and during his wash he noticed a lump on the back of his head. Both hands were scraped on the palms and the wrists. The general feeling was of burning all over his body. The bed was warm and his tense muscles eased as he lay on the pillow. He could feel himself drifting off when Stella quickly turned over and looked at him.

'Was it worth it?' Stella was wide awake 'your call to duty was it worth it?' She sat up.

'I'm not sure' Bridle sighed and lay motionless.

'After all that you are not sure' Stella folded her arms.

'What are you on about Stella?' Bridle felt confused.

'Oh come on you staged this late duty just to get out of the ball tonight.'

'I told you I will go to the ball just like Cinderella' Bridle was too tired to argue.

'Everything is a joke to you, what kind of state will you be in?'

'I'll be fine, I promised to go so I will.'

'So you are going because you promised, not because you want to be with me.'

Bridle sighed quietly. He didn't look up but he knew she would be sitting upright with her arms folded and her mouth pouting like a child. He hated this peevish side to Stella.

'I want to go Stella. I haven't been sneered at by your family in such a long time, I miss it.'

'You always revert to that chip on your shoulder.'

'If you say so' Bridle sighed and tried to turn over.

'I do say so, look I want this to be special for us, we can go there and show them all how happy we are, how fabulous we look together. They didn't think we'd last five minutes and here we are.'

Bridle rolled over and lifted himself up on his elbow. She looked at him with a sulky pout and he started to chuckle. Stella followed suit and they began to laugh until Bridle made a lunge for her and she jumped out of bed with a squeal.

'You are far too tired for that Mr. Bridle' Stella stood away from the bed with her hands on her hips and Bridle rolled over onto his back in frustration.

'I'm happy to chance it' he said with a smirk then pulled the blanket up to his shoulders as he remembered his injuries and didn't want Stella to worry.

'I'm going to mummy's house this afternoon to get ready with Caroline and Elizabeth can you come over for six thirty?'

Bridle was already starting to drift and Stella's voice was like an echo in the background.

'Are you going to wear that velvet dress on the mannequin?' His voice fell into a whisper as he drifted away and Stella giggled.

'No I told you it's for a client' she could tell by his breathing that he had dropped into a heavy sleep 'I'll leave you a note' she said tenderly and crept out of the room.

The sun was just beginning to show itself as Callum Riley made his way along the deserted street in Toxteth. A milk cart appeared plodding along the far end of the street but Riley judged the milkman to have one foot in the grave and incapable of noticing much. It amused Riley to see the old man having a conversation with his horse every time he stopped the cart. The rain had stopped but Riley was still wet from the night before. He had slept in an old shed off the Dock Road for a couple of hours after he evaded Bridle and the police search. He learned many years ago that the best way to hide from an enemy was to stay as close as possible to him. So he had stood in the shadow of a warehouse door and watched the police running backwards and forwards never realising he was there.

He reached the steps leading down to Vance's tenement just as the door opened. He leapt back silently and pinned himself behind a wall. Riley watched Mrs. Vance walk up the steps with a young sailor and they stopped just a few feet from him.

'Ah that was a great shag lad, best one I've had in years. I'll see yer next time you're in dock.' The young sailor walked off sheepishly and Mrs.Vance gave him the vee sign behind his back then made her way down the steps unaware that Riley was waiting for her. As she reached the door he calmly stepped out and pushed her forward into the hall where she fell flat on her face. She rolled over and was about to scream when he darted forward and rammed his hand over her mouth. Her eyes bulged with terror and Riley baulked at the smell of her. He caught hold of her cardigan and lifted her to her feet. Still clenching his hand over her mouth he pushed her into the parlour then threw her across the room. She crashed into a table and onto the floor where she lay moaning. He strolled back and closed the front door quietly then swiftly made his way into the parlour.

'Where's the lad yer bleach-headed old whore?'

'Please don't hurt me I'm a fallen woman, a sinner in need of forgiveness, can I just say a prayer to the blessed Virgin?' She looked at him pitifully and Riley gave her a dazzling smile.

'Just tell me were yer lad is me darlin' girl.'

'I think he's with … ' her words were cut short by the back of Riley's hand. She grunted and began to tremble violently.

'Thinking isn't good enough where is he?'

'With the Finch gang' she moaned 'he lodges with one of them on Smithdown Road. Please don't hit me again. I won't get work with me fuckin' face battered God forgive me. Look I'm bleedin' all over me best carpet.' She tried to wipe the blood from her nose but her hand shook too much. Riley looked down at the carpet with disgust then shook his head slowly.

'You've been talkin' to coppers haven't yer darlin'?' Riley put his face close to hers.

'I swear by St Francis I haven't spoken to no scuffers – honest to God.'

'St Francis now is it, how many saints are yer gonna call on?'

'As many as I fuckin have to' she muttered through her tears.

'In that case start sayin' yer prayers'…

As he finished speaking he struck her hard with a straight punch that split her nose and spurted blood over her clothes. She fell back and squealed clutching her face.

'You told the coppers where I'd be didn't yer?'

'That bastard of a Jack wanted Joey. He said he would collar me for whorin', I was scared' she was hardly coherent but Riley wasn't listening.

'So yer squealed on me didn't yer?' The look in Riley's eyes terrified her.

'No I swear on me fuckin' life'…

'You must have told someone yer pox ridden bitch.'

'And there was me thinkin' you were a fuckin' charmer. I fuckin' hate men' she moaned and Riley caught her by the throat and lifted her up.

'I nearly got shot last night, you must have told someone, now who was it?' He threw another back hand across her face and she crashed to the floor groaning.

'Why doesn't anyone believe a fuckin' word I say?' She was face down crying into the sticky carpet and Riley leaned over and whispered in her ear.

'Say hello to St. Francis for me.'

She raised herself up slowly and looked over her shoulder with terror in her eyes. He gave her a charming smile then swiftly caught her head in both hands and twisted it violently toward him. Her neck snapped with a loud crack and he let her lifeless body fall back to the floor with a look of disgust on his face. She had soiled herself and the smell was overpowering. He quickly looked around the room for any evidence of his visit then strolled to the door and glanced back at the foul-smelling body.

'I think I've just done you a favour' he grinned and turned into the gloom of the hallway.

Bridle could hear the ringing in the distance like a cowbell that was getting closer and closer. He woke and looked around the room in a sort of numb trance. The ringing was coming from somewhere. It was the telephone downstairs and it was still ringing. He sat up on the bed and hoped it would stop. It didn't, which meant it had to be work. He slid out of bed and ambled downstairs but the phone kept on ringing. Bridle held his hand above the receiver and hoped it would stop but it didn't. He knew he had no choice so he reluctantly picked up the receiver and gradually brought it to his ear.

'Bridle'

'This is Radford' Bridle braced himself 'I want you and Lodge down here for five o'clock today. I've got Webster, Crowley and Mcleish on my back and I want some answers.'

'It's my day off Sir' Bridle knew what the response would be.

'I want you and Lodge here at five o'clock sharp' Radford exploded 'get your fucking arse down here Bridle or I swear to God you'll be back in uniform on point duty outside Lime Street Station on Monday morning.'

Radford slammed the phone down so hard it made Bridle wince. Bridle replaced the receiver then saw the note Stella had left him next to the telephone. Six thirty at her mother's house. He had no chance of making it. He dropped onto the armchair like a deflated balloon and stared up at the ceiling. Stella was right the ceiling did need painting.

He jumped up and kicked the armchair across the room and

cursed loudly. Glancing at the clock he picked up the receiver to call Stella. He dialled the first number, then hesitated, then slammed the receiver into the cradle. She had to know. He cursed himself again then picked up the receiver and forced himself to dial but threw it back into the cradle before he dialled the last number. He didn't know what to say to Stella. She was in her parent's house with her family and friends enjoying every moment. That made him feel isolated enough but to give her the bad news would push her further into the family wilderness.

He pulled the armchair back into position and dropped into it. He had slept badly and the throb from the swelling on his head made him feel nauseous. He thought about the Irishman and how close he had been to having his brains spread around the docks. Lodge believed the mysterious car was a black Austin saloon with the registration plates covered up with sacking. They both agreed there were two men in the car but who was the target? Was it Joey Vance, the man he was talking to or both? Who was the Irishman? Now he had to face the post-mortem with Radford and his superiors and he didn't know what to tell them. He didn't know what to say to Stella either and he was beginning to wish that he hadn't got out of bed when the phone rang again.

'Bridle'

'John I didn't wake you did I?' Stella's voice was animated and excited.

'No Stella you didn't wake me' Bridle could feel a dark cloud descending.

'I forgot to tell you that I've hung your suit in my work-room with a clean shirt and you won't forget to polish your shoes will you?' Stella giggled and Bridle realised that she was playing to an audience probably Elizabeth and Caroline. He felt dreadful.

'Elizabeth thinks you may have a look of Clark Gable about you in your dinner suit' she giggled again and Bridle knew why he loved her so much.

'I don't have a moustache' he said half-heartedly.

'I could pencil one on your top lip just for the evening.'

Bridle smiled at her joke and took a deep breath. There was no easy way to break the news.

'Stella there was a serious incident last night and I've been ordered into headquarters at five o'clock to report to my superiors. I'm going to be late but I promise you I will be there as soon as I can.' There was a loud silence on the other end of the line and Bridle heard her draw a sharp breath. 'How late?' she asked icily.

'I'm not sure. I'll take my suit to the office then come straight over the river afterwards. I am really sorry Stella.' He closed his eyes and braced himself for her response.

'There's no need to rush John, Guy Charlton doesn't have a partner tonight and I'm sure he'll be happy to escort me to the ball' Stella said calmly. Bridle felt as though his stomach would drop out. He expected an angry response but this left him confused.

'Guy Charlton' Bridle repeated numbly.

'Yes Guy is an old friend and it will give us a chance to catch up. He is such good company, very outgoing and amusing. I'll see you whenever you turn up.' The line clicked and Bridle stood in a daze holding the receiver to his ear. He felt sick as he put the receiver down and tried to gather his thoughts. Guy Charlton? Outgoing and amusing? Bridle could manage Stella's anger especially when the job kept him late but he couldn't manage her calmness.

'She's trying to make me jealous' he said out loud as he kicked the armchair across the room for a second time. Glancing at the look on his face in the mirror he knew she had succeeded.

CHAPTER ELEVEN

Joey Vance walked up the street at a fast pace nodding to neighbours as he passed. He shrugged off any attempts at conversation and swiftly made his way down to his mother's tenement. He opened the door and slammed it shut behind him but as he turned toward the parlour the stench hit him in the face.

'Mam' he said cautiously as he entered the parlour. He could see she was lying face down on the floor with her head and neck twisted unnaturally to the right. A feeling of horror came over him as he could see her face from the neck up had become black and the smell made him wretch. He ran into the scullery and vomited into an enamel bucket then slowly rinsed his face in cold water. Then he slumped onto a rickety wooden chair and put his face in his hands and wept.

Joey wiped his nose on his sleeve then made his way back into the parlour. He could see her eyes were wide open and bulging like they were when she screamed at him or when she beat him with a leather belt. Now she was dead and he couldn't believe it. He reached out with his foot and pushed it against her shoulder as if she might wake up. A cold shiver ran through him. He had never been alone in a room with a dead body before although he had been to plenty of funerals in the street. Bodies were always left in an open coffin for the neighbours to call and pay their respects and get a glass of sherry or whiskey for taking the trouble. As a child his mother had dragged him to every funeral in the street and the neighbouring streets just to make the most of the free drink.

He had many good reasons to hate his mother but he could never abandon her. But now he was free of her. He kept his hand over his nose and mouth as he looked around the room and stuffed his pockets with anything he thought he might be able to sell. Then he remembered the Ogden's tobacco tin on the mantelpiece. That's where she kept her 'knockin' money as she liked to call it. He picked the tin up and rattled it then flicked the lid off to find an assortment of coins and an old ear-ring which she kept just in case it was worth a few bob. He pressed the lid back on the tin and dropped it into his pocket.

Joey made his way to the parlour door then took one last look at his mother. As he stared at her his imagination ran out of control and he expected her to leap up and start ranting at him. A powerful shiver ran up his spine and he could feel panic taking over his mind. His breathing became faster and his heart pounded against his chest. With a surge of will power he turned and ran to the front door and threw it open. He sprinted up the steps frantically and ran straight into Constable Locke walking his beat. Constable Locke caught him by the shoulders and held him at arm's length.

'What's up with you Joey me lad?'

Joey panicked at the sight of the uniform and the familiar glare of Constable Locke. He couldn't speak because his breathing was too rapid so he pulled himself away and sprinted down the street.

'He's a fast little bugger' Locke said as he watched Joey sprint away. He could see the front door swinging open so he made his way down the steps shaking his head and muttering to himself.

Locke was about to close the door when the smell hit him and made him gag. He stepped inside and an instinctive dread came over him.

'Hello anyone home?' Locke shouted in the vain hope that his instinct might be wrong but when he entered the parlour he let out a sigh of resignation. He took a handkerchief from his pocket and put it over his mouth and nose as he inspected the corpse. It was obvious from the position of her head that it was no accident but he knew it wasn't his place to decide if it was murder or not. He thought about Joey and he hoped he hadn't murdered the old bitch even if it was long overdue. Locke made his way up the steps and pondered how he had seen Joey grow up over the years and how much abuse he had taken from his mother. At the top of the steps he took his whistle from the breast pocket of his tunic and blew the alarm across the streets.

Bridle and Lodge sat together looking into the stern faces of Chief Superintendent Crowley, Superintendent Mcleish, Detective Superintendent Webster and Detective Inspector Radford. They had just finished giving their account of the previous night and the group of officers seemed speechless for a few moments as they considered the story. Lodge stared at Crowley and tried to understand how the rat had scurried so far from the sewer and up the promotion ladder. Crowley's affected manner and even worse his pencil moustache irritated Lodge like a stone in his shoe. Lodge glanced at Bridle. He was sitting in his dinner suit and black tie and it made him look like a matinee idol although Lodge would never tell him that. Bridle looked uncomfortable and Lodge noticed that the scrapes on his hands looked painful and inflamed.

Lodge turned his attention to Mcleish's granite face. This was the kind of copper Lodge was comfortable with, hard as nails and a total bastard. He liked officers to be bastards because he knew exactly where he stood with them. Not like Radford. Lodge looked at his beer-bloated face and narrow eyes. Lodge knew Radford liked to be every Jack's best mate and drinking partner. But he always had that sharp little knife concealed for any exposed back. Lodge shifted in his seat and released a wide yawn.

'Are we boring you Lodge?' Mcleish's steely glare was enough to make Lodge sit up straight and clear his throat.

'Sorry Sir not had much sleep' Lodge said with half a smile and glanced at Bridle in the vain hope of a supporting comment but Radford went off on a rant.

'You had no reason to be out there last night Sergeant Bridle. I gave you basic tasks relating to the Grant case and that didn't include gallivanting round the docks in the dead of night chasing gunmen. Who do you think you are Bulldog fuckin' Drummond?' Radford thought his joke would get a reaction around the table but it didn't. Bridle didn't respond as he knew he was on dangerous ground. Crowley sat up straight and glared at Radford.

'Inspector Radford you know I don't approve of bad language' Crowley sniffed. Radford's narrow eyes glared down at the desk.

'Sorry Sir'

'Why were you there Sergeant Bridle?' Webster asked looking over his spectacles.

'I was looking for Joey Vance Sir. I have reason to believe he's involved in the Grant case.' Radford sniggered then shook his head.

'It's all bollocks I've got two witnesses who put Billy Doyle with David Grant minutes before he was killed. My lads are looking for Doyle now and we'll nail the bastard for this murder'

Radford thrust his head forward and stabbed his finger on the desk as he spoke.

'Language Inspector' Crowley sniffed again and Radford's face turned crimson.

'Who gave you the information that Vance would be there Sergeant?' Webster asked quietly ignoring Radford.

'An informant Sir but not one of my usual snouts' He replied cautiously.

'Sergeant Bridle you need to know of a development where Vance is concerned' Webster said as he linked his fingers and looked up at the ceiling. 'His mother was found dead a few hours ago' Webster was solemn and Bridle and Lodge cast a quick glance at each other and Bridle's mind was racing. 'It seems strange that her son was being shot at last night and she turns up with a broken neck today' Webster continued then looked at Bridle for a response.

'Broken neck Sir' Bridle was incredulous.

'Joey Vance was seen running from the house by Constable Locke just before he discovered the body. The Police Surgeon's estimate for time of death is about five hours before the body was found' Webster said as he kept his eyes fixed on Bridle.

'Joey couldn't kill his own mother even if she was a monster. He probably found the body and ran for it Sir' Bridle said quickly.

'Facts, facts, facts that's all I ask Sergeant Bridle. I don't listen to guess-work. Did you have any contact with Mrs. Vance in relation to your investigations?' Webster stared at him and Bridle knew he had already worked it out.

'Yes Sir I did' Bridle said reluctantly.

'Did she tell you where Joey would be?'

'Yes Sir' Bridle felt like an idiot.

'It signed her death warrant' Webster said coldly.

'The Irishman, what do we know about him?' Mcleish asked.

'Nothing Sir' Bridle responded flatly.

'But you saw him speaking to Vance and got a clear view of him in the car headlights didn't you?' Crowley asked impatiently. Lodge cleared his throat noisily and looked at Crowley.

'With all due respect Chief Superintendent Crowley, it was pelting down with rain, the man wore a flat cap pulled down over his eyes and his collar turned up, the only light was from a dim lamp above the door of the doss house. When the driver hit his headlamps he started shooting and the big man dived into the shadows, we could only get a basic description. Oh and the other thing Sir, how do we know the big man and the Irishman are the same person? Sergeant Bridle couldn't turn around with a revolver stuck in his ear could he Sir?' Lodge didn't hide the contempt in his voice and everyone knew it. Crowley rolled his pencil through his fingers and nervously twitched his moustache.

'It's intriguing' Webster said with enthusiasm as if he had just discovered a challenging crossword puzzle.

'It's got nothing to do with the Grant case' Radford said through gritted teeth.

'It may be connected, it may not, perhaps Billy Doyle is your murderer Inspector but I think Bridle and Lodge should continue to investigate Vance and the Irishman' Webster said clasping his hands together and studying Radford's reaction.

'I agree' Mcleish said firmly and looked over at Crowley.

'Yes, yes, I agree also' Crowley said glancing to his left and right.

'Detective Constable Lodge saved my life last night and deserves a commendation' Bridle said quickly.

'Hang on' Lodge interjected 'Sergeant Bridle rolled over the top of a moving car to save my life, he deserves the commendation not me.'

'Why don't you just buy each other a nice bunch of flowers and we'll call it evens?' Mcleish said with a sneer and Bridle and Lodge bore the resulting laughter with good grace.

Bridle waited at the junction of Hardman Street and Rodney Street just as the sun was beginning to drop behind the liver building in the near distance turning the liver birds into dark silhouettes standing on their domes. The town was beginning to liven up for Saturday night and even though the economic depression had ravaged the city people still flocked to the music halls and pubs. A tram clunked to a halt a few feet away from Bridle and spilled the excited crowd onto the street in search of a good night out. Two young girls walking arm in arm looked Bridle up and down and he felt self-conscious in his dinner suit. One of them gave out a long wolf whistle and winked at him. This added to his embarrassment as they looked very young. He glanced hopefully up the street for his taxi and cursed the driver Alfie Morretti for being late.

The taxi pulled over from behind a tram just as two uniformed officers strolling along Rodney Street caught sight of Bridle in his finery and were about to give him some banter but he leapt swiftly into the cab before they had the chance.

'Sorry I'm late Mr. Bridle had to sort out some trouble with a fare.'

Bridle smirked as Morretti clicked the trap down on his meter. Small and wiry Morretti gave the impression of being a pushover but the broken nose was a warning sign, he was one of the fastest and hardest featherweights Bridle had ever seen.

Moretti was from a big Italian family on Gerrard Street in the heart of the city's little Italy district. He was fluent in Italian which he spoke with a heavy local accent and he was a sparring partner for the great featherweight champion Dom Volante who lived on the same street. 'Hobnobbin' with the elite tonight Mr. Bridle?' Morretti grinned over his shoulder but Bridle wasn't in the mood to smile back. 'Very nice suit, very classy, must be Italian.'

'It's rented Alf' Bridle murmured and Morretti could sense the tension in him. They had known each other for years as Morretti was one of Bridle's most reliable sources in a small network of local snouts.

'Guess yer not lookin' forward to the posh do then' Morretti said trying to be chirpy.

'Not one bit' Bridle mumbled.

'Try a good swig of this' Morretti said thrusting an ornate hip flask through his window at Bridle.

'Bit flashy for you Alf' Bridle said turning the flask over in his hand.

'Yeah it was left in the cab by a toff. I was gonna flog it but it's handy for the cold nights.'

'It's mid-summer' Bridle said unscrewing the top cautiously and Moretti laughed as Bridle sniffed the contents. The power of the rum hit his nostrils and he recoiled slightly.

'It'll put steel in yer nerves Mr. Bridle looks like you need some Dutch courage.'

Bridle didn't disagree and took a swig of the rum. Bridle knew it was important to take a drink with informers. Snouts would never trust a man who refused a drink. He took another heavy swig and replaced the top. It was basically very strong rum but he could taste something else in it. He didn't ask what it was but he felt warm and mellow almost immediately.

'Feel better already?' Morretti asked grinning.

Bridle nodded in reply and Morretti swung the cab into Haymarket and up to the Mersey Tunnel. He looked over his shoulder at Bridle as he pulled into the tunnel and opened his mouth to speak.

'I know Alf the tunnel toll is extra on the fare.' Morretti chuckled at Bridle's response and his shoulders bounced up and down.

'You know us Italians we breed like rabbits I got four kids now. I have to work hard.'

'Alf you were born on Scotland Road' Bridle said.

'Mam and dad are Italian and I'm Italian in spirit, what more can I say?' Morretti laughed and Bridle grinned. The Mersey Tunnel was still a novelty to Morretti as it hadn't been open very long. He felt nervous driving under the river and gripped the wheel tightly as he concentrated on the winding lanes.

'Not used to the tunnel yet Alf?' Bridle asked.

'I keep thinkin' of all that water over our heads, it worries me.'

Bridle laughed and tried to loosen his collar as the starch was beginning to irritate his neck. He didn't speak to Morretti again until they left the tunnel as it was obvious he was struggling to concentrate. At the toll booth on the Wirral side Bridle noticed Morretti had a line of sweat on his forehead as he paid the toll attendant.

Bridle sighed and tried not to think about the ordeal ahead. He still felt sick at the thought of Stella going to the ball on the arm of another man. His masculine instinct was to break his jaw but he knew that was far too unsophisticated for the class of people there. He would just be confirming their opinion of him as an ignorant lout. Bridle decided that his best plan was to be cool and aloof just like them. He knew they would all be watching his reaction to Guy Charlton so he planned to shake Charlton's hand and thank him for escorting Stella but with a look in his eye that would warn Charlton to back off or lose his front teeth. Bridle cursed himself. He cursed his jealousy and his feelings of inferiority but in his heart he knew that with a woman like Stella there would always be a Guy Charlton. The swelling on the back of his head still ached and the pain spread to his forehead.

'Alf any word on Joey Vance?'

'Heard about his mother, that news went round faster than the black-death, you don't suspect Joey?'

'I don't but some people do.'

'Joey's been runnin' for someone lately but I've heard they are dangerous people, not local, but you know what rumours are like.'

'He's linked to the Grant murder. He saw a few things and now his mother is dead. I need to find him Alf.'

'I'll do my best Mr. Bridle but you know what he's like, he's like a greyhound, now yer see him now yer don't' Morretti shrugged 'he hangs about with Paddy Finch's gang most of the time.'

'What's he doing with that gang of thugs?' Bridle asked.

'Survival, that's what it's all about Mr. Bridle.'

They carried on in silence along the road through Heswall. Bridle and Stella had wondered down the main street many times during their courtship. It had been a tough job to win Stella and he was determined not to lose her. He took another swig of the grog and nearly choked. Morretti wasn't comfortable with silence and gave Bridle a quick glance over his shoulder.

'Do yer know about this unemployment rally next week-end?' Morretti asked as he swung the cab off the main road and into a dark lane.

'Yeah Mcleish is policing it. Its right up his street' Bridle said idly.

'I've heard a few rumours, there could be trouble Mr. Bridle.'

'Any sign of trouble and Mcleish will quell it fast, he's got the mounted section at his disposal and he's had experience of riots before' Bridle said with wry grin.

'You know me Mr. Bridle I'm a labour man through and through, no messin' about, but there's been a different atmosphere lately, more aggressive and more organised. If yer know what I mean.'

'No I don't know what you mean' Bridle said pushing for details. Morretti sighed in frustration as if he wanted to say something but couldn't bring himself to do it.

'Jack Finney is a good councillor and well respected but he's not himself lately. He's gettin' aggressive in his speeches whippin' everybody up for this rally' Morretti said carefully.

'Is he inciting trouble?' Bridle asked.

'It's not Finney's way. He keeps everything close to his chest but lately some characters have wormed their way into his inner circle. They haven't been here five minutes.' Bridle picked up the resentment in Morretti's voice and wondered if it was just jealousy on his part. Bridle didn't consider in-fighting among political groups as suspicious but he did respect Morretti's instincts.

'What characters are you talking about?' Bridle asked.

'This Harry Croft comes back from Spain like some socialist hero, full of stories, so people follow him, he's got Finney wrapped around his little finger.'

'You don't trust him?'

'My backbone doesn't trust him Mr.Bridle.'

'Your backbone' Bridle said with a laugh.

'Yeah, I get a shiver right through it when I meet someone who can't be trusted, my missus swears by it.'

'And this Harry Croft fails your backbone test?' Bridle couldn't hide his amusement.

'Dead right he does and that Irish bastard that hangs around with him, too cocky for his own good, he failed my backbone test straight away.' Morretti laughed but Bridle didn't. Bridle had a strong gut feeling when Morretti mentioned the Irishman but he knew he had to be careful. There were hundreds of Irishmen in the city and many of them involved in politics but the feeling stayed with him.

'An Irishman' Bridle said quietly.

'Yeah he came over from Spain with Croft both of them just walked in and took over. Don't know what Jack Finney is thinkin' of, the man needs a kick up the arse.' Morretti turned the cab into a long gravel drive and motored slowly up to the house. Bridle was thinking quickly.

'The Manor House My Lord' Moretti said as he stopped the cab.

'So this Irishman was fighting in Spain?' Bridle asked.

'Yeah, too loud, too cocky you know the type.'

'Do you know his name?'

'Riley, Callum Riley, don't think it's his real name though.'

'Is that your backbone talking again?' Bridle smirked.

'Don't take the piss Mr. Bridle. He shouts his name out every chance he gets, draws attention to himself like he wants everyone to remember him.'

'You should have been a copper Alf' Bridle said casting a

doleful look out of the window at the Edwardian mansion house lit up with the party atmosphere.

'Me a copper, wash yer mouth out with soap Mr. Bridle' Morretti laughed 'look at the state of that lot' Morretti said nodding toward the line of luxury marques parked up on the far side of the drive with uniformed drivers smoking and chatting together. They cast a sneering eye over morretti's taxi cab and one driver sniggered behind his leather-gloved hand. Bridle climbed out of the cab and swiftly walked around to the driver's door as he knew what was coming next.

'What's that bastard sniggerin' at?' Morretti said as his short fuse ignited and he went for the handle of his door. Bridle pushed the door back forcefully and stood at the window.

'Not tonight Alf I've got enough on my plate, here's your fare and keep the change.' Morretti took the fare and the generous tip and slipped back into his seat.

'I'll find out what I can about Joey Vance Mr. Bridle but no promises.' Morretti nodded to Bridle as he swung the cab around and rammed the pedal down hard. His spinning wheels sprayed gravel over the line of well polished marques as the drivers leapt aside and shouted abuse. Morretti sped up the drive waving two fingers from the window as the angry drivers looked at Bridle. Bridle smiled and shrugged his shoulders.

'Taxi drivers they're all the same.'

The police vehicles crawled along the dark tenement lined streets like a funeral procession. Inspector Radford posted a Black Maria at each end of the street and three cars moved forward to the central tenement block. Radford heaved himself from the car and looked up at the building then scanned up and down the street. He gave the signal and police officers spilled from the cars and the vans and entered the central block on the double.

Officers were posted in the alleys behind the tenements to prevent any chance of losing their prey. Shouts and screams started to echo along the landings as the officers began their search. Dogs barked and children cried and a drunken old man lurched over to Radford and shook his fist.

'What's goin' on here yer stinkin' Jack?'

'Mind your own business grandad' Radford dismissed the old man as he lolled backwards and forwards.

'Have some respect for yer elders. I worked all my life to pay your fuckin' wages lad so don't call me grandad' he wobbled as he spoke and a young constable next to Radford began to laugh.

'Do you find this man funny constable?' Radford glared at him and the constable froze.

'No Sir… sorry Sir.'

'Place him under arrest for being drunk and disorderly' Radford fumed 'get him in the van.'

'Yes Sir' he said as he started forward but the old man threw down his cap and put up his fists.

'Add resisting arrest to the charge sheet' Radford shouted.

'Yer not takin' me to the fuckin' bridewell yer lanky bastard' the old man shouted as the young officer towered over him and tried to work out the best way to make the arrest. The old man swung a punch into fresh air and nearly fell over. A crowd had gathered and were goading the tall officer as he wrestled with the wiry old man.

'Watch were yer puttin' yer hands yer shirt-lifter' the old man squealed and the crowd howled with laughter.

'You are making a fool of yourself constable' Radford barked.

'Yes Sir' the fumbling officer replied as the old man dropped to his knees and crawled between his long legs causing the crowd to scream with laughter. Radford marched off in disgust and walked into the tenement block where he caught hold of the nearest uniformed Sergeant.

'Sergeant' Radford barked. Sergeant Dean turned around slowly and looked down into Radford's bloated face.

'That officer, number forty seven, he's incompetent, a total fool. Get him transferred out of this division I don't want to set eyes on him again' Radford seethed.

Sergeant Dean walked calmly over to the door with his hands clasped behind his back and viewed the scene outside. He smirked slightly then walked back to Radford in the same cool and unruffled manner.

'Yes Sir if you feel that's wise' Sergeant Dean's eyes glinted under the peak of his helmet and his dark moustache expanded as he stretched his neck under his chin strap.

'Why would it not be wise Sergeant?' Radford asked quietly as he knew something was coming.

'He's the Chief Constable's nephew Sir, just started with us.'

Sergeant Dean stood rigid with his hands behind his back. His face was expressionless but his eyes were smiling. Radford held his breath for a moment and was about to reply when he was distracted by a commotion on the stairs. Two officers were dragging Billy Doyle down the stairwell. He was struggling and shouting hysterically until Sergeant Dean cracked him on the knee with his truncheon. They threw him down in front of Radford and he rolled around sobbing and clasping his knee. Radford squatted down and got close to Doyle's ear.

'If you think that's painful Doyle wait till you get the rope round your neck' Radford whispered then stood up as Doyle shouted his innocence.

'I didn't kill Grant, I'm not swingin' for it Radford.'

'Oh you killed him alright and I can prove it. You will swing my lad, you will swing and dance on that rope in Walton. I only wish I could open the trap myself.'

'You'll be sorry for this Radford – I've got friends' Doyle was desperate.

'How do you think we found you Billy boy? Your mates sold you down the river. Scum like you don't have friends.' Radford nodded toward Doyle and two big constables rushed forward and picked him up under his armpits. They frog-marched him into the street followed by the rest of the officers. Outside constable forty seven was sitting on top of the old man who was kicking and shouting.

'Let me up and I'll kick the shit out of yer.'

Sergeant Dean calmly walked over to the scene with his hands clasped behind his back and stood over the two combatants. He had seen many things in his time and he had learned to take everything in his stride.

'Having problems making the arrest lad?'

'No Sergeant I think I've got him now.'

Sergeant Dean leaned forward and spoke to the old man in his flat drawl,

'Arthur, the officer says he's got you now.'

The old man let out a howl and rammed his knee upward into his opponent's groin. The constable fell sideways onto his back and coiled himself up in agony but manfully stifled a groan. The old man let out a squeal of delight as he wobbled off to the cheers of the crowd. Sergeant Dean watched him go then turned back to the young officer writhing on the ground.

'That was Arthur, he's well known in these parts. You won't forget him now will you constable?' Sergeant Dean turned and ambled away as constable forty seven pondered his hard lesson from ground level.

CHAPTER TWELVE

Climbing the steps to the front entrance of the hall had been hard enough for Bridle but actually walking through the door was an ordeal. A liveried doorman checked his invitation then opened the inner door to allow him into a classically decorated hall with a high domed ceiling. The room was bustling with people chattering and laughing all dressed in their finery with a glinting display of jewellery. The women sat in groups making small talk while the men stood in circles with well-charged glasses and burning cigars trying to solve the problems of the nation, loudly.

Bridle could hear the dance band playing in the other room and guessed that the event had split into two factions. Those who were happy with the introduction of a dance band and a crooner were dancing in the main room and those who wanted the traditional orchestra were in this room bemoaning it. He recognised one or two of the faces in the crowd and was surprised to see Sir Edward Grant holding court with a group of men at the far end of the room. Bridle picked his way between the guests and glanced around but saw no sign of Lady Grant or his daughter Amelia.

Bridle eased his way into the main ballroom. It was a warm evening and the room was aired from two open doors that led on to a terrace and further on to a wide lawn that was littered with tables and chairs for guests to enjoy the garden. There was no sign of Stella in the room and as he looked around he had that sick feeling in his stomach again. The band played a South American dance number and the over-crowded dance floor swayed to the rhythm. The men looked stiff and formal in their suits but the ladies wore a stunning collection of ball gowns that filled the room with colour.

Even Elizabeth and Caroline looked passable Bridle thought when he saw them dancing with their partners. Malcolm and Gerald darted their eyes in his direction but pretended not to see him. Elizabeth was casting him excited looks and trying at the same time to alert Caroline to his arrival. His attention was drawn to the sight of his father-in-law Sir Nigel dancing with young Amelia Grant. It was obvious Amelia was just excited to be there but Bridle could tell from the covert looks and glances in Sir Nigel's direction that people were in fear of Amelia's reputation. Bridle could see his mother-in-law Lady Marion sitting alone and stone faced refusing to see or acknowledge the looks of pity she was receiving from around the room.

Bridle took a glass of champagne from the tray of a passing waiter and made his way toward Lady Marion. She had always treated him coldly but he felt he had to make an effort for Stella's sake and she did look slightly crestfallen. She didn't acknowledge him until he reached the table.

'May I join you?'

She looked up sharply with a feigned expression of surprise but her face soon turned back to stone as she spoke.

'So you have come, do sit down.'

'Thank you' Bridle responded and sat down with a half-hearted smile.

'You turned a few heads as you entered, the suave image suits you.'

She spoke as if from a distance without taking her eyes from her husband and Bridle wondered what made this woman tick. She was elegant and intelligent and Stella had her beautiful eyes and yet she allowed her husband to embarrass and humiliate her regularly. She bore it with cool aloofness and Bridle wondered if she had lost all feeling or was she churning up inside like he was for Stella.

'I'm looking for Stella' Bridle said watching Elizabeth frantically trying to signal Caroline across the dance floor.

'Yes I'm sure you are' she said indifferently.

'Have you seen her?'

'Not for some time, she may be taking air on the terrace' she glanced at him sideways 'Estella has danced a lot tonight.' Bridle knew she expected him to react but he fought the impulse. 'We see very little of you these days.'

'I'm from the wrong side of the river' Bridle said sipping his champagne.

'Is the river such a great divide?' She replied staring straight ahead.

Bridle didn't answer as he watched Elizabeth and Caroline despatch their husbands to the outer room then make their way toward their mother's table. He braced himself as they approached and he thought he saw Lady Marion scowl but he wasn't certain. They sat down at the table with a noisy flourish and Elizabeth giggled annoyingly. Bridle was grateful to be spared their husband's company.

'Why it's been such a long time, how are you?' Caroline asked with little emotion.

Bridle could see that Caroline was like her mother, very controlled and with the same elegant aloofness. He had no idea where Elizabeth's flighty character came from but she was the funniest and the most entertaining of them. Bridle felt she had the look of a fluffy American film star and it amused him that she was a constant embarrassment to the family.

'I'm very well thank you Caroline' he said forcing a smile 'you both look very chic, I'm surprised Hollywood hasn't come calling for you Elizabeth.' Bridle winked at her and sipped his champagne. Elizabeth blushed and giggled at the same time, Lady Marion stifled a smile and Caroline fidgeted in her seat.

'You look ever so sophisticated in your black tie' Elizabeth responded and Caroline was aghast.

'Elizabeth' Caroline spluttered.

'Thank you Elizabeth' Bridle said smiling 'I'll drink to that' he finished his champagne and placed the glass on the table.

'What do you think of the party?' Caroline sniffed.

'It's a bit like a Dock Road pub on a Saturday night' Bridle replied flatly 'only here they wear the jewellery instead of selling it'

Elizabeth let out a snorting laugh and Caroline froze her with a glare.

'Have you found Estella yet?' Elizabeth asked mischievously.

'I know Stella came here with Guy Charlton' Bridle sighed 'and I guess she's danced with him for most of the evening and no, I am not going to punch him on the nose' Bridle smiled as he finished speaking but his stomach was churning.

'I'm glad to hear it' Lady Marion said just as the lights began to dim and the crooner came forward to the microphone under the spotlight. His hair was suspiciously dark and slicked back like a Rio lounge lizard but his accent was broad east-end of London.

'Now ladies and gentlemen please take your special partners for a slow and intimate experience on the dance floor.' His teeth glowed in the spotlight as he smiled and when the band began to play he sang with a deep and melodic voice that surprised Bridle.

Couples came out of the dim light onto the floor and pulled each other close to sway to the music. Bridle's stomach sank as he saw Stella and Guy Charlton appear from the terrace and walk slowly over to the floor. She held his hand playfully and led him onto the floor then they turned and held each other for a moment before they began to dance. They moved slowly and closely and Stella's head was almost resting on his shoulder. Bridle had to hold his breath to stop himself from shaking as he was aware that all at the table were staring at him. Charlton was tall, blonde and athletic, like the cricket aces in the comics Bridle read as a schoolboy. Stella looked relaxed and happy in his arms and Bridle thought she looked stunning in her ball-gown.

His mind raced and he felt cornered and out-classed. His instinct was to run onto the floor and break them up but he knew he couldn't do that. He had never seen Stella held by another man before and it hurt like a knife in his stomach. Bridle stood up slowly and made his way to the terrace being careful not to look back or let anyone see the violent tremble he could feel surging through his body. He leaned against a low wall and took a deep breath. The air was warm and it was a clear night. It was dark but there was that distant glow in the sky that never really allows pitch darkness in mid-summer.

He felt better for the air and looking out onto the lawn a number of people were drinking wine and champagne at the tables lit by candlelight. Further on he saw a young couple stealing away into the darkness for an assignation and his mind came back to Stella. He rubbed his forehead slowly to break up the tension he could feel building up. The swelling on the back of his head began to throb again and made him feel faint. All the pressures he was under at work were taking their toll. He could take all the stress of his job because he knew he was doing it for Stella. She was always there. Now he began to feel helpless at the thought of losing her. He told himself to grow up. So they'd had a row and she was getting even by flirting with an old boyfriend it was that simple. Bridle wrestled with his thoughts but became aware of glass chinking on glass behind him and he turned slowly. Sir Nigel Carver was standing behind him with a decanter of brandy and two glasses.

'I thought you might be in need of one.' He smiled his charming smile and Bridle nodded slowly as they sat down at a candle lit table in the corner of the terrace. Carver poured the brandy carefully and with a degree of reverence then sat back and took a silver cigarette case from the inside pocket of his jacket. Carver held the open case toward Bridle with a mocking grin as he knew that Bridle never smoked. Bridle ignored Carver's empty gesture and he took a sip of the smooth brandy then prepared himself for what might be coming next. He knew his father-in-law would make the most of Stella and Charlton. Carver smirked at his bit of mischief then took his time lighting and savouring the cigarette.

'I've always found women to be such odd creatures' Carver said eventually 'never sure of their emotions. They fall in and out of love. They can be tactile and warm one moment, the next moment tetchy and cold.' He cast a glance at Bridle to weigh his reaction but there was none so he continued 'you can shower them with gifts, you can pander to every whim, you can run yourself into the ground for them but still nothing pleases them.'

'Judging by your dance partner you could always try a teddy bear or a packet of sweets' Bridle said and Carver's face turned dark for a moment then became composed again within a few seconds.

'Your sense of humour was never subtle' Carver sneered.

'I'm not laughing' Bridle responded.

'I shall ignore your rather seedy insinuation as you must be quite tense seeing Estella with Guy.'

Bridle knew Carver was trying to draw a reaction but he was in no mood to fence with him so he took another sip of his brandy and ignored Carver's remark.

'I suggested the Grants come tonight' Carver continued 'it gives Sir Edward the chance to catch up with his old regimental friends and Amelia the chance to socialise with people of...'

'Her own age' Bridle interjected.

'Her own class' Carver said with a dark look and continued 'Lady Grant was too fragile to attend tonight.' Carver paused then changed tack. 'The Grant case is something of an embarrassment to your department so I've heard. No substantial progress at all.'

Bridle knew from Carver's tone that he was manipulating the conversation for a reason so he mentally prepared himself for confrontation.

'Softly softly' Bridle said off-hand.

'What if I told you I had some information that may be relevant?' Carver smiled and Bridle knew the game was kicking off.

'You have information that may be relevant' Bridle repeated slowly.

'It would certainly be to your advantage career-wise.'

'Are you trying to do me a favour?' Bridle asked with some suspicion.

'More a case of you scratch my back etcetera.'

'I don't do back scratching' Bridle said 'and I don't do etcetera, whatever that is.'

'How did you ever get as far as Sergeant?' Carver scowled.

'I was the only one who could make tea and type a report at the same time' Bridle said and finished his brandy. Carver almost laughed as he leaned forward and refilled Bridle's glass.

'I don't have to remind you about withholding information in relation to a criminal investigation do I Sir Nigel? After all, a man of your standing shouldn't have to be reminded of his duty.' Bridle couldn't help the sarcastic tone and the quality of the brandy was having an effect.

'There is nothing wrong with my sense of duty old boy my intention was to turn this information over to a more distinguished rank of my acquaintance' Carver said swirling the brandy around the glass.

'At a lodge meeting I guess' Bridle said as the silky warmth of the brandy went to his head.

'I think this Brandy may be a little too refined for your taste' Carver said smirking into his glass.

'Like everything else around here' Bridle murmured.

'Self-pity, come now I expected better from you' Carver smiled.

'If you have information on David Grant's murder you should report it.Whether you give it to the Chief Constable or to Doris the char lady down at the bridewell it makes no difference to me' Bridle said with a shrug.

'No ambition whatsoever, no wonder Estella is losing interest' Carver said casually and Bridle took a hard look at the man. Everything about him was theatrical. The cut of his clothes, the greying of his temples and the smoothness of his voice were all tools in his trade of manipulation. And he knew how to use them.

'Am I supposed take the bait?' Bridle could feel the warm numbness of the alcohol penetrate his brain as he drained his glass for a second time.

'You'd be a fool if you said there were no cracks starting to show' Carver tried to sound sympathetic as he poured more brandy into Bridle's glass.

'I work night shifts and day shifts sometimes without a day off. Stella has her own little business. We don't have much time together but we'll work it out.'

Bridle felt as if he was trying to convince himself rather than Carver and he took another heavy gulp of his brandy. He was trying to numb the incessant throb of his head injury.

'The information I speak of is actually a file compiled by a private enquiry agency. It details David's movements and dealings for the last two years. Valuable wouldn't you say?' Carver's attitude began to irritate Bridle.

'I could easily trace the enquiry agency. I could even arrest you on a number of charges in relation to obstructing a criminal investigation' Bridle slurred his words a little and took a moment to clear his head. 'But you are a clever man Sir Nigel. I'm sure you've covered your back from every direction so let's cut out all of this bullshit and get down to it. What do you want for the file?'

'I want you to leave Estella.'

Bridle was momentarily stunned by the directness of the response and the effect of the brandy caused him to chuckle but Carver's face was expressionless. Bridle was still laughing to himself when Stella and Guy Charlton stepped onto the terrace and made their way over to the table. Bridle looked at Stella and she gave him that pout of disapproval which he always treated as playful but tonight made him feel isolated. He thought she looked amazing in her red ball gown. Joey Vance was right Stella did look like a film star. Bridle drained his glass a little too quickly and his head felt like a train was steaming through it.

Carver stood up as they approached and Bridle followed suit but was alarmed to feel so unsteady on his feet. Stella could tell by his eyes that he had been drinking. She looked at the decanter then at her father and narrowed her eyes. Carver smiled and ignored his daughter's silent scolding.

'Do join us. Guy I don't believe you've met Estella's husband John.'

For a moment Bridle and Charlton weighed each other across the table like two boxers waiting for the bell when Charlton's face suddenly broke into a wide and genial smile as he held out his hand.

'Nice to meet you old boy Stella never stops talking about you. I expected some kind of Greek God.'

Charlton was so confident and good looking that Bridle guessed he made every man he met feel insecure.

'Mr. Charlton' Bridle said with a nod as they shook hands. The vigorous handshake reminded Bridle that his shoulder injury hurt like hell.

'My darling daughter you look stunning tonight' Carver said re-igniting his charm and Stella took the compliment with a coy grin.

'You must call me Guy' Charlton said jovially as he sat opposite Bridle but the fixed look between the two men gave away their mutual suspicion.

'Must I?' Bridle said and Carver grinned.

'So the old saying is true' Carver said and sipped his brandy.

'What old saying is that daddy?' Stella asked folding her arms as she knew by his tone that he was about to cause some mischief.

'You can't have two cocks in one hen-house' Carver and Charlton laughed but Stella's eyes narrowed and she stood up sharply.

'I'll leave you boys to your games' Stella said then strolled back to the ballroom and every man on the terrace turned to watch her go. Bridle looked idly into his empty glass and Carver immediately refilled it.

'Stella tells me you are a detective, sounds exciting' Charlton managed to sound interested and condescending at the same time.

'Detective work in Liverpool amounts to shoplifters in Woolworths or drunk and disorderly just about anywhere. Isn't that so John?' Carver said and exchanged smirks with Charlton. Bridle could feel the warm glow of the brandy moving through his veins making him feel mellow but he fought against it.

'If you say so' Bridle murmured.

'I am being a little unfair as John is involved in the Grant murder case at the moment. The case seems to be testing Liverpool's finest to the limit' Carver looked at Bridle over the rim of his brandy glass.

'I believe you knew David Grant very well – Guy' Bridle said without taking his eyes from Charlton.

'Our paths crossed, I wouldn't call him a chum.'

'I'm led to believe you were good chums' Bridle said making an obvious effort not to slur.

'Then I'm afraid you've been misled. He was an arrogant

hedonistic bore' Charlton shifted in his seat and Bridle wondered why he was lying.

'What about Sir Edward? Did you do business with him?' Bridle asked.

'As a matter of fact I did' Charlton looked uneasy.

'Profitable?' Bridle asked scowling.

'Reasonably' Charlton snapped.

'What kind of business?' Bridle persisted.

'Oh for goodness sake it's a party don't be such a bore' Carver interjected light heartedly. Bridle remained stone-faced.

'What kind of business did you do with Sir Edward?' Bridle repeated.

'Is this official or something? I'm not sure I like your tone old boy' Charlton took a large gulp of brandy and banged the glass onto the table.

'You have no business questioning Guy about the case here' Carver said and Bridle looked at him through heavy-lidded eyes. The lack of food and sleep over the last twenty four hours had drained him and the lump on his head seemed to ache to the beat of his pulse.

'Is Guy's name on this file of yours Sir Nigel?' Bridle couldn't hide the effects of the alcohol any longer and the pain in his shoulder was more irritating than toothache.

'What file? What's the man talking about?' Charlton asked looking at Carver.

'I'm sorry Guy I'm afraid he's tipsy he doesn't know what he's talking about' Carver said shaking his head.

'Sir Nigel offered me a file of information on David Grant in return for leaving Stella isn't that right Sir?' Bridle tried to focus his eyes and he cursed himself for giving in to the brandy and to taking too many shots of grog in the taxi.

'I think you've had too much of the sauce old boy' Charlton's good natured grin just irritated Bridle even more.

'Don't worry about me – old boy' Bridle snarled and tried to stand up quickly but his head throbbed and began to swim. He tried to steady himself on the table but as he pushed down the injury to his shoulder caused a bolt of pain to shoot across his back. He stumbled and fell to his knees tipping the table forward. The decanter and glasses crashed to the ground causing some alarm across the terrace. Bridle was on his knees holding his upper arm just as Stella, Caroline and Elizabeth stepped onto the terrace. Stella's joyful face turned to thunder as Bridle looked up pitifully and tried to smile.

'What's going on?' Stella asked looking at the horrified faces around the terrace. Charlton grinned and made a drinking gesture which made Elizabeth giggle and Stella burn with anger. Carver shrugged and shook his head in mock innocence.

'I'm fine I just slipped' Bridle slurred and everyone laughed except Stella.

'How could you do this?' The tears of anger and humiliation welled up in Stella's eyes and Carver stepped forward and put a comforting arm around his daughter's shoulder.

'Don't worry darling I'll get a car to take him home safely, don't let this spoil your evening.'

Carver said and winked at Caroline who saw her opportunity.

'Estella you must stay with mummy and daddy tonight, let him sleep it off alone' Caroline said and linked her sister's arm protectively.

'Come along Elizabeth' Caroline snapped her order and Elizabeth jumped to attention and linked Stella's opposite arm. They marched Stella from the terrace with stern backward glances at Bridle.

'I think it's the kennel for you old boy' Charlton said grinning.

'What a waste of fine Brandy' Carver said looking at the mess.

Bridle got to his feet slowly and looked around at the grimacing faces and for a moment felt like he was in hell.

'I'll arrange for a car to take you home' Carver said stifling a grin. Bridle looked at Carver's smug expression and realised that he had lost the fight and had to make a tactical withdrawal.

'I'll make my own way home' Bridle said as firmly as he could and straightened his jacket He walked slowly toward the gravel path that ran around the lawn knowing he would find a way out somewhere around the back. He was aware that Carver and Charlton were watching him but he was steady enough. The shock of falling and the humiliation had cleared his head almost immediately.

'Estella will never forgive you for this' Carver shouted as Bridle faded into the darkness of the garden.

The path crunched under his feet as he wrenched his tie loose and threw it into the hedge. He plunged his hands into his pockets like a sulking schoolboy then trudged along the path adjacent to a high wall looking for a gate to make his escape. Carver was right he pondered, Estella would never forgive him. He eventually came across an archway and a heavy gate with thick bolts. With some frustration he worked the bolts loose then threw the gate open and slammed it hard behind him. He turned onto the road mindless of the direction and just kept walking.

It was an isolated lane and dark except for a little light from a gibbous moon. He suddenly felt helpless as he cursed the deluded idea that he and Stella could ever make their marriage work. Perhaps a child would have made a difference but it never happened. Bridle could imagine Sir Nigel comparing him to Charlton like a mule to a stallion. He was low quality stock from the backstreets of the city. Charlton could probably sire offspring like a prize bull. Bridle began to disgust himself with his own self-pity when his senses were pulled together by the roar of a car engine and headlights casting his shadow down the lane.

After his experience in the alley the previous night his instinct was to brace himself as he turned to look into the headlights. The engine revved and screeched to a halt beside him and Miranda Shaw's demure face looked up at him from the driver's seat of an open-topped MG. She was wearing a sleek, jet black ball-gown that didn't hide the curves of her waist or the fullness of her breasts. But again it was her mouth that drew Bridle's attention. The darkness of the night highlighted the paleness of her skin and the ruby curves of her lips. She didn't smile. She spoke huskily.

'I saw you leave – shall we escape together?'

Bridle wasn't in the mood to ask questions. He climbed into the passenger seat without saying a word and her foot slammed down on the accelerator before he could close the door.

The next five minutes were a blur to Bridle. She threw the M.G. around the country lanes like a deranged racing driver and howled with delight each time they skidded on a bend or the rear of the vehicle swung across the road. Bridle held on to the dashboard with one hand and the base of his seat with the other. He hardly noticed the burning pain in his shoulder as most of his attention was focussed on survival. Her face was fixed with a rigid grin and each time she looked at him she whooped with laughter. Bridle felt completely helpless and he didn't like it. The combination of alcohol and violent driving made Bridle's head spin as he looked left and right to get a fixed idea of their location. It was impossible. The motion just made him feel more nauseous.

'Are we going to throw-up Sergeant?'

She squealed with laughter and put her foot down hard as they turned onto a straight section of road. Bridle looked from the speedometer to the road ahead and judged they would run out of straight road before she got the needle to hit the top of the dial.

'Death or glory Sergeant?' She screamed over the roar of the engine.

'I'll take glory if you don't mind' he growled back. Bridle could see the road ahead curved to the left but she maintained her speed. He looked from the road to her face which held that manic grin and a stare that seemed to welcome oblivion. Bridle knew in those brief seconds that she was making the decision whether they were going to live or die.

As they hit the bend at speed she slammed the brake pedal down then threw the gear stick into second. The brakes and tyres screamed in agony and the rear of the car slid across the road. The vehicle shuddered violently in the skid then slammed side-on against an embankment and came to a hard stop. Bridle was stunned for a moment and was about to crawl out when she threw the stick into first and pulled away at a more leisurely speed.

'I've had enough – I'll get out here' Bridle said and looked as though he was about to jump from the moving vehicle which made her laugh.

'Sergeant I thought you had more backbone, how disappointing. Shall I take you home to your little wife? Oh I forgot you're all alone tonight aren't you?' She gave him a coy smile and Bridle wondered what was going on in her head. Was she trying to set him up for something? He knew he had to get out of the car.

'Made a real fool of yourself back there didn't you?' she said giggling. Bridle didn't respond but he knew she was right. He closed his eyes and cursed himself as he thought about it. So many years on the force had thickened his skin but not for this. It was the worst place and the worst time and with the wrong people. He needed to get to the gym and take his frustration out on a punch-bag. Then he remembered his shoulder. Then he thought about the night before with all the action and the gun-play. Who was that Irishman? His thoughts played around for excuses to justify his condition. He dreaded to think what Alf Moretti had mixed with the rum in the flask. He thought about Stella and cursed himself again.

'What were you doing there tonight?' Bridle asked trying to redirect his thoughts.

'I was working.'

'Posing nude' Bridle said and she giggled.

'I don't pose nude I model artistically.'

'You wouldn't be washing dishes in a gown like that so how were you working?'

'You seem to have a very low opinion of me Sergeant'.

'I'm a policeman I have a low opinion of everyone. Are you going to answer the question?'

'I told you I was working' she smiled coyly.

'Doing what exactly?'

'I escort wealthy men to various functions. I hang from their arm and look adoringly at them. At the end of the evening they pay me lots of money.'

'Can't you just marry well, isn't that what girls like you do?'

206

'Girls like me?' Her tone flattened.

'You're from Oxford but you're father was a farm labourer. I guess you mix with the elite to get a slice of the cake' Bridle smiled at the dark look on her face.

'Dig up anything else about me?'

'Not yet, were you working on the night of the Grant murder?'

'Not exactly'

'What does that mean?' Bridle began to feel nauseous again.

'Do you think I was escorting David? He didn't need me, he could pick and choose.'

'So I've heard' Bridle sighed.

'Why would I escort David? I worked for him, he organised my clients, we socialised because he liked my company.'

'Are you saying David Grant was your pimp?' Bridle asked and she laughed out loud.

'That's a little harsh, I'm a gentleman's escort and David was my agent.'

'He took a percentage that makes him a pimp in my book.'

'So that makes me a prostitute in your book Sergeant' her eyes narrowed.

'A better class than a street walker but it's the same thing' Bridle said wearily but as he finished speaking she slammed her foot down hard and Bridle was thrown back into his seat as the car sped forward with screeching tyres.

'I guess I've upset you' he shouted but she didn't respond. Bridle's face turned to stone when he saw the bend ahead. 'Slow down' his voice waivered.

'You called me a whore' she screamed at him then pressed the pedal so hard she almost stood upright. Bridle knew there was no time to slow down for the bend so he cursed loudly then punched the gear stick into neutral and pulled hard on the handbrake with both hands. Miranda Shaw screamed and turned the wheel sharply which sent the MG into a wild spin. Bridle's nausea increased with the spinning motion which seemed to go on and on. He was aware of a powerful thud and then blackness.

'Are you alright?' Miranda Shaw's soft voice broke through the dullness of his mind as he slowly opened his eyes. 'Are you alright' she repeated.

His vision cleared to see her leaning over him with her breasts pulsing from the top of her gown as she breathed rapidly with shock. He pulled himself up and looked around. The engine was running and the car was at the side of the road but Bridle could see that there had been impact damage to his door and further along the nearside of the vehicle.

'I think I'm alright' Bridle said checking his head for cuts.

'Good' Miranda Shaw said then slapped him hard across the face. Bridle fell back into his seat and realised he had a bad headache as well as a sore face. 'You called me a whore.'

She jumped onto his lap and started slapping him hard with both hands. Bridle was stunned by her rage and was gagging on her heavy scent and the tobacco smoke that clung to her gown. He caught her wrists and threw her back into the driver's seat where she lay giggling with an odd look on her face. She obviously wasn't hurt when the car impacted Bridle thought as he looked around. He wasn't certain of the location but he could smell the River Mersey somewhere through a copse of trees to the left of the road.

'Are you alright to drive?' He jumped out of the vehicle before she had time to take off again.

'Do you care?' She pouted.

'No I don't' Bridle snapped.

'Bastard' her eyes flashed with rage.

'Your MG is a bit of a mess' he said ignoring her insult.

'It isn't mine' she purred. Bridle shook his head then turned and walked away.

'I wanted to talk to you about David's murder, that's why I followed you, I want to help you' she shouted louder as he got further away but he didn't look back. Bridle winced as the engine revved up then crunched into gear. The tyres screeched as the MG spurted past him in a wild acceleration.

'Bastard' her curse disappeared on the wind as the MG sped away leaving Bridle in darkness again.

He wandered along the dark lane until he found a sign and realised he was on the north side of Eastham village. Bridle decided his best plan was to get onto the main road and find a taxi if he was lucky. He ran his fingers over the swelling on the back of his head to check for bleeding but it was clear. Bridle wasn't sure if he had collided with the dashboard before he passed out in the car. He reached the main road within ten minutes but at that time of night it was deserted. As he trudged along in the dark he kept the thought of Stella in his mind.

He thought about the walk up the prom to the house and that feeling he had every time he saw the light on in Stella's workroom. For a moment he felt like punching Sir Nigel Carver's teeth out. Then he switched to the idea of punching Radford's teeth out. His thoughts degenerated into a raging attack on anyone who had crossed him and then he let out a long shout of frustration. He stopped and punched the nearest tree until his knuckles bled. He leaned against the tree with his eyes closed and breathed deeply in an effort to pull himself together.

'I'm not going to lose Stella' he said softly as he opened his eyes and straightened himself up. He resumed his march along the main road and started to chuckle to himself. His shoulder hurt like hell, his head was swollen and sore and now the knuckles on both hands were skinned and bleeding.

'Maybe I should stick to nicking shoplifters in Woolworths' he said then broke into a steady jog to burn off his frustration.

CHAPTER THIRTEEN

The crowd in the office relaxed as Inspector Radford finished his briefing on the arrest of Billy Doyle. Detective Superintendent Webster and Superintendent Mcleish sat on Radford's right side. Bridle, Lodge and Sullivan stood at the back of the room out of sight. Bridle had listened intently to Radford's diatribe but Lodge had taken advantage of the crowd cover to snatch furtive glances at his morning newspaper. Almost four days had passed since the ball and Stella hadn't returned home or taken any of Bridle's phone-calls. Bridle's mood had become gloomier by the day and listening to Radford had him bordering on belligerent.

'Doyle was always high on my list of suspects and the witness testimonies confirmed it for me.' There was a loud response of approval from the squad but Mcleish remained poker-faced and Webster looked as detached and crumpled as ever.

'So you haven't got a confession out of Doyle Inspector?' Mcleish asked cynically.

'Not yet Sir' Radford said looking around the room with a smirk 'but the case will stand up in court.' Radford's confidence was infectious and his squad murmured their agreement. At the back Bridle stood with his arms folded and his concentration fixed on Radford.

'I hope your case is water-tight Inspector, the department will be crucified if it's kicked out of court' Webster wiped his glasses on his handkerchief as he spoke but Radford didn't respond. Webster continued 'as for Margaret Vance, the Surgeon confirmed her neck was snapped by hand, not a nice way to go' Webster sighed.

'Even for a gutter whore' Mcleish added.

'It's straightforward enough' Radford said with renewed over-confidence 'the officer who found the body confirms seeing her lad running from the house. Joey Vance is simple-minded and could be capable of anything.'

'Billy Doyle is innocent and Joey Vance didn't kill his mother.'

All heads turned to the back of the room and glared at Bridle. Tommy Lodge looked up from his newspaper to see the whole room staring his way. He quickly shut the paper and joined the crowd in looking at Bridle with disbelief. George Sullivan looked down at his feet and sighed. To his mind Bridle had just done the career equivalent of throwing himself under a moving tram-car.

'The surgeon confirmed that Margaret Vance was killed hours before Joey was seen running away' Bridle said as he walked to the front of the room. Radford's face turned crimson.

'Vance could have murdered the old slut then cooked his dinner or played tiddlywinks for a couple of hours, who knows what goes through the mind of a mental case' Radford retorted.

'I've spent the last three days pursuing enquiries about Joey Vance and Billy Doyle with the help of Detectives Lodge and Sullivan' Bridle said and stopped in front of Radford. Lodge looked alarmed that Bridle had mentioned his name.

'We spent a day and a half on the dock working out distances and timings in relation to witness sightings of Billy Doyle and with the amended statements from Shaw, Porter and Swain we have come to the conclusion that Doyle couldn't have done it.'

'Put it in a report Sergeant' Radford said with a wave of dismissal 'and get back in your corner.' The jibe got a laugh from the squad and Lodge put a hand over his face and closed his eyes.

'I've done a report Inspector Radford, it's on your desk' Bridle responded.

'Must have got mixed up with my fish and chip paper' Radford said playing to the crowd.

'What have you found out Sergeant?' Webster ignored Radford.

'The main witnesses all confirm that Grant got out of the taxi further along the dock and that he was meeting with people that Grant described as dangerous. Grant's murder caused them to falsify their statements because of fear of intimidation or worse.'

'We didn't pursue the information in their amended statements Sir' Radford interjected 'because their testimony isn't reliable.' Webster nodded to Bridle to continue.

'All three witnesses agree he got out of the cab between five and ten minutes of leaving the fight and the cab crawled along at low speed because the driver was unsure of his way round the dock. We covered each direction from the warehouse at low speed for times between five and ten minutes, it didn't bring us anywhere near the murder scene.'

'He must have got into another vehicle' Webster said thoughtfully.

'Yes Sir, which proves he was meeting someone' Bridle responded.

'Yeah Billy Doyle' Radford quipped and Bridle continued

'the police surgeon places Grant's time of death at least two hours after the fight. Doyle was holding court at the bar of The Brigantine with his cronies and lots of witnesses by that time.'

'We checked that' Radford fired back 'The Brigantine was packed to the rafters that night no one would have noticed Doyle coming and going with or without accomplices. My witnesses place Doyle with Grant within at least an hour of estimated death – and don't forget the pocket watch – Doyle had Grant's silver pocket watch stashed away' Radford grinned with satisfaction.

'Stashed away in his waistcoat pocket' Bridle said dismissively 'Grant liked to play the big man in front of his friends. He had a habit of dropping expensive gifts on people from lady friends to taxi drivers. Doyle said Grant gave him the watch in gratitude for organising the fight.'

'There are no reliable witnesses to swear that the watch was a gift' Radford said flatly.

'You can't hang a man on that' Bridle said.

'Let the jury decide' Radford replied through gritted teeth.

The room was silent as the two men faced each other off. Mcleish and Webster looked at each other sideways then back to the men.

'Do you have any suspects Sergeant Bridle?' Webster asked.

'No Sir I don't have any suspects' Bridle said with a sigh as the inevitable chuckles went around the room.

'He's more concerned about saving Doyle' Radford shouted.

'Perhaps Sergeant Bridle is concerned about seeing justice done Inspector' Webster said vacantly scratching his nose 'he has made some very sound judgements.'

'But no results' Mcleish said to Radford's amusement 'have you found Joey Vance Sergeant?'

Bridle shook his head slowly and Radford threw his arms up in mock despair.

'Vance has got the mental age of a twelve year old it's just a case of pulling him in and getting him to own up' Radford said exasperated.

'Just like Doyle' Bridle said and Radford glared at him.

'What's your problem Sergeant Bridle, something on your mind, trouble at home?'

Radford's comment caused an outbreak of sniggering in the room and Bridle fought to contain himself. Lodge could see the blood pulsing through Bridle's neck and braced himself to lunge forward and hold him off Radford.

'I suggest you keep personal comments to yourself Inspector Radford or else save them for your alehouse cronies' Mcleish's granite-faced delivery silenced the room and Radford's face burned.

'Yes Sir' Radford glowered.

'Sergeant Bridle you need to put your personal problems aside' Mcleish said forcefully 'you should have found Vance by now especially as he's so important to your case. And if you are going to stand up and challenge a senior officer you need a more substantial argument do I make myself clear?' Mcleish stared hard at Bridle.

'Yes Sir' Bridle deflated under Mcleish's stare. Mcleish stood up and looked around the room with undisguised contempt.

'Just to change the subject next Saturday there is a rally and a march planned in the city. How it gained approval is a question for the politicians, all we have to do is keep it under control. A peaceful protest against unemployment so I'm told' Mcleish paused as a chuckle went around the room then he continued

215

'contingents are expected from all over the country – Newcastle –Nottingham – Wales… '

'All coal mining areas' Lodge mumbled 'if those lads turn nasty it'll be like wrestlin' angry bulldogs.'

Mcleish stopped mid-sentence and glared at Lodge.

'Stop your grumbling Lodge… I've got plenty of men in uniform including the mounted section. I need extra plain-clothes at Lime Street Station as we've had intelligence concerning agitators and I want any known troublemakers stopped at the door.'

'Is this paid overtime Sir?' Lodge asked and Mcleish looked up slowly.

'No Lodge, it's time off in lieu but I won't check your court books for a month. I think that's fair' Mcleish almost smiled.

'I'm on secondment Sir my court book won't be up to date anyway. So it's just time off in lieu for me then Sir' Lodge said wistfully and Mcleish ignored him.

'The final briefing on the rally will be on Wednesday. Details will be on the notice board. That's all, dismiss.'

The room became animated on Mcleish's sharp dismissal as the squad made a rush for the door. Sullivan turned to Bridle.

'What the hell are you tryin' to do? Finish your career?'

'Stella won't make contact with me George and I'm not sleeping well' Bridle sighed 'everything seems to be falling apart.' Bridle turned pale and Sullivan caught his arm.

'Pull yourself together man and get stuck into the job' Sullivan said firmly 'find Joey Vance.'

Bridle nodded slowly. He was beginning to feel ashamed of himself but then a spark seemed to ignite in his eyes. He turned suddenly to Lodge.

'Tommy let's pay a call on Mr. Finch.'

'Paddy Finch' Lodge spluttered,

'Yeah Paddy Finch – he gave you enough back-handers so you should know him' Bridle winked then smiled at the sight of Lodge frozen to the spot with his mouth wide open.

'You'll never get near him boss, his gang's got him covered' Lodge said quickly.

'Then I'll kick the crap out of his gang until I find him' Bridle said and stormed out of the office. Lodge turned to Sullivan with a look of bemusement on his pallid face.

'He's gone off his head George.'

'Watch his back Tommy' Sulllivan said quietly with a worried frown. Lodge grabbed his hat then snatched a packet of Woodbines from a neighbouring desk and slipped it into his jacket pocket. Sullivan grinned and shook his head.

'I hate the bastard who sits there' Lodge said on his way out.

Callum Riley and Harry Croft sat on the steps of St. George's Hall and watched the general bustle of Lime Street as idly as any of the other unemployed men dotted about the plateau. The trams and the taxis mingled with horse-drawn carts and barrow men. It was a hot afternoon and the huge neo-classical hall gave a good swathe of shade across the steps. A few yards away the Steble fountain gushed water over its large round dish and street urchins were having fun wading and standing under the overflows to get cool and washed at the same time.

Croft rolled a cigarette and passed it to Riley then set about rolling his own. Both men were silent and Riley's eyes were taking in every detail of the layout of the street. Croft rolled his cigarette with swift dexterity and clipped the lid of his tobacco tin down with a grin on his face.

'Nice to idle away an afternoon' Croft said striking a match and lighting Riley's cigarette and then his own.

'Harry me boy yer have some nice colleens promenading in this town.'

'Can't say I noticed' Croft said and spat across the steps below him. Riley had never questioned Croft's sexual preferences and he never would. Riley knew they shared a violent streak but Croft gained a satisfaction from it that even Riley found disturbing. Croft took a sheet of folded paper from his trouser pocket and opened it out slowly. He looked from the paper to the street and back again.

'The march will be coming into Lime Street from London Road' Croft said nodding toward the Empire Theatre 'they'll assemble on the steps in front of us here and the dais for the speakers will be between those two pillars on the top near the main doors.' Croft spoke with the cigarette in the corner of his mouth and the smoke made his right eye squint.

'I guess there'll be a wall of big coppers shoulder to shoulder along the street on the Station Hotel side directly in front of us.'

'What about the cavalry?' Riley asked casually.

'The mounted section will contain the march all the way and I guess they'll rank across the street in front of the station to bar the crowd from moving any further into the city' Croft said then re-folded the paper and slipped it back into his pocket.

'Good, I'll be on the plateau on the south side' Riley said nodding in the general direction.

'C.I.D. and Special Branch will be all over the place' Croft said.

'Sure enough but if there was no danger there'd be no fun Harry boy' Riley grinned. They both laughed as a group of Salvation Army ladies came up the steps from St. Georges Street.

'Tea and corned beef sandwiches are available at the town Citadel' the ladies chanted as they moved among the groups of dishevelled men scattered around the plateau.

'What's your name me pretty one?' Riley grinned at a young bespectacled Salvation Army girl who blushed slightly.

'Tea and corned beef sandwiches are available at the town Citadel' the girl repeated looking at the ground as she moved swiftly past.

'That bonnet makes yer look awful appealin' me darlin' Riley laughed out loud as the girl broke into a run to get away from him and Croft could feel his temper rising as he pulled Riley's attention back to the task in hand.

'I've got two groups of agitators mixed in with Finney's marchers. All hard men and all on a short fuse, they've had enough of peaceful protests' Croft said and Riley nodded.

'Finney wants a gentle protest' Riley paused then smiled 'you just want a fuckin' revolution eh Harry?' Croft ignored him and continued.

'When my lads kick-off in the crowd you and me will fire a few shots over their heads, me from the north side and you from the south. The crowd will panic and the coppers won't be able to hold it.' Croft paused 'Jack Finney won't know what the hell is going on. Mcleish will be humiliated for losing control and I want that bastard on his knees. He might even catch a stray bullet.'

'You won't have time Harry. If you go for a target you'll get nailed. Remember Barcelona'

Riley said sternly.

'We'll see' Croft whispered and threw his stub away.

Riley turned his attention back to the layout of the street. It didn't really concern him if Harry Croft shot a copper and got caught. It occurred to Riley that it might even be to his advantage. The Irishman smoked his cigarette and visualised the massive crowd on the plateau spilling across Lime Street. He imagined how the police would deploy their numbers around St. Georges Hall and he tried to anticipate where and how the undercover detectives would infiltrate the rally. He knew they'd be around the station looking for known political agitators to either detain or follow. Riley dismissed the problem from his mind because he knew they would never locate him once the rally was in progress.

Riley's concentration was broken as he became aware of police officers moving along the plateau ordering the idle men to move on. Riley and Croft stood up as a young constable approached. Riley doffed his cap and made an exaggerated bow.

'Thank you officer but we're off for tea and corned beef sandwiches at the town Citadel.'

Stella Bridle finished her cup of tea and placed the cup and saucer back on the tray. She sat in a comfortable lounge chair directly in front of the open French windows and contemplated the green lawn sprawling down toward the weeping willow. It was a beautiful afternoon and a B.B.C. broadcast of Chopin played from a wireless in the corner of the room. Her sojourn in the family home had given her time to consider the future calmly even though she was under a barrage of unwanted advice from family and friends alike. She had taken a step back from their influence and had spent a reclusive week gardening with her mother who had steadfastly refused to be involved and gave no opinion on Stella's situation. This was a tonic for Stella as her father had taken the opposite stance. Sir Nigel had never disguised his opinion that Bridle wasn't good enough for her.

Caroline called Bridle a city ruffian which actually made her laugh and she knew it would make Bridle laugh too. Why did he have to make such a fool of himself at the ball? She couldn't understand it. The attention from Guy Charlton was flattering but her father and her sisters were throwing them together at every opportunity and it was confusing her. Her thoughts rolled around and around in her head until she blew out a gasp of exasperation.

She picked up the volume of Thomas Hardy she had been reading and slipped through the French windows into the warm sunshine. It seemed appropriate to be reading Far from the Madding Crowd as that was where she wanted to be. As she made her way along the slate path toward the walled rose garden she could hear her father's agitated voice coming from the other side of the wall. She slowed her step as she approached and heard the more clipped tones of Sir Edward Grant responding to him in an even more agitated manner.

They were sitting on a stone bench built into the wall overlooking the rose garden. There was a small cast iron table in front of them with a tray of tea and coffee. An ash-tray teetered slightly on the edge of the table and tobacco smoke rose up over the wall showing Stella exactly where they were. Her intention was to sneak past and find herself a quiet corner of the garden but her attention was immediately caught by their conversation and she hesitated at the grilled partition in the wall directly above their bench seat.

'Then how did he find out?' Grant was furious.

'It's a bluff Edward he's testing you' Carver said dismissively.

'I can't go to the police – I'll have to pay.'

'Are there still grounds for blackmail Edward? So much dross has been published in the papers about David already how much more can there be to embarrass you?' Carver asked and Grant hesitated for a moment then stubbed his cigarette into the ash-tray.

'How do you smoke those damn things Nigel?' Grant took a cigar pouch from the inside pocket of his blazer. Grant flipped open the pouch and offered it to Carver. Carver declined and watched suspiciously as he fumbled about lighting his cigar.

'Edward have you told me everything?' Carver knew instinctively that he hadn't.

'Do you still have the file Nigel?' Grant asked and Carver nodded.

'Is it safe?'

'Of course it is Edward – why?'

'Some business dealings I had in partnership with David have turned out to be a little dubious. I thought I was giving David an opportunity but he and Guy let me down.'

'Guy Charlton?' Carver asked cautiously.

'Yes they wanted to get into the export business using Grant Hollister.'

Stella had to shift her weight carefully as her right calf began to cramp but she had no intention of missing the conversation.

'At the ball Estella's husband confronted Guy about doing business with David. He denied it but admitted doing business with you' Carver said.

'He did, technically I was David's partner… ' Grant hesitated.

'But you had no idea what the business was' Carver interjected 'so why would Guy lie about it?' Carver was becoming suspicious.

'He was talking to a policeman wasn't he?' Grant looked vacantly at his cigar.

'How dubious was this business Edward? I need to know.'

'Dubious enough for me to pay-off a blackmailer' Grant snapped.

'I don't like being used Edward, you gave me all this hogwash about saving your family pain and heartache' Carver didn't hide his disgust 'you were saving your own skin and Guy Charlton's apparently.'

'I had no idea what they were doing Nigel. I found out through the blackmailer and it was too late then. The damage was done and I couldn't risk my business. Grant Hollister have sailed the Mersey for over a hundred and fifty years, how could I risk that?'

'You have placed yourself in a very awkward position Edward. I advised you to take the file to the police, now I'm not sure.'

Behind the wall Stella held her breath and slipped off her shoes. She made her way back along the path in a crouched position until she was clear of the rose garden then she ran barefoot along the slate path and through the French windows into the house. She flopped into the armchair and threw her book onto the table. She slipped her shoes on and sat back to consider what to do next. A dark piece by Mahler was droning from the wireless as she pondered the conversation she had overheard. She stood up quickly then swept out of the room and into the hall. Her father's study was out of bounds to everyone in the house but it was never locked. Stella could feel the pulse in her neck as she nervously made her way into the study and closed the door softly behind her. She felt as guilty as if she was violating a church.

The room had what Stella considered a powerful smell of masculinity. It was an aromatic mix of tobacco, leather furniture, dusty books and whiskey. The window overlooked her father's beloved expanse of lawn and she could still see the wisps of tobacco smoke rising from the rose garden on the south side where Grant and her father were sitting. This gave Stella the confidence to sit in the dark leather chair behind what seemed to be a massive oak desk when she was a child. She had no idea where to look for the file. The desk was littered with newspapers and unopened letters.

She glanced around the room and wondered how men could relax in such gloomy clutter. One side of the room was a crammed bookcase that covered the entire wall and looked as if it hadn't been disturbed in a decade. The mantelpiece on the right side of the room had a rack of tobacco pipes of various shapes and sizes. A collection of exotic tobaccos stored in small boxes from the tobacconist Turmeau of Liverpool was stacked next to the rack. A monstrous antique clock stood in the centre of the mantelpiece that ticked so loud that Stella felt it would wake the dead.

Her attention was drawn to a heavy album on the desk to her right. She pulled it across and opened it with idle curiosity and immediately began to giggle. It was a scrap album of newspaper cuttings of her father's most successful cases. The first leaf of the album had a cutting with a striking photograph of her father in his prime. Bewigged and gowned he was standing in what Stella called his pose of righteous indignation which was how she often teased him when she was a teenager. Each flick of the page increased her giggles as the extent of her father's arrogance surprised even her.

Stella suddenly remembered where she was and why she was there. She closed the scrap book and stood up sharply. She glanced out of the window but couldn't see any smoke rising from the rose garden which sent her pulse racing. She pressed on the cover of the album but it wouldn't lie flat. Anxious to leave the album exactly as she found it she flicked through the pages. In the centre of the book was a thin, brown manila file. Her heart pulsed so rapidly she thought she might faint and her fingers trembled as she fumbled through the pages of the file. Stella couldn't believe her luck. She took the file and swiftly made her way to the door. She took a final glance around then slipped out into the hall and made a dash for the stairs and into the security of her bedroom.

CHAPTER FOURTEEN

Tommy Lodge could hardly keep up with Bridle's powerful stride as he marched down Duke Street and then cut through Kent Street to the maze of slums along Park Lane close to the cotton warehouses opposite Kings Dock. The streets were full of ragged and tired looking people. A group of men were sitting on battered old chairs on the pavement playing cards on a used fruit box. Black clad women were standing around in small groups chatting with arms folded or holding babies. Some women were sharing a dolly tub to wash their clothes and watched as a middle-aged woman with huge forearms twisted the wooden dolly-peg in the tub to agitate the washing. They cast suspicious glances at the Jacks who violated their space as they passed.

The street gangs of Liverpool were well established and held a long tradition of violence and intimidation. Bridle knew there was only one way to get their respect. There was only one language that they understood and he was prepared to take the risk to find Joey Vance.

'Don't be too hasty when we get there boss' Lodge was nervous, his association with the gang had always been questioned but he maintained it was purely a professional exercise in give and take.

'Go back Tommy – I'll sort this.'

'Sort What? Just a few questions you said' Lodge spluttered.

'I need Joey Vance.'

'That mad tart on the phone told George he was dead' Lodge stammered as he struggled to keep up with Bridle.

'Do we listen to mad tarts Tommy?' Bridle's cold manner disturbed Lodge.

'You don't know this gang you need to be careful boss' Lodge was slightly behind Bridle now.

'I know it's awkward for you Tommy, you've got connections with Finch, go back before they see you' Bridle cast a glance over his shoulder to see Lodge falling back rapidly.

'You know how it is boss, we all have to run with devil in this job' Lodge said as he retreated and Bridle strode on. Bridle didn't blame him. He knew Lodge had worked out what he was going to do and had decided it was madness. And it was. Bridle could feel a bitter rage deep in his stomach and he had to get it out of his system

Bridle marched on alone except for a group of tough looking teenage bucks keeping pace with him on the opposite side. He stopped suddenly and they all stopped with him.

'Tell Finch Detective Sergeant Bridle wants a word with him' Bridle called across the street then carried on walking. Two of the boys raced off ahead but the rest kept pace with Bridle and tried their best to look hard. At the top of the street Bridle turned into a slum court. A central courtyard was surrounded by high Victorian tenements. All of them were overcrowded with large families in various stages of deprivation. Lines of washing were slung above the courtyard from one building to the other. The yard itself was full of idle men sitting around smoking. Some women were scrubbing their doorsteps. In the upper floors people were holding conversations across the courtyard from their windows.

It was an amphitheatre of a deprived society and Bridle stood in the centre of it and looked around. The bustle of the court came to a standstill as all heads turned in Bridle's direction. The hard and deeply lined faces stared at the tall Jack standing in the courtyard and Bridle stared back at them. Gradually tough looking men began to appear from doorways. They stepped out into the courtyard and encircled Bridle. One man had a savage dog straining on a length of chain. The rest of the people drew back toward the walls and the whole macabre theatre watched in silence.

'I want Paddy Finch' Bridle's voice echoed around the courtyard.

'Who wants Paddy Finch?' The guttural accent came from a tall, lean faced man in his late thirties with a deep scar running across his chin under his lip.

'I don't talk to big-mouthed bucks' Bridle said firmly. The man made an angry lunge forward but was pulled back by a toothless roughneck.

'We don't talk to Jacks – Jacks are all shite' the roughneck spat on the ground.

Bridle looked around at the blank faces staring down from the windows and from the shadows of the court. Faces trapped by fear of one kind or another. Fear of hunger and sickness but worst of all fear of not being part of the gang. Bridle took a few steps backwards without taking his eyes from the group of roughnecks. The teenage bucks that had followed Bridle up the street were standing behind him. He took off his hat and his jacket and threw them to the smallest of the bucks. There was total silence from the crowd as Bridle walked back toward the roughnecks rolling up the sleeves of his shirt and loosening his tie. He stopped a few feet from the group and stared them down. The silent stand-off was broken by Bridle.

'Who's first?'

'Me' the toothless one thrust himself forward into Bridle's face.

'What's your name lad?' Bridle whispered.

'You can call me Saint Peter cos I'll be sendin' you through the pearly fuckin' gates.'

Bridle genuinely laughed at the joke as his opponent dragged off his ragged jacket and threw it to the ground. A circle formed around them as they squared-up and loud shouts for the roughneck echoed around the courtyard. Bridle held his guard in the classic boxing position but as he circled his opponent it became obvious that the man was a grappler. He had no discipline in his movement and Bridle managed to push him aside each time he made a wild lunge. Bridle could see he was very powerful and growing more furious. His attacks became more desperate as the crowd's baiting put him under pressure. Bridle knew that beating this man wasn't enough. He had to humiliate his opponent in front of his home crowd.

Sweat was pouring from the man's face as he made another desperate lunge for Bridle's head. Bridle ducked under his grip then immediately thrust upward with an uppercut that caught him under the jaw and lifted him off his feet and sent him backwards into the crowd. The crowd pushed him back at Bridle who immediately drove his fist into his solar plexus which bent him double. As his head dropped Bridle brought his knee up to his face and blood spurted across Bridle's shirt. A straight punch to his chin finished it quickly. The roughneck lay motionless on the ground and the crowd's murmuring rumbled around the courtyard. Bridle was breathless and he had lost some skin from his right hand but his blood was up.

'Is that the best you can do?' The crowd was silent. 'Who's

the cock of the gang? Come on bring him out' Bridle was burning. 'Is this all you've got? Where's the cock of the gang?'

Bridle's mocking tones echoed across the silent court. Four roughnecks moved menacingly toward him and Bridle knew he was in trouble. He backed away and the crowd began to murmur. One of the four pulled a length of chain from the inside of his jacket very slowly. Bridle knew that gang members concealed weapons in various ways. A length of chain running down the inside of a jacket sleeve was common. A second man pulled off his leather belt and wrapped it around his hand so that the iron buckle could be swung easily.

'I laid down a challenge, what happened to gang honour?' Bridle shouted as loud and as aggressively as he could but faces just stared back at him passively.

'Spineless bastards' Bridle shouted with contempt.

The two armed men moved forward with grins cracking their pallid faces. Bridle kept moving back but he was aware that the rest of the roughnecks had moved behind him to block his retreat. If his time was up Bridle was determined to take one of them with him. He waited for the chain to start its backward swing then he charged forward screaming wildly. The chain-man was startled at the sudden attack which gave Bridle the time to drive a kick into his groin. A collective groan went up from the crowd as Bridle's boot made contact and the power of the kick sent the chain-man backwards grunting in agony. Bridle recovered quickly. He spun around and ducked immediately to avoid the belt buckle swinging viciously at his head. As he ducked he lost balance and the iron buckle caught his injured shoulder on the return swing. He fell forward on to the ground but rolled over quickly onto his back and brought his knees up to cover his groin. The belt-man stood over him grinning as the crowd screamed for the Jack's blood. Death would be better than mutilation was the only thought in Bridle's head when the belt-man suddenly crashed sideways howling in agony.

Tommy Lodge's square bulk was unmistakeable even from the ground. Lodge grabbed Bridle's hand and pulled him to his feet. Lodge was holding his battered standard issue police truncheon so tight his knuckles were white.

'Where the hell did you come from?' Bridle said over his shoulder as they stood back to back in the middle of the mob.

'You wouldn't listen to me, now look, we're both fuckin' dead' Lodge growled.

'Blow your whistle Tommy, get some uniform over here.' Bridle kept his guard high and his eyes darted left and right.

'I forgot me whistle where's yours?' Lodge swung the truncheon when anyone got too close but he was more worried about the dog straining to get at them.

'In my jacket, but don't ask where my jacket is' Bridle said flatly.

'On the count of three, we go straight at them boss. I'll cut me way with old Bessie and you cover me back, what d' yer say?' Lodge said firing himself up but not really believing it. Bridle managed to grin at Lodge's affectionate name for his old truncheon.

'Start counting Tommy' Bridle shouted and Lodge nodded.

'One... two... '

'Tommy Lodge me old mucker, how the hell are yer?'

The voice boomed across the courtyard and stopped Lodge mid-count. The crowd fell silent but the dog snarled viciously. All heads turned to see Paddy Finch walking down the steps of the corner tenement. His square shoulders swaggered back and forth as he walked and he had a broad genial smile on his face.

'It's not like you to be a hero Lodgy what's goin' on?'

Finch laughed and the crowd pulled apart as he marched through them. As he got closer Bridle could see that he was tall, heavy-boned and well muscled for a man in middle age. His head was shaven and he had a black moustache, waxed and curved up at both ends under a substantial broken nose. He wore a grubby waistcoat over his shirt and a thick gold watch-chain curved from a buttonhole to a side pocket. His face lit-up as he grinned but Bridle could see that coldness in his eyes that could turn merciless at the flip of a coin. Finch had been a fair-ground wrestler in his younger days and had toured the booths all over the country. He had a fearsome reputation which brought him great respect and status in the circles he controlled.

'What the hell are you doin' to me boys?'

'It's my boss' Lodge said nodding toward Bridle 'he's a mad bastard.'

'I'm looking for Joey Vance' Bridle said ignoring the danger of the situation.

'And who are you hardcase?' Finch sneered.

'Detective Sergeant Bridle.'

'Bridle yer say, me boys told me you want a word with me. So what makes yer think kickin' the shit out of my lads will help yer?'

'I thought it might get me noticed.' Bridle couldn't think of a logical answer to the question and Finch threw back his head and let out a booming laugh.

'You're a hard man I'll give yer that. I thought Jacks spent their time proppin' up bars like Lodgy here.'

'I need to find Joey Vance, he could be in danger' Bridle replied.

'Why should I help a Jack? You come out here throwin' down challenges to me boys, you could've got killed and it would've been yer own fault hardcase' Finch waved the crowd away. Two men picked up the groaning chain-man by his arms and legs and carried him into one of the tenements. The rest melted back into the idle business of the court.

'Look Paddy someone took a shot at Joey. If yer can help us in any way for the lad's own safety' Lodge pleaded.

'I heard about the shootin' Lodgy. Maybe that's why the lad's gone to ground or maybe he's scared of Jacks, what do you think hardcase?' Finch looked at Bridle.

'I think Joey Vance knows something about the murder of David Grant. I think that's why someone tried to shoot him. He went to a doss house to meet an Irishman. I don't know why. Joey could've been on your business for all I know. Maggie Vance tipped me off about the meeting then she gets her neck snapped. I get a revolver shoved in my ear by an Irishman in a dark alley and and then he disappeared. So I think Joey's in real danger' Bridle was losing patience.

'You got something against Irishmen hardcase?' Finch asked narrowing his eyes.

'Only the ones who shove a gun in my head' Bridle retorted.

'How the hell will yer find him?' Finch boomed 'There are more Irishmen in this town than in Dublin's fair city.'

'And most of them are Priests' Lodge quipped and Finch broke into another booming laugh and pushed Lodge so hard on his shoulder that he almost dislocated it.

'I like this bastard's sense of humour' Finch shook his head

233

as he laughed and Lodge rubbed his shoulder and wondered how that was a joke.

'Does Joey work for you or not?' Bridle snapped. Finch turned to Bridle and fixed him with a cold stare.

'Why would he work for me?' Finch shrugged 'I'm unemployed like every other bastard round here Sergeant' Finch stared at Bridle and Bridle stared back. Lodge sidled up and pulled at Bridle's arm.

'I think that'll do us boss. He doesn't know where Joey is so let's go' Lodge was tense and Bridle pulled away from him in frustration.

'I heard they got Billy Doyle for that murder' Finch said taking a tin of snuff from his waistcoat pocket.

'Radford collared him' Lodge said quickly as Bridle recovered his hat and jacket from the grubby teenage buck.

'I suppose it takes a rat to catch a rat' Finch placed a pinch of snuff on the back of his right hand.

'Doyle didn't kill Grant' Bridle said flatly as Finch took the snuff from his hand and drew it up both nostrils.

'Is that so hardcase' Finch said with a sly grin as Bridle suddenly lunged forward and thrust his face close to Finch's.

'Look Finch, I know Joey didn't kill anyone, I'm not trying to set him up but I can't speak for every officer on the case. We need to sort this out and we need Joey's help' Bridle's face was contorted with frustration. Lodge took his shoulders from behind and pulled him away quickly.

'We'll be off Paddy thanks for yer time' Lodge said leading Bridle away and Finch stood with his hands in his pockets. Then he shouted across the courtyard.

'Are yer askin' me to be a snout for a Jack?' Finch laughed out loud and looked around for his cronies to follow suit. 'He wants Paddy Finch to be a snout for a Jack' Finch bellowed 'I'm the cock of this gang copper, always will be – remember that.' Finch laughed and his gang joined in as Bridle and Lodge moved slowly away.

'Just keep movin' boss and don't look back' Lodge kept smiling as he spoke.

'Waste of time' Bridle muttered.

'Oh I dunno boss you met Finchy, you made an impression on his boys and you're still alive. I think that's a good result.'

'You were right Tommy it was a bad idea.'

'Forget Joey boss, Finch will never let him talk to us.'

'What does Finch put on that moustache to keep it so black?' Bridle mused.

'Boot polish' Lodge replied biting his lip. They broke into a stifled laugh as they made their way down Park lane.

Superintendent Mcleish dropped the fourth spoonful of sugar into his hot mug of tea and stirred it vigorously. He stirred it so long and so loud that Detective Superintendent Webster and Chief Superintendent Crowley looked at each other and rolled their eyes. They knew they were in for a hard time.

'Special Branch' Mcleish said with a sneer and walked over to join his colleagues seated at the front of the briefing room. He slipped his mug of tea under his chair and stared impatiently at the door. Webster took out his pocket-watch and looked at the time.

'They're late' he said casually then took out his handkerchief and started to polish the watch with a slow rotating action. Mcleish wasn't sure if he was more irritated by the lateness of his fellow officers or by the unruffled calm of Webster. Mcleish hated not being in control and didn't hide the fact.

'We'll just have to wait' Crowley said.

Stating the obvious was only one of many things that irritated Mcleish about Crowley. Sitting next to him was another.

'I would prefer it if you didn't smoke' Crowley said as Mcleish reached into the breast pocket of his tunic for his packet of Players. Mcleish sighed heavily and slipped his hand away from the packet with a frustrated gesture.

'Why would that be Sir?' Mcleish didn't hide his scorn.

'I don't want our colleague from Scotland Yard to get the wrong impression of us' Crowley retorted 'It shows indiscipline and lack of respect Superintendent.'

Crowley stretched his neck in his over-starched collar and cleared his throat. Mcleish would never argue against discipline so he sat back and folded his arms. Webster held up his pocket watch to the light and admired the clarity of the polished glass. Then he breathed on the glass and started to polish it all over again. Mcleish grunted in exasperation and stood up sharply. Webster smiled to himself as Mcleish walked up and down the room with his hands in his pockets.

They looked to the door as they heard the voices growing louder along the corridor. Two well dressed Detectives entered the room. They knew Detective Inspector Latimer of Special Branch but the slightly taller and more distinguished man from Scotland Yard was new to them. Latimer introduced him as Detective Superintendent Allenby. As Latimer made the introductions Webster noticed the expensive cut of Allenby's suit and his gold cuff-links. Webster judged his bearing as military and his manner to be superior but not patronising which was unusual for Scotland Yard as they had a habit of treating any provincial C.I.D. as village idiots.

Allenby began his briefing by pinning two photographs to

the blackboard then took out a heavy briar pipe and began to fill it from a battered leather tobacco pouch.

'Now gentlemen if you would be so kind as to examine the photographs before I begin my briefing.'

Mcleish cast a glance at Crowley as they made their way to the blackboard but Crowley stared straight ahead. He had no intention of commenting on the Scotland Yard man smoking a pipe. It wasn't good politics. Mcleish just sneered and turned his attention to the photographs. One of the photographs had been taken covertly. It pictured two men standing in what looked like a dole queue chatting to the men in front of them. Their faces could be clearly seen. The other photograph was a typical group picture of uniformed men after basic training. In this case the photograph was marked – Auxiliary Division Royal Irish Constabulary. Webster noted it wasn't dated.

They took a good look at the photographs then filed silently back to their seats. Latimer sat at the table at the front of the room and Allenby paced slowly up and down in front of the blackboard.

'Now gentlemen can you identify anyone in the photographs?'

'One of the two men in the first photo is Harry Croft' Mcleish said folding his arms.

'Very good Superintendent and what do you know about him?' Allenby asked.

'Boy soldier, highly decorated but never commissioned as an officer, goes against his socialist beliefs so he says. His father Alan Croft was a syndicalist, a communist and then a socialist, not that there's much difference in my eyes. His father was also an alcoholic and a police informer but if you mention that he'll call you a liar. He might even kill you if he could get away with it.'

'Excellent Superintendent' Allenby was impressed so Mcleish continued.

'Croft is also a known political activist. He claims to be socialist but hates the labour party. He's an arrogant bastard, has to be the leader, has to be in control' Mcleish caught the raised eyebrows from Crowley and Webster and the irony wasn't lost on him.

'Thank you Superintendent' Allenby smiled with approval and pointed to the photograph with the briar.

'Henry Albert Croft as you say a distinguished soldier, he was recruited by Military Intelligence after the war for a number of covert operations. Brutal, sadistic, he's known to have a taste for violent sexual behaviour but only against prostitutes.'

'That makes it alright then I suppose' Webster said. Allenby ignored his remark and carried on.

'He has a dynamic personality, a natural leader, he became involved in the trade union movement then volunteered to fight for a socialist militia in Spain. Military Intelligence tried to recruit him again in Barcelona but he had developed anti-imperialist views so they dropped the idea.'

'Brutal, sadistic and a violent sexual deviant but Military Intelligence only dropped him for his anti-imperialist views' Webster said quietly 'and I thought we worked in a dirty world.' Allenby sighed but chose to ignore Webster's second remark.

'Who is the other man in the picture?' Mcleish asked.

'Callum Riley is his current alias, well known for his good looks and affable Irish charm, tends to use women callously, comes across as every man's favourite drinking partner...' Allenby paused and raised an eyebrow.

'But' Webster said idly and Allenby smiled.

'But indeed. Riley is a scarred individual. He was a teenager when officers of the auxiliary division shot members of his family in a skirmish. Riley took to arms for the rebels and hasn't stopped killing since.'

'By auxilliary division you mean the black and tans?' Webster asked tentatively.

'No Superintendent the auxiliaries were recruited from the officer class. The black and tans were recruited from… other sources. Both paramilitary with slightly different objectives' Allenby coughed.

'Same reputation' Mcleish sneered'why hasn't he been collared if he's such a busy killer?'

'Because he is very good Superintendent, very intelligent, Riley is hard to pin down. He spent some time in New York and you already know about Spain.'

'Did he meet Croft in Spain?' Webster asked.

'Met or targeted' Allenby responded.

'What are they doing over here?' Mcleish asked.

'I'll get round to that in a moment' Allenby replied and Mcleish folded his arms and let out a noisy sigh.

'What about the other photograph?' Webster asked scrutinizing the man from Scotland Yard.

'Yes it's a training cadre of the auxiliaries, as I mentioned earlier they were all ex-officers, their brief was to smash the rebels which led to some controversial incidents. Members of this cadre were in the unit that killed Riley's family' Allenby paused again.

'And the point is?' Mcleish's limited patience was almost spent.

'Three of these men have been murdered in the past seven years' Allenby replied.

'I don't find that surprising' Webster said 'surely you'd expect reprisals.'

'Lengths were taken to avoid it, new identities, many emigrated after their service.' Allenby said then paced up and down for a few moments. Crowley cleared his throat noisily and raised his hand.

'So you obviously suspect Riley of the murders in revenge for his family I presume.'

'That's too obvious' Webster said 'there must be some other connection to drag you up here from the Yard.'

Allenby grinned and nodded at Webster.

'This may interest you gentlemen, all of the dead men were found hanged, all with fatal head wounds' Allenby waited for a reaction but the room remained silent for a moment as if they were all afraid to state the obvious.

'When was the last man murdered?' Webster asked.

'Three years ago in New York City, he was working as a barman' Allenby replied.

'And Riley was in New York at the time' Mcleish said.

'We know he was in New York but that's all we know' Allenby responded.

'Can you connect Riley to the other murders in any way?' Webster asked.

'Tentatively, one was in London almost seven years ago, the victim was due to embark for Australia. The second victim was about two years later in Scotland.'

'And the third' Webster asked idly.

'Spain last year, the third victim had become a mercenary recruited by an American anti-fascist militia, a very tough man.' Allenby tapped the bowl of his pipe on the ashtray and glanced at Latimer.

'Not tough enough' Mcleish said 'why didn't you just alert the other officers in the picture?'

'It's difficult' Inspector Latimer interjected 'military records concerning this patrol are incomplete. It's hard enough to trace ex-soldiers around the world but many of these men changed their identities two or three times. It's an impossible task.'

'How close do you cloak and dagger boys watch him?' Mcleish asked and fixed Latimer with a stare.

'Riley is a very sharp operator' Latimer said as he stood up and moved to the front of the room. 'He doesn't rush, he's very methodical, even when you think he's drunk and incapable – he isn't.'

'So let me ask the obvious question' Webster said 'apart from the seemingly identical method how does David Grant's murder tie in with Riley? David Grant had no known connection with the military unless you know something we don't.' Latimer was about to respond but Allenby stepped in quickly.

'We have two reasons for being here gentlemen and both involve Riley. The similarity of the murders demands a deeper investigation into David Grant and that's your job. The second is our problem. There is a major political rally in this city at the week-end. Extremists and agitators are expected here from all over the country. Croft and Riley are heavily involved and we need to co-ordinate our surveillance with your department. We don't want any mix-ups and we don't want your department getting in our way' Allenby said and cast a stern look around the room.

'Amongst all of these anarchists and agitators would there be one or two decent union men making a stand for the unemployed?' Webster asked with his eyes fixed on Allenby.

'Decent union men are no threat Superintendent Webster and for that reason they are of no interest to me' Allenby said with cold detachment. Latimer coughed slightly and stepped forward to speak.

'Now gentlemen I suggest a short break for refreshments before we go into details, I also suggest you arrange to have these photographs copied and circulated.' Crowley looked sideways at Webster and Mcleish but neither moved.

'I'll arrange that' Crowley said and shifted in his chair self consciously.

It was a warm evening and the police gym had been busier than usual. Bridle had been subdued all through the session but it had nothing to do with the jibes and banter he received for the strapping on his shoulder. He had spent the evening coaching but it had been a mediocre class. It was mostly the sociable types looking for a good work-out and then the rest of the night in the Rose and Crown on Cheapside. Tommy Lodge had enjoyed the session and was placing his indian clubs carefully back on the rack. They stacked in pairs of the same size and weight and Lodge cursed under his breath when he found one club had gone astray. He took an agitated look around the gym then started shifting mats and benches to try and find it.

Bridle stood in front of the heavy bag and slipped on his bag gloves. He caught a look at himself in the mirror. His face was gaunt and the strapping on his shoulder made him look out of proportion. It didn't look good but he didn't care. There was loud banter coming from the locker-room as the men fired themselves up for a good pub session. One or two of the keen younger men were still hitting bags or lifting weights and Lodge continued grumbling as he wandered around looking for his stray club.

'Always the bloody same' Lodge mumbled 'can't trust anyone to put stuff back.'

Bridle ignored Lodge and started to pat the bag lightly and move around it smoothly to warm his body up. As he snapped and jabbed at the bag he turned his thoughts to Stella and when he couldn't stand that anymore he thought about the Grant case and Radford. As he got warmer he began to hit the bag harder but maintained a steady pace. He wanted to build up a sweat. He needed to purge himself of every dark and lonely thought that had invaded his mind since Stella left. The sweat began to pour from his head and run down his face. It ran into a cut on his cheek and began to sting and burn. But he refused to feel it. He increased his speed and power and became more and more oblivious to his surroundings. All he could hear was the crack of his glove on the bag and all he could feel was a pulse of rage coursing through him. His breathing grew harder and harder. His mind was focussed on the bag. It was like nothing else existed. He heard himself shouting hard with each impact on the heavy canvas. Each punch was harder than the last. Each shout was louder and more desperate.

As he reached a climax of exhaustion he fell against the bag and held on to it for support. He closed his eyes tightly as the blackness almost engulfed his consciousness. With rasping gulps he dragged the air back in to his lungs. He held on to the bag like a helpless child holding on to its mother. His breathing gradually slowed and he slid off the bag and opened his eyes. Tommy Lodge and all of the men from the locker room were standing at the back of the gym staring at him in total silence. Bridle stared back at them. There was nothing to say. He felt completely exposed as if he was standing in the middle of town stark naked. It seemed to Bridle that each face shared a common expression. A silent understanding of how he felt that would never be acknowledged or discussed.

'We'll be in the Crown if you fancy a pint later' Sergeant Dean said as they turned to make their way out. Bridle stared blankly into the mirror

'I'll lock up boss' Lodge said and picked up a broom and started sweeping. Bridle nodded slowly and made his way to the locker room.

Bridle's thoughts had wandered and swayed with the rhythm of the train carriage all the way through the dark tunnel under the Mersey. He hated the underground train journey and always took the ferry when he could. The underground was always cold and he hated the stink that swirled around the train at the station and he was always glad to get up the dark steps into fresh air. He strolled along the promenade with his hands in his pockets and tried to work out what was going on. It was difficult to focus his thoughts on his job without Stella and he knew instinctively that the Grant case was an opportunity to make his mark. The alternative was a miserable and tedious slide into retirement covering all the usual dross of petty crime in the city. His mind swung from self-pity to hard determination from self-doubt to ruthless courage within moments. If Stella never came back he knew it would poison his outlook. Even now he could hardly contain the anger. It was spilling out of him.

He stopped and placed both hands on the painted rail of the promenade and stared into the dirty river. The sun was almost set at his back as he looked toward the Liver Buildings in the fading light. The rattle of a train and carriages on the dockside overhead railway echoed across the Mersey. A beautiful transatlantic liner was moored in the middle of the river and dominated the waterfront. Tug boats were making their way down river in the shadow of the great ship. Bridle was brought to his senses by a rough voice behind him.

'You alright boyo' Bridle turned around to see a heavy, middle-aged man in dirty brown overalls with a cigarette stuck in the side of his mouth. His head was bald and glistening in the fading rays of the sun behind him. Bridle knew he lived locally and his overalls showed he worked in the sugar factory across the river.

'I'm fine thanks' Bridle said with a forced smile.

'For a minute there I thought you were gonna jump – top yourself like.'

'Do I look that bad?'

'Well, to be honest, yeah' he laughed as he replied.

'I just need a good supper and a bottle of brown ale' Bridle said pulling himself together but thinking that he wasn't going to get either.

'Thank God for that boyo cos I can't swim see, but being Welsh I could have sung you a nice hymn while you drowned.' He guffawed at his own joke and walked off shaking his head. Bridle smirked and carried on up the prom at his steady pace. He looked up at the villa. Normally at this point he would see the light in Stella's work room upstairs and his pace would quicken. But the house was dark.

Bridle made his way up the path and waved at next door's twitching curtain which abruptly stopped moving. There was no sense of joy to enter an empty house. No sense of expectation. As he stepped through the short hall and into the parlour his heart began to beat faster. He knew Stella had been there, a trace of her perfume was in the air. It was faint but it stirred him powerfully and glancing around he realised she had even tidied the room.

'Stella' he thrust his head into the tiny kitchen. The he realised the house had been in darkness and cursed his stupidity. But he knew she had been there. She hadn't left a note but she had left the message of her visit loud and clear. The tea towel folded on the rack. His breakfast dishes had been washed, dried and placed back in the cupboard. There was fresh water in the vase on the sideboard.

Bridle's stomach tightened as a dark thought suddenly crossed his mind. He dashed out of the room and covered the stairs in three long strides. The bedroom door almost came off its hinges as he shouldered his way in and threw open the wardrobe. Stella's clothes were still hanging there. He took a deep breath then blew it out with a long whistle of relief. He sat on the end of the bed for a moment and wondered why she had come back and not told him.

The next dark thought crossed his mind as he trudged slowly downstairs to the kitchen pantry. It was the realisation that there was no food in the house. He scanned the shelves of the pantry and decided that a slab of cheddar cheese wedged between two slices of roughly cut bread and cemented in with thick butter would do the job. He placed his culinary creation on a wooden tray with a deep mug of strongly brewed tea and sat at the small dining table. The wireless was within arm's reach and he decided that he would rather listen to the B.B.C. than the ticking clock.

It was only as he stretched over the table that he noticed the brown file standing on the mantelpiece with one edge of it behind the clock to stop it falling off. He stopped mid-stretch and stared at it for a moment. It could only have been Stella he thought as he quickly moved over to the mantelpiece but then hesitated. What was it? Why had she put it there? He took it down slowly and stared at the plain brown cover. Then he opened it quickly and saw David Grant's name and case number. He began to read the notes and by the time he had finished reading and re-reading them his deep mug of strong tea had gone stone cold.

CHAPTER FIFTEEN

Callum Riley slipped into the pub amidst a group of drunken stevedores who were half-way through a pub crawl from Park Lane to the Herculaneum Dock. He was wearing a soiled navy blue reefer jacket and a cap pulled low to obscure his face. He swayed and sang and rolled along with the group but slowly edged away through the crowd of ale-sodden men and squealing whores toward the taproom at the rear of the bar. Riley laughed and joked as he staggered across the floor but once he opened the taproom door he cast a glance of contempt at the throng behind him.

'You're late yer murderin' rebel bastard' Paddy Finch said suppressing a laugh.

'And yourself, still as big and ugly as the devil himself' Riley said with a beaming grin and the two men shook hands and slapped each other on the back to the amazement of Finch's companions.

'There's yer supper lad' Finch said and pointed to a dark pint of stout and a whiskey chaser on the table. Riley grinned and downed the whiskey then he picked up the stout and took a long, slow drink. He put the glass down with a sigh of satisfaction.

'You've been makin' a bit of noise round town' Finch said 'It's not like you.'

'Ah Padraig yer don't miss a trick' Riley took off his cap and threw it on the table.

'I keep hearin' things' Finch said.

'Hearin' things' Riley retorted 'is the statue of the Virgin still talkin' to yer Padraig?' Finch's men burst into a nasal laugh but cut it short when Finch glared at them.

'Alright so what is it yer want from me?' Finch asked and folded his huge arms across his barrel chest.

'A favour' Riley said with a confident smile.

'A favour is it' Finch said grinning 'yer might be able to charm the knickers off a Judy but you'll have to work harder with me lad.'

'Ah Padraig you're a fine lookin' man' Riley said and leaned forward 'but yer not my type.'

Finch's men held their breath to stifle a laugh as Riley took a folded sheet of paper from the inside of his reefer jacket placed it on the table and slid it over to Finch.

'What's this?' Finch asked glaring at his men.

'It's the favour I was askin' Riley replied. Finch picked up the sheet, unfolded it and read it with a serious look on his face. His face slowly broke into grin and he shook his head.

'What the hell are you up to this time my friend?'

'Serious business' Riley replied.

'To be sure and speakin' of business, we had a visit from a Jack yesterday' Finch said.

'Two Jacks' one of Finch's men butted in 'Tommy Lodge was there.'

'Number one, I don't count Tommy Lodge as a Jack' Finch said and suddenly leapt to his feet with surprising agility and punched his man full in the face sending him backwards over the chair. 'And number two, I don't like bein' interupted.' Finch's words were wasted on his man who was unconscious on the floor. Finch sat down and they resumed as if nothing had happened.

'Must have been a brave copper to call on you' Riley said with a grin.

'He could handle himself alright. He took out two of my boys, good lads too.'

'What did he want?' Riley was suspicious.

'Lookin' for Joey Vance, I never had a copper shoutin' the odds at me before. He's either off his head or he's got balls like a bull.'

'Did he find Joey?'

'Now why do you ask?' Finch noticed Riley's mood change.

'Joey knows some of our business that's all Padraig. Well now what about my list?'

'Like I said before my friend what are you up to this time? I don't want trouble for me or mine. You have a reputation and that makes you a marked man.' A fresh round of stout and whiskey was deposited on the table by a nervous barman overawed by the company. He grabbed his tray as the men downed the whiskey and left the room in a hurry.

'A marked man you say' Riley's face became dark.

'You upset a lot of people back home lad, I admire that, some people don't.'

'Some people' Riley spat the words out 'gutless bastards who wouldn't last five minutes if they tried to operate like me.'

'So what's this for?' Finch said waving the list under Riley's nose 'what's the target?' Riley's dark face broke into a slow grin then he sat up and finished his pint of stout.

'Probably the docks but I haven't decided yet, that's how I work' Riley grinned but Finch wasn't happy.

'Now I've got some good men at the docks and I look after me own. I don't want my boys injured, know what I'm sayin?'

'I said I haven't decided yet' Riley's eyes narrowed as he spoke and Finch drew himself up.

249

'Don't be givin' me one of yer murderin' looks laddo, this is my territory. I don't get used not even by you Kerry boy. I'll get this gear for yer when I know the target.' They stared each other down for a moment then Riley's eyes suddenly recovered their sparkle and the beaming smile slowly covered his face.

'I should know better than to fool with a man as sharp as you Padraig.'

'And save yer flannel for the Judies' Finch said and downed his whiskey.

'The barracks on the East Lancs Road' Riley said looking Finch squarely in the eye.

'The barracks is it?' Finch scanned Riley's face for any sign of deceit.

'The barracks it is' Riley said with a nod and a grin.

'Good I like military targets it's like a proper war so it is' Finch said grinning.

'So it is Padraig so it is' Riley said and nodded toward Finch's men 'can these two be trusted?'

'I hope so as they'll be goin' with yer' – to the barracks' Finch grinned at Riley's alarmed expression.

'No I do this kind of work alone – that's why I'm still alive.'

'My boys go or you don't' Finch grinned.

'You don't trust me Padraig' Riley held his hands up in mock contrition and looked at the two roughnecks. One was nursing his broken nose and the other drew on a tiny stub of a cigarette which he held with the tips of his fingers.

'Which one is the clever one?' Riley asked with a straight face. Finch let out a booming laugh and slapped the table.

'Milo can nick a van for the job and Brady can carry heavy stuff' Finch looked pleased with himself.

'Perfect' Riley said with grin.

Bridle and Lodge made their way down Water Street toward the Royal Liver Building. They had left the office early and Bridle had left a cover story with George Sullivan. All spare detectives from other divisions had been drafted in for the tedious duty of door to door enquires relating to the Maggie Vance murder. Every Jack hated door to door enquiries and Bridle and Lodge were no exception. Bridle was glad the department was under pressure for lack of progress in the Grant murder but it didn't suit Lodge one bit. Lodge hated the pantomime of clueless Jacks jumping through hoops for superior officers and they were quickly running out of hoops.

Lodge had grumbled constantly since he left the office and only calmed down when Bridle treated him to bacon on toast from the cafe on Bold Street. Bridle had spent the previous night reading and absorbing the file on David Grant. He was intrigued because he had realised it was the same file that Sir Nigel dangled under his nose if he was prepared to leave Stella. Bridle began to chuckle.

'What's so funny?' Lodge asked.

'I wish I knew' Bridle said pulling himself together and Lodge shook his head. They crossed The Strand and passed under the overhead railway then strolled up to the main entrance of the Liver Building. Bridle stopped and checked Lodge for any bits of bacon on his jacket or ketchup stains on his shoes after his breakfast at the cafe.

'Keep this up boss and you'll be makin' your own dresses by next week' Lodge said then cast a quick glance through the swinging doors 'are we goin' in a lift?' His face lit up with the question and Bridle rolled his eyes.

'Unless you want to take the stairs up to the eighth floor' Bridle said and led the way into the impressive ground floor of the building. Their footsteps echoed on the ornate tiled floor and the building had a striking atmosphere of business and commerce. Dark suited gentlemen in bowler hats or straw boaters wandered around carrying papers and files with an air of urgency. Lodge was distracted by a group of office girls walking along the corridor gossiping in whispers and looking very smart in pleated skirts and sensible shoes. Bridle ushered Lodge toward the lift and the gate was pulled back by a uniformed attendant in his fifties. As they got closer they noticed that he only had one arm and the empty sleeve was pinned back on his pristine tunic. He carried two military medals on his chest and he stood bolt upright as he turned to face them.

'Which floor Sir?'

'The Grant Hollister Line, I think it's the eighth' Bridle replied feeling a little intimated by his confidence and bearing.

'Very good Sir' he slammed the gate and they felt the unnerving sink in the stomach as the cage began its ascent. The attendant stood at ease with his arm folded behind his back then moved swiftly and efficiently to open the gate when the cage jolted to a halt. He stood to attention on one side as they left the cage.

'Thank you Sir'

'Thank you' Bridle responded.

'I wouldn't like to spar with him boss, one arm or not' Lodge said in a whisper and Bridle nodded in agreement.

Bridle opened one side of a double door that bore a large brass plaque with the name and insignia of the Grant Hollister Shipping line. They stepped into an outer office onto a thick comfortable carpet. The room was lit from a window on the left side and the walls were each dominated by a large oil painting of a ship of the line. There was a desk directly in front of them with a door to an inner office to the left of it. A slim, middle-aged woman sat behind the desk and looked at them blankly as they approached. She wore round wire framed spectacles and her hair was in a bun. Bridle noticed that her lips were thin and she had them slightly pursed in an attitude of terminal impatience.

'Can I help you?' She asked looking somewhere between them.

'Detective Sergeant Bridle and Detective Constable Lodge we're here to see Sir Edward Grant.'

'Is Sir Edward expecting you?' She said hastily looking at an itinerary on her desk.

'No' Bridle said.

'Then I'm afraid it's quite impossible, Sir Edward's diary is full today.'

'In that case I will have to ask Sir Edward to accompany us to the station for questioning.'

Bridle held her stare firmly as her eyes widened and her thin lips turned into a slight pout.

'One moment please' she stood up sedately and made her way through the door behind her.

'Her husband needs some lead in his pencil' Lodge mumbled and Bridle was about to respond when the door burst open and Sir Edward Grant stormed into the reception office followed swiftly by his secretary. Grant looked taller than Bridle remembered as he stood in the centre of the room with his chest inflated and his eyes burning into both men.

'How dare you turn up here and demand to see me I hope you have an explanation Sergeant.' Grant was genuinely enraged and Bridle noticed the smug look on the receptionist's face.

'I'm sorry to disturb you Sir Edward but we have received some information relevant to the case. We can discuss it here or at the station' Bridle spoke calmly and Grant's eyes began to bulge.

'What are you talking about man?'

'I'm talking about a business partnership you had with your son and Guy Charlton. I'm talking about your son's relationship with Miranda Shaw. I'm talking about blackmail and I'm talking about the withholding of information relevant to a murder investigation, shall I go on Sir?' Grant was stunned for a moment then a look of realisation spread across his face.

'Come this way' Grant said curtly then turned abruptly to his secretary 'Mrs. Danby we are not to be disturbed.' She sniffed and cast a sideways glance at Bridle and Lodge.

Grant led the way followed by Bridle but as Lodge held the door he looked back at Mrs Danby and winked. He grinned at her look of horror then quickly followed the others. Grant led them along a narrow corridor with busy offices leading off it. It was quite noisy on the corridor but when Grant closed the heavy door of his office there was hardly a sound from outside. Grant sat behind his imposing desk and Bridle looked up at the painting on the wall behind him. It was a portrait of the founder of the shipping line looking stern and business-like with a hard face and mutton chop whiskers. He was depicted with the ocean behind him and a number of sailing ships leaving an exotic coastline.

'They are slave ships in case you are wondering Sergeant' Grant said looking for a reaction from Bridle 'does that not shock you?' Grant's tone was challenging.

'This city was built on slavery Sir Edward why should it shock me?'

'The open celebration of slavery in a painting is that not reprehensible?'

'I guess the painting depicts the attitude of the times Sir Edward.'

'Indeed Sergeant. Very discerning of you but I choose to hang it today complete with its celebration of slavery so what does that make me?'

'A free man Sir'

Grant reacted with a slight sneer bending the corners of his mouth. His eyes darted to Lodge as he took out his notebook from the inner pocket of his jacket.

'I assume Sir Nigel Carver gave you the file.'

'Why would Sir Nigel give me a file Sir?' Bridle responded.

'Because he... oh never mind just get on with it Sergeant' Grant waved his hand airily.

'You engaged a private enquiry agency to follow your son can you tell me why?'

'I was concerned about his conduct – this is old ground Sergeant.'

'His social conduct was well known to you Sir, were you more concerned about his business dealings?''Perhaps you were concerned about his partnership with Guy Charlton.'

'I was pleased to see him making his own way believe it or not.'

'Pleased enough to engage an enquiry agency to keep an eye on him.'

'I was a silent partner not a dead one Sergeant.'

'What was the nature of the business Sir?'

'Exports, they had a tobacco contract for southern Europe. They transported from the bonded warehouses on the dock. Guy Charlton co-ordinated the business at the European end.'

'They chartered ships from your line to carry out this business Sir?'

'They did.'

'When we interviewed you at your house Sir Edward you denied any knowledge of your son's business with Guy Charlton' Bridle watched Grant's response carefully.

'Did I deny it Sergeant or did I just avoid the question?'

'Why would you avoid the question Sir' Bridle watched Grant's eyes but there was little reaction.

'I have no time for Guy Charlton he's not a businessman he's a gold chaser. I never wanted David to associate with him. I became a silent partner mainly to keep an eye them. Charlton was charging around Europe doing deals and making decisions without consultation. Money dropped through the man's fingers but he always had enough for himself.'

'Guy Charlton said he hardly knew your son when I questioned him' Bridle said and Lodge looked up from his notebook.

'I've no idea why' Grant's face gave nothing away 'he must have known the police would find out eventually' Grant leaned over his desk and took a cigar from an exquisitely carved wooden box. Lodge inhaled the aroma of the tobacco as it wafted across the room.

'Do you mind?' Grant asked holding up the cigar and both men shook their heads.

'Guy Charlton admitted to doing business with you Sir Edward but spoke of David with disdain, why would he do that?' Grant took his time answering the question as he concentrated on lighting his cigar. Bridle gave Lodge a sideways glance.

'You should ask Guy Charlton that question Sergeant.'

'I intend to Sir' Bridle said flatly 'which is why I'm giving you the opportunity to declare any misdeeds now.'

'Do you have any idea who you are talking to Sergeant? I am a highly respected businessman.

This shipping line brought prosperity to this city for over a hundred years how dare you infer that I would… '

'Why were you being blackmailed Sir Edward?' Bridle interrupted his rant and Grant was stunned for a moment then he slumped into his chair.

'It had nothing to do with the business' Grant said pointing his smoking cigar emphatically as he spoke.

'Then I suggest you clarify the matter now Sir' Bridle knew his technique was irritating Grant like a bad itch and for a moment Bridle thought he was defeated but he suddenly thrust forward on the offensive and jabbed his forefinger at Bridle.

'I have always put my family and my business above all else. David put his mother through hell with his constant indiscretions of one kind or another. A certain party threatened to expose some of David's more immoral pastimes, I had no choice but to comply, I had to protect my family' Grant slumped back and rubbed his forehead.

'Do you have any idea who the certain party was Sir?'

'No I assume it was someone involved in David's sordid business.'

'What sordid business was that Sir?'

'How long are you going to keep up this naive pretence?' Grant's eyes bulged 'I know you've seen the file'.

'If you would answer the question Sir, for Detective Lodge's notes' Bridle held his gaze and Grant sighed heavily.

'Apparently David would organise… sordid parties… orgies… for otherwise respectable people.' Lodge suddenly sat up and paid attention. 'He would use a country house in a secluded part of Cheshire for week-ends of organised debauchery. Many of his clients were old university friends now in politics or business or government service. David supplied the whole package and yes I am very ashamed of it.'

'I'm sure you are Sir and I'm sure Lady Grant would be distressed but keeping silent hasn't helped us. This information has opened up the whole investigation.'

'I am sorry Sergeant but I hope you understand my position.'

'I'm not convinced you are telling the truth about this blackmail Sir Edward' Bridle watched Grant's reaction 'you have told me lies before.'

'I beg your pardon Sergeant' Grant exploded and Lodge looked at Bridle and hoped he knew what he was doing.

'You smoke a very distinct cigar Sir Edward a special Cuban blend that you order from Turmeau's on Water Street am I right Sir?'

'Go on Sergeant' Grant glared at Bridle.

'Apparently you are their only client for this strong blend of Cuban cigar.'

'It's an excellent cigar and your point is?' Grant's face grew darker.

'My point is you told me that you had never met Miranda Shaw.'

'Miranda Shaw' Grant mumbled incredulously.

'Yes Sir Edward, when we interviewed Miss Shaw at the studio there was a cigar stub in the ashtray, a very distinctive smell but I couldn't place it. Then I smelt it on Miranda Shaw's gown on the night of the Whitley Ball.' Lodge stopped writing and looked over at Bridle then motioned toward his notebook.

'Keep writing Constable Lodge – can you explain that Sir Edward?'

'This Miranda Shaw could have been in proximity of me at the ball and picked up the smoke on her gown' Grant blustered.

258

'And the cigar stub at the studio Sir?'

'I don't know. I give them out sometimes as gifts, it could be anyone.'

Bridle paused for a moment as the sweat formed on Grant's forehead then he and Lodge exchanged a well rehearsed knowing look which they often used during questioning. Bridle sat back in his chair and fixed Grant with a hard look.

'Do you have a sexual relationship with Miss Shaw Sir?' Grant's mouth fell open and his face began to burn. 'Is that why you were being blackmailed Sir Edward?' Bridle maintained his composure as Grant began to mutter and mumble. 'We will have to follow this line of enquiry very thoroughly Sir Edward, we will expose every detail, name every name unless of course you co-operate now.'

'I can't tell you about the blackmail… I can't… but it's not over Miranda I swear.'

Grant slumped in his seat again and Lodge thought for a moment he was about to pass out, then he sat up quickly and pulled himself together.

'I have to ask for your total discretion. I admit I do have a relationship with Miranda Shaw but the blackmail is not related to that relationship I give you my word Sergeant. I can't have this made public it would destroy my reputation.'

'Not to mention your family Sir.' Grant looked cut by Bridle's sarcasm but Bridle knew a man like Grant showed no mercy in business and Bridle wasn't about to show any now 'I'm afraid I can't guarantee discretion Sir Edward, I will have to submit my findings to my superiors and… '

'Alright… alright – just give me a moment' Grant stood up and walked over to the drinks cabinet. His shoulders were stooped and he held the back of his hand to his mouth. Lodge looked at Bridle and drew his finger across his throat and winked. Grant opened the cabinet and selected a decanter of malt whiskey. As Grant poured the dark malt into the crystal tumbler Lodge watched every drop fall and couldn't resist licking his lips. Grant took a gulp and made his way slowly back to his seat then sat for a moment staring into his glass.

'First of all I have to make it clear about Miranda' Grant paused and took another heavy gulp of the malt 'we have a professional relationship.'

'Does that mean you pay her Sir Edward?' Grant threw Bridle a hard look but realised he had no grounds to protest.

'I maintain her – in the sense that I... '

'In the sense that you pay for her services Sir' Bridle knew he was getting under Grant's skin and Lodge had to bite his lip.

'I pay for her apartment and I give her a small allowance' Grant couldn't hide his disgust.

'You are aware that she is a professional escort Sir.'

'Of course I am aware of that what do you take me for?' Bridle and Lodge exchanged another glance and Grant's face turned dark.

'Don't mock me with knowing looks. I know what I am. Like most stupid old men I thought I was fascinating to women. I thought I was in control, but I became obsessed with her and she knew it. David manipulated the relationship-it gave him control over me. He was very shrewd, ruthless.'

'Sir Edward I have to warn you everything you say is being taken down... '

'Yes yes Sergeant I don't intend to incriminate myself' Grant sneered.

'I need to know why you were being blackmailed Sir Edward.'

Grant began to laugh quietly then drained his glass, slammed it onto the desk and pointed at the painting behind him.

'You see old Mathew Grant up there gentlemen? None of us are fit to wipe his shoes. A man of industry and commerce he actually believed in slavery. He believed he was helping the African, see how we all delude ourselves to satisfy our desires.' Grant began to laugh again and Bridle looked over at Lodge who was tapping the side of his head to indicate Grant was beginning to crack.

'If the blackmail wasn't over your adultery what was it Sir Edward?' Grant looked up at Bridle from his slumped position in the chair then sat up slowly.

'Adultery you call it?'

'The law calls it adultery Sir.'

'The law, oh yes of course, where everything is black and white.'

'I'm not concerned with your private life Sir.'

'Not unless you can use it to threaten me Sergeant.'

'Sir Edward, do you sleep with your wife?' Lodge could see the look on Bridle's face and knew he was serious.

'What kind of question is that?' Grant had an incredulous look on his face.

'Just answer the question Sir.'

'It's none of your damn… '

'On the night of your son's murder where did you sleep?' Grant's face was frozen into a grim mask but Bridle persisted 'Detective Constable Lodge make a note to enquire with Lady Margaret Grant… '

'I… my wife… has problems sleeping… I was in the spare room that night.'

'That affects your alibi Sir, as I recall from your statement it is based on the fact you were at home with your family and retired to bed on or around ten thirty.'

'Yes that's correct.'

'By your own admission after ten thirty no one can vouch for you Sir Edward.'

'That's absurd.'

'Sir Edward I want to know why you were being blackmailed and unless you tell me now, I swear I will arrest you under suspicion of murder.'

'You are mad.'

'No Sir I am not, I want answers and if you don't cooperate I will arrest you. Your name will be all over the papers again and details of your private life will be accidentally leaked to the press I promise you.' Bridle's eyes burned into Grant.

'So you are a bastard Sergeant Bridle.'

'The blackmail Sir Edward, I need to know' Bridle and Lodge glanced at each other as Grant stared into his empty glass for a moment then clasped his hands and took a deep breath.

'Guy Charlton and David were not exporting tobacco, not for long anyway' Grant paused 'I didn't know about it until the blackmailer made contact with me, I was a fool.'

'What were they exporting Sir?'

'They were trading in weaponry, illegally' Grant looked down at his desk 'rifles, small arms, ammunition and explosives' Grant shrugged and Lodge whistled through his teeth.

'Who were their customers?' Bridle asked glaring at Lodge.

'Any theatre of war Sergeant' Grant laughed 'isn't there a conflict in Spain at the moment?'

'The government has banned the supply of weapons to Spain' Bridle said naively.

'Yes of course Sergeant' Grant laughed again.

'Which faction did they supply?' Bridle asked ignoring his sarcasm.

'All of them Sergeant, fascists, communists, discounts for cash' Grant laughed at his feeble joke then made his way to the drinks cabinet and refilled his tumbler.

'I assume you stopped the trade when the blackmailer approached you.'

'Of course I stopped it. I won't have spivs destroying the reputation of this shipping line even if one of the spivs is my son.'

'Is there any evidence of this trade?' Bridle asked already knowing the answer.

'Evidence is your business Sergeant.' Grant took a heavy gulp of whiskey and made his way back to the desk and Bridle stood up slowly.

'Excuse us for a moment Sir Edward.' Bridle nodded to Lodge who slapped his notebook shut and followed Bridle into the noisy corridor.

'I could smell that malt from where I was sittin' Lodge said with a grin and Bridle shook his head.

'What do you make of that lot?' Bridle leaned against the wall with his hands in his pockets.

'Shower o' bastards' Lodge said.

'Yeah but apart from that' Bridle said in the hope of a useful comment from Lodge.

'I liked that bullshit about the cigars, very clever, have you been readin' Agatha Christie?'

'I made that up' Bridle said.

'Yeah and I've got tits like Mae West' Lodge responded with contempt 'he fell for it easy enough though.'

'Come on Tom how long have you been a Jack?' Bridle stared

hard at Lodge 'what did you call him after the first interview?' Lodge looked at the floor partly to think and partly to avoid Bridle's condemning stare.

'A thoroughbred bastard wasn't it?' Lodge squirmed with the effort of thinking.

'Yeah and thoroughbred bastards don't crumble that easy.'

'He's up to something then' Lodge had a gormless look on his face.

'Tommy I haven't seen a face like that since the last George Formby picture' Bridle started to laugh but stifled it when the door to the outer office opened and Mrs. Danby strode down the corridor carrying a box file. Her lips were pursed tightly and her gaze was fixed on Grant's office door. As she approached they pressed their backs to the wall and she glared at Lodge as she passed by. Lodge was tempted but thought better of winking at her again. She closed the door to Grant's office with a thud.

'Is it me or is it snowin' in here?' Lodge said pretending to shiver.

'He seemed keen to drop Charlton in the dirt all of a sudden' Bridle said.

'Yeah but we can't nail Charlton without evidence can we boss?' Lodge gave Bridle a look but Bridle ignored it. 'Why did he mention David Grant's parties?' Bridle pondered.

'Yeah the orgies, those bastards know how to live eh boss?'

'He knows the press would have a field-day if that one got out' Bridle was puzzled.

'Maybe Grant wants that. If it's all made public there'd be someone else dragged through the mud for a change' Lodge said with a sly grin.

'I can't see that' Bridle said shaking his head 'anyway you take a full statement from Sir Edward and I'll get George Sullivan to contact Customs and Excise about the gun-running. Then meet me at the bridewell I want to question Billy Doyle.'

'I thought you'd go straight for Guy Charlton' Lodge said with a grin and a wink. Bridle looked at him sideways then turned and made his way down the corridor.

CHAPTER SIXTEEN

Lady Marian Carver had tolerated a frosty atmosphere at breakfast. She knew when her husband was troubled but she hadn't seen him so agitated since Stella defied him and married the policeman. The presence of Stella usually lifted his spirits but he had thrown cold looks in her direction over the breakfast table. Stella in turn had been cold and aloof and Lady Marian had invited Elizabeth and Caroline to lunch in an attempt to lighten the mood. Mrs. Marsden the housekeeper had put together a nice selection of sandwiches and some of Sir Nigel's favourite sweet-cakes. The picnic table was laid on the lawn under the shade of the weeping willow. Stella, Caroline and Elizabeth were all seated and chatting about the latest films to come out of America as Lady Marian approached and took her seat in the shade.

'We were just talking about Clark Gable and Laurence Olivier mama, aren't they just dreamy?'

Elizabeth gushed as her mother sat down.

'I don't recall your English tutor teaching you words such as 'dreamy' Elizabeth.'

'No mama but Laurence Olivier is such an idol and Edith Cummings told me she bumped into him coming out of a tea shop in London and he was so gracious she just swooned.'

'Swooned' Lady Marian looked incredulously at her daughter then looked to Caroline and Stella for some sensible conversation but they were giggling into their napkins.

'Elizabeth you are such a giddy girl you make my head spin.'

'Shall I pour mama?' Caroline said as she threw a chastising look in Elizabeth's direction.

'Thank you dear – have you seen your father?'

'He was in his study practising a passage from Great Expectations rehearsing for his big night' Caroline said as she poured tea into her mother's cup.

'Yes the big night' Lady Marian said with a smile and cast a furtive glance at Stella.

'Is that enough tea mama? I think it's just the way you like it, sugar?' Caroline held the sugar bowl toward her mother and Lady Marian shook her head. She had never taken sugar but Caroline always offered it as a matter of protocol. There was an attention seeking side to Caroline that had begun in her childhood and had progressively irritated Lady Marian as her daughter matured.

'Have you heard from… John?' Lady Marian turned to Stella.

'I haven't spoken to him since the ball mummy' Stella said and Lady Marian winced, she preferred to be called mama but Stella knew that.

'What a fool he made of himself mama, of all of us. Poor Estella I felt for you' Caroline said in her usual stinging manner and Stella felt every muscle in her body go tense.

'He had been out all night on a case' Stella said quickly 'he'd had very little sleep and… '

'Oh he was obviously drunk, everyone said so. You are far too loyal Estella and he doesn't deserve it' Caroline said with a dismissive wave of her hand and Stella felt consumed by frustrated anger.

'He has to work very hard Caroline, sometimes he has only a couple of hours sleep between shifts if he has to be in court next day' Stella's defence sounded desperate to her family.

'That's the life he chose' Caroline replied knowing she had the full agreement of everyone at the table.

Sir Nigel Carver strode across the lawn at a good pace. He was dressed in casual slacks, a white shirt and a sleeveless cricket pullover and had a copy of The Times under his arm. He chose to sit opposite Stella and looked fleetingly at her as he sat down. The look was noted by Lady Marian who glanced from one to the other with pursed lips. Carver dropped the newspaper under his chair and rubbed his hands with mock delight at the table before him.

'Ah yes Mrs Marsden has done me proud with my favourite cakes.'

'A sandwich first I think Nigel' Lady Marian said holding a plate toward her husband.

'Yes of course Marian as you say.' Carver took a sandwich and placed it on the small plate in front of him.

'We were talking about Clark Gable daddy' Elizabeth said with a smile.

'Really' Carver said with a blank look 'do I know him?' Elizabeth giggled uncontrollably and Carver frowned and looked at Stella. 'Have you made any decision about your future Estella?' He asked brushing an imaginary speck from the knee of his trousers and ignoring the glare from his wife.

'I'm not sure' Stella said knowing that this was only an opening shot.

'Not sure, that's strange I feel certain you have paid him a visit recently' Carver forced a smile and took a sip of tea.

'I called to the house for some of my things' Stella folded her arms and waited for his next move.

'Really is that all?' Carver picked up his sandwich and looked at it suspiciously. Stella looked him in the eye but he turned his head away. Caroline and Elizabeth looked uncomfortable and Lady Marian fidgeted in her chair until she finally snapped.

'What is going on Nigel?' 'You two have been circling each other all morning, I want an explanation.'

'Ask Estella, she started it' Carver said childishly and Lady Marian turned to her daughter for a sensible response but Stella turned her head away and looked across the garden. Lady Marian's shoulders dropped and she heaved a sigh of frustration.

'Estella you were always wilful and you would always ride roughshod over me, I know that's my fault, my weakness. I should have used a firm hand, guided you into a suitable marriage, I've failed you in every way.'

'Oh for goodness sake mother what are you talking about? This is the twentieth century we've had a war that slaughtered thousands of people. We are in an economic depression and people are homeless and starving on city streets. This is the modern world and John and I have tried to make our way in it. You didn't fail me mother you were too busy being a cool, statuesque beauty on daddy's arm. I make all of my own choices and I always will.'

'You see Nigel she always treats me like a fool, it doesn't happen with Caroline or Elizabeth' Lady Marian's voice cracked with emotion which irritated Carver. He reached over the table and snatched his favourite cake from the tray and dropped it onto his plate with a petulant look in Stella's direction.

'Stella saw fit to remove a document from my study and place it into the hands of the authorities, namely her husband' Carver said and took a sharp bite out of his cake.

'Is this true Estella?' Lady Marian was shocked.

'Yes mummy' Stella replied 'the file held information

relevant to the Grant murder and you were holding it daddy.' Caroline and Elizabeth sat up and paid attention as they were both jealous of Stella's spirit and they knew how tough she could be when she was crossed.

'You are not in a position to judge my girl' Carver pushed his head back and spoke down his nose which infuriated Stella.

'Don't patronise me – you are supposed to be a man of the law' Stella's eyes flashed as she spoke and her sisters turned to see their father's reaction.

'It holds some very sensitive information' Carver retorted.

'It exposes David Grant as a sleazy rat and shows that just about anyone in his circle had a motive to kill him or to see him dead.' Stella folded her arms and sat back with a furious look on her face. Carver smiled at the sight of Stella's angry frown and began to laugh in a tactical move to make her angrier.

'Such indignation Estella, perhaps you see Guy in a different light since you read the file is that why you are so upset?' Carver chuckled again but Stella remained cool.

'I am upset because I look up to you – who were you trying to protect daddy?'

Lady Marian stared incredulously at the table but Caroline and Elizabeth swung their heads from one to the other in avid concentration.

'I did advise Edward to go to the police but it's complicated and the police are so inept. In my experience if a case isn't cut and dried they bungle it. I built my legal reputation on the idiocy of the police force' Carver knew that would get to Stella and he sat back and waited for a reaction.

'I won't rise to the bait daddy you had no right to withhold that file.'

Carver let out a long sigh and then smiled at his daughter.

He knew this was why he loved and missed her so much and why he felt she had wasted herself on Bridle.

'We did intend it to fall into police hands after some prudent editing but that opportunity is gone now.'

'Who do you think you are daddy the judge and the jury? You have no right to edit the file.'

'I was in a very difficult position with Edward and it is now almost impossible.'

'Perhaps you should get away for a while till it all blows over. David Grant had a quiet little hideaway in the Cheshire countryside, lots of his friends went there to relax. You might know it daddy?'

Stella stared firmly into her father's eyes but he avoided her gaze. She noticed him freeze for a moment before he took a slow bite of his sweet-cake. They sat back in an unspoken truce and everyone at the table seemed to deflate, except Carver. He surveyed his garden as if deep in thought and savoured his cake with relish then turned slowly and smiled at his wife.

Bridle had caught the tram at the Pier Head and it made its steady way up James Street to its first stop on Derby Square. As a few passengers clambered aboard Bridle watched a group of Union men standing on the steps of the Victoria monument calling for solidarity and support for the unemployed rally on Saturday. They were a mixed age group but all were passionate and driven and they had drawn a good crowd on the square. Bridle counted up to twenty four bystanders as the tram started to pull away and he caught a glimpse of an older man walking through the crowd handing out flyers.

He recognised Jack Finney immediately and Bridle turned to look as the tram moved away. Finney had aged a lot since their last encounter. Bridle cast his mind back to the events in the town hall many years before. He remembered how naive he was and how his baptism of fire in that riot almost made him change his job but Finney's words had influenced his decision. Finney was that kind of man, Bridle mused, charismatic and inspirational and after all those years he was still trying.

As the tram made its way up Hardman Street Bridle could see the queue for the labour exchange stretching down the hill. A long line of sullen men stared ahead and hoped for some movement in the line. Most of the men were general labourers dressed in dirty working clothes but there were a number of well groomed men looking for clerical work. Bridle knew that Finney was generating support for his unemployment rally at the weekend. He also knew that Mcleish was in charge of police supervision for the rally. Those two opposing each other again Bridle pondered.

When Bridle entered the office Inspector Radford and Detective Sergeant Morgan were standing by the notice board drinking mugs of tea. Radford cast a glance in his direction then turned his attention back to his conversation. Radford and Morgan burst into a loud laugh and Morgan glanced over at Bridle as he made his way to his desk where George Sullivan was typing.

'Sergeant Bridle you need to look at this' Radford pointed at the board as he shouted across the room. Bridle hesitated then walked across to the notice board.

'Superintendent Webster wants you to look at this Bridle' Radford pointed to the two photographs pinned to the board. 'He seems to think one of these gobshites was at your gunfight at the OK corral the other night' Morgan snorted a laugh and Radford smirked. Bridle sighed quietly and took a good look at the photographs. There was a short, typewritten biography pinned next to the photographs and Bridle took his time taking in the detail.

'Well' Radford said.

'Never seen them before… Sir' Bridle responded

'Can't believe you didn't get a look at the gunman' Morgan said and looked to Radford for approval. Bridle ignored Morgan and turned to Radford

'I've left a file in your pigeon-hole Sir, it's full of interesting information about David Grant you might find it useful.' Radford looked at Bridle with suspicion.

'Where did you get this information Bridle?' Radford asked.

'An informant Sir' Bridle said turning back to the photographs.

'A snout, do you know how much shit we've had from snouts trying to make a few quid from this case?' Radford clenched his teeth 'every little bastard on the street is touting information on David Grant.'

Bridle shrugged his shoulders 'I've duly notified you of the information Sir. The duty Sergeant has also made a note of it in the Day Book' Bridle said and turned slowly toward Radford who glared back at him. Morgan saw the look on Radford's face and backed away to his desk.

'Covering your back Bridle?'

'It's procedure… Sir.'

'Is it now?' Radford said and turned toward the open office 'Sergeant Bridle is trying to tell me about procedure' Radford laughed and his squad took their cue to laugh with him. 'Why don't I like you Sergeant Bridle?' Radford asked as he walked across the office.

'He doesn't fit in boss he's always out of step with the rest of us' Morgan said laughing and Radford nodded in agreement. 'Spot on Sergeant Morgan' Radford said and stopped in the middle of the floor.

'Go easy on him boss' Morgan said with grin 'I've heard some posh bloke is shaggin' his missus.' Radford and his squad laughed long and loud and Bridle tensed up with rage. His instinct was to grab Morgan by the throat but he knew if he did he would be finished. Bridle stared hard at Morgan but he refused to meet his gaze.

George Sullivan finished a call and replaced the telephone receiver in the cradle. He had been watching Bridle carefully and knew he was about to snap but hoped he wouldn't.

'Excuse me Inspector Radford' Sullivan's voice was strong and assertive and everyone in the room turned to look at him. 'That was Sergeant Campbell they've found a body in Kings Dock and it's been identified as Joey Vance.'

Bridle turned pale and stared at Sullivan in disbelief and Radford's face turned blood red.

'You and Lodge were supposed to be looking for that bastard' Radford screamed at Bridle from across the room 'you pair of useless tossers now we've lost a suspect and got another stiff. I had his card marked for killing his mother.' Radford threw a chair across the room then turned to Bridle. 'Get out of my sight Bridle, Morgan you come with me' Radford stormed from the office with Morgan in tow. Bridle sat down at his desk and put his head in his hands for a moment then sat back and let out a long sigh.

'One of these days George… ' Bridle said with a dark look on his face.

'You can't do anything and you know it' Sullivan said 'so keep a cool head or Radford will see you off.'

Bridle knew Sullivan was right and there was no way around it. He had to take whatever Radford threw at him.

'So Joey is dead – my mysterious caller was right' Sullivan said casting a concerned glance at Bridle 'was Joey your only way into this case?'

Bridle put his head back and looked at the nicotine stained ceiling for a moment then sat up straight and shook his head.

'I thought Joey was the key now I can't even see the lock.' Bridle laughed a little desperately and Sullivan gave him a grim look. Sullivan had seen desperate Jacks many times before and knew all the signs. Sullivan had always stepped back from being ambitious and had taken the deliberate move toward clerical efficiency as his strong point. He left the pressure to other people.

'Stay balanced or you'll make yourself ill, I've seen it all before' Sullivan said firmly with very little sympathy in his voice. Bridle nodded slowly and stood up.

'This case is getting to me George.'

'Then let it go' Sullivan replied.

'I can't' Bridle shook his head.

'Walk away and let Radford sink with it' Sullivan urged.

'And go back to nicking bookies and burglars. Is that what it's all about George?'

'I've read every report on this case, I've typed most of them for this brainless lot, it's not straightforward, too many names in the hat, too many motives. Radford will be looking for a sacrificial lamb and that could be you.'

'I know George I know but what can I do?'

'You could go back to Division and be a solid, ordinary Jack' Sullivan replied.

Bridle understood what Sullivan was telling him. There is

nothing wrong with being mediocre and ordinary and it's far safer. Bridle nodded and grinned at Sullivan.

'I know what you're saying George but I can't do it, I'm not walking away from this one.'

Jack Finney stood outside the tram driver's cafe at the Pier Head with a mug of hot tea and watched his men sort-out refreshments for a gang of hungry miners disembarking from a battered charabanc. It was the kind of atmosphere that Finney had hoped for. The loud camaraderie was infectious and Finney was excited about the success of the rally even though the organising process had strained him to the limit.

'It's looking good Jack' Harry Croft said as he pushed his way through the miners without spilling a drop of his tea.

'Yeah it's a great atmosphere Harry. This rally will be a landmark for us' Finney grinned and raised his mug.

'It's all down to you' Croft said.

'Don't tempt fate it's not done yet. It's got to be a peaceful march Harry I don't want any cock-ups. It's the subversive elements that worry me.'

'Leave them to me and Riley that's our job' Croft said and slapped his shoulder 'we'll keep it all under control.'

The miners were in high spirits as they passed plates of bacon sandwiches down the line. Each time a tram passed by the driver would crank the bell in loud support and the miners would shout back and punch the air.

'Look at that Jack solid as a rock' Croft said giving the driver a thumbs-up sign.

Finney didn't reply as his attention was focussed on a Black Maria that had just crossed the Strand out of James Street and was passing slowly under the overhead railway and moving in their direction. Croft saw the look on his face and turned to see the police wagon swing around just behind the charabanc. Mcleish's dark eyes stared out from under the razor sharp peak of his cap as he leaned through the passenger window. He looked over the scene with his face as grim as a death mask then turned back to Finney and Croft. Both men stared at Mcleish with undisguised venom. Croft had developed a hatred for Mcleish that could only be satisfied by violence.

'Councillor Finney I advise you to get this vehicle moved' Mcleish said and nodded toward the charabanc 'it's causing obstruction.'

Croft started to move forward but Finney caught his arm and pulled him back. Mcleish cracked his hard face with a grin.

'I hope to see you at the rally tomorrow' Mcleish called out as the Black Maria slowly pulled away.

'You can rely on it' Croft said quietly.

CHAPTER SEVENTEEN

Bridle nodded to the officer on duty as he stepped through the gate of the bridewell and strode across the courtyard to the cell block. The corridor had that familiar smell of vomit and urine from the drunk's tank at the far end of the block and Bridle gave thanks that he didn't have to deal with the Saturday night asylum anymore. As Bridle strolled along the corridor holding his breath to avoid the smell he could hear Lodge arguing with the Duty Sergeant over football.

'Sergeant Bridle, how do ye cope with this mad Evertonian for an entire shift?' Sergeant Reith's gruff Scottish accent barked down the corridor. Bridle was amused by the banter but he wasn't in the mood to laugh. He had cadged a lift across town in a police van on its way to the magistrate's court and had tried to read the report of Billy Doyle's interview but couldn't concentrate. The implications of Joey Vance's death felt like another nail in Bridle's well nailed coffin.

'Hello Gordon' Bridle nodded to Sergeant Reith 'how is our mate Billy Doyle today?'

'Poor lad is feeling sorry himself' Reith replied.

'I'm sure you're full of sympathy Gordon' Bridle said and Reith smirked.

'I got the statement from Sir Edward boss. He didn't like it one bit' Lodge said noting Bridle's grey pallor and sullen look. Bridle nodded.

'Can we see Doyle now Gordon?' Bridle asked and Sergeant Reith picked a heavy bunch of keys from his desk and led the way along the corridor.

'How can you stand this stench all day?' Lodge asked screwing his face up.

'A man gets used to it laddie.'

Their voices and the rattling keys echoed down the stone corridor. As they passed an occupied cell something hit the door from the inside and powerful voice boomed out.

'All you Jacks are bastards.'

'Who's that?' Lodge asked pointing with his thumb.

'The Chief Constable' Reith said over his shoulder. Lodge burst into a wheezy laugh and even Bridle managed a grin.

Reith led them down a flight of stone steps and along another corridor then stopped and unlocked a heavy door. Billy Doyle was sitting on a wooden chair and leaning on a table with his head in his hands. The walls were bare white tiles and the light came through a grated window glazed with thick glass. The interview cell was restricted so Reith nodded and left the room. Lodge sat on a chair opposite Doyle but Bridle sat on the edge of the table. Doyle looked up at Bridle. His eyes were dark and haunted and his reptilian face was gaunt and drawn. Bridle found it difficult to even recognise the man. Doyle dropped his head and looked at the table.

'You don't look well Billy' Bridle said

'Fuck off' Doyle replied without looking up.

'Give him a cigarette Tommy'. Bridle said.

'You won't buy me with a fuckin' ciggy' Doyle folded his arms tightly and Bridle shrugged his shoulders. 'I didn't say I didn't want a ciggy... I just said ... ' Doyle's head trembled as he spoke.

'I know what you said Billy I'm not deaf' Bridle said.

'I just said you won't buy me… ' Doyle hesitated and Bridle butted in.

'With a fuckin ciggy… that's what you said… isn't that what he said Tommy?'

'I think that's what he said boss… so do yer want a ciggy or not Billy?'

'Fuck off' Doyle began to rock backward and forward slowly.

'Give him a cigarette Tommy' Bridle said.

'You won't… ' Doyle paused.

'Won't what Billy?' Bridle asked forcefully.

'You won't buy… '

'Buy what Billy?' Bridle moved away from the table and closer to Doyle.

'Me with a… ' Doyle began to shake violently.

'We won't buy you with a fuckin' ciggy' Bridle shouted into Doyle's face and he recoiled then dropped his head 'it's like listening to a record with the needle stuck.'

Bridle caught hold of Doyle's arms and hauled him to his feet then he spun him around and pushed his face against the cracked mirror. Bridle held Doyle firmly as his whole body trembled and tears began to flow from his swollen eyes.

'You see that face in the mirror? Can you see that screwed-up whingeing face in the mirror? Who is it? Tell me.'

Bridle screamed at Doyle and he tried to say his name but he choked on his tears.

'It's Billy Doyle' Bridle shouted into his ear 'big foreman on the dock. Look at yourself man you've cracked like that mirror you worthless gutter rat. What would all your dock men say now eh Billy? All those men who have to crawl to you for work, day after day, look at you now, open your eyes' Bridle shook Doyle until he opened his eyes and stared at his own tear streaked face in the mirror.

'Look at that face Billy, is that the face of a man?' Bridle whispered menacingly 'no it's the face of a spineless shit and that's all you are.'

Doyle tried to speak but all he could do was tremble. Bridle slipped his hand around Doyle's throat and his eyes bulged with fear.

'Can you feel how tight that is around your throat Billy?' Bridle squeezed until Doyle began to choke. 'That's like the rope that Radford is slipping over your head. You will swing and writhe and choke and die for a murder you didn't commit. Is that what you want?' Bridle looked into Doyle's cracked reflection in the mirror. 'See how that crack in the mirror twists your face up? That's you Billy, cracked, twisted and broken.'

Bridle threw Doyle across the cell and he hit the wall and slid to the floor. He lay face down and wept like a baby. Bridle left him for a moment then pulled him up and made him sit up straight with his back against the wall. Bridle took a handkerchief from his own pocket and wiped the tears from Doyle's face until it was dry then dropped it onto Doyle's lap. All three men remained silent for a moment then Bridle leaned back against the wall.

'Give him a cigarette Tommy' Bridle said.

'Do you want a ciggy Billy?' Lodge asked and Doyle hesitated for a moment.

'Yeah – I'd like a ciggy – please.' Doyle tried to nod as he answered but his neck went into a nervous spasm and he had to hold his head in both hands to stop the tremble. Lodge took out a cigarette and lit it then handed it over to Doyle who took it hungrily and sucked the smoke deep into his lungs.

'You wanted to see me before Radford collared you' Bridle said.

'Yeah, bit late now isn't it?' Doyle's face was bitter as he blew the smoke out.

'Billy you just can't take it' Bridle looked at Doyle with contempt.

'No I can't take it' Doyle shook his head and it went into spasm again.

'Radford will break you soon Billy, he'll make you confess to the murder' Bridle spoke softly and watched Doyle's reaction carefully.

'I didn't kill anyone I haven't got the guts' Doyle drew hard on his cigarette.

'I believe you Billy but I can't help you unless you help me' Bridle said and Doyle tried to laugh but broke into a cough.

'Maybe we should just walk away boss' Lodge said 'leave this bastard to rot.'

'Radford hates your guts Bridle' Doyle said quickly 'he wanted to set you up for that unlicensed fight on the dock. He wanted me to say you were riggin' the fights for big cash payouts.' Bridle and Lodge glanced at each other.

'Why didn't you?' Bridle asked.

'I hate Radford' Doyle said 'why should I help him?'

'Start helping yourself Billy' Bridle said softly 'give him another cigarette Tommy.'

Lodge gave Bridle a sharp look then grudgingly lit Doyle another cigarette.

'How did you get to know David Grant?' Bridle asked as Doyle blew out a plume of smoke.

'Did him a few favours.'

'What favours?' Bridle sensed that Doyle's confidence was returning.

'Stuff like the fight, Grant's crowd loved all that. I'd set up a cock-fight and he'd bring a few toffs along, pissed up usually, lay a few bets, you know how it goes'.

'What else?' Bridle stepped closer to Doyle 'what other favours did you do? Stow an unspecified cargo?' Bridle stood over Doyle 'I'll tell you what business you were in Billy, gun-running. You got cases of arms on board Grant Hollister ships for David Grant and Guy Charlton. I don't know what you made out of it but my guess is not much, not with two operators like them.'

'I never knew what was in the crates Mr. Bridle, honest to God' Doyle's face began to contort again.

'Are you lying to me Billy?' Bridle asked staring down at Doyle.

'No I'm not lyin' I swear to God Mr. Bridle' Doyle clasped his hands to hide the tremble.

'You didn't care what was in the crates. Stolen goods, guns, drugs, you just didn't care did you Billy? Did you?' Bridle screamed out his question and Doyle shook his head and pulled his knees in close to his chest.

'How much did they pay you?' Bridle asked in a whisper 'how much per shipment? Come on Billy' Bridle suddenly caught hold of Doyle's shirt and hauled him to his feet then he threw him onto the chair with contempt. Doyle sat and whimpered for a few moments.

'I got different amounts each time but it was never enough. I had to pay off the lads as well.'

'Is that why you blackmailed Sir Edward Grant?' Bridle stared hard into Doyle's frightened eyes but he showed genuine shock at the question.

'Blackmail, no Mr. Bridle not me, you can't stitch me with that one. I know nothin' about it I swear to God.'

'There he goes again boss swearin' to God – have you taken up religion or somethin' Billy?' Doyle squirmed at Lodge's mocking tone.

'I'll tell you what I think Billy' Bridle said and leaned back against the wall 'I think you got sick of being short-changed by Grant and Charlton. I think you argued with Grant on the night of the fight. I think you and your boys tried to intimidate Grant for more cash but it all went wrong. You killed him by accident then hung him up on a meat hook to make it look like some kind of gangland killing. Then you had the brilliant idea of blackmailing his dad over the arms shipments.'

'It's all shit' Doyle said shaking his head slowly.

'Is it Billy? Will you say that when you step onto the trap-door with a hood over your head?'

'That's not what happened' Doyle said staring at Bridle.

Bridle slipped his hands into his pockets and let out a bored sigh.

'So what happened? You've run out of options Billy.'

Doyle looked from Bridle to Lodge and back again then clasped his hands together tightly.

'I arranged to meet Grant after the fight at the gangway of the ship we'd loaded that day. We'd stowed loads of his merchandise in the hold. I saw him get out of the taxi full of himself he was, showin' off to his snooty friends. I kept in the shadows till he got closer. He gave me some cash, not much, I argued for more but he just laughed in me face.' Doyle paused and looked at Bridle.

'So what did you do?' Bridle said calmly.

'What could I do? He was bread and butter to me' Doyle said.

'Alright go on' Bridle wasn't convinced.

'He said he was seein' people later on the dock and he was expectin' some big money from them, said he'd see me straight. He told me to get three of my toughest lads and meet him by the dock bridge in half an hour, said his paymasters were dangerous men and he wanted some muscle to watch his back, then he just walked off, whistling like he was pissed or something.'

'What direction?' Bridle snapped.

'Toward the dock bridge, I went back to the warehouse to get some lads.'

'Did you see Joey Vance on the dock?' Bridle asked softly.

'I saw him leggin' it cos he nicked some cash from a bookie, someone will sort him out if he's not careful' Doyle took another long drag on his cigarette.

'Someone already has Billy' Bridle said quietly and Lodge threw him a worried look 'his body was found floating in the dock.' Lodge realised then why Bridle had looked so ashen when he arrived at the bridewell. Doyle stared at the wall with a strained look on his face.

'When we got back to the dock bridge we saw Joey sprinting fast with some bastard behind him.'

'Did you recognise the man?' Bridle cut in sharply.

'When he saw us he stopped in his tracks, glared at us then shot away fast. I'd say he was Spanish or Portuguese, vicious looking bastard.'

'What did you do?' Bridle asked.

'Nothing' Doyle shrugged 'we found Grant by the bridge arguing the toss with another Spaniard who took off when he saw us' Doyle chuckled 'Grant was glad to see us, he was scared stiff.' Doyle paused and his face went dark 'Grant didn't have our money, he said they cheated him but we didn't believe that. One of the lads lost his temper and winded Grant with a punch. He dropped faster than a tart's drawers. We left Grant on the dockside gruntin' like a pig but he was alive I swear it.' Doyle sank back exhausted. He drew on the stub of the cigarette until it was completely spent while Bridle turned over Doyle's story in his head.

'Did you and the boys kill him Billy?' Bridle asked casually.

'No we left him on the dockside I told yer Mr. Bridle.'

'I want the names of your boys' Bridle said flatly and Doyle sat up.

'I can't do that Mr. Bridle and you know it. If I spill it to you I'm a dead man.'

'It seems to me you're dead either way Billy. If you tell that fairy story in court you might as well pull the trap yourself' Bridle said with contempt.

'What about the Spaniards?' Doyle's eyes were pleading 'that's something isn't it?'

'It's not enough, let's get out of this stinking dump Tommy' Bridle turned away in disgust and his ploy worked as Doyle leapt from his chair in panic.

'I knew Grant was alive because when I looked back I saw a ship's officer helpin' him to his feet' the desperation in Doyle's voice made Bridle and Lodge exchange glances.

'So that's two men of foreign appearance and a ship's officer, anyone else Billy?' Lodge asked with a smirk 'a chinese cook or Marlene Dietrich on a night out?'

'Don't take the piss' Doyle said and hung his head again.

'Billy no ship's officer has come forward in the investigation, you're getting desperate and to be honest so am I' Bridle was exasperated.

'It was Grant Hollister' Doyle said quietly.

'What was Grant Hollister?' Bridle asked with a heavy sigh.

'The uniform on the officer, I know all the uniforms for all the lines' Doyle saw the glare on Lodge's face and dropped his head.

'Do you know how much extra work is involved in checking that information?' Lodge said stabbing his finger in Doyle's direction 'if this is a lie Billy I'll make you pay for it.'

Bridle turned away and hammered the door with his fist. He had to get out of the cell and out of Doyle's company as he was beginning to feel suffocated. Sergeant Reith opened the door and Bridle nodded to him as he stormed out. Bridle marched up the corridor with Lodge scurrying behind.

'Lost yer' rag there boss' Lodge said trying to keep pace with Bridle 'Doyle can't take it, he's panicking, shifting blame, you can't believe a word he says.' Bridle ignored Lodge's comments until they stepped out of the cell block and into the courtyard. Bridle stopped so abruptly that Lodge almost marched into his back.

'Joey Vance saw Grant talking to a foreigner, I suppose it could have been a Spaniard' Bridle said quietly 'but Joey didn't say anything about a ship's officer.'

'Because there was no ship's officer, Doyle is just stirring it up boss. Have I got time for a quick smoke?' Lodge cast a hopeful grin in Bridle's direction but got a glare in response.

'No, we're going for Guy Charlton, now.'

Riley had worked carefully in the back of the stolen morris for over an hour. He had positioned Finch's cronies Milo and Brady at each end of the wide alleyway were the car was parked, but every so often one of them would wander down to poke their face in for a look. Riley had removed the top cushion of the back seat and had placed dynamite and a crude timing device in the space under it. He had also packed loose steel nails around the device to maximise the damage of the explosion.

'Looks nasty that does feller.'

Milo's voice made Riley jump slightly. Riley turned around to see Milo's ball shaped head leaning into the car. His breath reeked but when Riley saw the cigarette in his fingers he leapt up and kicked Milo in the stomach which sent him stumbling backwards into the alley. Riley sprang forward and punched Milo hard in the face before he could recover his balance and he fell onto the cobbles with a grunt. Riley calmly stamped on the cigarette with the sole of his boot as Milo sat upright on the cobbles and rubbed his jaw. Brady came running down the alley and Riley instinctively turned and braced himself.

'What's goin' on Riley?' Brady shouted looking at Milo's condition.

'I said no cigarettes and this gorilla almost shoves one in my ear' Riley said through gritted teeth.

'Uhh I forgot' Milo mumbled and looked sulkily toward Riley.

'Is it finished yet?' Brady asked looking into the back of the car 'that looks like an alarm clock down there.'

'It is an alarm clock' Riley replied 'the last alarm clock you'll ever hear.'

'I don't like these bleedin' things Riley they make me nervous' Brady said stepping away.

'Don't worry' Riley said recovering his smile 'it's not connected up so no nasty bangs, yet' Riley laughed.

'How the hell does an alarm clock set off a bomb?' Brady was incredulous.

'Simple enough' Riley said as he pulled Milo up from the cobbles 'the clock is connected to a battery and to the caps that ignite the dynamite, the clapper hits the bell at the set time which completes the circuit to the cap which blows the sticks, and everything else, as high as the Angel Gabriel.'

'Riley you've got brains to throw away so yer have' Brady shook his head in admiration.

'I can't help agreein' with you there' Riley laughed 'now go and get the van while I put the seat back together.'

Riley's broad grin turned to a dark sneer as the two men made their way up the alley to the street. He climbed into the back of the Morris and made certain that the device was safe and secure then he carefully replaced the seat cover and fixed it with two heavy screws. The noisy diesel engine of the van growled down the alley and Riley walked up to meet Milo and Brady. Riley leaned in through the passenger window and winced slightly at the smell of body odour rising from the two men.

'Follow me up to the north-end and we'll head out along the East Lancashire Road. We'll stop at Carr Mill Dam and park on the north side of the lake, just like we did on the dry run remember?' Riley looked at their blank faces and wasn't hopeful.

'Course we remember' Brady sounded insulted 'we park-up on the north side and we wait till it gets dark then… '

'Yeah yeah you got it now pull up a bit so I can get the morris out of the alley' Riley turned quickly and walked down the alley, Brady shouted after him.

'We won't be stayin' too close behind yer though eh' they both laughed and Riley grinned and nodded. 'I got me fishin' rods in the back' Milo shouted 'we can try our luck in the lake while we're there.'

'Pair of bloody idiots' Riley whispered to himself as he climbed into the morris and eventually started the croaking engine. He pulled the choking car out of the alley and turned the vehicle north. The morris was in bad shape and Riley guessed by the chugging acceleration that there was a problem with the fuel line. He looked into his rear view mirror at the boys following behind and laughed. They couldn't even be trusted to steal a decent car.

Riley drove through the city at a steady pace and could see in his mirror that the boys wanted to go faster. He had no intention of drawing any attention to himself and kept his speed down. Riley took the car through Walton and began to accelerate as they moved further out of town onto the East Lancashire Road. The road was busy with heavy goods traffic running to and from Liverpool Docks. The road was a main corridor through to the industrial areas of Manchester and Lancashire and the diesel engines of the wagons were deafening as they growled past Riley's struggling vehicle.

Riley eventually turned left at Carr Mill and followed the road around the lake to the north side. He pulled the car into a wooded area on the edge of the lake close to the noise of the main road but hidden from the passing traffic. The van pulled in alongside the morris and Riley secured the hand-brake and left it in gear before he switched the engine off and climbed out. As Riley approached the van Milo cranked the window down and grinned at him.

'It's a bit noisy on this side Riley I won't be catchin' many fish here' Milo said with a grin. Riley nodded then took a swift look around the immediate area. The nearby industrial traffic was noisy and Riley had to shout to be heard.

'I think you're right Milo we should move, but your engine sounds a bit rough to me. Give it a few revs and I'll have a listen' Riley said and moved around to the front of the van. He nodded to Milo who pressed the accelerator. Riley turned his head slightly to listen until Milo lost patience and took his foot off the pedal.

'Once more' Riley shouted and a disgruntled Milo rammed his foot down on the pedal. At the same moment two heavy wagons roared past and Riley took advantage of the noise. He swiftly drew a revolver from the inside of his jacket and fired two shots in rapid succession. The windscreen shattered and the two men were thrown back against their seats as blood, bone and brain-matter splattered on the panel behind them. Riley deftly slipped the gun back into his jacket and walked around to the driver's side. He opened the door and looked at the carnage with a grin.

'You'll be feedin' fish today Milo not catching them.'

Riley gave a sly grin then leaned across Brady's twitching body and dropped the handbrake. Then he switched off the engine and slammed the door with contempt. He took a more careful look around then made his way to the back of the van which had begun to move slowly on the incline toward the lake. Riley placed both hands on the back doors, dropped his body weight and pushed hard. He broke into a run as he pushed because he knew the van needed momentum to get it as far into the lake as possible. Riley cursed as the forward motion took him into the shallows up to his knees but he laughed out loud as the van submerged with a gurgle and a flurry of bubbles. He shook the water from his trousers as he walked back to the morris and climbed into the driver's seat.

'If this motor doesn't start now I'll murder you boys' Riley said with a chuckle. The engine choked into life and he drove calmly around the lake and back to the main road. At the junction Riley turned right and took the vehicle and its contents back toward the city.

CHAPTER EIGHTEEN

Bridle and Lodge had sat in the back of the police car and listened to Constable Thomas and Constable Jones talking about rugby in their native Welsh all the way from the city to the outskirts of Chester. Bridle's thoughts wandered from Stella to worrying about the job. He guessed Radford would get him off the case now that Joey Vance was dead but he was finding it hard to care. The death of Joey Vance had shaken him more than he realised.

'I hope you two aren't talkin' about me in yer native lingo' Lodge said folding his arms.

'We can't talk about you in Welsh Lodgy' Constable Thomas said with a grin, 'Welsh being a beautiful language there's no word to describe a Jack' both uniformed men laughed out loud. Lodge cast a smirk at Bridle but could see from the look on his face that he wasn't in any mood for a joke.

'You two should be minding sheep on some freezin' hillside' Lodge said with a grin.

'Oh there's bitter for you' Thomas said nudging Jones with his elbow 'it's not our fault if the illustrious Watch Committee recognises the crime fighting talents of the Welshman against the drinkin' smokin' whorin' local applicants. Which begs the question, how the hell did you get in Lodgy?'

Lodge refused to take the bait as the two massive frames of the Welshmen rocked with mirth on the front seat. They laughed so hard that Thomas almost missed the left turn on the map he was reading. Jones swung the car left off the main road and down a country lane just about wide enough for a vehicle.

Bridle had tried to keep his personal feelings detached from the case but there was satisfaction in knowing that Guy Charlton was basically a crook. He was clever, well connected and successful but still a crook. Is that what Stella found so attractive about him? Bridle's thoughts were driving him mad. He questioned the wisdom of being on the case. Did it look like he was being vindictive? Would Stella even speak to him again? Lodge suddenly whistled through his teeth which pulled Bridle out of his mournful thoughts.

'You won't find one like that in Anfield' Lodge said waving his thumb out of the window. They looked across the field to a Georgian house which fleetingly appeared between the trees. Bridle immediately thought that this was the world that Stella should be living in and his stomach sank. Jones turned the car into the lane that led to the house then slowed to a stop as a group of estate workers approached them.

The workers looked suspiciously at the two uniformed officers in the front seat as Bridle pulled his window down and scanned the group. A tall, lean and distinguished man in his late forties stepped up to the car. He was wearing a clean, white shirt and a waistcoat and his shirt sleeves were rolled up because of the heat of the day. He wore light brown trousers and soft leather boots and he approached the car with an air of authority.

'This one must be in charge' Lodge said looking him up and down 'he's not covered in shit.'

'You see Bryn' Thomas said turning to Jones 'that's why Lodgy is a detective he has powers of observation denied to mortal men like you and me.'

Lodge smirked as the two uniformed men had their fun but Bridle threw them a dark look and they stopped laughing abruptly.

'Can I help you?' The tall man asked leaning toward the car window.

'We're looking for Guy Charlton' Bridle said 'is he at the house?'

'No Mr. Charlton is at the stables on the other side of the estate. If you take this lane and follow it around for about half a mile you can't miss the stable block on the right hand side. He's just sent us over here, he's got visitors.'

'Thanks' Bridle said and Jones reversed the car back and turned on to the lane. The car dropped into a dip then came up over a hill but had to swerve suddenly to avoid a car that was parked in a shallow lay-by with the rear end jutting out.

'Bit early for courting' Jones said recovering the vehicle. Bridle swung around in his seat and stared at the parked car as they passed.

'Look at that car Tommy' Bridle said gripping Lodge's arm.

'Isn't that… ' Lodge muttered.

'Stop here Jones' Bridle shouted and Jones slammed his foot on the brake pedal and they all lurched forward as it came to a halt.

'What's going on?' Constable Thomas shouted above the revving engine.

'We've seen that car before' Bridle said 'Thomas you stay here and watch that vehicle. Arrest anyone who tries to take it but be careful they could be armed, don't take any risks' Bridle's face was enough to make Thomas feel butterflies in his stomach.

'Yes Sergeant I won't take any risks if you don't mind see. I'm getting married to Gwladys in a fortnight and we've got family coming from Glamorgan… ' Bridle and Lodge looked at each other incredulously then Lodge leaned forward and shouted in Thomas's ear.

'Taff shut yer gob and get the hell out.'

Lodge scrambled out of the car and opened the driver's door. He pushed Jones aside to take over the driving then slammed the door and thrust the stick into gear. The tyres screeched as it sped off down the lane leaving a nervous Constable Thomas standing in the middle of the road.

'Don't worry about me boyos I'll just guard this vehicle, alone, against armed assailants.'

Lodge threw the vehicle around the lane so violently that Bridle was tossed from one side to the other. Constable Jones braced himself in the front seat and didn't like the look in Lodge's eyes. Lodge smirked at the terror on Constable Jones's face but Bridle just grinned. He knew it was pointless trying to reason with Tommy Lodge when he was enjoying himself. Lodge took the next bend so fast that he almost over-shot the entrance to the stables and cursed as he slammed on the brakes and swung the car through the gate. He brought the vehicle to a violent halt on the gravel of the stable courtyard and Bridle leapt out of the back almost before the vehicle stopped. He stood in the courtyard and looked around but there was no sign of anyone. Horses peeked over the top of their stable doors but they looked unruffled by the dramatic arrival. Lodge and Jones were bickering as they caught up with Bridle but he silenced them with a glower.

'Shut up and listen' Bridle snarled.

They could hear the rooks overhead and the odd clump of hoofs as the horses stirred restlessly. But then they heard a muffled sound from a stable at the top end of the courtyard.

Bridle started to run forward but almost immediately the stable door burst open and a man ran out and stood defiantly in the middle of the yard. He was mid-height, dark-haired and lean with olive tanned skin and he was holding a pistol at arm's length pointing at Bridle. Bridle stopped his run abruptly and Lodge and Jones almost ran into his back. They looked across the yard to the source of the choking sound and Jones let out a loud curse in Welsh. Guy Charlton was gasping on a rope slung around his neck and over a beam of the stable roof. The rope was held taut by another man and he had Charlton up on the balls of his feet with both his hands tied behind his back. It was obvious that Charlton had been knocked around by the blood on his face and his eyes were bulging with fear.

Jones started to move forward as he was in full uniform and rashly judged that they would accept his authority but Bridle caught his arm and kept him back

'Can you speak English?' Bridle asked and the gunman nodded 'we are all police officers. Drop your weapon and let him go, do you understand?' Bridle said slowly.

'Si I understand, you do not have to speak so slowly Senor. I am an educated man and I speak good English, in Espagna I was a teacher.'

'Must be a tough school' Lodge muttered but Bridle ignored him.

'You are policemen so you understand the meaning of justice?' The gunman asked.

'Yes after proof of guilt presented in a court of law' Bridle replied.

'We have judged this man today and we have found him guilty.'

'It doesn't work like that' Bridle said

'You hang murderers in this country Senor. This man is guilty of murder in my country.'

'What are we waiting for?' Constable Jones said 'let's take the scrawny bastards' but Bridle held his arm firmly.

'You are brave but very stupid. You see this revolver Senor? It is German, high quality, accurate and reliable. Not like the weapons that this man supplies. He trades inferior weapons, unreliable weapons. That is why this man is a murderer and a thief. He is guilty, why should we not hang him today?'

'If you hang him today you will be guilty of murder' Bridle said firmly.

'Men like him are pigs they prey on the misery of better men. In Espagna we are in civil war, we fight for freedom. Idealists come from all over the world to fight with us for glory but they come and go and we still have dead children on our streets. All my people need are the weapons to fight for themselves and this pig takes our gold for useless weapons. We are here for vengeance Senor and this man will die today.'

'It'll save you a job boss' Lodge whispered but backed off when he saw the look on Bridle's face.

'I guess you've already murdered David Grant so I suppose you've got nothing left to lose' Bridle said and the Spaniard laughed and shook his head.

'Policemen, always you have to solve the crime even looking down the barrel of a gun. I salute you Senor, you have courage, but look at this pig dancing on the rope he is very afraid, so scared to die.'

He nodded to his companion who pulled the rope tighter and Charlton gasped as he desperately fought to keep his weight off the rope by shifting on the tips of his toes. They watched Charlton in his macabre dance for a few moments then the

Spaniard nodded once more to the grinning hangman. They all knew this would be the end for Charlton but they could only watch helplessly.

'If you pull that rope you will never see Spain again' Bridle shouted and the Spaniards glanced at each other. Bridle steadied himself and prepared to lunge forward but the hangman suddenly released the rope and Charlton collapsed choking to the floor.

'He even snorts like a pig' the Spaniard said and pointed his gun at Jones 'you help the stinking pig.'

Jones walked over to Charlton and pulled the rope from his neck but never took his eyes from the gunman. Charlton writhed on the ground gasping for air as Jones untied his hands and he could see the rope had burned the skin from Charlton's neck and wrists. The two Spaniards stood in the centre of the courtyard and the hangman produced a cruel blade from a sheath strapped behind his back.

'We are not murderers Senor.'

'So what are you?' Bridle asked with some contempt.

'He took our gold for weapons and we came to take our gold back. Pigs will always make money from war, from misery. Look around Senor, this pig has privilege yet he takes money from peasants.'

'Did you kill David Grant for the same reason?' Bridle asked and the gunman cursed in Spanish then had a short and animated conversation with his partner.

'This pig and Grant made promises – all lies. They wanted more gold. Emilio was angry he beat Senor Grant a little but he did not kill him. We wanted our gold.'

'We were in the alley when you took a shot at Joey Vance' Bridle said quickly. The Spaniards spoke a few words together then shrugged and looked puzzled.

'Was that you who rolled over the car Senor?'

Bridle and Lodge cast an awkward glance at each other and Bridle nodded. The gunman turned to his partner and spoke fast in Spanish then they both laughed.

'Thank you for the entertainment Senor but we followed him to that alley.' The Spaniard pointed the gun at Charlton. 'We had already warned him – we wanted to put fear in him but someone else fired back at us – from the darkness – so we got out fast – unfortunately you were in the way Senor' Bridle looked at Lodge.

'So that was Charlton in the alley with Joey' Bridle said and Lodge shook his head.

'I need a pint of mild and a ciggy boss' Lodge said 'I'm gettin' a headache with all this.' The Spaniards started to back away and Bridle moved forward then hesitated.

'We can't just let you walk away from this' Bridle said.

'You cannot stop us Senor – if you try you will lose a kneecap – the choice is yours.'

'There's a constable guarding your car. You've got nowhere to go so drop the weapons.'

Bridle moved forward slowly as he was talking and the Spaniards spoke rapidly to each other as they backed away. They grew more agitated as they spoke and started to argue and gesticulate then the gunman suddenly pointed his revolver at Bridle's legs and he froze to the spot.

'Do not move Senor – my friend Emilio is angry – he wants me to hurt you. We would rather die at home in our civil war than rot in your prison – so we must try to go – we hope your constable will not be foolish.'

They backed away to the end of the stable block then sprinted across the field and through a copse which was a short-cut to the lane where they had left the car. Jones stood up red-faced and his powerful frame was tense with rage.

'Taff's on his own' he shouted at Bridle.

'He's not stupid' Bridle responded.

Jones glared at Bridle for a moment then threw off his helmet and charged out across the field toward the lane. Bridle turned and looked at Charlton sitting on the ground with his back propped against the wall then turned to Lodge.

'Get after them Tommy' Bridle said and Lodge ran to the car as fast as his bulk would allow muttering curses under his breath. He started the engine and revved it hard then powered it through the gate as Bridle turned toward Charlton with a grim look on his face.

Charlton was breathing through his mouth in short gasps. His right eye was swollen and closed over. His top lip was also cut and swollen and there was a slight trickle of blood from his nose. Bridle took a slow walk over to Charlton and stood over him. Charlton leaned his head back and to the right so that he could look at Bridle through his good eye. The two men seemed to consider each other for a moment then Charlton tried to smile but his lip was too swollen and it made him look grotesque.

'Thanks old boy just in the nick of time. Nice to see you sober.'

Charlton spoke in a rasping voice and Bridle just stared blankly at him. Bridle put out his hand and Charlton reached up and grasped it. Bridle pulled him to his feet and Charlton leaned back against the wall with a gasp. At that moment the crack of a pistol shot echoed across the field and Bridle glared at Charlton.

'If my men are injured I swear I will throw that rope back around your neck and string you up myself' Bridle said quietly and Charlton tried to pull his swollen lip into a defiant smile.

'Have you got the guts old chum?' His flippant response turned Bridle cold.

'Why did you meet Joey Vance that night in the rain?'

'Can't recall the name, the night or the rain – sorry' Charlton rasped.

'You told me you had no business with David Grant.'

'That's true, the man's dead you know.'

Charlton tried to laugh but just coughed. Bridle stared at Charlton with contempt and wished for a moment that they had turned up too late to stop him swinging.

'Is that stern look supposed to intimidate me?' Charlton asked and Bridle turned away in disgust to gather his thoughts. 'I'm beginning to see why Estella left you Sergeant – sheer boredom.'

Charlton coughed and laughed at the same time and Bridle felt a bolt of anger hit him in the chest like a punch. Bridle pivoted on his right foot and spun around. At the same time he brought up his right arm and hit Charlton with a powerful back-hander across his face which sent him sideways and onto his back. He lay gasping on the ground and Bridle stood over him trying to contain his fury. Bridle looked at his hands. They were shaking with rage and he loathed himself for losing control.

'Easy target old chum' Charlton rasped 'you will never be good enough for Estella and you know it.'

'Shut your mouth' Bridle shouted and had a powerful urge to hit him again.

'You've lost her old boy' Charlton began to chuckle and cough and Bridle clenched his fists until his fingernails dug into the palms of his hands. Charlton pulled himself up and sat with his back against the stable wall. Bridle glared at him.

'I think you were blackmailing Sir Edward Grant and you used Joey Vance as a go-between. I think Sir Edward suspected you that's why he told us about your arms dealing, he wanted to sort you out' Bridle spoke calmly to focus his mind away from hitting him again

'Sir Edward Grant' Charlton spat the name out 'what kind of man allows his own son to pimp for him for God's sake?' Charlton winced.

'He set you up Charlton and you'll pay for it' Bridle said.

'We had a legitimate business, prove otherwise if you can' Charlton sneered.

'Billy Doyle is stuck in a prison cell and his nerves have gone. He can't take it. He couldn't wait to talk to me and get it all off his chest' Bridle moved closer to Charlton.

'I need a Doctor' Charlton said coughing 'get me to a hospital.'

'I don't understand' Bridle said with contempt 'all this will be yours eventually so why all the dirty deals? You're no different from any other thieving buck that I meet every day, in the gutter where I come from' Bridle shook his head and Charlton smiled defiantly.

'It's just the game old boy' Charlton said affably 'do you gamble?' 'No of course you don't, perhaps a flutter on the National with the lads at the station. Did you ever take a risk in your predictable life? I feel ashamed for Estella' Charlton gasped and broke into a long cough. Bridle gritted his teeth to control his temper. He could feel Charlton turning the tables on him and he didn't like it.

'It's the game is it?' 'Well I've had enough of games Charlton.

I don't care what we have to nail you for, blackmail, gun-running, murder anything will do for me.'

'Murder, now where did that come from?' Charlton sneered.

'The Spaniard just confirmed you were in that alley with Joey Vance' Bridle said.

'What Spaniard?' Charlton said shrugging his shoulders.

'Joey Vance is dead – murdered, get my drift old boy?' Bridle leaned forward and glared in Charlton's face.

'Joey is dead?' Charlton repeated 'he was a harmless boy.'

'But he was just part of the game, your game, now he's dead. But the game is the thing, like you said.' Bridle turned and walked away just as he heard the sound of two vehicles speeding down the lane.

The Spaniard's car screeched through the gate first and Bridle could see Jones's grinning face at the wheel. Thomas's huge bulk filled the back seat with the defeated Spaniards crushed on either side of him and handcuffed to his thick wrists.

'Wales two – Spain nil' Jones said with a grin and Thomas's laugh boomed out from the back seat. Lodge followed and brought the police car to a halt on the courtyard and climbed out casually.

'There was a gunshot' Bridle said.

'There was indeed Sergeant' Thomas said 'he took a low shot at me as I went in for the tackle see, just missed my wedding present for Gwladys so to speak, but Bryn took the other feller down and we soon had it sorted out as you can observe' Bridle couldn't help grinning despite himself.

'We'll never hear the end of this one boss' Lodge said shaking his head.

'Give me a minute with Charlton' Bridle said and Lodge

nodded then wandered off toward the stables to roll a cigarette. Bridle strolled back to Charlton

'Are your parents at the house?' Bridle asked.

'I would prefer it if you didn't go up there' Charlton was emphatic.

'Why?' Bridle asked.

'Because that's the way I want it' Charlton said. Bridle began to laugh quietly and shook his head. 'What are you laughing at?' Charlton snapped.

'I'm laughing at you Guy' Bridle responded still laughing 'if you keep that attitude in prison you'll be spitting your teeth out in no time.'

'I see what you're trying to do Sergeant but you won't get to me' Charlton grinned 'I need to go to hospital I have been strangled.'

'Yeah so you keep saying.'

'They would have murdered me' Charlton stroked his throat 'I wonder if your constable would have a spare cigarette' Charlton said raising his voice in Lodge's direction and Bridle lost patience.

'Why were you in that alley? Why did you meet Joey Vance? Who else was there?'

'If you want any answers you'll have to arrest me old boy' Charlton sighed.

Bridle nodded, turned away and walked over to Lodge who was stroking a placid horse's nose at the stable door.

'I always wanted to ride a horse' Lodge said with a wistful look 'like cowboys on the flicks.'

Lodge looked at Bridle's pale and drawn face. 'It's gettin' late boss and we'll be stuck in the magistrate's court tomorrow with these bloody arrests. You've got nothing to stick on Charlton and you can't lock him up for shaggin' your missus.'

Bridle didn't respond and just stood with his hands in his pockets looking at the ground.

'I'll get Charlton in the car' Lodge said and threw the stub of his cigarette across the yard.

CHAPTER NINETEEN

The Greystone Village Theatre vibrated with the sound of laughter and applause as the evening performance reached its finale. Bridle stood in the foyer and read the elaborate poster for the production which was billed as a celebration of Charles Dickens and his works. He was in a dour mood but he cracked a thin smile when he saw Sir Nigel Carver KC billed as the foremost interpreter of Dickens work on the Wirral peninsular. The poster almost shouted: Sir Nigel will read from David Copperfield in the guise and manner of the odious Mr.Wackford Squeers of Dotheboys Hall with sketches performed by the local amateur dramatic society. Judging by the applause Bridle had to admit that Sir Nigel had gone down a storm.

As the applause faded the audience began to spill into the foyer and the first rush surged through to the street. Bridle worked his way into the auditorium against the flow of the crowd. He scanned the theatre from the rear of the auditorium as people made their way up the aisles. There was too much clamour so he stepped back and leaned casually against the wall and watched the crowd moving through. Bridle looked unkempt with a shadow of stubble on his chin and people eyed him suspiciously as they scurried past.

He was oblivious to the attention as he caught sight of Stella with her mother standing just below the stage chatting to a tall and distinguished man. A pang of jealousy coiled inside Bridle every time he saw Stella talking to a man but a closer observation eased his fears. The man was very tall with a thick mane of grey hair dramatically swept back across his head. He wore a maroon, velvet smoking jacket with a cravat and he gesticulated airily as he spoke.

'Oh I thought Nigel was inspired tonight Marian, just so completely inspired. He painted such a canvas' he waved his hand as if he was painting with an imaginary brush 'I've always said that the law robbed us of a great theatrical talent' he waved both hands skyward to end with a flourish.

'Oh I don't know Oliver' Lady Marian said 'I think Nigel made full use of his dramatic skills in court.'

'Yes yes of course he did my dear' Oliver said laughing but stopped suddenly and caught his breath as he saw Bridle standing at the top of the aisle in the dimmed light.

'Oh my goodness, tall, dark and brooding – surely this is my reward from heaven' Oliver clasped his hands in mock prayer.

'Oliver you are outrageous' Lady Marian said shaking her head with a thin smile that hardly disguised her annoyance at the appearance of her son in law. She looked at her daughter who was staring at Bridle with the kind of look that only another woman could understand. Lady Marian gave a resigned sigh and linked Oliver's arm in her own.

'We are joining your father for drinks backstage Estella. I suppose we shall be about an hour or so.'

'Thank you mummy' Stella said without taking her eyes from Bridle and Lady Marian led the reluctant Oliver away. Bridle moved slowly down the central aisle and held his breath as he approached Stella.

'You look fabulous' he said quietly.

'Thank you' Stella said as if she knew it already.

'Did the show go well?'

'Very' Stella looked at the floor to avoid his eyes. Bridle took another deep breath as the pause in the conversation was uncomfortable.

'I'm sorry about the ball Stella'

Bridle had considered small talk but that time had passed. It was all or nothing.

'Are you coming home?' He looked so deeply into her eyes that she had to turn away again.

'You haven't shaved' she said looking anywhere but at him 'are you eating? You seem a little thinner.'

'I eat enough' he said dismissing the question.

'You can't even toast bread without burning it' she said with a glare.

'Come home and toast my bread or I might die of starvation' he gave her a smile that always made her submit and she turned away quickly in case she did.

'Daddy was very good tonight' she said awkwardly.

'Stella I know you think I'm hitting the bottle again but I promised you seven years ago I would never give in to it.'

'That's not what it looked like.'

'I know, I know but I was very strung up about the ball and that brandy was so smooth I hardly felt it going down' he tried not to sound desperate.

'Daddy should have known better.'

'Stella you know I have to drink in my job. I have to drink with informants or they won't trust me. I have to have a beer with colleagues or they would never accept me. I was tired, I'd been up all night I'm sorry.'

Stella could see by his face that he was sorry but there was a part of her that had heard it all before and part of her wanted to forgive him.

'Was that file of any use to you?' She said making an awkward job of hiding her emotions. Bridle felt that a door had closed in his face and it reprised that sick feeling in his stomach.

'It was very useful thanks.'

'I stole it from my father's study. I felt like a foreign spy – it was very exciting. I thought it might lead you to the killer' she said raising her eyebrows dramatically.

'It might yet' he said and fought back the urge to tell her that her father had offered him the file if he was prepared to leave her.

'Stella I have to tell you we arrested Guy Charlton today' Bridle tensed as he waited for her response but she smiled in resignation.

'Guy was always going to be arrested for something someday' she said.

'I want you to know it was nothing personal' Bridle said.

'There was nothing between us. The old flame was well and truly out. You had nothing to fear.' She stepped forward and kissed his stubbly cheek 'now I'm going backstage to drink a toast to my father – thespian extraordinaire.'

Stella giggled and was about to say something else but her voice broke a little so she turned quickly and walked away. Bridle watched her fade into the shadow of the doorway.

'Goodbye Stella' Bridle said in a hoarse whisper then turned and made his slow way back up the aisle until he was swallowed by the darkness.

'Mcleish can kiss my fat arse' Tommy Lodge said when he read the standing orders for the unemployment rally on Saturday.

'What's up with you Tommy?' George Sullivan smirked as he knew exactly what Lodge was fuming about as he had typed Mcleish's orders himself.

'The devil's second cousin has stuck me on Lime Street Station tomorrow for the rally' Lodge cursed and threw the order sheet across the desk 'this is because I get mixed up in Bridle's cack-handed investigation. They've all got it in for me now especially Radford. A month ago my only worry was gettin' enough collars to fill up my court book. Now I've got the same disease as Bridle.'

'What disease is that Tom?' Sullivan asked not even trying to hide his amusement.

'Leprosy' Lodge snarled and leapt up from his chair. He considered slipping out of the office for a smoke but he caught Radford's eye and knew he had no chance. Radford started to walk toward him and Lodge cursed under his breath and turned to the notice-board and stared at it with intense concentration. Radford stepped up beside him with his hands in his pockets and an unconvinced look on his face.

'Solved it Tommy?' Radford said nodding toward the untidy chart of suspects and occurrences relating to the Grant case.

'Lookin' at stuff on the Joey Vance killing Sir, thought there might be a link with the Grant murder' Lodge cringed as he said it but it was all he could think up.

'A link' Radford said and whistled through his teeth 'hear that lads?' Radford shouted across the office 'Lodgy thinks there might be a link with Vance's murder.'

Lodge half-closed his eyes and tried to blot out the humiliation.

'Now isn't that unlikely Tommy as we've got Billy Doyle locked up for killing Grant. He couldn't kill Vance if he was locked up could he?' Radford sniggered through his nose.

'No Sir' Lodge said gritting his teeth.

'Lodgy I recall a conversation we had not long ago when you came onto this squad' Radford whispered as he looked over the notice board casually. Lodge's mind went blank for a moment as he pretended to scan the notice-board. His attention was suddenly caught by the photographs circulated by Special Branch. He almost said something but quickly changed his mind.

'I told you Tommy boy that the only reason I tolerated a burned out old duffer like you on this squad was to keep an eye on Bridle and report back to me.'

'There's a lot goin' on at the moment Sir. What with the Grant case and the Vance murders and now this stuff from Special Branch' Lodge knew he was babbling and was even confusing himself but he knew he couldn't bluff Radford for long.

'Didn't you agree to keep an eye on Bridle for me Tom?'

'Yeah – well – to be honest – Bridle's starting to disappear up his own crack Sir' Lodge said with a slight air of desperation.

'Good' Radford smiled.

'He's havin' trouble at home, his wife's playin' away and his in-laws hate his guts. In fact he's collared the bloke whose shaggin' his missus – brought him in for questioning.'

'He's done what?' Radford grimaced.

'It's in the report Sir, about Guy Charlton' Lodge said but almost immediately regretted it.

'Lodgy are you telling me that this Guy Charlton is the one knockin' off Bridle's wife?' 'That's priceless Tommy lad' Radford couldn't contain his delight and Lodge felt suddenly drained and closed his eyes as he considered how much he despised himself.

Radford slapped Lodge's back as he walked away and Lodge just stared blankly ahead. What could he do? The question went round and round in his head. Self-preservation was in his blood. He had a wife and family to support and he knew it was only a matter of time before Bridle's enemies nailed him. He had probably done Bridle a favour in the long run he reasoned. Thirty pieces of silver? Not even that much Lodge thought as he was overcome with an urge to punch the notice-board off the wall. He glared at the sepia photograph of the auxiliaries and wondered if any of those soldier boys ever had his problems. How many of those smiling faces had his level of hard luck, debts and misery. As he wallowed in self-pity a figure in the picture that he had noticed earlier caught Lodge's eye again and pulled his mind into focus. Lodge turned away from the notice board slowly as he knew it was important to contain his excitement. He leaned over the desk and smiled at Sullivan who thought for a moment that Lodge had become deranged.

'Have you cracked up at last Tommy?' Sullivan looked oddly at him and Lodge shook his head.

'Have you still got that magnifying glass in your desk George?' Lodge said a little sheepishly.

'The one you always take the piss out of Tommy?' Lodge nodded. 'You mean the one where you call me Sherlock Holmes every time I use it?' Lodge nodded again and Sullivan produced the glass from his desk drawer. 'Would yer like to borrow the deerstalker as well Tom?' Sullivan grinned and Lodge furtively motioned Sullivan to follow him over to the notice board. Sullivan took the hint as Lodge held the glass unsteadily to the photograph. He drew it in and out until the figure he was looking at was in sharp focus.

'What have yer found Tom?' Sullivan whispered.

'I think I've found redemption George.'

Bridle hadn't slept all night. At least he couldn't remember sleeping as his mind had wandered in and out of nowhere since he slumped into the armchair. He was still dressed and his unshaven face had much thicker stubble than the day before. His eyes were dark and sunken and his appearance on the street would probably get him arrested for vagrancy. The curtains were still drawn but a beam of sunlight streaked through a gap and threw a bright, fine line across the table in front of him. An unopened bottle of scotch stood in the centre of the table and Bridle pondered the way the sunlight changed the shade of the amber coloured whiskey. His arms were draped over the sides of the chair and his legs were splayed out in front of him. If his eyes had been closed he could easily have been mistaken for a corpse but his eyes were wide open and staring vaguely in the direction of the bottle.

Bridle made no reaction when Tommy Lodge stepped carefully into the room. Lodge looked from Bridle to the bottle and back again. He wasn't prepared for the sight in the chair which he could have understood it if the bottle was empty. Lodge picked up the bottle just to check that the top was secure then he slammed it hard on the table to shock Bridle into a reaction. Only Bridle's eyes moved as he glanced at Lodge and then resumed his stare from a dark space in his head.

'How long have you been in the chair?' Lodge asked but got no reaction 'the front door was wide open – anyone could have walked in.'

Lodge walked over to the window and pulled the curtains open sharply which made the room explode with light. Bridle screwed up his eyes and turned his head away as the light was like a slap in the face.

'So you are alive then' Lodge said and tipped his hat back on his head. Lodge picked up the scotch and lovingly caressed the curves of the bottle. Then he looked at the mess Bridle was in and sighed.

'Fancy a drink?'

There was no reaction from the chair. Lodge walked into the kitchen and left the door ajar so Bridle could see what he was doing. Lodge held up the bottle then turned his head slowly and looked at Bridle slumped in the chair. Bridle stared at Lodge helplessly but Lodge had seen the look before on a lot of men. Lodge let out a heavy sigh then in a swift movement struck the neck of the bottle on the edge of the sink. The neck came off cleanly.

'Oh look I broke it.'

Lodge held the bottle high as he poured the whiskey slowly down the drain. He licked his lips as he watched the last drop fall then placed the bottle on the draining board and strolled back into the room and stood looking down at Bridle.

'Is she worth this?' Lodge asked and Bridle turned his head aside.

'I said is she worth this?' Lodge raised his voice and Bridle ignored him. 'Call yourself a man Sergeant Bridle? Sat there like a lovesick teenager get up and get back to work.' Lodge stared hard at Bridle but got no reaction.

'She's just a piece of posh totty. God only knows who's shaggin' it now' Lodge bellowed. Bridle's face grew darker. He started to rub his hands on the arms of the chair as his anxiety intensified.

'You know nothing about her' Bridle whispered.

Lodge took a deep breath as he knew he had to go one step too far.

'She's probably over a table right now with some tennis playin' posh bloke bangin'…

Bridle launched himself from the chair and grasped Lodge's throat with both hands and slammed him into the wall. Bridle pushed his bodyweight into Lodge as he choked him and Lodge pulled desperately at Bridle's wrists as he could feel himself losing consciousness. Lodge raised his right knee and drove his heel down onto Bridle's instep. Bridle screamed in agony and released his grip enough for Lodge to throw a short head-butt into his face. Bridle let out a grunt and fell backwards onto the floor clasping his bloody nose.Lodge slid down the wall and sat holding his head in his hands trying to catch his breath. They recovered in silence. Bridle on his back looking at the ceiling and Lodge sitting with his back against the wall.

'You could have tried a bucket of cold water' Bridle said eventually.

'Next time it'll be the bucket without the fuckin' water' Lodge said so seriously that Bridle began to laugh.

'Thanks Tommy' Bridle said quietly and Lodge shrugged it off. Lodge despised any kind of emotional expression. It jarred on him because it was unmanly. Lodge dismissed Bridle's weak moment from his mind and his face lit up with a grin.

'I found something that might interest you boss' Lodge said thankful that the drama was over.

Bridle picked himself up and sat cross-legged then wiped the blood from his nose with his sleeve.

'Go on' Bridle said.

'Did you see those photos Special Branch posted up?'

'Yeah, Webster thought the Irish bloke might be our gunman – what about it?'

'That group picture of the auxiliaries – recognise anyone?' Lodge raised an eyebrow to punctuate his question which was a signal to Bridle that Lodge felt he had been very clever.

'No I didn't' pay it much attention' Bridle said.

'He's a lot younger but as you know I'm pretty good with faces' Lodge said grinning and Bridle just nodded as he knew Lodge would string it out for as long as possible.

'It's not dead obvious' Lodge looked expectantly at Bridle. 'No guess?'

'If I guess it right you'll sulk for a week' Bridle said.

'That's true enough boss. Alright then I'll tell yer, one of the young officers in the group is Sir Edward Grant, I'd put your last quid on it boss' Lodge looked pleased with himself. Bridle looked at the floor and pondered the implications.

'I don't know what the connection is boss but there's got to be one' Lodge said hoping Bridle would eventually switch himself back on. Bridle rubbed the stubble on his chin and had a vague impression of body odour.

'I need a wash and shave.'

'I'll wait in the car and smoke a roly' Lodge said pulling himself to his feet.

He made his way out to the promenade. The sun was high and the river was heavy with traffic as Lodge dug into his jacket pocket for his tobacco and cigarette papers. He deftly rolled a thin but essential cigarette and began to whistle as he made his way down the prom to the car. Lodge was happy that his world was back to normal.

The two pit-bulls growled savagely and pulled hard on their chains to tear into each other. Their handlers had to dig their heels in to prevent being dragged into the fight. Paddy Finch crossed his arms and grinned at the bestial display.

'Fine pair of killers' Finch said with satisfaction 'you've earned yer money training them.'

The tall Romany bowed his head slightly to acknowledge the compliment.

'Will they give us a good show in the ring?' Finch's eyes widened.

'Good as any fighting dog in the country' the Romany said 'bloodlust is in them.'

'I can see that by God' Finch replied.

'You promised me cash money' the Romany said abruptly and Finch broke into a powerful laugh.

'I always pay my debts' Finch said 'Mrs O'Grady here looks after all my transactions' he nodded toward an elderly white-haired woman smoking a pipe in the corner of the room. She was dressed in black and her appearance was clean and disciplined unlike many of the women around Finch.

'We'll do business again' Finch said and shook his hand.

Finch pulled a battered clay pipe from the pocket of his waistcoat and blew out the debris from the pot as he made his way out into the yard in front of the court. As he recharged the pipe with tobacco he took a good look around then beckoned a rough looking teenage buck who was idling at the corner of the court.

'Any sign of Milo and Brady?' Finch asked as he struck a match and put it to the bowl. The hard-faced buck looked Finch in the eye and slowly shook his head. Finch drew on the pipe as the tobacco started to burn then flicked the match away. He walked slowly down the court smoking his pipe but the teenager knew from experience that Finch wasn't finished with him yet. The smoke rose above Finch's head as if his thoughts were manifesting and blowing away on the wind. He turned on his heel and slowly walked back. His eyes were narrowed and the furrows were deep on his shaven head as he blew the smoke into the air.

'Go and find Tommy Lodge – tell him Finch wants a word.'

Bridle held the magnifying glass close to the photograph and ignored the sniggers he could hear from the detectives sitting at their desks behind him. George Sullivan was on the telephone and Tommy Lodge sat on the edge of the desk with an expectant look on his face. Bridle put the glass down and nodded discreetly at Lodge and Sullivan. Lodge was so pleased with himself that he started to whistle through his teeth. George Sullivan put the receiver back in its cradle and looked up at Bridle.

'Sir Edward Grant is in London on business. He's due into Lime Street this afternoon at four thirty.'

'Thanks George' Bridle said 'how did you get on with customs and excise?' The look on Sullivan's face was enough to give Bridle the answer.

'Radford blocked it, he also released Guy Charlton' Sullivan looked contrite but Bridle knew it had nothing to do with him. The door to Radford's office opened with a flourish and Detective Sergeant Morgan shuffled out with his usual air of appearing to be busy in order to prevent it.

'Sergeant Bridle, Inspector Radford would like a chat if you have the time' Morgan looked to his colleagues to respond to his hint of sarcasm but got no reaction. Bridle immediately walked across the room and into Radford's office. As Bridle entered the room he swung the door shut behind him. His timing was perfect as it caused Morgan to walk into the closed door with a grunt. Bridle could hear the muffled laughter in the office as he sat down opposite Radford.

'What are they laughing at?' Radford said looking over Bridle's shoulder.

'No idea Sir' Bridle lied.

'So what exactly have you and Lodge been doing Sergeant?'

'Investigating Sir'

'Are you being flippant with me Bridle?' Radford's narrow eyes narrowed even more.

'No Sir.'

'Because if you try and take the piss out of me I'll make sure your feet don't touch the ground lad.'

'Yes Sir'

'Don't say 'yes sir' like that to me' Radford's face began to burn.

'No Sir'

'You're doing it again Bridle' Radford seethed.

'Doing what Sir?'

'Being flippant, taking the piss.' Bridle ignored Radford's insecurity and looked him straight in the eye.

'I've submitted detailed reports on all of our investigations Sir and you chose to release Guy Charlton yet we know he's been involved in illegal exports. Gun-running' Bridle could see Radford's face was glowing.

'The man was assaulted on his own property by foreign vagrants. It's an open secret that Mr. Charlton has had an illicit relationship with your wife Sergeant Bridle. With your personal involvement it was inappropriate to detain him.'

'In your opinion Sir'

'Do you have evidence to back up your allegations against Charlton?' Radford thrust his face forward.

'Give me time to question those Spaniards, they dealt with Charlton and Grant, they may even have killed Grant' Bridle tried not to sound desperate.

'I've assigned Detective Sergeant Morgan to handle that' Radford smiled.

'What the hell does Morgan know about this case?' Bridle fought to subdue his rage.

'Who do you think you are Bridle? I am the senior officer on this case and you work under my direction is that clear Sergeant?' Radford's eyes were almost bursting out of his head and Bridle knew he had pushed too hard.

'Yes Sir'

'It's my intention to submit a report to my superiors and recommend your suspension Sergeant Bridle' Radford sat back with obvious satisfaction.

'Can I ask on what grounds Sir?'

'Abuse of police authority, personal feelings affecting your professional judgement, false arrest of Guy Charlton' Radford shrugged his shoulders and grinned.

'If you read my report Sir you'll find that Sir Edward Grant was fully aware of Guy Charlton and his son's criminal activities.'

'Sir Edward Grant has made a formal complaint against you and Lodge through his solicitor. He says you've been harassing him, putting him under undue strain and pressure at a sensitive time for himself and his family.' Bridle despised Radford when he was useless but he despised him more when he was winning.

'Detective Constable Lodge is a witness to Sir Edward Grant's admissions… '

'Tommy Lodge won't support you Bridle he knows which side his bread is buttered. Who do you think told me about Charlton and your missus?' Radford sniggered again and Bridle knew he had to leave the room quickly or throw a punch in Radford's direction.

'Is that all Sir?' Bridle said gritting his teeth.

'Isn't that enough Sergeant?' Radford grinned 'you're dismissed.'

Bridle left the room quickly and walked over to the notice board. He picked up the magnifying glass and scrutinised the image on the photograph. Sullivan and Lodge glanced at each other and knew that an approach wasn't advisable. Bridle walked up and down clicking his fingers then turned sharply and started to walk toward the door when Sullivan waved a file at him.

'I've got Sir Edward Grant's service record and that stuff you wanted on Guy Charlton.'

'Thanks George' Bridle said without turning or stopping and slammed the door as he left the room. Lodge turned to Sullivan and shook his head.

'I'm goin' downstairs for a ciggy' Lodge said.

Bridle tried to focus his mind as he made his way down flights of stone steps at a fast pace. He was oblivious to other officers on the stairs and earned a few curses as he crashed through them. He reached the basement and strode purposefully along the dimly lit corridor to a set of double doors at the end. Disregarding the sign that indicated a meeting in progress he burst through the doors and stood scowling at the cabal of officers sitting at a circular table in the middle of the room. The room became immediately silent as they turned and saw the tall and tough looking officer standing before them. Webster and Mcleish glared at him while the Special Branch officers exchanged puzzled looks.

'Sergeant Bridle did you see the sign on the door indicating a meeting in progress?' Mcleish said with a cold stare.

'Yes Sir I did.'

'Then I suggest you offer us a good reason for your intrusion or face the consequences.'

'I want to question this Special Branch officer from Scotland Yard on a matter of some urgency regarding the Grant murder.'

It was obvious to everyone at the table that Bridle was intense and agitated and had no intention of backing off. Webster and Mcleish exchanged anxious glances.

'Sergeant Bridle we are co-ordinating our plans for the workers rally tomorrow and we do not have time for this' Mcleish spoke firmly in the hope that Bridle would leave and prevent any further action.

'I have no objection Superintendent Mcleish' Allenby said genially 'the officer is obviously in earnest. What can I do for you Sergeant?'

'Sir, were you aware that one of the officers in that photograph is Sir Edward Grant?' Bridle stared intently at Allenby who let out a small sigh of resignation.

'Yes Sergeant I was aware of that' Allenby replied.

'But you didn't consider it important to point it out?' Bridle responded.

'I didn't conceal it either, although it is matter of security' Allenby said calmly.

'So you knew it was possible that David Grant was murdered by this Irishman you are looking for, as an act of revenge against Sir Edward?' Bridle stared hard at Allenby who responded with a patronising smile.

'It was possible but Sir Edward was aware of the revenge killings. We had warned him quite early on. He was a very experienced soldier, more than capable of protecting himself and his family.' Allenby clasped his hands across his chest and Webster and Mcleish looked at Bridle for a response.

'Billy Doyle is in custody for the murder Sergeant' Mcleish said.

'Yes Sir I know' Bridle responded.

'We know you don't agree with Inspector Radford' Webster said.

'No Sir I don't' Bridle replied.

'You don't like each other apparently' Webster said idly scratching his ear.

'It may appear that David Grant was killed in exactly the same way as these other men, but that isn't necessarily the case' Allenby said.

'You've led us to believe they are exactly the same' Bridle said containing his impatience.

'No Sergeant I said they were similar. My objective is Riley. I have no interest in your murder investigation' Allenby was inscrutable and both Mcleish and Webster cast a suspicious look at him.

'If Riley is killing for revenge why kill the son and not the father?' Bridle asked.

'I understand members of Riley's family were killed in that skirmish' Webster said 'perhaps it's a case of an eye for an eye.'

Allenby sat back in his chair and looked at Bridle with a slight grin cracking his narrow mouth.

'Perhaps' Allenby said.

'Enough is enough we'll take this further on Monday morning, you're dismissed Sergeant' Mcleish stared at Bridle as if he was challenging him to disobey but Bridle took a deep breath and nodded his head.

'Yes Sir'

Bridle turned and walked toward the door with a feeling that every eye in the room was burning into his back. His anger had subsided and he began to realise the enormity of his action. He was facing a request for suspension from Radford and he knew that this incident would add weight to Radford's argument. As he reached the door he almost began to laugh at his situation when a simple thought struck him and compelled him to stop and turn around. Mcleish glared in his direction but Bridle fixed his stare at Allenby.

'Sir, just to confirm, when you warned Sir Edward of the killings did you tell him the details?'

Allenby looked at Bridle with cool detachment.

'Details Sergeant' Allenby repeated.

'How the bodies were found and cause of death Sir' Bridle replied.

'As a matter of fact we did but Sir Edward was familiar with the method.'

Allenby finished his sentence with an enigmatic smile then turned away and spoke to Latimer. Bridle was about to ask another question but Mcleish's voice barked out.

'You are dismissed Sergeant.'

CHAPTER TWENTY

Lodge wandered down the street smoking his thin cigarette and pondered jumping on the next tram to anywhere. He stopped and leaned against a wall and let the world pass him by as he enjoyed his smoke. Lodge always convinced himself that he had a hard life and that's why he had to be the way he was. He had no interest in office politics and believed in backing the horse with the best form. Any moral decision that involved loyalty was to be avoided at all costs. Get the job done, get pissed and get home to the wife. That was all a man could ask for and Lodge did his best to aspire to it.

The dole queue across the road stretched its way out of the dole office and down the street. Lodge looked at the blank faces staring aimlessly toward the front of the queue. The occasional shuffle forward broke the monotony for them and gave them some hope.

'It's like a queue for a train with one-way tickets to hell.'

The deep, melancholic voice pulled Lodge together and he looked up at Sergeant Dean as he stared sadly toward the dole queue.

'Thanks for that observation Dixie. I was feelin' a bit brassed off now I think I'll just go and jump in the Mersey' Lodge whined and Sergeant Dean broke into a bass laugh.

'You wouldn't do that Lodgy' Dean said with a wide grin 'not while the pubs are open anyway.'

Lodge watched Sergeant Dean chuckling down the street as he continued his beat and could only shake his head in amusement until he saw the thin and scruffy teenager staring moodily from across the street in his direction. Lodge cursed as he knew he was one of Finch's bucks. Lodge threw the stub of his cigarette into the gutter and moved swiftly away. He immediately turned left into Temple Street then cut into the first doorway he came to which happened to be solicitors chambers. Lodge was familiar with that musty smell of legal documents, polished wood panels and desperation.

He was in a small foyer with a highly decorative tiled floor which ended at the base of a dark varnished staircase. On the first landing two crusty looking legal types were talking and glancing apprehensively in his direction. Lodge waited a few tense minutes to see if Finch's buck passed by but there was no sign of him. A tall, wiry figure with pince-nez spectacles began to descend the stairs staring at Lodge with his nose pinched in distaste.

'Do you have business here?'

The man's accent was so polished that Lodge immediately felt both contempt and inferior at the same time.

'I'm a Police officer following a suspect and I apologise for the intrusion Sir' Lodge fumbled for his warrant card but the man waved his hand dismissively.

'You are obviously a police officer, what else could you be?'

The man's thin, pursed lips broke into a sneering grin which Lodge thought was probably a novelty for his facial muscles.

'I'll be off now Sir.'

Lodge touched the tip of his hat and as he pulled the handle of the door he cursed furiously under his breath.

'Yes you be off now and follow that suspect there's a good chap.'

Lodge ignored the tall, grinning death-mask and pulled the door tightly behind him as he stepped into the street.

'Kiss my fat arse' Lodge said as he scrambled in his pockets for his tobacco and cigarette papers.

'No thanks.'

The thick, local accent came from behind and Lodge knew immediately it was Finch's buck. Lodge rolled his eyes to heaven and shook his head slowly.

'Why me Lord?'

Lodge whispered then turned slowly to see the stick-thin teenager leaning casually against the wall. His trousers fell short of his boots which were laced-up tight with no sign of any socks. His shirt was out of his trousers and his thin jacket was threadbare at the elbows.

'You need a good dinner lad' Lodge said looking him up and down.

'Finch wants yer' he responded without any expression on his face.

'I'm busy' Lodge replied.

'Not busy enough' his young face was hard and his eyes were deep in his skull.

'Don't talk to me like that you're just a bloody kid' Lodge said with contempt.

'And you're just a stinkin' Jack. Mr.Finch will be in The Brigantine tonight. Be there – he wants yer.'

He turned fast and moved swiftly away before Lodge could reply or object. All Lodge could do was stand and watch him go as light rain began to speckle the pavement. It became torrential within minutes and Lodge cursed his luck again as he looked up at the grey clouds.

'Shower of bastards.'

The rain was still thrashing the pavement late in the evening as Bridle sat in the police car parked halfway down Percy Street. The gloomy weather made the evening darker than it should have been for the time of year and Bridle had to squint through the rain-mottled windscreen. He had been there for almost an hour when Morretti's taxi pulled up and for a moment they had a stand-off as to who was getting out in the rain. Bridle conceded and took a short run through the downpour and into the cab. He sat back and brushed the water from his jacket and trousers.

'Good to see you again Mr. Bridle' Morretti said over his shoulder.

'Alf what did you put in that grog you gave me?'

'My special mixture – I only share it with men I respect.'

Morretti looked puzzled but Bridle decided not to pursue it. He took a banknote from his wallet and passed it over to Moretti.

'What have you got for me Alf?'

'Very generous Mr. Bridle as always' Morretti said and slipped the note into his top pocket.

'I kept my eye on the place all week. She has an interesting life, out all hours of the night' Morretti grinned and exposed gaps in his teeth. 'Loads of people around, lots of parties, last few nights there's been one bloke about' Morretti leered over his shoulder.

'Might be her dad' Bridle said looking out of the window.

'Her dad yeah – that's a good one' Morretti began to chuckle.

'Description Alf' Bridle said abruptly and Morretti got the message.

'About your age, tall but not heavyweight, lean, blonde hair, clean looking bloke.'

'When did you last see them together?'

'Saw them on the door-step last night, they argued and he stormed off. That was about ten past midnight, she's a fiery one Mr Bridle.'

'You should see her drive a sports car' Bridle said squinting through the rain.

'I won't ask how you know that Mr. Bridle' Morretti said with a wink.

'Joey Vance?' Bridle said ignoring his innuendo.

'Bad news that was, the lad didn't deserve the knife' Morretti took a swig from his flask and offered it over his shoulder but Bridle's look was enough.

'Sorry, I forgot' Morretti replaced the cap sheepishly and slipped the flask under the dashboard.

'Have you heard anything?' Bridle asked but he was distracted by another taxi as it pulled up a few yards ahead of them. Miranda Shaw jumped out and ran up the steps to shelter under the porch as her companion paid the driver then sprinted up the steps to join her. Bridle couldn't see the man as he had his hat pulled down tight and his collar turned-up against the rain.

'Bob's yer uncle' Morretti said 'that's the feller.'

Bridle watched as they disappeared into the house then turned his attention back to Morretti.

'Go on' Bridle said.

'Yeah Joey Vance was runnin' around for Finchy, you knew that. I heard it was a blackmail job and it must have been for big money. Not Finch's normal style. It's all a bit odd. Joey was just a go-between, I guess they knifed him to cut him out, one less to pay.'

'Any names come up, anything at all?' Bridle wanted more value for his money.

'No one's talkin' much since Joey got gutted. I know Joey was shouting about the bloke who killed his mam, said he knew who it was and he was goin' to ask Finchy to sort him out. I know that's not much but that's life – you're the Jack.'

'Thanks for reminding me Alf.'

Bridle didn't wait for reply as he opened the door and stepped into the rain. He slammed the door so hard Morretti winced then he jogged across to the house and up the steps to the heavy front door with unpolished brass fittings. He hammered the brass door-knocker till it echoed around the street and when he got no response he hammered it again.

The door opened partially and Miranda Shaw stood in the narrow gap. She was wearing the same silk kimono that she wore at the studio and Bridle could see that nothing hindered the shape of her figure underneath. Her pose was provocative and she turned her hip just enough to expose the length of her naked thigh through the gap of her gown. Her make-up was sparse which highlighted the ruby line of her lips. It was her mouth that fascinated Bridle and somehow she knew it. But she knew by the stone-cold look on his face that no amount of pouting was going to distract him.

'Oh Sergeant you found me at last' she said with a smile that would melt steel.

'Save it for your clients' Bridle said pushing her against the wall as he barged past.

'Bastard' she said and stormed after him. She leapt onto his back and tried to hold on as he walked into the living room but he flipped her over his shoulder and she landed on the sofa with a squeal. Bridle still had the kimono in his hand.

'Bastard' she squealed again and tried to hide her naked breasts with her hands but changed her mind and threw the nearest plant-pot at him. He dodged it easily and it knocked an aspidistra from its stand with a crash. She stood, naked, with her hands on her hips glaring at him so Bridle threw the kimono in her face. She let the gown fall to the floor and calmly pointed her finger at him.

'I'm going to scream very loud and very long and I am going to say you tried to rape me. I'll give you ten seconds to get out' she smiled and pushed her breasts teasingly toward him.

'Count slowly while I search the place' Bridle said and she clenched her fists and screamed at him in frustration.

Bridle walked across the hall and pushed open the nearest door but the room was empty. He moved quickly through the small kitchen to the back door. The door had two heavy bolts, the lower one had been drawn across but the top bolt was still in place. Bridle guessed that her companion had tried to get out that way but didn't have time so he had to be somewhere inside. Miranda Shaw stormed into the kitchen tying her gown tightly around her waist.

'Bastard' she growled.

'Where is he?'

Bridle glared at her and noticed her glance fleetingly over his shoulder. He turned quickly and looked at the thin door of the broom cupboard as Miranda Shaw lunged forward and grabbed a carving knife from the table and held it toward him. Bridle smiled at her for a moment then threw a sharp and heavy kick at the broom cupboard door which disintegrated like matchwood. The figure inside launched himself out but Bridle chinned him with a straight right punch and he crumpled easily. Bridle caught him and swung him around onto the wooden kitchen chair where his head lolled back and he let out a short groan.

'Hello Guy' Bridle said.

When Tommy Lodge stepped into the back parlour of the Brigantine Paddy Finch was already holding court. The room was a thick haze of tobacco smoke and Lodge cursed his luck as he worked his way across the bustling floor. He tried to catch the barman's eye in the hope of a pint but he was too busy.

'Mr. Lodge' Finch boomed.

Finch waved his hand dismissively at a small group of roughnecks who were at his table and they all left silently. The hollow-eyed teenager was one of them and he gave Lodge a long, hard stare as he moved away.

'What's his name?' Lodge asked as he sat down 'the artful fuckin' dodger?'

Finch laughed and slapped the table 'that's Mickey Higgs. Higgsy is sharp as a razor but he hates Jacks.' Finch laughed again and pushed a dark pint of beer toward Lodge.

'Cheers Paddy' Lodge said and took a long gulp.

'I've got a problem Lodgy and I think you can help me.'

Finch's words were enough to make Lodge's stomach sink so he took another long swig of his pint.

'Two of my lads have disappeared, Milo and Brady.'

'I'd try the nearest knockin' shop Paddy.'

Lodge hoped to keep it light but he saw the dark look in Finch's eyes.

'They were on a job for me and they had orders. If they haven't come back it's because they can't' Fince growled and Lodge cleared his throat.

'What can you tell me Paddy?'

'I can tell you that their carcasses might turn up soon but I doubt it.'

'What's goin' on Paddy? What do yer want me to do?' Lodge knew that Finch would only tell him what he needed to know and that worried him.

'There's a rebel lad on the loose in town and he's got the means to do a lot of damage' Finch watched Lodge's face turn pale.

'What 'means' Paddy?' Lodge felt sick.

'I'm no traitor to the cause Lodgy. This lad was one of the best in the brigades, tough and clever. But he got twisted up inside and he's got no loyalty anymore. He's a danger to all of us. I should never have trusted him.'

Lodge nodded his head slowly as if he cared about what Finch was telling him. His main thought was how quickly he could off-load the information so someone else could deal with it. Then he thought of the photograph posted up by Special Branch.

'Would his name be Riley by any chance?' Lodge whispered.

'Could be' Finch said quietly and Lodge leaned forward with a wink.

'I shouldn't tell yer' this Paddy but Special Branch are waitin' for him. They've got the city boxed-off for the rally tomorrow. Those bastards will sort him out' Lodge sat back and grinned with satisfaction but his face dropped as Finch started to laugh.

'No scuffer will get near this lad believe me Lodgy' Finch sneered at the thought.

'Paddy there'll be armed officers in the crowd and that's confidential information. I'd be kicked out on my arse for tellin' yer' that' Lodge said.

Finch sneered again and raised his arm above the crowd and within moments a barman appeared with a tray of pint pots and Lodge's eyes widened. They remained silent while the barman deftly placed the glasses on the table and made a hasty retreat.

'Cheers' Lodge grinned and took a long swig of dark mild. Finch lit his clay pipe and threw the match into the grey mush in the ash tray.

'I won't argue with a Jack so just listen to what I'm tellin' yer.'

Finch's eyes were cold and Lodge knew better than to interrupt.

'He told me he was after a military target so I helped him. I went against my own gut feeling so I sent Milo and Brady along. I should've known they'd be no match for him.'

Finch paused to take a drag on the clay pipe and Lodge could feel his stomach sink a little more.

'I'll make a long story short Lodgy – he's rigged a bomb in the back of a motor' Finch said and Lodge almost choked on his pint.

'A bomb' Lodge said and wiped the spillage from his chin.

'You heard me. It'll be in town somewhere if I know that bastard, somewhere on the route of that unemployment march. It'll cause too much bad blood. Every gang in the city will blame each other. It could go on for years and I don't need it.'

Lodge sat back as the colour drained from his face. Finch noticed that the clay pipe had burned itself out so he threw it into the ash tray with a grunt.

'Give me the details of the motor Paddy and I'll get it circulated, we'll find it in no time.'

'I'll tell you what's going to happen' Finch said and Lodge closed his eyes. They were words he didn't want to hear. 'You and Higgsy and some of the boys will find it' Finch said.

'Me, the artful dodger and a gang of street bucks lookin' for a fuckin' bomb in the middle of a political rally what chance have we got?' Lodge's fear overcame his tact.

'More chance than with me Lodge' Finch said with menace

and Lodge felt that hopeless feeling in the pit of his stomach like a low punch from a heavyweight.

'Paddy the bomb could be anywhere, we need manpower, let me report it and...'

'All you need is a backbone Lodge' Finch said with contempt 'I'm no snout – I won't rat on a brother in arms even if he is a head case.'

'I've been assigned to Lime Street Station tomorrow, I can't just leave my post' Lodge spluttered.

'Find a way' Finch spat back 'you owe me Lodge.'

'What if we don't find it? What if it goes off?' Lodge stammered.

'You and Higgsy will find it, but if you don't then my conscience is clear, I tried.'

Finch shrugged and sipped his pint slowly. Lodge felt sick. He glanced across the room and Higgsy was staring at him through the dark cavities he called eyes.

'How old is he?' Lodge said nodding toward Higgsy.

'Seventeen, but he's got bigger balls than you Mr. Lodge' Finch laughed and Lodge raised his pint to his mouth and whispered.

'Shower of bastards.'

'How's your neck Guy?' Bridle asked.

'A little longer than it used to be' Charlton said shaking his head as he recovered from Bridle's punch.

'Do you always hide in broom cupboards?' Bridle forced a grin.

'That depends entirely on whose broom cupboard it is old boy' Charlton said with a bright smile. Miranda Shaw still held the carving knife in a threatening stance and Charlton looked at her and squirmed.

'For goodness sake Miranda' Charlton whined 'put it away and make some tea there's a good girl.'

'I'm not your skivvy' she said and threw the knife across the table.

'Be a dear' Charlton insisted.

'I'm not making tea for that bastard' She said and tightened the cord of her robe. Bridle looked at her and wondered how he had ever thought she was interesting. When he first saw her at the warehouse she held some fascination for him but each experience of her since then had dissolved the illusion.

'Where do we go from here Sergeant?' Charlton asked as he leaned across the table and helped himself to a cigarette from a packet that lay open. Bridle could see Charlton oozed confidence and if he was honest Bridle had no idea where it was going.

'I was released with no charge' Charlton continued and lit his cigarette 'an innocent man.'

'So why were you hiding in the cupboard?' Bridle asked and Miranda Shaw started to giggle as she lit the gas ring with a match and slipped the heavy kettle onto it.

'I wish I knew old boy. All I want to do is get out of this damn country – it's gone to the dogs' a peevish look drifted over Charlton's face. 'What are you giggling at Miranda? I thought you were on my side' Charlton looked at Bridle. 'Are you looking for another reason to arrest me Sergeant?'

'It's an offence to assault a police officer Guy – especially from a broom cupboard.'

Charlton rolled his eyes and blew out a plume of smoke as Miranda Shaw giggled again.

'But you chinned me old boy doesn't that cancel it out?'

'I believe you are a suspect in the murder of David Grant' Bridle said with a bored sigh.

'Guy didn't kill him' Miranda Shaw said and slammed the heavy brown teapot onto the table.

'Where do you plan to go?' Bridle asked ignoring her outburst.

'Abroad' Charlton shrugged.

'There's a war in Spain Guy, oh I forgot you've already made a profit from that one. Are you jumping ship before your Spanish friends convince my superiors of your guilt?'

'Guilt is something you have to prove so I should have plenty of time for a trip' Charlton smirked 'unless you try to stop me.'

'Do I look as if I care?' Bridle asked flatly.

'To be honest old boy I can't say you do.'

Miranda Shaw placed three large mugs down next to the teapot. Both men watched as she poured the dark, stewed tea into the mugs and Charlton heaped three spoonfuls of sugar into his and stirred it slowly.

'You were in the alley with Joey on the night of the shooting' Bridle said and sipped his tea.

'I thought you said you wouldn't make this bastard a cup of tea'? Charlton said avoiding the question.

'I can change my mind can't I?' She replied with a giggle.

'Do you know how Joey died Guy?' Bridle saw Charlton baulk slightly at the question. 'He was knifed in the stomach continuously, he was gutted like a fish' Charlton closed his eyes in disgust and Miranda Shaw covered her mouth. Charlton took a long drink of his hot tea then just stared at the contents of his mug as if he was reading the tea leaves.

'Joey was just a runner he didn't deserve that' Charlton said quietly.

'Sir Edward Grant told me about the blackmail' Bridle said and Charlton looked up.

'Is that so?' Charlton replied glancing at Miranda Shaw.

'He said you and David blackmailed him over his relationship with Miss Shaw. I guess you two set him up for that one' Bridle sipped his tea and watched their reaction.

'Keep guessing Sergeant' Charlton said and dropped the burning stub of his cigarette into an ashtray. But Bridle noticed that his face had lost that bright light of confidence and his eyes had developed dark rings under them.

'I can guess all night if I have to' Bridle said 'you look like a man who hasn't slept for a while Guy.'

Charlton heaved a sigh of frustration and pulled another cigarette from the pack. He lit it with sharp, angry movements then threw the spent match across the room. Bridle looked around the kitchen and squirmed slightly.

'Is this Sir Edwards love-nest Miranda? Doesn't spoil you does he?' Bridle squirmed as he glanced around. Miranda Shaw's eyes ignited and she was about to respond when Charlton held up his hand to stop her.

'Sergeant, what exactly do you want?' Charlton asked with a puzzled look.

'I want the killer of David Grant' Bridle responded.

'Isn't this case a little too complicated for provincial coppers like you?' Charlton suddenly smiled 'oh I understand now, this is all about you isn't it Sergeant? A last chance to prove your mettle before your career sinks without trace. Success might even bring Estella running back' Charlton broke into a sniggering laugh 'glory hunting is such a seedy business Sergeant.'

'Why were you in that alley with Joey?' Bridle said resisting the urge to drag Charlton across the table by his expensive lapels. Charlton shook his head slowly then stared blankly at the table for a moment.

'Think about this Sergeant, would a man like Sir Edward Grant worry about being exposed over a tart like Miranda?'

Miranda Shaw's face darkened but she held her tongue when Charlton raised his hand again.

'He has a lot of power in this city. He knows many eminent people if you understand me, any hint of scandal would be quashed easily by his circle of influence.'

'If it wasn't sex then what was it?' Bridle said and noticed Miranda Shaw's hands were shaking slightly.

'When I was in Spain I met an Irishman. A bit of an adventurer, good company we got to know each other... ' Charlton hesitated.

'Go on' Bridle said.

'We got on very well. We had the same attitude to life, lots of energy and drive.'

'Is that what you call it?' Bridle said with sarcasm and Charlton ignored him.

'David came over to Spain with a shipment and we all got smashed together. That is, we got smashed our Irish friend was a bit more sober than the rest of us. David went on and on about how much he hated his father which was tedious. Then our Irish companion tells us a story about Sir Edward Grant. He served in Ireland during the rebellion. Apparently his unit was involved in a controversial gunfight in a village. They over-stepped the mark so to speak and our Irish friend had proof of their guilt.'

'So that was the basis of the blackmail' Bridle said with a sigh of resignation.

'When David heard the story it was like music to his ears. He said it would give him power to manipulate his father but then our Irishman weaved his persuasive charm and suggested blackmailing Sir Edward. He convinced David that it would cause his father far more distress to be under threat and paying out large sums of money. David agreed and realised he could wallow in his father's prolonged misery' Charlton paused as if he was arranging the story in his head.

'What about Joey?' Bridle asked.

'Cash drops were arranged by the Irishman, Joey was the runner that's all I know' Charlton flopped back in the chair as if a heavy weight had just lifted off his shoulders.

'Your friend goes by the name of Callum Riley' Bridle said and Charlton broke into a smile.

'I'm almost impressed Sergeant.'

'Be thankful you're still in one piece, the man kills without hesitation' Bridle said and Charlton's face drained of colour.

'I warned you Guy I could see it in his eyes' Miranda Shaw whispered.

'He's disappeared' Bridle said 'gone to ground – he's a dangerous man and he might come looking for you Guy.' Bridle smirked at his own mischief as Charlton's face turned ashen.

'I knew he was mad' Miranda Shaw said 'his ego was out of control. His personality would change with the wind. Always telling us of his exploits and adventures and giving us advice on avoiding the law. If he's in hiding Sergeant I can tell you the advice he continually gave to us.' She looked at Charlton and he just nodded. 'He said the best place to hide from your enemy is as close to him as possible.'

'Maybe I should double check your broom cupboard' Bridle said and Miranda Shaw broke into another fit of giggling. 'So I guess you deny any involvement in the blackmail and you deny being in the alley with Joey Vance' Bridle said without hiding his sarcasm and Charlton avoided his stare.

'Unless you can prove otherwise Sergeant, I'm not in the

business of incriminating myself' Charlton hastily stubbed out his cigarette.

'I don't suppose you have a uniform of the Grant Hollister Line hanging in your wardrobe' Bridle asked casually and Charlton looked puzzled.

'Are you grasping at straws now old boy? Why would I? Go and look for yourself' Charlton shook his head.

Bridle said nothing. He looked at the two beautiful people before him and wondered when and how far they would eventually fall. Bridle pushed back his chair and stood up. He thought about saying something but knew there was no point so he just strolled out of the kitchen, along the hall and out onto the damp porch. The rain had turned into a fine drizzle and looked like bright needles against the flickering streetlight. He turned his collar then stepped out into the misty drizzle. He was dreading the journey home and that slow walk up the promenade to a cold house. As he climbed into the police car he wondered if Hagan's chip shop would still be open on Park Road. By the time the engine ignited he was already looking forward to a bag of cod and chips laden with salt and drenched in malt vinegar.

CHAPTER TWENTY ONE

The protesters had gathered early in the morning at Islington Square and Jack Finney led the march proudly across town and down London Road toward Lime Street. The weather was fine and the atmosphere was like a carnival as the different trade union groups marched with brightly embroidered banners and a small colliery brass band played marching tunes. Spirits were high and even the police escort joined in the banter. The mounted police trotted a few yards ahead of the forward marchers with an air of controlled authority. Finney was pleased and proud of the way the whole operation had gone. He was especially pleased to see the crowds of bystanders showing their support for the marchers on the route.

Finney had expected some kind of disruption and experience wouldn't allow him to discard the possibility until the whole day was over. Some men had been stopped at Lime Street Station on their arrival but Finney and the other organisers had been expecting that. It was something that Finney as a councillor would take up with the Watch Committee in the course of his duties

'Are yer' orange or are yer' green?' A guttural voice bellowed from the crowd and Finney stepped forward.

'Orange or green we've all got to put food on the table' Finney shouted 'employment is a basic right and that's what we're marching for.'

Finney had emphasised at every organisational meeting that he and the party would not tolerate violence or incitement to violence during the rally. Even so Finney had taken the precaution of posting his best men with the known troublemakers and they had a constable shadowing them all the way. The whole organisation of the event marked a turning point for Finney as all interested civic parties had participated in the meetings including the police. It was situation that Finney had worked for all his life, the right to peaceful protest with the full co-operation of the authorities. Harry Croft shouldered his way through the marchers and joined Finney at the front.

'Well done Jack' Croft said and shook his hand as they marched. 'This is all your hard work.'

'Thanks Harry' Finney said with a wide grin of satisfaction 'I hope you'll say a few words when we get to the plateau.'

'This is your day Jack not mine' Croft smiled and made a forced effort to look humble.

Finney strode out with enthusiasm as the throng spread across across Lime Street and up the steps to the plateau of St. Georges Hall. He led the leaders to the dais on the top between two pillars as the crowds continued to spill out of London Road onto Lime Street. Finney and his colleagues looked at the massing crowd with pride and disbelief. The mounted Police formed a cordon across Lime Street directly in front of the station and Finney thought what an impressive sight they looked even though their role was to keep control. Finney was full of excitement for the day but didn't let it affect his judgement. He knew how quickly events could turn.

The excitable crowd made the job much harder for Tommy Lodge and Higgsy. They had been searching and watching the area around the station and the plateau for over three hours without any success. Lodge's nerves stretched to capacity every time Higgsy or one of his gang smashed the quarter light window of a parked car and pulled out the back seat to find nothing. Lodge and Higgsy leaned against a wall on Copperas Hill and watched the marchers filling up Lime Street. Some of the younger, agile men climbed lamp posts and a few were perched on the lion monuments turned black by soot and smog of the city. Lodge finished rolling a cigarette and held it out to Higgsy who had both hands in his pockets and the usual surly look on his face. Higgsy snatched the cigarette and thrust it between his lips then resumed his brooding stance without saying a word.

'No thanks required' Lodge murmured as he quickly filled another paper with a line of tobacco and rolled it between his fingers. Lodge struck a match and Higgsy swiftly caught his wrist, leaned forward and lit his own cigarette first then released Lodge's arm with a jerk. Lodge was stunned for a moment but then was almost consumed by the impulse to deck Higgsy with a sharp punch.

'You skull-faced little... ' Lodge seethed but Higgsy strolled away with a look of contempt on his face. Higgsy strode down Copperas Hill and Lodge struggled to keep up with him and light his cigarette at the same time.

'I'm a police officer you can't ignore me' Lodge fumed.

'You're a Jack... you don't count' Higgsy said in his deep, broad accent.

Lodge threw down his cigarette in frustration and was about to snap back when Higgsy stopped suddenly on the corner of Skelhorne Street and pointed at an Austin van parked outside a cafe.

'That wasn't there five minutes ago' Higgsy said in his monotone accent.

'It's a bread van he'll be gone in a few minutes' Lodge said in the hope that Higgsy would leave the van alone but the toffee hammer deftly appeared from his sleeve. Lodge cursed Higgsy as he moved toward the van with that dead look in his sunken eyes. Higgsy walked to the back of the van and paused as he looked around then tried to open the doors. They were locked. The milling crowds made his work easier and Lodge had no choice but to stand and cover him. Higgsy sidled up to the driver's door and with a swift flick of his wrist smashed the quarter light glass with the toffee hammer. He reached inside and pulled up the catch of the door lock and was in the driving seat within seconds. The van was full of empty bread trays and Lodge leaned in and groaned.

'Empty' Lodge cursed again but Higgsy ignored him as usual and rifled through the glove compartment. He found a set of keys then leapt from the van and moved to the rear with a speed that made Lodge's head spin. Higgsy unlocked the doors quickly and stared blankly at the interior. Three tiers of empty trays were stretched across the van and Lodge savoured the lingering smell of buns and scones. Higgsy pulled the bottom two trays out and pulled back the canvas sheet that lay on the floor of the van. Higgsy made no reaction but Lodge's jaw dropped.

'Don't do this to me Lord' Lodge whispered.

Under the canvas sheet was a crude device made up of tight bundles of stick dynamite wired to a battery and what looked like an ordinary alarm clock. Six inch nails were packed all around the dynamite and wires coiled their way from the battery to the clock and then to a terminal somewhere under a bundle of dynamite.

'You're the Jack, what happens now?' Higgsy asked and a thin smile cracked his skeletal face.

Bridle watched Harry Croft with some admiration as he stirred up the crowd with a rousing speech. Then Croft made a glowing introduction and invited Jack Finney to the dais to speak. Bridle was in a raised position at the base of the Duke of Wellington's column and had a good view of the speakers. Finney stepped forward to roaring applause and he waved both arms and grinned till his jaw ached. It was obvious to Bridle that Finney had earned a great deal of respect over the years since their first encounter. Bridle recalled the defiant man who lay on the floor of the town hall with a gashed head and a broken arm who ranted until he passed out. It was that spirit that earned Bridle's respect and assistance all those years ago.

The undercover police officers that were meant to blend with the crowd stood out like sore thumbs to Bridle. They stood too tall and too straight as if they had just stepped off the parade ground. He had no idea who the Special Branch men were but he knew that some of them were carrying firearms. Bridle looked around the crowd for Tommy Lodge. He heard that Lodge wormed his way out of duty on Lime Street Station and assumed he had found a cushy post to smoke a roly and read the paper.

Jack Finney gave a powerful speech about freedom to protest but was distracted as Mcleish appeared on the plateau to the right of the dais. His uniform was immaculate and he carried a swagger stick under his arm as he marched a rank of uniformed men across the plateau. Bridle watched with fascination as he posted each man between the pillars flanking the dais in full view of the protesters. To Bridle's mind this was just a little too provocative but he knew of the grudging history between the two men.

Finney ignored Mcleish's strategy and carried on emphasising how much progress the unions had made through organised and peaceful negotiation. The crowd began to murmur and Finney knew he was losing their attention and looked around for Harry Croft to rally their support but he had disappeared from the plateau. Finney introduced the next speaker who stepped forward, took Finney's hand and shook it vigorously. Finney smiled, waved and turned away in search of Mcleish who was standing a few yards away, bolt upright with his swagger stick clamped tightly under his arm. Mcleish stared directly forward although his vision was impaired by the peak of his cap.

'This wasn't agreed' Finney growled at Mcleish and pointed at the line of policemen between the pillars. Mcleish didn't flinch or reply.

'We had approval for this rally, we agreed the route, we agreed the police deployment and it was sanctioned by all parties in advance' Finney stabbed his finger toward the line of policemen 'that was not discussed or agreed.'

'It is my duty to maintain civil order Councillor' Mcleish responded.

'This is provocation, if anything happens today Mcleish I'll hold you responsible' Finney's rage caused him to gasp and he began to rub his chest with his fist.

'You don't look well Councillor Finney.'

'You won't do this to me again Mcleish, this will stay a peaceful protest, I swear to God.'

'My men do not incite violence Councillor they respond to it.'

Groups of men at opposite ends of the plateau began to shout and heckle simultaneously then they pushed the crowd forward to create a surge. Bridle could see the agitators from his vantage point and it was obviously a co-ordinated effort. The rank of officers at the rear of the crowd stood to alert at the order of the duty Sergeant and the mounted police tightened their line and steadied the horses. Years of experience at football matches had honed their discipline and skill at crowd control. The speaker at the dais called for calm but men had begun to shout and jostle from all sides of the crowd.

Finney leaned against a pillar and cursed as the mass of people began to surge in waves across the plateau. Union leaders tried to contain the troublemakers but it was getting out of hand and soon it was difficult to tell the difference. Finney turned back to Mcleish with a look of desperation on his face.

'Don't order your men to draw batons Mcleish you know the crowd will panic' Finney was ashen and his breathing was shallow. Mcleish looked at the increasing madness on the plateau and turned back to Finney.

'When will you ever learn Jack?' Mcleish stared hard into Finney's eyes. 'How many years have you wasted on this rabble?' 'All of your peaceful protesters are back in the jungle, again.'

'No we've shown the way today' Finney's voice grew increasingly desperate as Mcleish pointed his stick at the crowd.

'Can you see what I see?' Mcleish turned on his heel and strode down to the rank of men standing to attention.

'Draw batons' Mcleish shouted and the men drew their heavy truncheons, wrapped the cord tightly around their wrists then stood ready. Finney leaned back against a pillar and slid down into a squat position on the cold stone floor. He held his arm against his chest to ease the pain and watched helplessly as Mcleish ordered his men forward.

Beads of sweat formed on Lodge's forehead regardless of how many times he mopped it off. He stared helplessly at the dynamite and cursed his misfortune.

'How long are yer gonna stare at it?' Higgsy droned into Lodge's ear.

'As long as I fuckin' have to' Lodge snapped back.

'Feelin' the strain Lodgy?'

Lodge cast an evil look at Higgsy but they were suddenly distracted by the commotion coming from St. Georges Hall. People were running up the street in a panic and it was obvious a disturbance had broken out on the plateau.

'What the hell…' Lodge whispered as the van was surrounded by people running away in desperation.

'Something's kicked off on Lime Street' Higgsy said in his emotionless drawl. Lodge closed the doors of the van to shield the bomb from the people spilling out of Lime Street.

'We've got to get help, we need the army' Lodge said and wiped more sweat from his brow as Higgsy sneered at him.

'Look around scuffer it's too late, you've got to move it' Higgsy said.

'Movement might trigger it' Lodge mumbled. Higgsy lost patience and wrenched the van doors open.

'Look, its set for three o'clock you've got about five minutes to shift it. Make a decision Lodgy.' Higgsy's expressionless drawl grated on Lodge. He looked at Higgsy standing with his hands in his pockets and absolutely no expression on his face. No sign of fear. Lodge wondered if he even had a heartbeat.

'Are you scared of dyin' Lodgy?'

Lodge looked from Higgsy to his gang of bucks standing up the street. They all looked back at Lodge with contempt because they could see his fear.

'I've got a family' Lodge whispered.

'In five minutes you'll have fuck all' Higgsy drawled.

Lodge slammed both rear doors shut and marched around to the driver's door and leaned in. He pulled the crank handle from the door pouch and rattled the gear stick to ensure it was in neutral. Higgs and his gang watched in silence as Lodge moved to the front of the vehicle and pushed the crank handle into position at base of the engine. Lodge turned the handle sharply and the engine grumbled slightly, he turned it over again and the engine ignited but coughed out. Lodge took a deep breath and turned it over a third time and the engine ignited and ticked-over sweetly. He pulled the crank handle out and threw it into the gutter then marched around to the driver's side just as Higgsy leapt into the driver's seat, slammed the door shut and locked it.

'What are you playin' at Higgsy?'

Higgsy looked at Lodge for a moment. His skeletal features showed no expression or emotion as he rammed the vehicle into gear and roared up Copperas Hill despatching people left and right as they threw themselves out of his way. The bucks sprinted off up the hill after him and Lodge pulled his pocket-watch from his waistcoat and checked the time. If Higgsy was right about the clock he had less than three minutes.

Bridle watched numbly as the ranks of constables advanced with batons drawn. The mounted section contained the mayhem from the south side as the two ranks squeezed the protesters from the east and west side. Their only escape was to the north end and the police had placed Black Marias across that route and were arresting fleeing protesters at random. Bridle stayed as high on the plinth as he could to avoid the crush and he could see agitators trying to rally the protesters to turn and fight the police below him.

The gunshots came from opposite ends of the plateau almost at the same time and everyone including police instinctively recoiled and ducked for cover. The shots threw everyone into disarray and the horses of the mounted section reared and broke the line as their riders struggled to control them. The police cordons broke and people ran in all directions as a second volley of gunshots went off and caused widespread panic. Bridle caught sight of the gun-smoke on the second volley only a few yards from his position on the north side. He leapt from the plinth and pushed his way through toward the right side of the hall when a powerful constable caught him by the back of his jacket. Bridle knew a truncheon was likely to follow so he spun quickly and covered his head with his left arm and swung an uppercut to the jaw with his right. The constable grunted and wobbled for a moment so Bridle ducked away and sped up the steps to the north side.

Bridle sprinted across the plateau but stopped short when he saw Jack Finney slumped on the ground with his back to the pillar. Bridle wasn't sure if he was concious so he crouched down and shook his arm.

'Councillor Finney' Bridle shook him again and Finney reluctantly opened his eyes. Finney stared at Bridle and a faint look of recognition swept over his face.

'No need to carry me away from this one lad' Finney laughed painfully.

'You need a doctor Mr. Finney' Bridle said quietly.

'No lad a doctor is the last thing I need.'

Bridle was about to reply when the heavy crump of an explosion from the east side of town startled them.

'What the hell was that?' Finney spluttered.

'God only knows Mr. Finney' Bridle said looking at the black smoke rising above the Station Hotel building.

'Did you stick with it lad?'

Bridle paused for a moment as he recalled their first encounter.

'Yes Mr Finney I stayed with it.'

'Plain clothes man eh' Finney said with admiration.

'I saw gunfire from this end of the plateau Mr. Finney did you see anything?'

Finney sighed and nodded his head slowly.

'A man called Riley fired over their heads to panic the crowd, this is my fault' Finney said with despair in his voice. Bridle looked around and wondered where the hell the Special Branch men had got to. They were supposed to deal with Riley.

'Which way did he go?' Bridle asked.

'The man is armed and dangerous lad' Finney said with a cough.

'We've got armed officers around somewhere, so I'm told' Bridle tried to sound convinced.

'Riley ran off toward St. John's Gardens, he could be anywhere by now' Finney put his head back against the wall.

'Will you be alright Sir?' Bridle said standing up and Finney nodded slowly. Bridle turned and sprinted toward the north end of the plateau then dropped down the steps into St. John's Gardens at the rear of the hall. Protesters and police were still running in all directions as Bridle looked through the gardens and across to the Walker Art Gallery but it was impossible to identify anybody in the mayhem all about. Bridle knew it was hopeless. He had only seen a photograph of Riley and knew he could never pick him out of the chaos. As he turned to walk way the rear service door to the hall caught his eye. The door jamb was protruding marginally from the closed position and he had learned to spot an insecure door from years on the beat. He pulled the door open carefully then took a deep breath and stepped into a long corridor. He left the door ajar to avoid making any noise then moved slowly and quietly along the corridor toward the main hall.

Tommy Lodge had kept on running up Copperas Hill even when he heard the explosion. By the time he reached Russell Street his lungs were burning and he had to stop. He could see a dark cloud of smoke rising from somewhere near Brownlow Hill and children were running around shouting about a bomb. People rushed out of their houses toward Brownlow Hill and Lodge had that sick feeling in his stomach again as he watched them rush by. He cursed Higgsy to the devil and dreaded to think where he had abandoned the van. Lodge broke into a jog along Russell Street together with a growing mob of semi-hysterical people concerned for the safety of their children.

The bells of the fire engines alerted more children and they rushed off to see what the excitement was all about. Lodge had to stop again and gasp for air. He turned over different excuses in his mind as he desperately tried to think of how he could handle the situation he was in.

Then it occurred to him that nobody knew of his involvement with the bomb except Paddy Finch and his cronies. He gasped with relief as he realised he was off the hook and carried on jogging around the corner and up the hill toward the rising smoke.

Lodge slowed to a walk and blew out a sigh of relief when he saw that Higgsy had managed to drop the van on waste ground that had been levelled for building work. A powerful Fire Sergeant with a handle-bar moustache was keeping the growing crowd back. Lodge knew him well.

'Keep clear – get back to the pavement – no bystanders or children have been hurt.'

'Alright Tosh' Lodge said stepping out of the crowd.

'What are you doing here Tommy?' Tosh said.

'Saw the commotion Tosh, thought I'd better have a look.' Lodge had a great sense of relief that no one around was injured or killed. 'Thank God no one was hurt eh.'

'No bystanders hurt Lodgy, can't say the same for the driver though' Tosh replied.

'Where is he?' Lodge's stomach sank 'has he gone to hospital?'

'No he's still here' Tosh said pointing with his thumb 'what's left of him.'

Lodge suddenly turned pale and began to retch but managed to hold back the vomit.

'Did you know him Tommy?'

Lodge hesitated to answer the question then shook his head.

'No I didn't know him.'

'You ain't got the stomach for this work Tommy stick with the shoplifters' Tosh said dismissively.

'Yeah, I'll leave it to you Tosh see you around' Lodge said and walked slowly back toward the road. Lodge started to walk down Brownlow Hill when he saw Higgsy's gang staring at the burning wreck. He approached them cautiously. Every face in the gang looked capable of killing him.

'I was going to drive it – you all saw that – he just jumped in, why?' Lodge looked incredulous as a tall buck with red hair swaggered up and put his hardened face close to Lodge's. Then he dropped his head and spat on the floor.

'That's why' he said then turned away and led the gang down the hill in silence. Lodge looked down at the spit on his shoes then noticed that his hands were trembling. He slipped his hands in his pockets and followed the gang down the hill in a mournful procession.

Harry Croft gripped Jack Finney by the arm-pits and lifted him to his feet but Finney slumped onto the pillar for support.

'I'm alright Harry, I get these attacks, I'll survive' Finney's voice was less pained.

Harry Croft looked agitated and kept his head down as the protesters moved up the steps and began to re-group along the outside wall near the main entrance to the hall. Croft looked around quickly then moved in close to Finney and slipped a revolver into the belt of his trousers under Finney's jacket.

'Stash this for me Jack' Croft said pulling away with his head darting left and right. Finney could smell the cordite rising from the revolver.

'This has been fired Harry' Finney said wearily.

'Yeah that's right I fired it' Croft's admission turned Finney pale again.

'It was you and Riley together, you wanted all this chaos' Finney looked defeated. 'I've been a total fool.'

'What good is peaceful protest Jack?' 'It changes nothing. These men are fighting back now. The whole country needs to fight back. We need change even if it means a revolution.'

'No' Finney shook his head 'you've betrayed us Harry.'

Croft was about to reply when he saw two men pushing through the crowd toward him. He turned quickly and elbowed his way down the steps but caught sight of Mcleish advancing toward him with a squad of constables. Croft dashed back up the steps in an attempt to get the revolver from Finney when a tall, well tailored figure slid from behind a pillar and aimed a pistol at his head. Croft immediately raised his hands and smiled.

'I'm not armed' Croft said affably.

'Get on your knees and get your hands behind your head' the armed man spoke with assured authority. He went forward cautiously and pat-searched Croft then looked up and shook his head at Allenby and Latimer as they approached.

'No weapon Harry' Mcleish said marching up behind 'where did you hide it?'

'This man is in our custody Superintendent' Allenby said firmly.

'What charge?' Croft asked with defiance.

'Whatever we can muster' Allenby said flatly.

'We'll see' Croft said with a grin.

Mcleish shook his head and smiled as he stood over the kneeling man. Mcleish's presence alone was enough to stir Croft into a rage and he was beginning to seethe.

'So it's come to this' Mcleish said grinning 'Harry Croft hero of Spain, on his knees, like father like son eh?' Mcleish winked.

'Shut that evil face of yours Mcleish' Croft snarled.

'Remember his dad Jack?' Mcleish called to Finney 'Alan Croft was a good snout when he was sober' Mcleish jeered but Finney was too sick at heart to respond.

'Liar' Croft screamed.

'Alan Croft ratted on anyone for money, now his son has ratted on you Jack, betrayal is in his blood.'

Croft trembled with subdued rage as Mcleish laughed and turned away. Mcleish's final act of turning his back on Croft sent him over the edge. Croft drew a short blade from inside his boot and launched himself from his kneeling position toward Mcleish with a wild scream and a speed that took them by surprise. The Special Branch officer calmly fired two rounds into Croft's back and he pitched forward as Mcleish turned. Croft was dead before he hit the stone floor but one bullet had passed straight through him and creased Mcleishs's cheekbone. Mcleish wiped the fine line of blood from his face then kicked the blade away with contempt.

'Scum' Mcleish whispered at Croft's twitching corpse.

The two gunshots sent the crowd into another panic so Finney took advantage and slipped away from the pillar and made his way down the steps into St John's Gardens then slumped onto a bench. He put his head in his hands and wept.

It didn't surprise Bridle that local villains might take advantage of the situation to raid St. George's Hall but it did surprise him that there was no sound coming from anywhere inside the building. At the same time Miranda Shaw's words about Riley kept running around in his head. Riley said that the best place to hide from an enemy was as close to him as possible. Bridle controlled his breathing as he moved softly down the corridor because he was aware that even a fly couldn't land in the empty hall without creating an echo. He took the handle of the door to the main hall and eased it gently but it clicked and the echo made Bridle wince. He froze to the spot for a few moments as the echo faded then slipped quietly through the door and into the hall.

The Minton floor tiles were exposed across half of the hall and Bridle guessed that the regular cleaning process was underway during the week. He looked up at the galleries surrounding the hall and at the impressive ceiling. Outside he could hear the muffled sound of chaos but inside was so quiet it was almost sacred. Bridle crept further into the hall but was careful not to walk on the exposed tiles. He held his breath and listened intently. There was no hint of noise, not even a soft echo that might give away intruders. It occurred to Bridle that intruders could be watching every move he made from somewhere up in the galleries. He remained motionless and listened for a few minutes more then turned away with a sigh of resignation and made his way toward the exit. Bridle made no reaction when he saw a fleeting shadow to his right but his heart rate increased as he kept a steady pace across the hall.

'Take one more step and it'll be yer last copper.'

The mock gangster tones came from behind and Bridle recognised the voice immediately. Riley began to chuckle. 'I've always wanted to say that since I saw it on the flicks.'

'Can I turn around this time?' Bridle asked.

'Be my guest' Riley replied.

Bridle turned slowly to see Riley leaning against the wall on the right side of the hall. He wore a navy blue reefer jacket and a cap pulled low on his face. Riley held a revolver in his right hand and fumbled in his pocket with his left. He beckoned with the revolver and Bridle walked slowly toward him. Riley took a packet of Capstan cigarettes from his pocket with his left hand and slipped one between his lips.

'That's far enough copper' Riley struck a match with his thumb and lit his cigarette then threw the spent match onto the exposed ornate floor tiles.

'Shall I put my hands up like you see on the flicks?' Bridle said drily and Riley grinned.

'You can stick yer hands up yer arse for all I care. If yer make any move I don't like I'll shoot yer stone dead believe me.'

'I believe you.'

Riley blew out the cigarette smoke then took off his cap and threw it onto the floor.

'Spoils me hairstyle don't yer think?' Riley grinned.

'People are after you' Bridle said.

'To be sure, lots of people, so many people I've lost count' Riley turned his head slightly to listen to the noise outside.

'How many people have you murdered?' Bridle asked. Riley looked up at the ceiling then shook his head and shrugged.

'I'm a sort of soldier – the people I kill are casualties of war.'

A dark look swept across Riley's face for a moment then a second later his face lit up with a grin and he took a drag on his cigarette. Bridle had seen the same kind of look on old boxers and damaged war veterans. As though the aggression they had to call on to fight had totally consumed them.

'How many had a chance to fight back in this war of yours?' Bridle decided to play for time as he had no idea how to handle Riley.

'I'm the one fighting back copper' Riley pushed himself away from the wall and began to circle Bridle slowly. Bridle looked straight ahead as he spoke.

'You were involved in blackmail with Guy Charlton and David Grant that's why you were in the alley that night in the rain. Why blackmail Sir Edward Grant? Why didn't you just kill him like you killed the other officers involved in that skirmish?' Bridle spoke calmly as Riley continued to circle slowly then he suddenly stopped in front of Bridle and shrugged his shoulders.

'Money' Riley said.

'Money talks louder than revenge for your family' Bridle smiled and Riley's bright grin dropped into a dark scowl. Bridle knew he'd prodded a wound so he continued.

'I guess it was better to kill David Grant. It brought out all that scandal in the papers, damaged the reputation of the whole family, gave them shame and guilt, sounds like good soldiering to me.' Bridle winked as he finished the sentence and for a moment Riley looked as if he was about to lunge at him. Then Riley's expression brightened again and he poked his forefinger at Bridle.

'You are very good copper, I nearly took the bait, and you've done your homework that's for sure' Riley nodded with respect. 'I was on to a good thing with that blackmail it was my pension plan. Why would I kill Sir Edward? He was a goose laying my golden eggs, and I've got news for yer copper, I didn't kill David Grant. So think about that one while yer can.' Riley grinned and Bridle had a sinking feeling that he was telling the truth.

'Like you said copper Grant's world is falling apart, his son is dead, his business is under investigation, his wife is ill. Oh and there's the young colleen who does all that naked modelling stuff, the papers will love that one. Grant will be a leper, apoplexy all round. I think Sir Edward should stay alive and enjoy it.' Riley nodded with satisfaction and took a long drag on his cigarette.

'Why kill Joey Vance? He was harmless' Bridle asked.

Riley blew out the smoke and shook his head.

'Am I to be blamed for every backstreet murder in this stinking city? What did yer do for murderers before I came along?' Riley looked incredulous and Bridle almost laughed.

'So where do you go from here?' Bridle's only strategy left was to keep Riley talking.

'I fancy Australia or the Americas where a good man can do well for himself, what d'yer think copper?' Riley grinned.

'You've got to get out of town first' Bridle replied and Riley almost choked.

'Who the hell is goin' to stop me?' 'I've done what I please in this town so far.'

'Special Branch men are everywhere and their armed' Bridle knew he was wasting his time trying to worry Riley. His arrogance matched his confidence.

'That's the game I'm in and I'm the number one player' Riley said and kept his eyes fixed on Bridle as he knelt and picked his cap from the floor then pulled it firmly on his head. Then he straightened his reefer jacket. To Bridle he looked like any one of the hundreds of seafaring men that walked around the port. Riley checked the chambers of his revolver then slipped it into the broad leather belt of his trousers just under his jacket. He nodded toward the door.

'You lead the way to the back door. When we get outside we walk away like we're the best of mates. Stay at my left side and stay very close' Riley tapped the pistol in his belt.

'Why should I?' Bridle asked 'you'll have to kill me either way.'

Riley shrugged his shoulders.

'Because you've got no choice and because it gives you time to think copper. You might take a brave risk and rush me, you might even win. Then you'd be a hero and I'd be a fuckin' legend.'

Bridle realised that Riley had no fear of death and was even inviting it. He was right, there was no choice but to play out Riley's game.

Riley held his arm out toward the door and Bridle led the way across the hall and into the corridor. Their footsteps echoed all around the building as they approached the outer door which Bridle had left open. Bridle took hold of the door handle and hesitated. Riley stood directly behind him.

'It's not the place to make a move' Riley whispered.

'I was thinking about my wife' Bridle answered quietly.

'Ah and I bet she's a sweet one.'

Bridle pushed the door open and stepped out into St. John's Garden's and Riley followed him closely. People were still rushing through the gardens and around the steps to the plateau. There were groups littered around the gardens, some of them nursing injuries and others just looked exhausted. Riley stayed tight to Bridle's side as they made their way along the path dodging people rushing from the other direction. Bridle had already decided to make a break from Riley as the crowd built up around them and he glanced about for any police uniforms in the vicinity. Bridle and Riley were both so focussed on their thoughts that they failed to notice the dishevelled figure staring at them from a bench as they passed.

The sight of Riley almost tore the heart out of Jack Finney as he sat hunched on the bench. His hatred turned immediately into rage and his hand fell onto the grip of Croft's pistol which he drew from his belt as he stood up. He strode behind Bridle and Riley for a few seconds holding the pistol tightly at his side. Finney stared at Riley's exposed back as the anger rose in him like steam under pressure. He stopped and raised the gun.

'Riley' Finney screamed.

Riley turned, drew and fired his revolver in an acute reflex action. Finney had hardly finished calling Riley's name when the bullet struck his chest. The impact projected him backwards and the recoil forced him to pull the trigger of his pistol as he fell onto the path. The angle of the shot caused the bullet to ricochet off the ground and strike Riley in his right side just under his rib cage. Riley screamed in agony and fell back against the wall as panic broke out all around the gardens at the sound of more gunfire.

Bridle was initially stunned by the gunshots but recovered fast enough to dash toward Finney as he crumbled to the ground. People were throwing themselves behind any cover they could find as Bridle snatched the gun from the path next to Finney. He walked back toward Riley with the gun raised and levelled at Riley's slumped body. Riley was on the ground but supported himself against the wall on his left side. Blood seeped out of his jacket and formed a dark pool on the ground and his head lolled forward as if he was losing consciousness.

Bridle stopped about six feet away with the revolver held firmly in two hands and pointed directly at Riley. He looked incapacitated but Riley still held his revolver limply in his right hand and Bridle wasn't about to take a risk with a man like him.

'Throw the gun down Riley' Bridle said firmly but every muscle in his body felt as if it was shaking. Riley's shoulders began to tremble with laughter and he lifted his head and looked at Bridle.

'Can't yer see I'm shot man?'

'Just throw the gun down' Bridle shifted his stance but kept the weapon fixed on Riley.

'You're nervous copper, not used to this kind of thing eh' Riley said softly.

'I'll shoot you if I have to' Bridle said.

'Is the old feller dead?' Riley said ignoring Bridle's response.

'I don't know' Bridle replied.

'Jesus that was one hell of a shot I pulled off there?'

'Throw the gun down' Bridle repeated.

'Look at all these lovely people skulking around the place we've got an audience so we have' Riley gasped and pulled himself up a little.

'Give up Riley. I'll hold fire but I can't vouch for other officers' Bridle could feel the sweat on his brow but he held a firm grip on the pistol.

'If you stall long enough copper someone else will do the job eh?' Riley grinned.

A number of constables and mounted policemen had followed the sound of gunshots into the gardens and stood back at a distance in total silence. Bridle glanced at them fleetingly and cursed under his breath.

'Put the gun down – you've got no chance Riley.'

Bridle was saying the words for the audience to hear but in his heart he knew exactly what Riley wanted. Riley looked up and saw Allenby and Mcleish moving slowly along the path with two armed Special Branch men. Riley gave a sneering laugh.

'The game's up then' Riley shouted for the benefit of his audience. He turned back to Bridle and spoke softly.

'Remember what I said copper?' 'I'll make you a hero and you'll make me a legend.'

'Don't do it Riley.'

Bridle could feel the pulse beating in his neck as he braced himself. Riley gave out a beaming smile then raised his revolver sharply. Both men fired at the same time and the entire crowd ducked their heads instinctively at the crack of the double discharge.

The mounted men had to rein their horses but the crowd started to move cautiously out of their cover to get a better look. The police line kept them back and Mcleish went forward with the other officers. Riley lay dead on the ground. The bullet had passed through his forehead and had blown the back of his head away. Blood and brain matter spilled across the ground and the spectators craned their necks to get a look at the mess.

Bridle threw the gun down with disgust and strode over to Finney who was covered in blood and gasping urgently. A young policeman was trying to stem the flow of blood from Finney's chest but he had a hopeless task. Finney looked at Bridle with desperation but couldn't speak as blood was filling his lungs rapidly. Bridle nodded his head slowly. Finney seemed to understand then closed his eyes and his rasping breath stopped and rattled in his throat.

'You were very lucky Sergeant.'

Bridle turned slowly to see Allenby smiling at him. Mcleish was standing at his shoulder but he just stared at Finney's lifeless body.

'I can't believe he missed you, the man was a crack shot' Allenby said looking puzzled 'you are a very lucky man.'

Bridle's face was pale and gaunt and he looked at Allenby but ignored his comment. Mcleish looked at Bridle and was about to speak but the look on Bridle's face changed his mind. Bridle turned away and started to walk slowly down the path toward the town. He didn't notice but the police officers holding the line all looked at him with a mixture of awe and respect as he passed. A wiry figure suddenly jumped in front of Bridle and shouted.

'This way Sir' a flash bulb exploded in Bridle's face as he looked up. The agile photographer from the Liverpool Post and Echo darted away before Bridle could react. Bridle tapped his right pocket and pulled out a crumpled white bag. There was one glacier mint left and he slipped it into his mouth as he made his way down the steps into the town.

CHAPTER TWENTY TWO

Bridle, Lodge and George Sullivan sat at a grease stained table in the police mess and sipped hot mugs of tea. Bridle and Lodge had spent the day being de-briefed by senior officers and were completely spent. Sullivan had given up trying to make any conversation with his companions as they just stared at the table or looked at the ceiling. Lodge was on his third packet of Woodbines and Bridle dunked the last fig biscuit into his tea as he prepared himself for the next round of high spirits from the rank and file. He'd lost count at the number of times the Daily Post had been waved under his nose with his photograph on the front page or the number of men who had pointed their fingers and pretended to shoot at him. It was all banter but it was beginning to wear thin with Bridle.

'I'm starvin', my belly's moaning like a whore on a Saturday night' Lodge stubbed out the remainder of his cigarette in the ashtray then immediately took another from the packet.

Inspector Radford walked in with a newspaper under his arm and joined a group of his cronies at a table on the far side of the room. Sullivan and Lodge glanced at each other and then at Bridle but he was lost in his thoughts. Within minutes Radford had the newspaper on the table and sneering glances were cast in Bridle's direction. Bridle was oblivious to the attention but Sullivan looked at Lodge and nodded toward the door. Lodge rolled his eyes and was about to move when Bridle came out of his reverie.

'Riley said he didn't kill David Grant' Bridle mused as he tapped the table with his forefinger.

'Don't start this now boss I'm ready for the knackers yard' Lodge snapped and lit his cigarette.

'And he didn't kill Joey Vance' Bridle said ignoring Lodge.

'He would say that, wouldn't he?' Sullivan said.

'Why would he?' Bridle replied 'he wasn't afraid of being caught because he had already decided to go out in a blaze of glory, to be a legend.'

'A dead legend' Lodge said.

'They're the best kind' Sullivan quipped 'what are you getting at?' Bridle sat back in his chair and gave out a heavy sigh.

'I'm not sure George.'

'Good so we can get down to the pub then crawl home to bed' Lodge said rubbing his hands.

'I could do with a lift over the river Tommy, I'm dead on my feet' Bridle said with a mournful look on his face. Lodge opened his mouth to snap his refusal but he could see Bridle's tired, dark-ringed eyes and sunken face. Lodge knew that killing Riley had diminished Bridle and shaken his confidence. A chastising look from Sullivan also helped his decision.

'Alright but let's get going now so I can get back for a few pints' Lodge said grudgingly just in case anyone thought he was going soft. As they made their way out two detectives at Radford's table started shooting at them with their fingers. Bridle just kept moving but Tommy Lodge turned and fired back with a two fingered vee sign.

'You lot still firing blanks?' Lodge said and the laughter erupted across the room. They stepped into the corridor and Sullivan almost walked straight into Superintendent Mcleish.

'Sorry Sir' Sullivan moved to one side and Lodge moved to the other.

'I'd like a word with you Sergeant Bridle' Mcleish's gravel delivery showed no tolerance for refusal. Sullivan and Lodge glanced at Bridle then moved off along the corridor.

'How do you feel Sergeant?' Mcleish took a packet of Players from the breast pocket of his tunic and offered one to Bridle, who shook his head.

'I feel numb about the whole thing Sir.'

'That's natural. How do you feel about Jack Finney?' Mcleish lit his cigarette then put the smoking match on the windowsill.

'I was sorry for the man. It all happened so fast he didn't stand a chance' Bridle was weary and it was beginning to show.

'You couldn't save him this time' Mcleish said and drew on his cigarette. Bridle looked puzzled.

'Sorry Sir… '

'I saw you on the night of the town hall riot many years ago. You carried Finney out, let him get away' Mcleish fixed him with a stare that demanded an explanation but Bridle had no answer to the question.

'Yes Sir… I did.'

'Can I ask you why you did that Sergeant Bridle?' Mcleish said in a whisper and for a moment Bridle felt trapped.

'Because… ' Bridle paused and thought about all of the humanitarian reasons and any other excuse he could think of to please Mcleish. But then he rejected them all and looked into Mcleish's stern features.

'Because I felt it was the right thing to do at the time Sir.'

Mcleish stared at Bridle for a few moments then nodded.

'Thank you Sergeant.'

Bridle couldn't be certain but he almost detected a faint

smile on that cold face as Mcleish turned and made his way into the mess. He wasn't sure if that was good or bad and he was too tired to care.

Tommy Lodge sat in the passenger seat with his arms folded and a dour look on his face. It was bad enough losing drinking time by agreeing to take Bridle home but it was more irritating when Bridle insisted on driving. Bridle had resisted all of Lodge's attempts at conversation and was driving like a man in a trance. Lodge huffed and puffed and did his best to make Bridle feel guilty but got no response so he had to resort to a sulky silence.

They emerged from the Mersey tunnel and Bridle turned north toward Wallasey but as they approached the turn for the promenade Bridle swung the vehicle the opposite way and headed west across the Wirral. Lodge was confused for a moment and looked around as if they might be taking another route to the promenade but Bridle accelerated away like a man who had just made a firm decision.

'It's a bit late for an excursion boss. I don't suppose we're headin' for a pub?'

Lodge looked hopefully at Bridle but he knew that look on his face so he just sat back and resigned himself to another late night. It took around twenty minutes to drive across the Wirral and into Caldy. Lodge cast an occasional look at Bridle's expression throughout the drive but it never altered.

The sun was dropping low over the Welsh hills as they turned into the gravel drive of Sir Edward Grant. Lodge said nothing to Bridle as they climbed out of the car and made their way to the steps of the house. Lodge cast a swift look over the drive to see if there were any discarded stubs of Sir Edward's cigars as he had done on their last visit but had the same disappointing result. They strode up the steps to the imposing front door and rang the door-bell. Lodge didn't try to keep up with him and just made it to the top of the steps as the door was opened by the Grant's tall and poker-faced butler. He raised an eyebrow at the sight of Bridle's dark and surly features and then recovered his haughty look at the sight of Lodge.

'I'm afraid Sir Edward is entertaining guests for dinner tonight Sir.'

'Really' Bridle said and pushed his way into the hall forcing the butler back against the door. The butler gasped as he watched Bridle disappear into the house and Lodge stopped and tapped the butler's chest with his finger.

'Put your tongue back in Mary the man's married.'

Lodge followed Bridle through the hall and into the dining room where Lady Grant was sitting with her daughter Amelia and Lady Marian Carver. Both men removed their hats and Bridle nodded to Lady Grant.

'I'm sorry to disturb you Lady Grant we're here to see Sir Edward' Bridle nodded to his mother in law who drew a sharp breath and turned her head away. Amelia Grant's eyes lit up when she saw Bridle and was about to speak when Lady Grant silenced her with a look. Lady Grant's face was grey and drawn and heavy lines looped down from her eyes.

'Do you always enter a room unannounced?' Her voice was weak and her head shook slightly as she spoke. Bridle knew her to be the same age as Lady Marian but her illness had taken its toll. Lady Marian was the usual picture of grace and cool elegance but Amelia was almost jumping up and down with excitement.

'I'm sorry m'am' Bridle turned to leave the room but was stopped by Lady Marian's voice which Bridle noticed for the first time was very like Stella's.

'We saw your photograph in the newspaper under rather unfortunate circumstances.'

Bridle thought about making a reply but decided against it and nodded to Lodge to keep moving.

'Estella was… concerned' Lady Marian said with hesitation as if she wanted him to know but didn't really want to tell him. Bridle kept moving along the hall behind Lodge. He didn't want to think about Stella and he had no intention of discussing her with Lady Marian. The butler approached them with a slight flush to his cheeks.

'Sir Edward is in the library with Sir Nigel Carver if you would like to follow me.'

Both men ignored his polite request and brushed him aside as Lodge led the way into the library and the wonderful aroma of Havana cigar smoke. Lodge hesitated for a moment as he sucked in the aromatic smoke but he came down to earth as Bridle forcibly pushed him aside and strode into the room.

Carver and Grant were sitting in high-backed leather bound chairs either side of a grand fireplace. A low fire was burning in the hearth and the room temperature was comfortable. Sir Nigel was smoking a newly lit cigar. Grant's face was screwed-up into a dark scowl but Carver grinned in his usual affable and charming way.

'Hello John, have you brought your six-gun with you?' Carver grinned and rolled the cigar around his lips but Grant appeared to snarl as if the words he was about to speak were burning the inside of his mouth.

'You had better have a good reason for this Sergeant' Grant spoke through gritted teeth and he poked his cigar toward Bridle.

'I'd like to arrest you for the murder of David Grant and for the murder of Joey Vance Sir' Bridle said with contempt 'but unfortunately I can't.'

Carver was paralysed for a moment but Grant didn't react.

'My God I think the man is serious Edward' Carver said and sat forward in his chair 'what are you suggesting?'

'I'm not suggesting Sir Nigel I'm accusing.'

Bridle took out a folded and crumpled sheet of paper and dropped it onto Grant's lap. He picked it up with a look of disgust and unfolded it then looked at the sheet incredulously. After a few moments he shook his head and threw it to Carver.

'Matchstick men and boats' Grant said and began to laugh. Carver looked at the sheet with disbelief.

'This is a child's drawing, I am seriously worried about you' Carver said.

'That was drawn some time ago at my house by Joey Vance. I didn't realise at the time but he was telling me who murdered David Grant.'

Bridle's dark and serious face made Carver a little uneasy. Lodge couldn't believe what Bridle was saying and backed off toward the desk in the hope that no one would notice he was there. Carver stood up and moved closer to Bridle with a genuine look of concern on his face.

'John has been under a lot of strain lately Edward' Carver turned his head and whispered in Bridle's ear 'have you been drinking again?'

Bridle looked up slowly into Carver's face. Bridle's features were set like stone and his eyes burned into Carver. Lodge knew the look well and moved forward in case he had to intervene for the sake of both men. The darkness in Bridle's look caused the smug grin to slide from Carver's face and he realised for a moment that he was on dangerous ground. Bridle stepped toward the hearth and stared into the fire.

'Look at the picture again Sir Nigel' Bridle said quietly 'look at the boats – Joey has drawn the Grant Hollister insignia on the side of the boats – a triangle inside a circle – now look at the matchstick men – one on the floor and one clearly hitting him with something.'

'John this is really… '

'Look at the matchstick men Sir Nigel – the head of each figure is a circle – inside each head Joey has drawn a triangle – the insignia of your line Sir Edward – drawn on both figures – Joey is saying both figures are Grants – David Grant on the floor – and you Sir Edward standing over him.'

'Absolutely absurd' Grant laughed.

'John I think you could be seeing what you want to see' Carver said shaking his head.

'I killed a man on Saturday, shot him dead. He was a killer himself, very conceited. He shot Councillor Finney and then congratulated himself on the skill of his shot, that's the kind of man he was. When I got home I threw up for an hour.'

'Is there any particular reason for sharing your weakness with us Sergeant?' Grant asked.

'It was the same man who blackmailed you Sir Edward. The same man whose family you and your squad encountered in Ireland all those years ago – but you knew that. You knew who he was because Special Branch had warned you – they told you how he killed his victims.' Bridle turned away from the fire and walked back toward the desk.

'Exactly what is your point?' Carver asked.

'It's not easy for a normal person to kill someone violently they have to be provoked by emotion or self-preservation. It takes a certain kind of person to kill without compunction.' Grant and Carver exchanged impatient looks and Carver nodded his head slightly as if to imply that he would sort out the situation.

'I asked you if David was fluent in any language and you denied it and dismissed him as an idiot, in fact he had picked up Spanish during his trips to Europe. He was a very sharp and intelligent operator that was your first lie Sir Edward.'

'Really John, I think you should go home to bed and have a good sleep' Carver smiled and placed a comforting hand on Bridle's shoulder but was startled to feel his arm being gripped firmly and pulled away by Lodge.

'Excuse me Sir' Lodge said 'I suggest you allow Sergeant Bridle to finish' Lodge pushed Carver back toward the fireplace and Carver pulled his arm away in disgust.

'I couldn't understand why Joey Vance was so frightened, I thought he was scared of Paddy Finch and his gang but that didn't really make sense as Joey was one of them. Then it occurred to me that Joey wasn't running from Paddy Finch he was running from you Sir Edward. He was terrified of you – for good reason.'

'What reason would that be Sergeant?' Grant looked at Carver and shook his head.

'Because he saw you on the dock that night dressed as a ship's officer – he saw you kill your son.'

'I was at home Sergeant' Grant sneered.

'We established the weakness in your alibi some time ago Sir Edward. Joey turned up on the promenade near my house because he was running away from you and you knifed him because he witnessed the murder. As I said before it takes a certain kind of person to kill without compunction and you have a history of it Sir Edward.'

'If you are talking about my military career I was involved in irregular warfare Sergeant. The strategy is different. Why would I murder my own son?''What kind of man do you take me for?' Grant took a sip of whiskey. Bridle walked over to the fireplace again and leaned on the mantle. Lodge was standing back behind the desk and Grant and Carver stood in the centre of the room looking at Bridle with expectation.

'I don't know why you killed your son' Bridle said and both men laughed out loud 'but I think you are a man without any compassion – you and Riley are very alike – conceited and ready to sacrifice anyone to your conceit.'

'Really John, I think you need to go back to the drawing board' Carver continued laughing but Grant stared at Bridle intensely.

'You battered David around the head with a blunt weapon then you strung him up. You wanted to imply that Riley had done it because you knew Special Branch were after him. So that would rid you of a feckless son and a blackmailer. You also knew of Riley's unstable character – you guessed he was likely to kill you anyway.'

'Very good Sergeant' Grant said and attempted a smile 'you don't have any evidence and you don't have any witnesses.'

'Exactly' Carver said 'you have nothing and you call yourself a professional.'

'I suppose you would like to see me breakdown and confess Sergeant? Fall on my sword as it were' Grant said and looked to Carver to appreciate his joke.

'No Sir' Bridle said with a cold look 'I'd like to see you drop through a trap-door in Walton Prison with a hood over your head and a halter around your neck.'

Lodge considered pulling Bridle through the door by the scruff of his neck. It was one thing to commit professional suicide alone but Lodge didn't want to go on the scrap heap before he made it to his pension.

'I think that's quite enough John, I suggest you leave immediately or I'll advise Sir Edward to take legal proceedings' Carver said as he marched over to the door and pulled it open. Lodge cleared his throat and tugged Bridle's arm but Bridle pulled away.

'There is a man in custody and about to stand trial for your son's murder' Bridle said turning to Grant.

'Good' Grant said and finished his whiskey 'I intend to take this further Sergeant, I have a lot of political influence. I'll see you in the dole queue before I'm finished' Grant thumped his glass down on the table and Bridle glared at him.

'It's my intention to expose your relationship with Miranda Shaw and to expose your involvement in your son's vice den in the country' Bridle paused for effect 'I don't care how many eminent people I have to interview and implicate in the sex parties but my investigation will be thorough. If any of my findings are accidentally leaked to the press then I will be very outraged and will assure the public that all the people named are innocent until proven guilty. But you know what people are like Sir Edward, they enjoy a good scandal from their betters.'

Bridle held Grant's stare for a moment then turned to the door. Carver still held the door handle but had a slight frown as if he was deep in thought.

'You look worried Sir Nigel, try and get some sleep' Bridle winked at Carver and followed Lodge through the hall to the front door. Lodge opened the door and stepped out onto the porch which was lit by two carriage lights on adjacent pillars. He was glad to be out and hurried down the steps and into the driver's seat before Bridle could beat him to it. Lodge had the engine ticking over sweetly by the time Bridle slipped into the passenger seat.

'Where the hell did all that come from?' Lodge said pulling away hard, spitting gravel in all directions.

'I've had long nights alone to think it through' Bridle said staring blankly at the windscreen.

'Well do me a favour boss start shaggin' someone soon before you get us both sacked.'

Bridle started to laugh quietly and Lodge shook his head.

'You really think it was Grant?'

'Without doubt' Bridle replied.

'So he's got away with it' Lodge said.

'He won't hang but I'll make sure he suffers' Bridle said quietly.

'What about Billy Doyle?' Lodge said glancing at Bridle.

'What about him?' Bridle replied shrugging his shoulders.

'He could hang if Radford gets his way' Lodge replied.

Bridle looked sideways at Lodge and both men began to laugh as Lodge rammed the pedal down with the intention of making the last pint before closing time.

'Stop here Tom' Bridle said as they approached the end of the promenade. Lodge slammed down heavily on the brakes and the car jerked to a stop.

'Are you sure boss?' Lodge said half-heartedly.

'Yeah I need the air' Bridle said and climbed out. He closed the door and leaned in through the window.

'Enjoy your pint Tommy' Bridle said and was about to turn away but hesitated 'oh yeah and enjoy those cigars you nicked from Sir Edward Grant's cigar box.'

Lodge tapped the cigars in his breast pocket and shook his

head as he watched Bridle's shadowy figure disappear into the gloom of the promenade.

Bridle walked slowly and kept his head bowed to an uncomfortable breeze coming off the river. It was dark and murky and Bridle had given up trying to see anything too far ahead of him. He slipped his hands into his pockets as his fingers were beginning to get numb in the fresh breeze. A stray dog came out of the darkness and sniffed around him before it cocked a leg on the nearest post and disappeared again. Bridle picked out the lights from the houses as they ran up the promenade toward New Brighton as he always did but the breeze made him drop his head again and he held on to the rim of his hat in case it blew off.

Flecks of colour reflected off the black river from ship's mooring lights as a young couple hurried past him arm in arm, rushing to their warm destination. He looked up briefly from under his hat to get his bearings but stopped dead as if a bolt of electricity had shot through his body. The light was on in Stella's work-room. He stared for a moment then started to jog then broke into a run until he reached the house. Bridle stopped at the bottom step and looked up at the light in the window. Did he leave it on by mistake? His stomach sank at the thought as he walked slowly up the steps and fumbled with his keys. He opened the door nervously and flicked on the hall light then closed the door and stood motionless.

Stella appeared on the top landing of the stairs. She was wearing the velvet dress that had been hanging on the mannequin. The straps were slightly off the shoulder and her jet black hair was fastened up which exposed her long neck and the low cut emphasised the fullness of her breasts. The dress hugged her trim waist then ran over the firm curves of her hips. As she moved slowly down the stairs Bridle could see she was wearing high heeled shoes and sheer stockings. Her mouth was drawn in ruby lipstick and as she got closer Bridle could smell her perfume. It was a dream. It felt like dream and Stella looked like a dream.

Stella reached the bottom step and Bridle was about to speak but she swiftly put her finger on his lips. Bridle caught her arm and pulled her firmly to him and kissed the nape of her neck. She sighed quietly and the odour from her perfume made his head spin. He kissed her hard on the mouth and she opened her lips to him as he lifted her from the stair and spun her around to the wall. They pressed firmly into each other and Stella raised her knee and squeezed her thigh against his as she moaned for him.

Outside the breeze had turned into a biting wind. Somewhere across the coal black river a lonely dog howled in the night.